KISS OF STEEL

BEC McMASTER

sourcebooks
casablanca

Photos by Gene Mollica
Type/Layout Design by Joanna Metzger

Published by Sourcebooks Casablanca, an imprint of Sourcebooks, Inc.
P.O. Box 4410, Naperville, Illinois 60567-4410
(630) 961-3900
Fax: (630) 961-2168
www.sourcebooks.com

Printed and bound in the United States of America.
VP 10 9 8 7 6 5 4 3 2 1

To Byron, for encouraging my dreams
and being my very own hero

Chapter 1

If only she'd been born a man... A man in Whitechapel had choices. He could take up a trade, or theft, or even join some of the rookery gangs. A woman had opportunities too, but they were far more limited and nothing that a gently bred young lady would ever aspire to.

A mere six months ago Honoria Todd had owned other options. They hadn't included the grim tenement that she lived in, hovering on the edges of Whitechapel. Or the nearly overwhelming burden of seeing her brother and sister fed. Six months ago she'd been a respectable young woman with a promising job as her father's research assistant, hovering on the edge of the biggest breakthrough since Darwin's hypotheses. It had taken less than a week for everything she had to be torn away from her. Sometimes she thought the most painful loss had been her naïveté.

Scurrying along Church Street, Honoria tugged the edge of her cloak up to shield herself from the intermittent drizzle, but it did no good. Water gathered on the brim of her black top hat, and each step sent an icy droplet down the back of her neck. Gritting her teeth, she hurried on. She was late. Mr. Macy had kept her back an hour at work to discuss the progress of her latest pupil, Miss Austin. Scion of a merchant dynasty, Miss Austin was intended to be launched upon the Echelon, where she just might be fortunate enough to be taken in as a thrall. The girl was certainly pretty enough to catch the eye of one of the seven dukes who ruled the council, or perhaps one of the numerous lesser Houses. Her family would be gifted with exclusive trade agreements and possibly sponsorship, and Miss Austin would live out the terms of her contract in the extravagant style the Echelon was acclimatized to. The type of style Honoria had once lived on the edges of. Before her father was murdered.

Church Street opened into Butcher Square. On a kinder day the square would be packed with vendors and thronging with people. Today only the grim metal lions that guarded the entrance to the Museum of Bio-Mechanic History kept watch. The city wall loomed ahead, with the gaping maw of Ratcatcher Gate offering a glimpse of Whitechapel beyond. Fifty years ago the residents of Whitechapel had built the wall with whatever they could lay their hands on. It stood nearly twenty feet high, but its symbolism towered over the cold, misty square. Whitechapel had its own rules, its own rulers. The aristocratic Echelon could own London city, but they'd best steer clear of the rookeries.

If Mr. Macy found out Honoria's address, he'd fire her on the spot. Her only source of a respectable livelihood would vanish, and she'd be facing those damned *options* again. She'd wasted a shilling tonight on a steam cab, just to keep the illusion of her circumstances intact. Mr. Macy had walked her out before locking up the studio where he taught young ladies to improve themselves. Usually he stayed behind and she could slip into the masses of foot traffic in Clerkenwell, turn a corner, and then double back for the long walk home. Tonight his chivalry had cost her a loaf of bread.

She'd disembarked two streets away, prompting the cab driver to shake his head and mutter something beneath his breath. She felt like shaking her head too. A shilling for the sleight-of-hand that kept her employed. It didn't matter that that shilling would keep her with a roof over her head and food on the table for months to come. She still felt its loss keenly. Her stockings needed darning again and they hadn't the thread for it; her younger sister, Lena, had put her fingers through her gloves; and fourteen-year-old Charlie…Her breath caught. Charlie needed more than the pair of them combined.

"'Ey!" a voice called. "'Ey, you!"

Honoria's hand strayed to the pistol in her pocket and she glanced over her shoulder. A few months ago she might have jumped skittishly at the cry, but she'd spotted the ragged urchin out of the corner of her eye as soon as she started toward Ratcatcher Gate. The pistol was a heavy, welcoming weight in her grip. Her father's pistol was one of the few things she had left of him and probably the most precious for its sheer practicality. She'd long ago given up on sentimentality.

"Yes?" she asked. The square was abandoned, but

she knew there'd be eyes watching them from the heavily boarded windows that lined it.

The urchin peered at her from flat, muddy-brown eyes. It could have been any age or sex with the amount of dirt it wore. She decided the square jaw was strong enough to name it a boy. Not even the constant rain could wash away the dirt on his face, as though it were as deeply ingrained in the child's pores as it was in the cobblestones beneath their feet.

"Spare a shillin', m'um?" he asked, glancing around as though prepared to flee.

Honoria's eyes narrowed and she gave the urchin another steady look. If she wasn't mistaken, that was a rather fine herringbone stitch riddled with grime at the edge of the child's coat. The clothing fit altogether too well for it to have been stolen, and it was draped in such a manner that it made the child look rather more malnourished than she suspected he was.

She took her time drawing her slim change purse out and opening it. A handful of grimy shillings bounced pitifully in the bottom of it. Plucking one out with reluctance, she offered it to the little street rogue.

The urchin reached for the coin and Honoria grabbed his hand. A quick twist revealed the inside of the child's wrist—and the crossed daggers tattooed there.

His wary mud-brown eyes widened and he tried to yank his hand away. "Leggo!"

Honoria snatched her shilling back and released him. The boy staggered, landing with a splash in a puddle. He swore under his breath and rolled to his feet.

"I've more need of it than you," she told him, then swept her cloak to the side to reveal the butt of the pistol in her skirt pocket. "Run back to your master and tell *him* to give you a coin."

The boy's lip curled and he glanced over his shoulder. "Worf a try. Already bin paid for this." He flipped a shilling out of nowhere and then pocketed it just as swiftly. A stealthy smile flashed over his face, gone just as quickly as the coin. "'Imself wants a word with you."

"Himself?" For a moment she was blank. Then her gaze shot to the child's wrist and that damning tattoo of ownership. She tucked her change purse away and tugged her cloak about her chin. "I'm afraid I'm not at liberty this evening." Somehow she forced the words out, cool and clipped. Her fingers started to shake. She thrust them into fists. "My brother is not well. And I'm late. I must see to him."

She took a step, then shied away as a hand caught at her cloak. "Don't. Touch. Me."

The boy shrugged. "I'm jus' the messenger, luv. And trust me, you ain't wantin' 'im to send one o' the others."

Her mouth went dry. In the ensuing silence, she felt as though her heartbeat had suddenly erupted into a tribal rhythm. Six months scratching a living on the edges of the rookery, trying to stay beneath the notice of the master. All for nothing. He'd been aware of her, probably all along.

She had to see what he wanted. She'd caught a glimpse of the *others* who were part of his gang. Everybody in the streets gave them a large berth, like rats fleeing from a pack of prowling toms. Either she could go of her own volition, or she could be dragged there.

"Let me tell my sister where I'm going," she finally said. "She'll be worried."

"Your neck," the urchin said with a shrug. "Not mine."

Honoria stared at him for a moment, then turned toward Ratcatcher Gate. Its heavy stone arch cast a shadow of cold over her that seemed to run down her spine. Himself. Blade. The man who ruled the rookeries. *Or creature*, she thought with a nervous shiver. There was nothing human about him.

By the time Honoria found Crowe Lane, she was drenched and her cotton skirts clung to her. The rain had finally let up, but the hour's walk had done its damage. Though little more than a fine mist, the rain had managed to seep through to her skin, leaving her flesh pebbled with cold and her corset tight and constrictive about her ribs. Or perhaps it was the thought of what was ahead causing her shortness of breath.

Before heading out, she'd made herself snatch a mouthful of the fried cod that Lena had burned again. It sat in her stomach like a greasy weight, but she hadn't eaten for a good eight hours and her knees needed the strength. At barely seventeen, Lena had no innate skill at cookery, but she was often home earlier than Honoria, her shift at the clockmaker's finished well before dusk started to settle. They'd had their usual strained argument over nothing at all—and everything—before Charlie's cough had broken the tension. Lena had hurried in to take him his supper and try to get him to eat something, an ordeal Honoria didn't envy her. But, then, her sister wouldn't envy

Honoria's task either if she'd known about it. Honoria had slipped out of the door before Lena could ask, not even bothering to change her clothes.

A thick yellow fog was beginning to settle over the rookery. There were no gas lamps here, and she had no flare stick to light the way. At a sovereign apiece, she couldn't afford one.

Footsteps scuttled in the shadows, but the fog carried every sound, and they might have been next to her or fifty feet away. She wasn't concerned. This close to the master's lair, nobody would dare attack her without his leave. For a moment she felt strangely fearless, her booted heels striking the cobbles with a ringing sound. She'd been afraid for so long: afraid of starving to death, afraid the Echelon would find them and drag her brother and sister away, afraid of being attacked in the streets by one of the Slasher gangs—those who drained a person of their blood to sell to the factories down by the wharves. It had worn her out with its familiarity, worn her down. She'd thought she had little fear left.

And yet that familiar hollow feeling pooled in her stomach as she paused in front of the derelict building. The fog eddied away from the roughened brick walls as though something kept it out. A pair of crossed daggers was carved into the wooden sign that hung over the door, the sign that all the Reapers gang wore, proclaiming which gang they ran with.

The Roman denarius that hung around her neck suddenly felt heavy. She knew the words inscribed on it as if they were engraved on her soul: *fortes fortuna juvat*. The motto her father had taken for himself when his experiments caught the eye of the duke of Caine, catapulting them into the gleaming world of the great Houses and earning them untold patronage.

"Fortune favors the bold," she whispered under her breath. Then she raised her fist and rapped sharply on the door. They would have seen her coming and sent word, no doubt.

The door swung open. A man filled the doorway, and Honoria took a half step back. He loomed over her by a good foot, a short black beard trimmed neatly over his jaw, and his head shaven. It wasn't the evil look in his green eyes that scared her, or the scars that dissected his face. It was the heavy bio-mechanic arm that had been fitted to his right shoulder, and the pair of glittering knives at his belt. His entire appearance spoke of violence.

Breathe, she reminded herself, still staring up at him. *Just breathe.*

As though her stare unnerved him, he gave a low grunt and jerked his head. "Inside. 'E's waitin'."

Honoria couldn't resist a closer look at the arm as she stepped past. The metal spars were bare, the hydraulics clearly defined by the hoses that provided the pressure needed to move it. It was crude work. She'd seen better, a thousand times over, when her father worked for Lord Vickers. There wasn't even a scrap of synthetic flesh to cover it, though perhaps in this trade it would be more costly to constantly patch it against assault. And it was hardly likely that he could have gone to the Echelon's blacksmiths or metalworkers. This was a job created in the rookeries.

"Up the stairs," he muttered. The door closed behind her with a sharp slam. Then the lock snicked.

That nervous little fluttering started again, deep in her stomach. The hall stretched ahead endlessly, the timbers rotted and dusty. Hardly the place she'd have expected to find the master of the rookeries.

To stall, Honoria reached up and started unpinning her hat, with its wilted black feathers and bedraggled scraps of lace. She could have sold it, and the dress she wore too, for both were far finer than her circumstances, but that would only lead Mr. Macy to ask questions. *Smoke and mirrors*, she thought. Her entire life was an illusion.

"Ain't got all night," the doorman said.

The hat finally came free, and she turned and shoved it at him. "I wouldn't want to disturb his breakfast."

When he took the hat, as though surprised to do so, she started tugging on the stained leather of her kid gloves. Her fingers were cold and the leather fought her.

The big man gestured up a flight of stairs. "After you."

Honoria stalked past in a swish of skirts.

The stairs were narrow and dusty. They creaked alarmingly, and she gripped the rail, half afraid they were going to collapse beneath her. There was a landing at the top, and she glanced around, wondering which door to take. Light glowed beneath one of the doors, a welcome sight.

The doorman held it open, yellow light spilling out into the hall, and despite herself, she started toward it hungrily. It had the warm glow of a good fire, and she almost thought she could smell the scent of lemon wax in the air. Which was ridiculous.

"Come in, Miz Pryor," a man called in an atrocious accent, using the name she'd assumed months ago.

Garbled cockney from the sound of it, mixed with a healthy dose of…the upper classes?

She frowned. A peculiar combination, but her ear had never been wrong before. That was why Mr. Macy kept her on. She had a talent for speech and could teach a parrot to sound like a duchess.

The parlor could have belonged in any merchant's home. Honoria stopped in her tracks, surprised by the polished timber floors and the fine gilt-lined furnishings. In front of the glowing fireplace was a stuffed armchair, shadowing the man who sat within. She caught a glimpse of pale blond hair and the sheen of firelight sparking off his eyes. With the fire at his back, his features were indeterminate and even his build was difficult to define. Nothing but shadows and hints of movement.

Despite her prejudice, she found herself peering at him curiously. The only blue bloods she'd known were of the Echelon, those born to the Great Houses and offered infected blood during the blood rites when they were fifteen. Only the extremely well born or influential were allowed the rites, but accidents occurred, of course, when the virus could be spread by the merest scratch or droplet of blood. Blade himself was considered a rogue blue blood, unsanctioned, his very existence an insult. If the Echelon could have killed him, they would have.

She'd never met a rogue before. The only others who survived became Nighthawks, a guild of hunters and thief takers, or if they could claim some minor aristocratic connections or blood, they might be offered a place in the elite Coldrush Guards who stood watch over the Ivory Tower. Neither were the type of people she'd come into contact with when she served on the very edges of the Echelon. She hadn't been considered well bred enough to attend the Ivory Tower functions, nor was she lowborn enough to come across one of the Nighthawks.

"Good evening..." She paused. What did one call a man who went by only one name? "You sent for me?"

"Warm yourself by the fire," he said in that atrocious accent.

Honoria took a hesitant step forward. The hulking giant followed her in, shutting the door behind him. But at least he didn't leave her here alone with the master of the 'Chapel.

She slid a sidelong glance at the man in the chair, concentrating superficially on tucking her gloves away. A step to the right gave her a better view—a chiseled profile with a strong nose and heavy brows. Firelight gleamed on his hair, gilding it, his eyelashes stained almost silver by the light, and she realized he was looking down, stroking something that rested in his lap.

A cheroot dangled between the bare fingers of his left hand. The other was gloved and curled over the back of an enormous tomcat that regarded her with an evil expression. She sensed a glint of green watching her and realized that Blade was examining her as carefully as she was him.

"What's wrong, luv? Cat got your tongue?" His fingers stroked the cat's black throat. The tom arched its neck, its yellow eyes shutting with pleasure. A scar slashed across the tom's face, distorting its features, and the left ear was a ragged mess. The deep rumble of the cat's purr filled the air.

Honoria gave a start. "Is that a threat? Or simply an uncouth method of welcoming a person?" Her voice didn't betray her. Years of schooling kept her tone crisp and bereft of inflection. Almost bored, even.

Living among the Echelon for ten years had taught her the benefit of managing her emotions. One hint of fear and they would turn their pale eyes on her like sharks smelling blood. This man might rule the rookeries with an iron fist, but she had faced down the prince consort himself, with his colorless, red-rimmed eyes and too-pink lips. Blade was dangerous, but she couldn't afford to let him see how much he frightened her. That wasn't how the game was played. And the cursed blue bloods liked their games so very much…

Honoria took a deep, steadying breath and crossed to the fireplace, holding out her pale hands to warm them. She could feel his gaze between her shoulder blades. It lingered, almost like the sensation of a pair of lips brushing against her neck. Every hair down her spine rose and her nipples tightened painfully.

The silence stretched out. She let it, knowing he was testing her mettle. The fire crackled in the grate, a wall of warmth against her front. The wet cotton of her dress began to steam.

He broke first. "It weren't a threat. If it were"—his voice dropped to a murmur—"you'd know it. You wouldn't need to ask."

Honoria closed her eyes and let the warmth wash over her. This was a waste of time. She should be home, using these last few precious hours to help Lena with the mending she took in for extra coin.

"What do you want?" She was tired and wet and hungry, and if he was trying to frighten her, then he had best get on with it.

"I want you to turn and look at me."

Honoria half glanced over her shoulder. It was foolishness to give him her back. One last act of defiance. She'd learned how to take such punitive steps and still make her obeisances. It had amused her father's patron, Lord Vickers. Her small rebellions were the only reason he hadn't simply taken her. It made him wait, made him drag out the hunt.

Honoria held the pose just long enough to imply that she turned only of her own accord. Then she met Blade's gaze again, the warmth curling up her back.

"And then?" she asked, tipping her chin up.

He put the cheroot to his lips, his features disappearing in a wreath of smoke. The embers on the end glowed red and then faded, and he breathed out, dispersing the sweet-smelling smoke across the room.

"You've been six months in me turf and not paid a visit," he said. "That ain't polite, dove. It ain't wise for a woman to be without protection. You been lucky so far. People been wonderin' if you and I 'ad struck a deal. Now they're wonderin' if I would care if you went missin'." He flicked the cheroot over a small tray and the ashes crumbled. "Consider this a *polite* warnin' and an offer. You won't be unmolested for long."

The pistol was a heavy, reassuring weight in her skirt pocket. "Then they shall receive a little surprise if they do. Only a fool walks these streets without protection."

"That little barker in your pocket and the pig-sticker in your boot?" He laughed, low and husky. "Won't do you much good when your throat is slit."

That *little barker* was highly modified. Her lips thinned. If he made a move toward her, she would show him just how clever—and distrustful—her father had been. One shot could rip a hole through a man's chest the size of her head and explode on impact. Not even a blue blood could survive such a shot at close range, and it had been designed for precisely that. Her father had known Lord Vickers would turn on him someday.

"It's served me well so far," she replied.

"Aye. That knuckler on Vertigo Street and the pair of bludgers in Butcher's Square," he said, proving how closely he'd been having her watched. "A child and a pair of idiots. I ain't impressed."

"How about now?" she asked, drawing the pistol smoothly and pointing it at him.

He smiled.

There was a blur of movement and something grabbed her from behind. Honoria gasped, the knife a sharp warning against her throat as Blade drew her back against his hard body. Her chin tipped up and she swallowed hard, the edge of the knife hovering directly over her carotid artery. His arm was a steel band about her waist, hugging her close.

His lips brushed her ear. "Still not impressed," he whispered.

The fire spat. Her wide eyes took in the room: the cheroot sitting in the ashtray and still smoking, the abandoned cat giving them a disgruntled look from the floor as it turned and sauntered away, and the long stretch of shadow that showed them locked together in a parody of an embrace.

"Put it down, luv," he said. "And don't ever draw on me again unless you intend to use it."

Honoria lowered the pistol. "I was proving a point. I didn't bother to cock it."

"Just as I were provin' *my* point," he replied in that husky whisper. His cool breath stirred the curls at her throat, pebbling her damp skin. "Who do you think won?"

"I may have been…somewhat precipitous," she admitted.

His hand slid along hers, closing over her fingers. "Give it to me."

No. Honoria shut her eyes and took a deep breath. She forced her fingers to relax. To let him take the smooth weight of the pistol.

He thumbed open the barrel and examined the shot inside with a soft grunt. "What the bleedin' devil are you usin' for rounds?"

"Firebolts," she replied. "My father designed them." And then she shut her mouth. He didn't need to know anything about her father. It was safer that way. Vickers still had a price on her head, and who knew what this man would do for that much money?

Blade snapped the pistol barrel back into place, then tucked it away somewhere on his person. The razor-edged knife against her throat kept her locked in place. The pressure was perfect. She couldn't move an inch, but it hadn't broken the skin either.

Then suddenly it eased. Honoria took a deeper

breath, her head spinning with the sudden rush of oxygen into starved lungs. With the knife gone, other impressions started leeching into her. The hard body imprinted against hers, separated only by the thickness of her bedraggled bustle. The press of his belt buckle, tugging at the fabric of her skirts. And the sound of his breathing, quickening just slightly.

His arm slid around her waist again. "And now you're disarmed. And at me mercy. Now what do you do, Miz Pryor?"

A sharp heel to the instep. Her father's voice echoed in her head. *Then a brutal knee to the unmentionables.* But that was how to bring a human man down. Not a blue blood. Nothing short of decapitation could bring one of *them* down. Unless…

Honoria slid a hand over his, feeling the coolness of his skin. The steel ring she wore on her right forefinger brushed against his knuckle. It resembled a band of thorns, the sharp barbs curling around a delicate steel rosebud. One flick of her finger and the sharp thorn needle contained within the rosebud would pop out, smothered in a particular toxin that could incapacitate a blue blood.

Ten minutes before it would wear off. Not long, but perhaps long enough to escape. The concentrated toxin was one of many weapons her father had discovered for Vickers. And she had only enough toxin for one use.

Honoria took a slow breath. Then drew her hand away and bowed her head. It was her own foolish sense of pride that had seen her into this situation. She should never have drawn the pistol.

"I'm sorry." The words burned on her tongue, but she said them. "I mishandled the situation. I meant only to prove that I was not wholly without defense. You may unhand me, if you will."

"And what will you do..." he asked, "if I do not will it?"

Honoria turned her head. Met his gaze. This close, she could see the intense green depths that flickered with firelight. His pupils darkened, expanding as though to swallow the irises. Her breath caught. Memory flashed of another man holding her, his fist tight in her hair and his cold lips brushing against the vein in her throat. Whispering what he was going to do to her...

Suddenly the arm about her waist felt like a cage. She pushed at it, heat burning through her cheeks. "Let me go. Please." His hand tightened and she felt a scream bubbling up in her throat. "Let me *go*!"

Blade released her and Honoria staggered forward. Her hands fell on the back of one of the armchairs in the room, her fingers digging into the stuffed embroidery. She felt as though she'd been running up a flight of stairs, her pulse throbbing through the artery of her throat and thundering in her ears. She couldn't breathe. The damned corset...

Blade moved in front of her, his feet crossing over like a swordsman carefully circling an opponent. For the first time she got a good look at him.

His hair was close-cropped and guinea-gold. Some of the panic went out of her at the sight. He was close to the Fade—when the color leeched out of a blue blood just before he displayed symptoms of turning—but not standing on the edge. Still in control of his inner demon, thank goodness.

Firelight gilded the muscle in his arms, delineating the veins that ran up the inside of his wrist and curled over his bicep. A white shirt opened at the throat, a black scrap of silk knotted and looped twice around his neck. A hint of a tattoo peeked out from the rolled-up sleeves of his shirt.

And her pistol was tucked behind his belt.

Honoria eyed it hungrily, shivering a little as she caught her breath. There was no more pretense left in her. She just wanted to be gone.

"What do you want?" she asked. "I won't be your blood whore." She was not that desperate. Yet.

His hands hovered in the air as though to reassure her. Those penetrating eyes locked on her face. "I can't offer you protection for nothin'. It don't work that way, luv." His eyelids narrowed lazily, his voice dropping to a silky whisper. "And I think we've proved that you need protection."

"Only from you," she retorted.

His lips thinned. "Per'aps…Per'aps I mis'andled the situation too."

Honoria stared at him. Was this a trick? All blue bloods lied. She licked her dry lips, racking her brain. "Do you want payment? I could find money…" Somewhere. There was little left to sell. Her clothes, the ones she wore to fool Mr. Macy. They were made of fine wool and printed cottons. Charlie's clockwork soldiers. Or even her father's diaries.

She shied away from that thought. Those diaries had cost her father his life. He'd made her swear to keep them safe. Too many lives depended on it. She couldn't sell them, not even to protect her innocence.

The clothing it would have to be. And perhaps her job with it.

A swell of anger rose in her throat, threatening to choke her. Every time she thought she found her feet, something swept them out from under her. Struggling, always struggling, to keep out of the mire of debt and starvation. If she lost her job, then she would find herself facing this same dilemma, but a month from now.

She wanted to scream again in frustration. It wasn't fair. Tears burned in the backs of her eyes. There were only two things she had that were worth anything to him: her virginity and her blood. And she wasn't prepared to sacrifice either. Not just yet.

"Find money?" His eyes narrowed. "Where? The Drainers?"

Honoria shook her head. She'd seen too many people forced by starvation to sell their blood to the Drainers. Every man and woman over the age of eighteen had to donate two pints of blood a year for the blood taxes, but there were those who took advantage of the poor to find a cheap way to find more.

In the last six months she'd seen a man slowly bleed away his life week by week to feed his family, before he finally died. Honoria had spared what she could of their own food supplies, but within two weeks the man's wife was dead too and the children vanished. The only ones who made any profit out of the venture were the Drainers.

"No," she replied quietly. She would be his blood

whore before she went anywhere near the Drainers. They were the lowest of scum. At least Blade would have some interest in keeping her alive. Tradition stated that a thrall—a blood whore—was to be protected and looked after.

"Then we're at an impasse." He sank back down into the armchair and ground out the smoldering cheroot. "I can't afford to be lenient. And you ain't prepared to offer me anythin' o' worth."

She winced at his butchered words. And then her eyes went wide. "I could teach you to speak," she blurted, then clapped a hand over her mouth.

His gaze flickered up, his fingers pausing on the cheroot stub. A scowl drew his eyebrows down. "Ain't nothin' wrong with 'ow I speak, luv."

"I never meant…It's what I do. I correct the sounds of people's speech and teach them genteel mannerisms. I'm a finishing tutor for young ladies. And the occasional gentleman."

He ground the stub down to nothing. She eyed it nervously.

"And what would I do with fancy talk?" He deliberately placed harsh accent on the words. A sneer curled his lip. "Join the Ech'lon?"

"Whatever you wished to do with it. It's the only thing I have that I can give you."

His gaze made a slow perusal of her figure.

"*Will* give you," she corrected, a flare of heat burning in her cheeks.

"Am I to visit your place o' employment, then?"

Honoria blanched. "*No*. No. That would be inconvenient for you and uncomfortable for Mr. Macy."

Not to mention what Mr. Macy would say about her continued employment prospects. She barely suppressed a shudder. An image sprang to mind—of this dangerous ruffian stalking among the fluttering young ladies whom she taught. A wolf set among innocent young chicks, practically licking its lips.

Blade sat back, making a steeple of his fingers. "Then you will come 'ere. Three nights a week."

"*Three?*"

"Three," he confirmed.

It would leave her exhausted. She barely had the strength to get through the days as it was. And yet she would have this dangerous man's protection. She could walk through the roughest alleys of the slums without even a pistol on her. Lena wouldn't have to walk an extra mile each day merely to arrive at the clockmakers safely, and they could leave Charlie alone at the house without worrying about thieves.

Suddenly what had seemed a hopeless situation became the best stroke of luck she'd had all year.

"Three nights a week," she heard herself say. "Two hours a night. I can't sacrifice any more. Night might be your day, but I've work to do when the sun is up. I'll need some sleep."

A hint of satisfaction glinted in his eyes. Honoria stilled again. Then the look was gone and his face remained admirably blank.

"You do realize what people'll think," he said.

Honoria folded her hands in front of her. She knew precisely what he meant. Visiting him three nights a week would have everyone assuming she'd paid for his protection with her body. It stung. She'd thought six months of poverty had desensitized her to the worst, but there was still a tiny, deeply buried part of her that remembered what it had been like to be respectable. Her voice was soft when she said, "That is the least of my concerns."

"Done then." Blade's smile curled over his mouth. "My protection, for your lessons."

It hit her. She had survived. She had *won*. Coming here tonight, she didn't think she'd have left without losing something important to her. Instead she had gained the power of Blade's name without losing anything. Teaching him to speak and behave properly would cost her nothing but a few hours' sleep a week.

Dizziness washed over her. Relief or hunger, she wasn't quite sure. She suddenly felt the urge to sit down hard. But she didn't dare show any sign of weakness in front of this man.

He might have consented to an agreement that was advantageous for her, but he certainly wasn't any less dangerous. She'd seen the hunger burning in his eyes. That was all a blue blood was. Sooner or later it showed in all of them, no matter how carefully they hid it.

She couldn't let down her guard, not even for a moment.

"When shall we begin?" she asked, forcing her knees to straighten. If she clutched at the armchair a little too firmly, his gaze never turned toward it. It was locked on her face, as though memorizing her features.

"Tomorrow," he said. "At ten."

Chapter 2

"Well?"

Blade stared into the crackling flames, his hand resting against the brick chimney. The slight scent of mechanical oil drifted past, and the whir of the hydraulics on Rip's arm as he shut the door made a quiet hiss. It almost masked the faint scent of musk and man that accompanied him.

"She's mine." She just didn't know it yet.

"I don't understand why she's so important?"

Blade turned, his gaze alighting on his two lieutenants. Rip scowled, crossing his arms over his chest. Most people thought him merely muscle, but he had the kind of cunning that could have ruled a rookery gang. Instead he'd thrown his lot in with Blade. Fewer knives in the back that way.

Blade's second lieutenant, Will Carver, crossed toward the fireplace on silent feet. He held his hands out, the firelight gleaming in his amber eyes. He topped Rip by a hand, and his shoulders were nearly twice again as broad.

Blade leaned against the mantel. "Well? Will?"

"She smells good. Clean." Will shrugged. "Ain't your usual sort."

Blade smiled. "Vickers wants 'er."

Both lieutenants stiffened.

"What's *'e* got to do with 'er?" Rip scowled.

"Now that's a question I can't answer, me ducks," Blade replied. If he breathed in, he could almost smell Honoria's scent lingering in the air. The hunger crawled up his throat, and he closed his eyes, forcing his body to release that scent-laden breath. He'd fed only last night. He shouldn't be this close to the edge yet. Something about the girl stirred him. Perhaps her fear, an intoxicating scent. He didn't deny it. Or maybe the defiance in her eyes as she'd stared him down despite the racing throb of her heartbeat.

"Six months ago, Vickers put a price on 'er head," he said, forcing the words out. "He's given the Nighthawks a contract to find 'er, a younger sister, and a brother."

Will whistled soundlessly. "And they ain't found 'em yet? That's—"

"Almost unheard of," Blade interrupted. He wasn't sure how she'd escaped Vickers, but she'd left very little trace if the Guild of Hunters hadn't tracked her. "Her real name's Honoria Todd. Goes by Miz Pryor. Works out o' the city, for a man named Macy. Keeps 'er head down." He considered her. "Stubborn. Arrogant. Proud. The only thing I don't know is why Vickers wants 'er."

It didn't matter. If Vickers wanted her, then Blade would have her. But he would have liked to know why Vickers had offered such a high reward for a mere slip of a lass, just so he could play the game right. Maybe she'd heard something that could help Blade bring down that pasty-faced maggot who called himself a duke. Or maybe she knew of a weakness.

"She mighta spurned 'im." Rip squatted down and offered his fingers to Puss to sniff. The cat allowed him to scratch between its flea-bitten ears. "You know how his lordship gets when he sets his sights on somethin'."

"Maybe." Blade slid his hands into his pockets. "It's a big reward for a spurned lover." With those dark, flashing eyes and that weary, determined way she'd glared back at him, she was just the type to set Vickers's cold heart aflutter. If he had one.

She wasn't young enough for Vickers, but he would have liked her courage. He'd have wanted to crush it. Blade had spent half a century staring into the eyes of someone and working out whether the person would fight to the death or collapse at the faintest amount of pressure. Hell would freeze over first before Honoria Todd gave anyone the pleasure of seeing her succumb.

"What's so amusin'?" Will growled.

Blade looked up, and felt the smile on his lips die. "Nothin'." He rubbed at the back of his neck, ignoring Will's piercing gaze.

"So how'd you find her," Rip asked, "if the Nighthawks couldn't?"

"'Cos I know everythin' that goes on in the rookeries, bucko. Two young women in my turf with a young lad? All three with the crisp, cultured tones o' Oxford?" He sneered. "You know I likes me puzzles. And I'm possibly the only one as knows 'bout the price Vickers put out for three fugitives. I can put two and two together."

"You want I should find out what Vickers wants with 'em?" Rip asked.

Blade reached for his gold cheroot case. "Hmm. No. Already got eyes in that corner. You keep well away from Vickers." His gaze flickered to Will as he tugged out a slim cheroot. "You too." Will gave him a nasty little smile.

"Then what do you want with us?" Rip asked.

"I want an eye kept on the 'ouse." He bent and lit the cheroot in the fire. "Will, I want you on watch in particular. With your nose and 'earing, Vickers won't get close." Taking a deep breath, he let the smoke curl through his lungs. "And make sure everyone knows she belongs to me."

"Why not mark her?" Will held up his wrist, with his tattoo visible.

"Not yet," he murmured. An insane urge struck him. He wanted his mark on her skin. But he wouldn't force her to it. She would ask for it herself, when she was ready. When he looked up, both of them were watching him, particularly Will with those bloody amber eyes of his. "Go on," he growled. "You've got your orders."

Puss attacked Rip's boot as he stood. The big man grimaced and tried to disentangle the cat without hurting it.

"'Ere now, Puss." Blade knelt down, clicking his fingers.

The cat gave him a look, considering the entreaty. It rolled to its feet, letting Rip step away, and then slowly strolled over to Blade to investigate.

"Bloody cat," Will muttered, giving Puss a wide berth.

Puss's lip curled up as Will slipped past. The cat hissed, fur standing on end and glaring at the youth.

Blade grabbed him by the scruff of the neck. "That's enough now," he said, settling the cat in his arms. "Will's our friend."

Will smiled darkly, flashing his teeth. "One day I'm going to eat that creature."

Blade stroked the cat. "And one day I might just have me a wolf-hide rug for me floor." He smiled. "But it ain't today. Now, go and make sure Miss Todd has a safe night's rest."

Charlie was coughing again. Honoria had her hands buried in the sink when she heard the familiar *hark-hark-hark* noise begin in the small room that Charlie and Lena shared. Her head shot up and she cocked it. She'd had plenty of practice in judging the severity of the sound over the last month.

"Not again," she muttered, wiping her hands on her apron. Weak dawn light crept through the windows. She didn't have time to linger. Mr. Macy would be expecting her at nine. But Charlie was her brother.

Their small flat had a kitchen and two tiny private rooms. She and Lena had shared a room when they first came to the 'Chapel, but when Charlie started getting the night tremors, Lena had moved her small cot in to be with him. The two of them had always had a special affinity, and her presence—though it frequently vexed Honoria—seemed to calm Charlie.

"Now, come on," Lena was murmuring when

Honoria opened the door. "Take a deep breath. That's my boy. Deep and slow."

Honoria's shadow fell across the bed. Lena looked up, dark circles beneath her eyes. Charlie's face was so pale that Honoria could have counted each freckle on his cheeks, and his arms stuck out of the sweat-soiled nightshirt like a scarecrow's.

He gave her a weak smile. "Honor..." And then he broke into another coughing attack.

Lena's lips thinned. "He *was* doing fine."

Honoria ignored her, sitting on the bed and reaching across to rub Charlie's back. Her fingers ran over the knotted protuberances of his spine. No matter how much he ate, his body kept getting thinner and weaker, as though he simply could no longer find sustenance from food.

"I'll fetch some water," Lena muttered, disappearing through the door.

Honoria held Charlie's face against her shoulder as he coughed. "There, my boy," she crooned. "Let it out. It'll be better soon." A bitter taste filled her mouth. "I'll make it better." Another promise she couldn't keep. She was getting heartily sick of them.

By the time Lena returned, the coughing had stopped. Honoria rocked him gently, stroking the silky strands of hair off the back of his neck. It was day now and his skin was feverishly cool, almost pallid. At night he would twist and sweat, his teeth grinding together for hours.

"You'd best be going," Lena said, holding the glass for Charlie. "Or you'll be late. Again. You know what happened last time."

Mr. Macy had given her a lecture about tardiness with the implied hint that he'd dock her pay next time. "I won't be late. I'll run if I need to."

"In that?" Lena's eyebrows shot up.

Honoria clenched her jaw. The dress she wore was her finest, with a cream-colored, floral brocade overdress and a flounce of cream pleats. Against the dull brown wool of Lena's homemade gown, the dress looked beautiful. It was also a point of constant contention between them. Honoria's job relied on keeping up appearances. Lena's did not.

"Yes," she snapped. "In this."

"Don't," Charlie muttered hoarsely, grabbing her hand. "Don't fight."

The two sisters looked down at him.

"We're not fighting," Honoria said instinctively. She stroked her hand through his hair, tipping his chin up. "We're..." And then she stopped.

"Charlie?" she whispered.

There was blood on his lips. His glassy eyes met hers. "What?"

"Oh, my goodness." Lena sat up. "Oh no! Your dress!"

Honoria looked down in shock. Her shoulder was stained bright vermilion. Charlie touched his mouth, then stared at the blood on his fingertips.

"It's nothing," Honoria blurted. "You must have bitten your tongue. Lena, stop being such a...such a..." The blood was slick between her fingers. His condition couldn't have gotten as bad as it had so swiftly. She'd been rigorous with Blaud's iron pills and the injections of colloidal silver. Poor Charlie's arm looked like a pincushion.

He gazed hypnotically at the blood. "There's rather a lot of it," he said. His little pink tongue darted out, licking at his bloodied lips. Something, some flash of darkness, swam through the pale blue of his irises.

"The rag!" she ordered, gesturing at a piece of stained flannel near the washstand. She snatched his hand and held it down, wiping the blood off with the rag Lena gave her. "There. Nearly done."

"Honor. He's..." Lena's whisper died away.

Charlie was staring at Honoria's bloodied shoulder. Hungrily.

"Lena." Somehow her voice was cool and composed. Inside she was shaking like a leaf. "Run and fetch Doctor Madison. Tell him Charlie's had another turn."

"I can't leave you with him—"

"Go," Honoria commanded. "And send a lad to Mr. Macy's to tell him Charlie's ill again and I can't make it in today." That would be another shilling to send the message. And more for the doctor, on top of what they already owed. But it couldn't be helped.

Lena spun on her heel and bolted in a flurry of skirts.

"Charlie," she said in a low voice. "Charlie, look at me."

His gaze lifted slowly.

"*Stop* it." The hard, flat tone had never failed to work before.

His nostrils flared. "I can't..." Suddenly he buried his face in his hands. "Can you go? Just go away a bit so I can't smell it."

Each step back from him felt like a weight settling on her shoulders. "Is this better?" she asked, staring at him from across the room. His face was almost as white as fresh snow. He looked so small against the bed, a little bloodied figure lost in the tangle of bed sheets. Seeing her brother in this condition was harder than anything she'd had to do before.

Charlie nodded, then erupted into another coughing attack.

Honoria could do nothing as another bloodied rain landed on the sheets. Heat burned behind her eyes. It wasn't fair. Why wouldn't fate simply leave them alone?

"Hmm." Doctor Madison thumbed Charlie's eyelid back.

Honoria hovered. "Well? Is he going to be all right?"

Madison stepped away from the bed and wrung his hands. "If I could trouble you for some tea, Miss Pryor?" He gave her a piercing look.

Honoria pasted a smile on her face. Inside, her stomach plummeted. "Of course, Doctor. If you'll join me in the kitchen?" Leaning closer to Charlie, she tucked the sheets up over him and kissed his cool forehead. "Get some rest. I'll bring you something to eat."

"Not hungry," he said in a quavering voice.

"Some of that nice stew Lena made the night before last," she said, as though he hadn't spoken. "I'll soak the bread in it too so that it's easy to get down."

Getting it down didn't seem to be the problem. Keeping it down was.

She closed the door behind them and crossed to the small stove and kettle. She'd sent Lena to work. There was no point in both sisters hovering over Charlie, and they needed the money.

"You know," she said in a quiet voice, concentrating on stoking the stove. "When Mama died, I promised her I'd look after them. Charlie was so sweet. So small..." Her hands fell to her sides and she stared through the stove, seeing Charlie's pink face and the tuft of silky blond hair on his head.

"How long has he been like this?"

"The coughing? Three weeks and five days. There hasn't been any blood before—"

"Not the coughing, Miss Pryor."

Though it was said gently, the words felt as though they'd taken her feet out from under her. "Five months. Five months since the first symptoms started showing up." There. She'd said it.

The doctor's eyebrows rose. "You've known what was wrong with him?"

She shook her head. Then nodded. "I know what the craving virus looks like, Doctor Madison...But it's impossible. Charlie shouldn't be able to..." She stopped then. More words that she didn't dare speak aloud.

"Shouldn't be able to?" he prompted.

"I simply can't believe this is happening." She smiled weakly and poured him a cup of tea.

The doctor gave her a look of fatherly concern, sipping at the tea. "You'd best be on your guard. I noticed the cot in his room. I don't think either of you should be staying in there with him in these circumstances."

"He would never hurt us." And yet the way Charlie had looked at her, at the blood...

"He might not be able to control himself," the doctor replied. "The monster inside him—"

"He's not a monster." But was that not what a blue blood was? What she'd always believed?

"Of course not. I meant only that Charlie might not be able to stop himself."

Honoria sank into a chair. She—more than anyone—knew what the craving virus turned a person into. She had taken her father's notes and helped him with the gentler patients at the Institute. There was even a scar on her shoulder where a young girl named Daisy—a sweet, mild-mannered girl before Vickers infected her—had gone for Honoria's throat with her bare teeth one day when Honoria hadn't kept her guard up.

If Charlie lost control—if he went after Lena—Honoria would never forgive herself. The infection was growing worse. If she didn't find some way to stop it soon, it would be too late.

"I'll move the cot. And I'll lock the door when we're asleep."

The doctor squeezed her shoulder. "I'm sorry. I'll have to report this."

"No." She surged to her feet. "No, please. They'll take him away. They'll kill him if he can't control it, or if he does, they'll lock him up and make him into one of their slaves." She'd seen the mindless brutes the Echelon kept chained, displaying them on leashes as though they were the latest accessory. And those were the ones who survived.

Tears burned in her eyes. "Please," she whispered.

"You have a month. It's the best I can do. I would advise you to stay away from him as much as possible. Perhaps sucking on some raw meat might assuage his hunger. If he becomes violent, then restrain him." The doctor hesitated on the doorstep. "There's no charge for today."

Honoria dashed at her eyes. "That's not necessary. I can pay you—"

"I won't be coming back, Miss Pryor. God have mercy on you." Then he slipped his bowler on and hurried down the steps into the alley.

Chapter 3

A LIGHT SHONE IN THE WINDOW. BLADE STALKED through the fog that clung to the ground, swirling about his thighs. He couldn't see a blasted thing, but he knew the cobblestones beneath his feet like he knew the back of his hand. It had been fifty years since he'd staggered into the 'Chapel, bleeding from a dozen stab wounds. He had decided then that this would be his home and that nobody—not even Vickers—could take it from him.

Blade's war with the Echelon had been short but bloody. The metaljackets hunting him had the numbers, but the terrain was perfect for the kind of guerrilla warfare that Blade excelled at. Vickers might have taken him from the gutters, but Blade had never forgotten them. In the end, he had knifed more than twenty of the elite Coldrush Guards and destroyed at least fifty of the metaljacket drones with them. The Echelon had withdrawn, ceding him the rookeries.

Running a hand over the cold iron banister, he climbed the steps to the peeling, pea-green door. She hadn't come. Miss Honoria Todd had reneged on their bargain. A kinder man might have asked why. But his first instinct was to work out how much advantage he could take from this.

Reaching out, he rapped sharply at the door. Three streets over a dog started barking. Blade smiled. He could smell Will trailing him over the rooftops as he'd strictly forbidden him to do. Rip and Will were like a pair of bleedin' nursemaids. The lad was good, almost invisible, in fact, but sometimes he forgot that Blade's senses were as finely tuned as his own.

Footsteps sounded from within. And a faint mutter as someone tripped over something. He leaned his palm against the doorjamb as the three locks were slipped.

The door cracked open an inch. A pair of liquid-dark eyes stared out then widened.

Blade examined his watch with exaggerated theater. "I coulda sworn I said ten."

Honoria clapped a hand to her mouth. Dark circles swam under her eyes, and the shawl around her shoulders barely disguised the indentation of her collarbone. She opened the door just enough to slip out, shutting it behind her. "I'm so sorry. I completely forgot."

Blade didn't back away. Honoria was forced to look up at him, her back pressed against the door, with just an inch between them. She cleared her throat a little and tugged the shawl tighter. The movement drew attention to her slim hands. It softened what he'd been about to say.

"You forgot?"

"My brother isn't well. We've had the doctor in. My visit with you completely slipped my mind."

He couldn't take his eyes off her wrists. Or the fine

bones of her face and the gauntness of her cheeks. Honoria was slowly starving herself. He'd seen enough of it to think himself unaffected. But somehow he found himself stepping back, giving her space. "Come. Walk with me."

Her face paled. "I can't."

"That weren't an invitation."

"I can't leave my sister alone."

Blade rapped on the door—with the pair of crossed daggers carved into it that morning. The mark of the Reapers gang and a sign of his protection. "Ain't nobody crossin' this threshold."

That was the benefit of his protection for those who accepted his price. Slasher gangs, murderers, thieves, or just the odd drunken lout, it didn't matter. He had a reputation to uphold. Cross him, or his, and Blade would come knocking.

Because of Blade, some said Whitechapel was as safe as the city proper these days.

Honoria chewed on her bottom lip. "I'll just tell Lena where I'm going." She had a hand on the door when she paused. "Where are we going? What time will I be back?"

"For a walk," he replied, reining in his frustration. Honoria had been gently reared. A brief stint in the rookery hadn't yet taught her that he was master here. He could afford to be patient. "'Bout an hour. Mebbe."

She slipped inside and shut the door in his face. Blade splayed a hand over the coarse bricks of the doorjamb. Bloody woman, shutting the door on him. Anyone would think she was ashamed of having him here at her home. With his eyes narrowing, he leaned closer to listen.

"...where? Walking out with whom?" a young girl hissed.

"No one. Just...a man," Honoria replied. "I've locked Charlie's door. Don't open it. I'll be back as soon as I can get rid of...as soon as I can."

"I see. Well, at least make sure he pays for it."

Silence descended. Then the familiar, icy-cold whiplash of Honoria's voice. "Don't you *ever* speak to me like that again." A chair squealed. "I'll be back."

Blade jerked back as he heard Honoria's footsteps stalk toward him. He caught a glimpse of the room beyond as she opened the door: a table with three mismatched chairs, a pair of hideous brown curtains at the kitchen window, and a young girl with a pile of mending in front of her. She looked up, and he immediately saw the resemblance. Their dark eyes were the same, though the girl was marginally prettier, with plumper cheeks. Maybe eighteen. He couldn't tell with her small frame.

Honoria shut the door firmly. "Don't even think about it. You go anywhere near her and I'll kill you. I swear it."

He looked down and met her indignant eyes. She might be exhausted and malnourished, but she was prepared to protect her family with her life. In that way he saw a little bit of Emily in her. "Does she know you're starvin' yourself to keep her fed?"

Color blossomed in her cheeks. "I don't know what you're talking about. Shall we? I have an hour, and I don't believe you wish to waste it."

She marched down the steps, shivering with the cold. Blade sauntered after her. He'd had vague plans of parading her through the gin shops just to show the world and "Miss Independent" who her master was. Instead he shrugged out of his leather coat and slipped it over her shoulders.

Honoria started, blinking up at him.

"I don't feel it," he said with a shrug. "And your shiverin's gettin' on me nerves."

Her fingers clutched at the edges of the coat. Blade thought for a moment that she would reject it. But then she drew it closer. "Thank you."

"You're welcome."

Honoria gave him an odd look. "Where do you wish to go?"

"This way." He gestured with his head.

"The docks?"

"I've a mind to share a pint."

Her head swiveled toward him.

"Of ale," he clarified dryly. Shoving his hands into his pockets, he strode forward into the fog. If he lingered, he just might be tempted to take her up on what she'd thought he referred to.

Honoria scurried after him. Blade listened for a moment, slowing his stride to match hers. She was puffing as she caught up, her cheeks rosy with exertion. He eyed her darkly. How she managed to walk to work each day was beyond him. The bloody woman was on the verge of collapse.

He paused at the intersection of Old Castle Street and Wentworth but then changed his mind. "This way."

"But the docks are that way," she protested.

He ducked through an alley leading out of the rookeries. An odd odor caught his nose and he stiffened. Honoria bumped into him.

"What are you doing?"

"Catchin' me breath," he muttered, looking around. It must have been his imagination. There was more than enough moldy food scraps and offal dumped in the gutters to account for the rancid, rotting smell that had wafted past. "Come on."

They came to the end of the alley, passing through the tiny improvised gate of Hoargate and coming out at Petticoat Lane. Some of the late-night vendors of the market were still hawking their wares. A couple of whores eyed him. One smoothed her skirts, then caught a glimpse of Honoria. The woman deflated and started looking around for another mark.

"You," he said, pointing at a vendor. "'Ow much for that pie?"

The man paled, then stammered, "For you? Ah, why, nothin' at all, sir."

Blade flipped him a coin anyway. The man snatched it out of the air, then hastened to wrap up one of his cold pork pies. Blade offered it to Honoria.

She stared at the package. "I couldn't. Thank you for the offer, but—"

He glared at her. "Just take the damn thing and eat it. This is the rookery, luv. Ain't no rules 'bout what you can and can't accept from a man. Your stomach rumblin's fit to drive a man barmy."

"I can't pay you back. I have to pay the doctor—"

"This one's free."

He gave her his back and started walking. Behind

him the sound of waxed paper rippled, and then came the swish of her skirts as she followed. Gravy and pig fat flavored the air. His lips curved in a smile.

He knew better than to turn around and watch her eating. Instead he led her across the street to a pneumatic rickshaw. The young Han Chinese boy nodded to him, then hopped up onto the cycle seat. "Where to?"

"The White Hart," Blade said, offering Honoria a hand. "Aldgate."

Honoria dashed pastry from her lips, then eyed his hand. After a moment's hesitation, she slid her warm fingers over his. Her eyes widened and he knew she felt how cold his skin was. Taking her by the waist, he lifted her into the seat and then jumped up beside her. The narrow seat pressed them together, thigh against thigh, and when she shot him a nervous look, he stretched his arm out casually and rested it behind her on the seat back.

"I've never ridden in one of these before," she said as the rickshaw gave a jerk and ducked out into the lane. It wove its way between market stalls and people with an ease he'd never gotten used to.

"They come out o' Limey when the Chinese moved in. Good way to get 'round the East End. Ain't no steam cabs or omnibuses 'ere, luv."

The young driver hurled them into the corner onto Whitechapel High. Honoria sucked in a breath, tumbling into Blade. He caught her close, tucking her protectively under an arm. Her palm was on his thigh. She realized it the same moment he did and jerked it away.

Blade's hand tightened on her shoulder, reluctant to let go. But then he felt her body tense and forced himself to release her. No point scaring her off. He'd have to move slowly, let her get used to him. For he intended to have her. It was just a matter of when.

Honoria cleared her throat and righted herself, patting an errant curl back into place. "Your accent. It isn't entirely cockney."

"Ain't it?"

Honoria gave him a sidelong glance. Whatever goodwill he'd won with the pie was gone with the enforced intimacy of the rickshaw. Her shoulders were squared like a woman facing the gallows. "You sound horrendous most of the time, but sometimes I find a trace of…of…proper speech in your words."

"You mean of inside the city walls."

Her head rested close to his arm. He could almost reach out and touch one of those errant brown curls that trailed from her rumpled chignon.

"The upper class," she corrected. "The Echelon."

His fingers brushed the soft silk of one curl. She didn't notice. "You think I sound like one o' those fancy lords?"

A pained expression crossed her face. "Not at the moment. Mostly when you forget yourself."

"Are you askin' where I come from?" He wrapped the curl around his finger, staring into her eyes. Her hair was very soft, like spun silk. And thick. What would it look like tumbled over her shoulders?

His mind took a swift detour. He wanted to taste that milky-white skin, to run his tongue over the naked curve of her breasts and the rosy, puckered nipples. His cock stirred. With her head bowed in thought, he could see the fine tracery of veins that traversed her throat. Saliva pooled in his mouth, and his vision narrowed to the pulsing, heady throb of her carotid artery, casting the world into a chiaroscuro landscape.

"I've heard several theories," she replied, her voice sounding as though it came from a great distance. "I heard you escaped from the Inquisition in the New Catalonian prisons, where you were infected with the craving virus. Or that you led the resistance in France when the revolution guillotined the entire blue blood aristocracy there." She was breathing rapidly, not quite as unaffected as her cool, crisp tone presumed. Blood pulsed through her veins, beating in time to the throb of her heart.

Want it... "What do you think?" he whispered, leaning closer.

"You don't have any trace of French or the Catalan dialects. You sound like you were born in the gutters and somehow learned to mimic the sounds of the aristocracy." Honoria chose that moment to look up, and he tugged the curl that he'd wrapped around his finger. She clapped a hand to the back of her head, her fingers sliding over his. Her eyes widened.

Take it, Blade thought. The knife against her throat, nicking her just enough to bleed her; his mouth on her skin, the sudden hot flood of blood against his lips as she struggled in his arms at first, then slowly, slowly succumbed...

He shut his eyes. *I ain't an animal.*

And then Vickers's voice, whispering in his ear. *Yes, you are. Remember the guards? Remember that old woman? Remember Emily?*

He would never forget her. And God help him if he did—God help them all.

Sound washed back in upon him. Blade opened his eyes. The world was a riot of color again, not the grim, stark shadows he saw when the hunger forced itself upon him. He could feel it receding, unsatisfied.

"What are you doing?" The words died on her lips as she saw his expression.

He gently disentangled his finger. "Your hair's as soft as silk."

He almost laughed to see the bewildered expression on her face as she evidently searched his words for some hidden meaning and failed to find it.

"I'll thank you to keep your hands to yourself," she finally said. "And you managed that sentence without a trace of the rookeries in it."

Blade ran the words back through his head. She was right. He'd sounded exactly like Vickers did, with his hard, crisp vowels and the slight sibilance he placed on certain letters. The comparison annoyed him. "You were right. I were born in the gutters, but I weren't always street scum."

"That's not what I meant."

"No?" He leaned back in the seat as they passed beneath the massive bricked edifice of Aldgate and into the heart of the city, hiding his face from the pair of metaljackets guarding the gate. The pair stood almost seven feet tall, with burnished metal breastplates and overlapping plates to protect the delicate steam-driven mechanisms that made them move.

The enormous spire of the Ivory Tower gleamed in the distance. Since Parliament had been overthrown, the Ivory Tower had become the heart of Echelon power, and its soaring tower served as a watchful reminder of who ruled over London.

There was no place in the city where you could escape the sight of it. Not even in the stews.

"Have you ever been inside it?" Honoria asked, following his gaze.

"Once." He tore his eyes away. "Painted the floors wet with blood."

Her gaze shot to his.

"Themselves don't like rogue blue bloods runnin' 'round. Only saw the sheriff's 'otel, mind. Spent a few months there, rottin' in the dark before I sprang meself. They come after me, but I convinced 'em it weren't wise to chase me down. Found me way to the 'Chapel and stayed there."

"Do you think this is wise then?" Honoria said. "Coming into the city?"

"Who's goin' to stop me?"

She gave him a dubious look.

Blade laughed. "They got better things to do than make sure I stay out. Too busy stabbin' each other in the back and pretendin' they didn't do it."

"I think," she said, "that you like playing cat and mouse with them. Proving that you can go where you like, when you like."

"Mebbe." He smiled. "There's a bit of the blue blood in me after all."

"Manipulation isn't a symptom of the disease," she replied primly. "But a manifestation of the individual's own nature."

"Near every bloodsucker I ever met'd sell 'is mother

for a bit o' the ready. And how do you know what the cravin' does or doesn't do?" He examined their surroundings as though the question was an idle one. "You ever met a blue blood before?"

"No," she replied. "But I've read a lot about the disease."

Liar. Blade smiled to himself. She'd spill her secrets to him one day. Half a century of life had taught him patience if nothing else.

The rickshaw came to a halt and the young driver ground the brakes on. "Here, sir. The White Hart."

Blade leapt to the ground and turned to offer a hand to Honoria. She blinked and he realized she'd missed the movement. "It's warm inside and the grub's good." He gave her a disarming smile. "Or so I 'eard."

She didn't want to take his hand. But her skirts were long and made the jump down somewhat precarious. The warmth of her fingers was somewhat intoxicating. That was what he missed most; he hated the clammy feel of his own skin. Sometimes he wondered if touching him felt like touching one of the Echelon's cold metal drones. Did Honoria find the sensation disgusting? Other women had turned away from him in the past.

He caught her around the waist before he could find out, and set her on her feet. She barely came up to his shoulder, and it felt as though there was more weight in the material of her full skirts and bustle than in her flesh.

"Wait 'ere," he told the driver, flipping him a bull.

The boy looked down in surprise. "Yes, sir. Thank you, sir."

Honoria watched as the five shillings disappeared and the boy dragged the rickshaw out of the way. "That's far more than what he earned."

"Aye." Blade shrugged, then set his hand into the small of her back. "After you, milady."

The White Hart was tucked between two buildings. It was probably a good thing, for the roof was crooked, leaning drunkenly against the building on its right as though that was all that held it up. A gas lamp lit the coat of arms hanging over the door and gleamed on the glass windowpanes that formed the front.

Inside, the room was in full roar. Timber panels with carved bas-relief lined the wall, and green leather booths offered a modicum of privacy. There was an embossed bronze panel—depicting a stag fleeing from hunters—over the bar, blackened by years of smoke from the enormous hearth in the corner.

Honoria stopped and Blade almost stepped into her. The heat from her body shimmered in the inch between them. He drank it in. So warm. So full of life. He wanted to sink himself into her, drown in her heat. But then she was stepping forward, toward a narrow booth near the window.

Blade caught the serving maid's eye and jerked his head. The woman flushed a healthy pink that spread all the way down her throat, and he paused, watching as the blood flushed through her pale skin. For a moment the color faded and he was left with a world of gray again. It was enough for him to shake it off and follow Honoria.

One of her eyebrows shot up. "See something you liked?"

He slunk into the seat opposite her, their knees bumping. The plump serving maid bobbed toward them, her breasts threatening to spill out of her neckline. She was everything that Honoria was not; full of fleshy curves, with a healthy shine to her hair that spoke of rich meals and good health.

"Yes," he replied, watching Honoria's lips thin. Was that jealousy in her eyes? Or cool disinterest? He couldn't tell with her and it drove him crazy. Honoria could give a cardsharp a run for his money.

"Well, don't let me stop you," she said.

"I've already eaten," he replied. He leaned closer. "Do you know what I see when I look at her?"

"A pretty young woman who would be more than happy to be with you. Unlike certain others."

"Do you?" He took another look at the serving maid. "I s'pose she's pretty enough. I 'adn't noticed."

Honoria snorted. Then looked horrified at her poor manners.

"I see blood. Flushin' up 'er neck, runnin' through 'er veins. 'Er skin's pale enough to show 'em, almost blue beneath the surface. Like a map showin' me where to go."

"Oh."

"But I don't dabble with strangers," he said, sitting back. "When I first saw the Ech'lon lords, with their blood slaves and thralls, I thought it barbaric. I understand now why they take 'em. Drinkin' from thralls is safer. They knows what to expect and what not to do when I'm bang up with the 'unger. In return I make sure they're well fed and sheltered, with enough coin to keep 'emselves as they wish. It suits 'em and it suits me."

"A very convincing argument. Do you tell that to them, or are they free to make up their own minds?" Heat flushed through her cheeks.

"I ain't ever taken an unwillin' thrall. You ain't got nothin' to fear like that. Only if you wish it, luv. All you have to do is ask."

Honoria's face paled and she tried to stand. He caught a handful of her skirts and held her there.

"One day you'll beg me to take you in," he whispered.

"When hell freezes over," she replied.

The serving maid arrived. "Sir?" she asked hesitantly.

"Damn your pride." He let go of Honoria's skirts. "What's the special?" he asked the maid.

"Mutton stew with bread and dripping."

Blade gave Honoria a direct look. "Do you want it?"

"I don't want anything from you." For the first time her facade cracked. He caught a glimpse of tears, and then she looked away, choking them back down as she slumped into the seat again.

"A bowl of it," he told the maid. "And two pints. Of ale."

"No!"

He ignored Honoria's protest and nodded to the serving maid.

"Damn you." Honoria started digging in her change purse.

Blade caught her hand. "Tonight's on me."

"No."

"Put the bloody money away."

She slapped a handful of shillings on the table between them. "I won't be your whore. I won't owe you anything."

He growled and caught her hand, holding it flat over the cold metal shillings. "All I want's for you to talk to me. A bit o' good conversation for the cost o' the meal. So I can 'ear 'ow you says things." He flashed her a smile. "Me first lesson."

He pushed her hand and the shillings under them back toward her. Honoria's gaze dropped first. He knew what she was thinking. She couldn't afford the meal, but she wouldn't let him pay for it. By turning it into a transaction, she could keep some semblance of pride.

The serving maid returned with two foaming mugs of ale. Honoria flushed and dragged her hand away, taking the shillings with her. The heat of her lingered in his fingers as if he'd stolen a touch of it. He rubbed them together, feeling the residue.

"Well, where you from?" he asked. "You appear six months ago out o' nowhere. Ain't no relatives visit. Ain't no friends. No suitors. Like you sprung from nothin'."

A minute thinning of her lips. She was good. A bleedin' Jack-in-a-box. He took a sip of the ale and forced it down. If he concentrated, he might be able to swill it all, but most of the time he had no need of food or drink. Still, he missed the taste of things sometimes.

"Oxford," she replied. "My father was a professor. I taught the local young women their finishing touches."

"What 'appened? How'd you end up 'ere in the East End?"

A flash of something real, something painful, flickered through her eyes. "He passed away. The lease was sold and we were without a roof over our heads. I had a cousin in London, but that didn't work out. I took a job with Mr. Macy, but the pay wasn't enough to support a life in the city, and I can't say I like the idea of being under the Echelon's thumb."

"Why the prejudice against 'em? You ever run afoul o' the Ech'lon?"

"No." A slight hesitation. "Everybody speaks of them, though, and they sound like something I'd prefer to avoid."

For a moment she almost relaxed. Then the mutton stew appeared. Blade spread his arms across the back of the seat and watched her stare at it as though she'd never eaten in her life…and had suddenly found a dead fly in her bowl.

"Try the fork," he recommended. "It's much easier than mentally consumin' the meal."

A hot little glare made him smile again. But she picked up the fork and started tearing off delicate pieces of bread. Blade looked away, enjoying the clink of silverware and the heady scent of lamb stew and ale. If he closed his eyes, he could almost smell her, the faint musk of *woman* lingering beneath the spicier scent of stew like the base notes of an aromatic. There was no scent of his own to add except the touch of oil he used to sharpen his blades and the soap used to launder his clothes.

A blue blood had no personal scent. No warmth. Sometimes he felt as though he were slowly turning to marble, devoid of any of the touches of humanity that surrounded him. Until nothing but the hunger remained.

Something caught his ear—the rustle of waxed

paper. He fixed Honoria with a hawkish glare, but she was dipping her fork into the stew again. The bread was gone. Too quickly for the small pieces she'd been breaking off.

He could smell pork now too. "God's teeth, you're a stubborn wench."

She looked up in surprise. "I beg your pardon?"

"The 'alf-eaten pork pie in your pocket and the bread." He shook his head. "Aye, give it away, even though you obviously need it more."

"My brother and sister are at home wondering where I am," she said. "The least I can do is bring something back. I can't eat all of this." She put the fork down. The stew was hardly touched. "I can't eat a thing more."

The way she eyed the bowl, with reluctance in her eyes, made him believe her. She'd been starving herself so long that now she had the appetite of a bird.

"Next time it'll cost you," he said.

Honoria's chin tipped up. "There won't be a next time. I agreed to three lessons a week. No more. No less."

He leaned closer, breathing in her scent. "We'll see."

"No. We wo—"

The door to the White Hart smashed open. Blade was on his feet with his razor tucked in the palm of his hand before he realized it was Will, breathing hard from running.

"Bodies. Two of 'em," Will said. "Torn up and drained, like a bloody blue blood went crazy down in Pickle Road."

Honoria's head jerked up and she went white as a ghost. "That's my street!"

Chapter 4

"Stay back," Blade commanded.

Honoria took one look at the crowd and hurried after him. They were three houses down from the small flat she rented. There was no way she was going to stay behind.

Blade pushed through the crowd of people ahead of her, forging a path through the swarm of goggling onlookers with his powerful body. Honoria stumbled along behind. People shot glares at them—until they saw who was pushing through. Then the way miraculously cleared and the master of the rookery found himself in the eye of the storm. It seemed being known as the Devil of Whitechapel was extremely useful in certain situations.

Blood sprayed the cobblestones, gleaming black in the moonlight. One of the spectators had located a flare stick, and the fluorescent glow highlighted the brilliant scarlet splashes near Blade's booted feet.

Honoria swallowed. She had seen blood before. In vials and tubes in her father's lab or on the samples she took from Charlie to examine his virus levels.

Not like this. Not painted across the flagstones as though someone had wielded an artist's flamboyant brush, flicking drips of it in every direction. The ghastly sprawl of the two bodies was almost garish in the moonlight. Some quirk of fate had found this part of London free of its almost perpetual ground cover of fog.

Blade turned and found her on his heels. "I tol' you to stay back." He looked around at the crowd. "Go on. You seen it. Now get."

The onlookers dispersed with a handful of whispers. The burly man who'd found them at the White Hart knelt beside Blade and surveyed the scene with his burning amber eyes. Two others hung around, and the tattoos on their wrists proclaimed them Blade's men. One had a steel cap riveted to his scalp and a wicked hook in place of his left hand. The other winked at her with a devilish smile.

"Cutthroat Nelly cried the alarm," the man he'd called Will said. "O'Shay sent me after you and came 'ere to clear the street."

The taller man, the one who'd winked, spat to the side. "Bleedin' vultures swarmed me before I could keep it quiet." A thick lilt of Irish filled his voice.

"Who are they?" Blade knelt down, fingertips pressed together and a burning look in his eye as he stared at the bodies. He didn't go any closer, and she realized that he was wearing that expression again. The one that made his nostrils flare and his pupils consume his irises.

No matter how hideous the scene was, he liked it. Or the smell of it, anyway.

Honoria shivered. She looked down the lane to the little house three houses down with the light blazing in the window.

"Smells like Jem Barrett o'er in Brick Lane and his brother, Tom," Will said.

"Jaysus," O'Shay swore. "He did a right number on 'em. Their own mother wouldn't e'en recognize 'em."

Blade reached out and touched his finger to a droplet of blood. "Nothing human did this."

"Aye." Will agreed. "Tore 'em apart. Throat first, at least. They weren't aware o' most o' it."

"Only blue blood in these parts is you," O'Shay muttered. "And you wouldn't lose control like this."

Honoria went cold. It started in her stomach, then crept outward, spiraling through her core. There was a bitter taste in her mouth. *Oh God. Lena!*

She broke into a run.

Blade caught her at the door of the flat, dragging her into his arms.

"No! Let me go!" She hammered at his chest. "I have to..." She couldn't speak. A gurgle of something, a sound of inarticulate pain, crawled up her throat.

"Let me go in first, luv." His voice and hands were gentle, but he controlled her as easily as if she were a fluttering bird in his hand. "Just let me make sure it's safe."

She collapsed against his chest, feeling the slow, inhuman thump of his heart beneath her cheek. His body was hard, firm. Strangely comforting. "No," she said weakly. "No. You can't." Because if he found Charlie, he'd kill him.

"Honor?" Lena called from the other side of the door.

Her knees chose that moment to give out. "Lena?" His arms closed around her, holding her close, with a quiet murmur against her ear.

The door opened. Lena peered out, her fingers trembling. Honoria pushed Blade away and dragged her frightened sister into her arms.

"I thought it might have been...That you were..." Honoria turned her face into Lena's hair, breathing in the sweet, familiar scent. *Safe*. Lena was safe.

"I could hear them all yelling, but I didn't dare go out." Lena swallowed.

"Charlie?"

Lena looked past her at Blade. "He's still in bed. I didn't unlock the door."

"Good. You did good." Her knees were still shaking. But Charlie was still in bed and Lena was...It dawned on her then. Her brother hadn't lost control and turned.

Which meant there had been another blue blood in Whitechapel.

A dash of ice water down her spine. But if Vickers had found them, he would have taken Lena and Charlie and tossed the house, searching for the diary with her father's secrets.

Or would he?

This was exactly the type of game he liked to play. Cat and mouse. Toying with her. Leaving a pair of bodies torn apart in the street just to prove that he could. That nowhere was safe from him.

You are nothing, he'd once whispered in her ear. *I could take you here and now, and you couldn't do a thing to stop me.*

But he hadn't, because it was far more enjoyable to watch her live in fear. Once he broke her, the game would no longer be as entertaining.

What could she do? Should she run? But where? And how could she take Charlie now when he was so ill? Where would she ever find another respectable job?

"Blade?" A man called, startling her back to the present.

She'd forgotten about him in the horror. And Blade was just as dangerous—if not more so—than Vickers. When she turned, she found him watching her, leaning back against the railing with that nonchalant way he had. With his leather coat over her shoulders, he wore only a white shirt and black velvet waistcoat. Despite herself, despite everything, she couldn't help remembering how *stroke-able* that waistcoat had felt when he had held her in his arms.

A laugh took her. She was going mad. She had to be to think such a thing at a time like this.

Blade held up a hand, instantly silencing O'Shay. His gaze met hers, and she felt as though she were falling into a bottomless well, her body straining toward him, her eyes unable to drop from his.

"All's well?" he asked softly.

She nodded, holding Lena's hand tucked safely in hers. "All's well." It was a whisper. Her palms itched as though they hungered for the touch of him.

"I'll see you tomorrow night," he told her. "Don't go out till morn. I'll make sure Will's on guard, just in case."

He looked away. The spell was broken and Honoria blinked, sucking in a deep breath. She felt as though something important had happened, something that her mind couldn't yet make heads nor tails of. Then he turned and strode back toward the bodies.

"Honor," Lena whispered. "That man just called him Blade. He's not *the* Blade, is he? Where did you go?"

Honoria held her sister's hand, watching as Blade sauntered down the steps. "He took me for a meal." It was starting to rain, a light drizzle that did little but dampen the air. In the distance, Blade knelt down over the pair of bodies, examining them with the trio of men at his side. "I don't know why."

"I don't like him," Lena said. "You shouldn't see him again."

Honoria turned and shut the door behind them. Her eyes were burning with exhaustion. There'd be little mending finished tonight. She desperately needed sleep.

"I don't have much choice. He's our new protector."

Blade examined the blood patterns as he knelt in the street like a statue. O'Shay shifted impatiently, but Tin Man and Will just watched, letting him do what needed to be done.

He shut his eyes and let the silence of the street filter through him. Small sounds and smells started jumping out at him. Whispers from nearby houses. A dog several streets over, harassed by a pack of street children. A young boy coughing. The stink of fried sole in the nearest house.

He shut them out, went deeper. Will's heart was hammering along at a clipping rate. O'Shay had excitement running through his veins, ready to fight or hunt. It lingered on his skin like an acrid scent. Tin Man's breath whistled through his iron lungs. And underneath it all was the faint, rotten smell of a blue blood gone wrong.

God 'ave mercy. Blade went cold. He'd never smelled that scent—except for that moment earlier tonight—but he knew what it was. He should have listened to his instincts. The bloody creature had been *watching* him.

"Let's hunt the limey bastard down," O'Shay muttered. "We wait any longer and the trail'll go cold."

Blade held up a hand. And opened his eyes. "No. No one goes anywhere."

His heart was starting to beat faster. One word of this, and the rookery would erupt like a stirred anthill as people killed each other trying to get out in a hurry. Right now a blue blood had murdered two men in Blade's turf. Right now it was just a game between him and the Echelon. Everyone would be waiting around to see who was left standing at the end. They'd be laying coin down at Whitey's and debating about what would change if the Echelon slit his throat and took over.

"We're workin' double shifts." Until the monster was caught. Or if… "Will, you and O'Shay watch the Todd 'ousehold tonight. Watch your backs."

"We gettin' any relief when it starts gettin' dirty?" O'Shay asked.

Blade stood and brushed the dust off his pants. "We're only watchin' the house at night. When the sun rises, you can seek your beds."

Because there was no need to guard the rookery

during the day. The creature—the blue blood gone wrong—couldn't tolerate direct sunlight. It would go to ground, and that was when he would hunt it.

"Tin Man, you're with me. Time to rouse the troops, get us ready for a dawn 'unt."

"What are we 'untin', Blade?" Will asked. His nose was wrinkling up in distaste. He could smell it too; he just didn't know what it was.

Blade paused. Panic never did a man good. But sending his lads out to face something they were unprepared for was sending them to suicide.

"A vampire," he replied. "But keep it fuckin' quiet, or we'll 'ave a riot on our 'ands."

Chapter 5

THE LAST DYING RAYS OF SUNLIGHT GLIMMERED ON THE horizon like a molten puddle of gold. Blade walked along the edge of the gutter, hands thrust deep into his pockets. It had been a long, frustrating day. He, Tin Man, and O'Shay had worked the northern end of Whitechapel while Will, Rip, and Lark had worked the south, hunting for a scent trail.

There was plenty of rot in the 'Chapel. Plenty of fetid stinks. The stench from the nearby draining factories filled the air, overwhelmed only by the splash of urine against an alley wall or the hint of garish perfume on a whore's throat. Blade closed his eyes and kept walking, letting his nose sort through all the distinct scents, through the layers, dropping lower and lower, hunting for that sickly sweet rot.

"Bloody 'ell," O'Shay muttered from behind. "I 'ates when you do that." There was a brief flurry of scrabbling feet on the slick tiles. O'Shay swore. "It's gettin' dark, Blade. If the vampire's out there, he'll be thinkin' 'bout breakfast."

Blade stopped. Then opened his eyes. The end of the rooftop was an inch from the toe of his boots.

"I'd rather not *be* breakfast," O'Shay called. "You know what I'm sayin'?"

Blade spun on his heel. O'Shay clung to a chimney. Tin Man rolled his eyes and hopped over him, sliding down the steep incline of the roof until he hit the gutters. He sunk the hook of his left hand into the tiles and caught himself in time. More metal than man, he'd shown up on Blade's doorstep ten years ago, mute, his body scarred, and willing to do anything for his master, as long as Blade took in the small bundle in his arms too. Rumor said he'd once worked the coal mines, where the black lung took him. How a poor coal miner ever got the coin to pay for an iron lung was never explained, though. Nor where Tin Man had gained his scars.

Blade didn't know where Tin Man had found Lark. She could have been his child or even a sister; he didn't know.

Tin Man stared at him. The man couldn't talk, but his eyes were eloquent enough.

Blade nodded. Lark was out there, determined not to be left behind. The rest of the men could handle themselves, but she was only fourteen. Or near enough.

"Time to regroup." Blade dug a whistle out of his pocket. The high-pitched noise shot straight through his ears, but neither Tin Man nor O'Shay blinked.

In the distance an answering whistle screamed through the onslaught of night. "There 'e is, lads. Back to the warren."

Night was edging closer as they made their way back to the warren. Blade felt it coming, felt it seeping its way through his body. The hairs on the back of his neck rose. He scrubbed at them sharply. Of late he'd been more aware of the moment the sun set.

"You all right?" O'Shay was watching him as they walked.

"Happy as a whore with a bottle o' blue ruin," Blade answered, forcing a smile onto his lips.

Will, Rip, and Lark were waiting at the warren. Rip stoked the fire with his usual patience, the flames reflecting off his green eyes. Will paced the parlor while Lark sat in his chair with her feet up on the footstool, scratching Puss's chin.

"Off," Will commanded, nudging Lark's feet.

The girl flashed him a cheeky grin, then darted out of the room.

"Got nothin'," Will said. "Nothin' but piss and stink. It's like he vanished into thin air."

"He went to ground," Blade said. "They always do." He poured himself a glass of blood, swirling it under his nose. He refused to buy it from the Drainers, but there were those who offered it in exchange for coin or protection. A man could get too used to taking direct from the vein. Sometimes it was good to drink it cold. "First thing a vampire does is find a lair to 'ole up in. They 'ates the sun—it burns 'em. So it'll be somewhere dark. Tucked up safe. A basement. An ole factory. Tomorrow we'll spread out farther. Check the abandoned warehouses down by the docks."

"And what about tonight?" Will asked.

"It's glutted for the moment," Blade said. "Won't

be out till the 'unger builds up again. We've got a day or two, at most. Tomorrow I want the word spread. I'm puttin' martial law down on the rookery. Let 'em think it's 'cos we're about to go to war with the Ech'lon. Nobody's allowed out at night past dusk."

"People won't like it," Rip said.

"They don't 'ave to like it," Blade replied. He slid into his armchair, hooking his left ankle up on his knee. "If they're caught out on the streets, they'll answer to me. And they'd better have a bloody good answer."

"So what'll we do?" Rip asked, kneeling down and offering Puss a piece of hardtack from his pocket.

"Get some rest," Blade said. "I've got the rookery lads keepin' watch for the night with whistles. So keep your boots on, boys, just in case we get a sightin'. Tomorrow I want maps. We'll mark out the areas we've searched and try to pinpoint where it mighta 'oled up—"

Will turned and sniffed at the air. "Someone's comin'."

Blade tugged his pocket watch out and examined it. Nine o'clock. If it was Honoria, she was early.

"Miss Todd," Will said, a flash of disapproval crossing his face.

Blade tucked his watch back in his waistcoat. "Go on, off with you. No drink. No women. And keep your knives close."

"That go for you too, ey, boss?" O'Shay shot him a leer.

"Miz Todd ain't the sort of woman you'd be likely consortin' with," Blade replied. "And this serves a purpose. I ain't forgotten 'bout Vickers."

Even the men could hear the sound of her footsteps now, and then the brief rap on the door. Lark stuck her head in. "Miz Pryor's 'ere. You want I should let 'er in?"

A brief swirl of Honoria's scent swept through him, reminding him of the previous night. His blood heated. "Aye. Send for a light supper." No doubt she'd barely eaten. "Some o' that kidney pie and fresh bread Esme baked for dinner. And a pot o' tea." Ladies liked tea, didn't they?

O'Shay snickered under his breath as he and the other men filed from the room. A cascade of striped skirts glimmered in the hallway, and each of the men took their fill of her. Honoria's eyes widened at the sight of them and she politely murmured greetings. Then her gaze lifted and met Blade's.

For a moment he felt as though the air was thick with the mysterious charged lightning the Echelon could produce. Though her cheeks were thin and pale, there was no sign of surrender in her eyes. She had come here with her defenses fully raised.

Blade dragged the stuffed armchair around, placing it close to the fire. The autumn nights were still long, yet a hint of winter's chill hung in the night air. "Come," he said, gesturing toward the chair.

Honoria tugged at her kid gloves. He pretended not to notice how thin and worn they were as he took her hat. Thick braids formed a coronet on her head, and her dress was an eye-watering confection of charcoal and white stripes. The cut of the cloth juxtaposed against itself, the stripes forming different slanting angles. A scrap of lace edged her throat, hiding the enticing glimpse of her carotid artery. Covered from top to toe. He almost felt like laughing. Did she really think it would be so easy? She reminded him of a present, just begging to be unwrapped. Starting with the buttons at her wrists. His lips, cool on the soft skin there as he licked the pale veins, feeling the pulse of her blood against his tongue. From there his mind took a detour. A slow exploration of the spill of lace at her throat. Tugging it free, revealing the smooth slope of her neck. Lips to throat, tasting the salt of her skin. His cock surged at the thought.

Of course, she was just as likely to conk him with the satchel in her hand if he tried.

"'Ere. Let me take that," he murmured. His fingers brushed hers as he took it. His imagination felt that touch in other, darker places, but Honoria looked far less affected.

"You're being entirely too charming," she said, turning on him with guarded eyes. "What are you up to?"

"Per'aps it's merely me nature to be charmin'."

"Unlikely." She gave him a reserved look as she seated herself. "You want something from me."

"A gentleman never professes 'is desires to a lady," he admitted. "It ain't polite."

A healthy flush of color touched her cheeks. "You're quite right, of course. But a gentleman should never admit to having such desires in the first instance."

Blade sank into the opposing armchair and hooked his ankle up on his other knee. He laced his fingers together across his middle, eyeing her with a slight smile. "Your notions are practic'ly middle class, luv." The Echelon was all about the pursuit of pleasure. As if in defiance, the middle and working classes had become somewhat conservative. They dressed in solid, work-a-day colors and sturdy fabrics and kept well-mannered households.

"I am middle class," she retorted.

"And I'm of the gutters."

"Your manners perhaps." She ran an appraising eye over him. "You have the gaudy instincts of the Echelon and a theoretical notion of etiquette, so it seems. When it suits you. I shall have my work cut out for me."

Dragging the satchel into her lap, she opened it and started assembling an array of papers and notes on the small table beside her. "I thought perhaps we should start with an overview of what is needed. I have none of the equipment I use at Macy's, but I'm certain we can make do. Your speech shall be the most difficult task. There are some books here that I borrowed from my brother..." She dug them out, relegating him to merely another student. He would just see about that. She looked up beneath thick, dark lashes. "Can you read at all?"

"Some," he admitted. It weren't the sort of thing he'd had much time for, between his early life on the streets and his later life in the rookery. "Me name. Dates. Numbers. I'm good with numbers."

Honoria uncapped a pen and made a brief notation. A knock sounded on the door and she looked up.

"Come in," he called.

Lark shoved the door open, giving an old automated drone a shove. The drone rumbled forward with a teakettle whistle of steam escaping from its vents. A gleaming silver tureen held Honoria's meal, with steam vents keeping it warm within, and the teapot jostled on the tray as the drone jerked toward them.

"Bloody 'ell," Blade said. "You've resurrected old Bertie."

They didn't bother to sit on formality at the warren. The drone had been fenced years ago, and with its faulty wiring it had never been sold on. Esme or Lark must have hauled it out of storage, though for what purpose he wasn't certain.

Lark hauled the drone up short just as it prepared to plow through Honoria's chair. "Bloody scrap o' tin."

Honoria stared in astonishment. "What is this?"

"An eighteen fifty-eight service drone," he admitted. "Either that or a rusted bucket of bolts with the steering capacity of an 'erd of stampedin' bulls."

"Yes, but..." Honoria gave the pot of tea a swift glance, then eyed the silver tureen with far more interest. "It's well after supper and you don't eat."

Blade lifted the lid. A steaming waft of kidney pie filled the air. He deliberately fanned it her way with the lid. To the side sat a small plate of biscuits and ginger cake. "I thought per'aps you might be 'ungry. Me 'ousekeeper's grub is delicious, I'm told."

"That's very kind of you, but I assure you I'm not." As if to defy her, her stomach gave an audible growl. She flushed. "You shouldn't have."

"Tea?" Blade offered.

Honoria stilled his hand with a touch of her fingers. "Allow me." She reached for the pair of cups and elegantly handled the tea service, her gaze darting between it and the plate of kidney pie.

Blade smuggled a smile.

"Anythin' else?" Lark asked, waggling her eyebrows at him.

"Get to bed," he muttered.

Lark left them alone with a sigh of relief. The drone bobbed up and down, occasionally erupting with an almost flatulent gasp of steam.

"I'm not some starving kitten you've fetched off your doorstep," Honoria said briskly, gesturing toward the lumped sugar and pitcher of cream. "You're utterly transparent, you know?"

He shook his head to the condiments and accepted the teacup and saucer. "I ain't the foggiest clue what you're referrin' to."

"Fattening me up," she snapped. "Like a Christmas goose. I'm not eating it."

"Let it go cold then. I don't give a damn, but me 'ousekeeper might think it rude."

Her mouth opened. Then closed. "You're incorrigible. I shan't enjoy a bite, knowing my brother and sister are at home without—"

"Take some cake 'ome then," he suggested, "if that'll ease your guilt."

She still looked cross. But she shot the pie a longing look. *If only she'd look at me like that*, he thought and rubbed at his jaw.

Still, it gave him an odd sort of pleasure to see her accept the plate and dissect the meat with the small fork. The urge to protect her was suddenly overwhelming. Honoria was not the sort of woman to welcome such attentions, and he wasn't sure why he felt such a strong inclination. After their first meeting, he was fairly certain she'd spit in the eye of the devil himself. She needed someone to watch over her, but she'd be damned if she'd admit it.

As she took a delicate bite, her eyes softened with pleasure. "Delicious."

A flake of pastry clung to her lips. He shifted uncomfortably as her tongue darted out and swept it away. "Aye," he muttered. He liked seeing the visible enjoyment on her face. A simple moment of sensory delight that he was privy to.

Imagine what other delights he could show her. Imagine her reaction, as delicious and uncensored as it was now, while she closed her lips over another bite.

Her gaze flickered his way. "You're staring."

"Can't 'elp meself," he replied. "You were made to be stared at."

A flicker of consternation crossed her face. She toyed with the fork. "As far as compliments go, it is crude but sufficient. But we shall cover that later, after we have begun the rudimentary matters."

"I were merely statin' the truth," he replied. "Can't take me eyes off you. Does it bother you?"

Another slant of those wide, almond eyes. "It's disconcerting," she admitted. "How should you like it if I stared so at you?"

Blade spread his arms wide. "Look all you want, luv."

Honoria stabbed the last of the pie, delicately sweeping it off the tip of the fork with her cherry-colored lips. Her gaze settled on his with a challenging gleam. Then slowly it started wandering down his body, cataloging each inch of flesh as though she were ruthlessly looking to find fault with it. An uncomfortable feeling.

"A woman is not encouraged to…to leer at a man,"

she said with a troubled look pinching her brows. She paused, seemingly quite taken with his thighs.

His cock stirred. *Thank the lord for tight leather*, he thought, feeling her piercing gaze upon that area of his anatomy. "Ain't you ever looked at a man, then?"

"Of course not."

Relief swelled in his chest.

Honoria shook her head as though clearing it. "How do you distract me so easily?" She put the empty plate aside and tugged a sheet of paper out of her sheaf. "This is a sheet of the alphabet. I shall go over it with you. We might as well begin there for tonight. The basics of appropriate conversational topics seem to be escaping you entirely."

Blade didn't complain. As she placed the paper on a small writing table between them, she dragged her chair closer. He hauled his alongside, and as she leaned forward, her shoulder brushed against his.

She shot him a startled look. "That's quite close enough."

"Can't see the paper." He squinted slightly.

"You're a blue blood." As such his vision was preternaturally excellent.

Teasing her was far more enjoyable than most of the interactions he'd ever had with women. Including the naked ones. It was so easy to fluster her.

Honoria readjusted her chair, then used her cup of tea to anchor the top corner of the sheet. There were twenty-six squares across it, filled with thick, dark letters. In this state he could recognize most of them; it was only when placed in a jumble that he could not always pick out the meaning.

"This," she said, pointing at the first letter, "is 'A,' as in airship."

He liked watching her mouth form the shape of the words. The flick of her tongue as she pronounced each vowel and consonant. The wet gleam on her lips as she moistened them.

She made him repeat the sound, which he did, perfectly. By the time she'd reached 'F,' she was frowning at him.

"Are you paying attention?" she accused.

"Aye."

"To the *letters*," she said. "Not my…my mouth."

"I know me letters," he said. "When they're like this."

An eyebrow arched. "Prove it."

"We've no ink," he said, sliding his fingers over the edge of her armchair. He stroked her hand gently. "'Ow do I prove it?"

Honoria tugged at his fingers, but he turned her hand over in his and exposed the bare skin of her wrist.

"I've an idea," he murmured innocently.

With his fingertip he traced the first slashing line of the "A" across her smooth skin. The touch was deliberately light. Her lips parted and she gave a helpless little shiver.

"Stop."

"'A.' For arm." He returned to the start and began the soft, lush curves of the next letter. "'B.'" His gaze traveled down her throat to her bosom, and he leaned closer, his voice lowering hypnotically. "For…brow." A devilish little smile.

Honoria's eyes went out of focus as she stared at his mouth. Her breath came a little heavier and she wet her lips. "That's quite enough." But the words lacked force.

"'C.'" Another suggestive curve. "For cheek." His breath brushed against her neck as he slowly leaned closer.

Honoria trembled, like a rabbit trapped in the hunter's hand, knowing that the soothing strokes of his touch were dangerous and yet not understanding how. He sensed the struggle within her; by rights she should pull away and slap him. With the melting softness in her body, she wanted to wait and see what else he could do. Curiosity would be her downfall. There was a passionate woman beneath the starch and tightly laced stays. But she could not be won by force, only by the sweet lure of desire.

Blade brought her hand up, lowering his mouth to the inside of her wrist. Her pulse gave an erratic jolt and she sucked in a sharp breath.

"'D,'" he whispered, feeling the coolness of his breath stir across her skin. "For dimples. Me favorite bit." Reaching out he started tracing the curve of the "D" across her wrist with his tongue. This close, he could smell the come-hither scent of her lush body.

"Stop," she breathed, her lips parted and quivering. A tremor ran through her entire body.

He looked up from her wrist, his tongue swirling through the intricate points of an "E." Their eyes met, hers wide and shocked. Blade stopped tracing the letter and suckled the tender skin into his mouth in a delicious parody of what he would do if the vein were cut open.

It was too much for her. She pushed him away with

a cry and clutched her arm to her chest as she put three staggering steps between them. There was a bruise forming on her wrist in the shape of his mouth. The sight of it stirred his blood. He'd put his mark on her. Dark satisfaction flavored the thought.

Honoria stared at him through passion-glazed eyes. She looked vulnerable, and he realized that the cool mask of indifference she often wore was gone. As she rubbed hard at the mark on her wrist, her eyebrows drew together. She was not happy. He had slipped past her emphatic barriers, and she would never forget how easily he'd done it.

"You..." With a growl, she gathered her papers up and stuck them in her satchel. "You have overstepped the line. That is *not* considered polite *or* acceptable. Good night."

"You forgot your cake," he called as she turned to leave the room. "For your brother and sister."

With another angry glance, she returned to fold the cake neatly into a napkin. "You have two days. I advise that you learn some restraint."

And then she turned and stalked out, leaving him laughing behind her.

"Miss Pryor, a word if I could?" Mr. Macy wrung his hands as he stood in the doorway, a habit she secretly found detestable.

Honoria plastered a smile on her face and put her teacup down. She couldn't help tugging at the sleeve of her gown, though she knew it covered the damning mark. Blade's mark. She could feel his mouth on her skin as if he'd etched the sensation into her body. The thought made her angry—yes, *angry*—that she could not escape him.

Her notes were spread across the polished surface of the walnut secretary desk, written in the spidery hand of the mechanical letter copier. She had just finished with Miss Lovett, who was making remarkable progress. The girl's stammer had almost completely submerged, except in times of emotional duress, and she could recite the names of the Great Houses of the Echelon by rote: Malloryn, Casavian, Bleight, Lannister, Caine, Goethe, and Morioch.

"Of course, Mr. Macy. I was just reviewing my notes on Miss Lovett. They say she's caught the eye of Mr. George Fitzwilliam of the House of Lannister. A minor offshoot but a coup for the academy, sir."

Mr. Macy allowed himself a small smile. "Indeed." Then it faded. He stepped into the parlor she'd been allocated for her lessons, shutting the doors behind him with meticulous care.

Honoria felt the air deflate out of her and put the spring pen down, smoothing out her skirts. This was going to be a difficult talk, possibly disastrous. She could tell.

Still, she kept the smile on her lips. "Would you care for some tea, sir?"

"No, thank you." Mr. Macy took his seat, sinking into the stuffed armchair. The drone hovered with the tea caddy, little puffs of steam erupting from the release valve on its head. "I'm afraid, Miss Pryor, that we need to have a serious discussion."

"I'm sorry, sir. I know yesterday was inexcusable. It

won't happen again, I promise. Charlie's illness caught me by surprise. I didn't—"

"I'm not here to discuss your brother's illness," Mr. Macy said. His watery blue eyes met hers from behind his steel-rimmed glasses. "I had a rather alarming visit this morning from a dear friend of mine, Mr. Bromley. He said that he saw you passing through Aldgate three days ago after work, on your way out of the city."

Her stomach plummeted. Somehow she kept the smile in place.

"I'm afraid it's led me to question certain inconsistencies in your story, Miss Pryor." He pulled a note from his pocket. "I sent a telegram to your reference in Oxford, Mrs. Grimthorpe. The response came back this afternoon." His gaze met hers. "Do you have anything to say for yourself?"

Oh, dear. "I've never given you any reason to doubt me, Mr. Macy. I've only ever had three days off, tending to Charlie, since I began working for you, and I've had remarkable success with my ladies."

He pulled an envelope from his pocket and slid it across the table between them. "I'm very sorry to do this, Miss Pryor. You have been an exceptional employee. But I cannot risk someone with a dubious past at the academy. As you say, Miss Lovett is discussing thrall contracts with the House of Lannister. It could *make* Macy's Academy of the Finer Arts, but it would also pull undue scrutiny from the Echelon. It is clear that you are hiding something. It would be rude of me to insist upon an answer, but the mere fact that you used a reference from a *woman who doesn't exist*, as well as the lack of Oxford-born speech to your tongue—and yes, I have an ear for accents too—tells me that it would be unwise to further our association."

"Mr. Macy, please..." There was something hot on her cheeks. Goodness, was she crying? She touched her gloved finger to it and stared at the wet lace. "Please, do not do this. I have a younger brother. A sister. They depend upon me."

Mr. Macy looked uncomfortable. "I've included a reference for you. An excellent one. And a bank check to see you through the next two weeks."

Honoria knew when the battle was lost. The decision had been made before he even entered the room. She eyed the envelope. Two weeks. And then they would have nothing but Lena's meager wage. It wasn't enough, and yet it was more than he ought to have given her after she'd lied to him.

A pity she couldn't use it, for she didn't dare show the bank her identity card. And *Miss Pryor* had none.

"I'm very sorry." Her head bowed in defeat. "I'll gather my things. Thank you for...for the reference."

He stood, evidently eager to have this over with. "Would you like me to call a steam cab for you?"

Honoria laughed under her breath. Five shillings for the cab. "No. No, thank you, sir." She stood, sweeping her skirts out behind her. What a strange relief she felt. No more snide comments from Lena about the fine dresses she wore to fool Mr. Macy. No more sneaking around, pretending to ride the tram to the address she'd given him in the West End.

She knew the shock would soon wear off and fear would settle in, gnawing at her belly. Those ever-present questions would begin circling her mind like vultures. *Where to work? How to feed them? How to pay the rent? How to find warm clothes for the winter that was looming around the corner?*

But she couldn't think about it now. She could only digest—slowly—this latest hand that fate had dealt her.

"Thank you, sir," she said again, and swept out into the hallway to fetch her hat and reticule.

❧

It took less time than she'd anticipated for the shock to wear off. The cold, bleak wind went right through her as she stepped outside clutching her letter of reference in her hand. It threatened to tear her hat from her head and dried the tears on her cheeks. She couldn't afford to cry, and there was no point really. Crying accomplished nothing.

It was only in the heart of night that she couldn't help herself.

Smoke hung over the chimneys of London. Somewhere behind the clouds the sun battled valiantly. The street stretched seemingly forever, a uniform parade of gray row houses lining its edges. It was still early afternoon. Pedicabs and steam carts lined the way, with a couple of pedestrians staring up at her curiously as she hovered on the doorstep.

Honoria took a step down. Then another. Macy's door had shielded her from the worst of the wind, but now it swept around her, traveling right through her threadbare stockings and the lightweight mauve cape that she wore. She hovered on the footpath, uncertain what to do. Go home? Charlie would be waiting. At least she could look after him now, without constantly worrying about leaving him home alone. Or should she start looking for a job?

She looked down at the envelope.

Whatever job she lied her way into, it would never be enough. Macy's hadn't been enough. Charlie needed good food, medications to slow down the rate of the craving virus, and a doctor who wouldn't ask questions or inform the Echelon about his condition. She'd been running herself into the ground, trying to pretend that she could provide him with what he needed when she knew she couldn't. Mr. Macy had only forced her eyes open.

She needed money. A lot of it. And there were only two things left to sell that had any value.

The mercenary little part of her brain that had seen Blade flipping gold sovereigns and shillings around with equal abandon knew exactly where she could get money from. She cringed away from the thought. Once she started down that path, there was no turning back. And a small part of her, the part that was still a young, naïve girl daydreaming about a white knight come to take her away didn't want to do that. Blade had been kind to her, and even though she knew he had ulterior motives in courting her as he had, she still couldn't stop herself from wishing.

Honoria took a step, then another. Toward the city. Her body knew where it was going, even as her mind resisted. There was one last option left to try. A dangerous, terrifying option that could see her in the depths of the Echelon's notorious dungeons before the end of day, but she had to try.

If she failed...Well, then she could bury her soul and take what was left of her pride to Blade and beg him to take her in as his kept woman.

~

The enormous metal eagle glared back at her, its wings outspread atop the hollow glass sphere that guarded the gates. A small electric orb pulsed in the heart of the globe, with the occasional spark of blue lightning shooting out, licking at the interior of the glass.

Honoria eyed the spark, her palms sweating inside her threadbare lace gloves. Pushing her identity card into the slot by the gate, she waited with bated breath as the metal teeth crunched down through the slots in the card. The stored lightning flickered but didn't lash out. Letting out her breath, she slipped inside the garden.

Before Vickers, her father had been sponsored by the duke of Caine. She'd grown up in this house and knew it almost as well as Caine did.

The servants' quarters were around the back. Honoria eased her way through the lush, overgrown gardens, keeping an ear out for the servant drones and any wandering thralls. The gardens were eerily familiar but not quite as large as she remembered. When she was a child they'd seemed endless, full of paths where she and Lena could chase each other along and thick with foliage in which to hide. She found the back door into the kitchen and eased it open. The room was empty, of course. Nobody to feed except the thralls, and the last time she'd heard, Leo kept only three.

Caine House had barely changed. That was one of the problems with being so long-lived. The blue bloods tended to stagnate after so many years, both at home and in their running of the country. It had been forty years since the prince consort took control, and since he'd first imposed his stifling rules, very little differed. The city walls kept the Echelon in and the poor out. Everybody had their place, and that was to serve.

Of course, such rule hadn't worked so well in France. With the majority of the French aristocracy infected with the virus, they'd thought themselves invulnerable. It wasn't until most of them were guillotined in the revolution that the English blue bloods sat up and took note. Humans were little more than thralls, but they could still be dangerous.

The prince consort was clever enough to know this. Officially his lovely young wife, Queen Alexandra, was in command, but everyone knew who pulled her strings. The people loved their queen, so the prince consort paraded her through the streets and held court from the balcony of the palace. He doted on her in public and played the handsome blue blood lover. If the queen's eyes wore a glassy look and her skin was a trifle too pale, then most of the commoners thought it was purely the height of fashion.

And then, of course, there was the metaljacket legion, in case things turned nasty.

Honoria found her way through the lower floors, fingers trailing over the fine white Chinese wallpaper that decorated the walls. The floors were ivory marble with a Turkish-red runner down the center. Several times she heard the low, distinct hum of a drone and ducked into one of the spare rooms to hide. The automated servants might not be programmed to deal with intruders, but they would certainly alert someone who could.

Honoria slipped into the servants' hidden warren of corridors and found her way to the third floor. There were voices in the library. Avoiding all of the creaking floorboards, she made her way to the main bedroom.

The massive four-posted bed dominated the room with heavy red velvet curtains tied to the posts. Late afternoon sunlight cast shining squares across the red carpets.

The pistol was heavy in her reticule as she dug it out. No need to take chances. Her father had said that if she ever needed help, she could come here, but the Leo Barrons she knew—the young boy who had put frogs down her dress and tricked her into touching one of the globes of stored lightning—wasn't the same as a man. He was one of *them* now.

The door opened.

"What the *hell* are you doing here?" Leo hissed. He slammed the door and took a menacing half step toward her.

Honoria held up the pistol and clicked the hammer back. "Stay where you are."

Leo froze. An inscrutable expression came over his face. She took the chance to examine him. He'd always been fair as a boy, but his silky moonbeam hair had darkened to an antique gold. He wore a crisp black velvet jacket with puffed sleeves, a loose white shirt, and a pair of tight leather trousers. Rings glittered on his fingers, and there was a flash of gold at his ear with a ruby dangling from the loop.

"You've changed," she said. His skin looked paler, almost...silvery?

He eyed the pistol then gave a fluid shrug. "It happens." Crossing the floor with catlike grace, he circled toward the liquor cabinet on the tallboy. "Care for a drink?" A sidelong look through silky lashes. He waved the bottle at her, the ruby-colored blood swirling around inside.

"Thank you, no."

Leo splashed a dash of blood into the glass. Though it shared the same color as claret, it was denser, lacking the gleam of liquor. No doubt it was bought directly from the draining factories down near Whitechapel. She eyed it with distaste. Did he know how many people sold their lives for what he drank so carelessly? Would he even care?

"Half of London's hunting for you." His eyes locked on her, black as night.

"I was careful."

"Are you going to shoot me?" He arched a brow. "No? Then put it away."

Honoria stared through the sight. The gun muzzle came into sharp focus, with Leo muting into a blur of black behind it. He moved and she looked up just as he clamped a hand over the pistol.

"Put it down, Honoria. Before somebody gets hurt." This time there was none of his boyish nonchalance.

Her jaw tightened.

"If I wanted to hurt you, I wouldn't have bothered coming all the way upstairs." He held both hands in the air. "I'd have simply sent Vickers up."

"*Vickers?*" She lowered the pistol in shock. "Vickers is here?"

"In the library." Leo's mouth twisted. "You're damned

lucky he didn't realize it was you, with all that scent he wears. What were you thinking, coming here? Surely you realize that the house is watched."

"I was desperate. And nobody saw my face. I kept my head down and my hat—"

"Damn it, your scent, Honoria. Those watching the house aren't simply using their eyes."

A kernel of suspicion burned in her. "Why is Vickers here?"

He did smile then, that familiar, mocking curl of the lips that she remembered. "Politics. Vickers is trying to play me. Your escape cost him a great deal of face."

Despite herself, she felt an odd twinge of discomfort. She shouldn't care, truly. Leo was nothing to her. But… "Are you going to be all right?"

"Do you give a damn?" Leo gave her a direct look.

"Of course I do."

He blinked. Then looked down into the glass. "You don't like me."

"I wouldn't wish Vickers on my worst enemy. Besides," she added softly, "Father always had a soft spot for you."

Their eyes met.

"You need money," he said, running his finger around the rim of the glass and dropping his gaze.

"I lost my job. My employer knew I was hiding something."

"Get a new one." Leo put the glass down and started for the door.

"I can't." She grabbed his sleeve. The effect as he froze was chilling. "I can't afford to look after Lena and Charlie, not even with a job. I need access to the trust that Father left for us. You're the executor. All I need is some money to tide us over until—"

He broke her grip. Caught her wrist. "You don't understand. If I access that trust, people are going to ask why. It was bad enough that your father named me executor. I can't explain why I'm withdrawing large sums."

"Then take it out of your own drawings," she said. "You can have whatever Father left. Just loan me enough to see me through the year. I promise I won't ever ask for more. You won't see me again."

"I can't."

Her blood boiled. "You mean you won't. You jealous son of a bitch. You're doing this because—"

"*Don't.*"

"They're your brother and sister too." Once the words were out, she regretted them. She'd never once told him that she knew why he'd tormented her so as a child, or why her father had spoken so often of him.

Leo's face closed over. "I'm a Caine," he replied. "It would be wise not to cast such aspersions, especially out loud. One might take offense at being called a bastard. You're lucky that I have some feelings of misguided benevolence toward you and your family. I can't give you money. You'll have to make do." His gaze ran over her, down the violet skirts and the elegant ruffles at the bottom that hid the frayed hem. "I cannot say that you look to be in dire straits. Perhaps you should part with some of the luxuries you evidently took with you."

Honoria ground her teeth together. "This was a mistake. I thought you were a decent man. I was wrong."

"You have five minutes." He crossed to the door in a loose-hipped saunter. "I'll keep Vickers distracted. And for god's sake, spray yourself with some of my aftershave to dilute your scent." He paused with one hand on the door. "By the way, you don't by any chance have the diary, do you?"

"The diary?" The lie came easily to her lips. "Father's diary?"

"Yes."

"I haven't seen it since I escaped from Vickers's house." And she wouldn't tell him if she did. "Why?"

"Are you certain?" Leo asked, his black eyes meeting hers.

"I'm sure."

He nodded once, the bright gleam in his eyes dulling. "If I were you, I wouldn't linger. And I wouldn't come here again."

"Don't worry. I won't."

Her last option walked out into the hallway and slammed the door shut.

"Damn it." After everything, she'd thought that perhaps he might find some trace of humanity within to help them.

Obviously she was wrong. And now she was trapped in the same house as the creature from her nightmares, and she could only hope that Leo wouldn't betray her.

She'd been such a fool. Trying to run from the inevitable. Honoria rubbed at her arms. Why bother? What was so wrong with selling herself? Perhaps a part of her had believed that they would escape this wretched mire and return to her former place in society.

There was no going back now. No escaping. She'd been starving herself for weeks for a principle. And the worst thing was, a part of her had always known it would come to this.

Perhaps it wouldn't be so bad. Blade had been kind to her so far. And though he was not classically handsome, still he made her breath catch and her body heat at the mere sight of him. They said that sometimes a woman could even find pleasure in it, though the very thought made her cringe inside.

Who was she trying to fool?

"Problem?" Vickers inquired as he stared out the windows, the sunlight highlighting his pale, powdery skin and blond, almost white curls. As was the custom in many of the older blue bloods, he wore powder in his hair. His lips were a girlish pink. Even his eyelashes had faded to a coarse white.

Leo closed the door behind him with a soft, controlled click. "Not at all. One of my thralls." He gave a slight smile, knowing Vickers would smell the blood on his breath. "She missed me."

The creak of the floorboards whispered outside. An overpowering waft of his aftershave caught Leo's nose as Honoria crept past. Vickers's eyes tracked the movement, but his face remained impassive.

"You should teach her not to interrupt." Vickers's tone held no inflection.

Leo quirked a brow and slung himself into his chair.

He lazed back in it, one leg slung over the arm of the chair. "I did. She won't bother me again."

Vickers nodded. "Good. Now, have you made any progress on the whereabouts of the Todd family? It's been six months, Barrons. Anyone would think you weren't looking hard enough."

From anyone else it might have been only a comment, not the threat it was. Leo toyed with his ring, watching the light gleam through the emerald. He wanted Vickers gone. His men were still searching, but Leo knew that so far no sign had been found of the vampire.

They'd find it soon enough. Or traces of it. The creature wouldn't be able to resist. It would start tearing its way through London, and then the Echelon would have a problem on its hands. It would be the last breath of air to knock down the house of cards that Leo was desperately trying to balance. Everything relied on saving face in his world, and if any of his many enemies could prove that he had known about the vampire, the House of Caine would be destroyed along with the creature.

Knowing a man was close to the Fade and not alerting authorities would earn a severe reprimand from the council, at the very least. If they learned he was directly responsible for the vampire, for causing his infection in the first place…

He had no time left for Honoria or the others. They would simply have to fend for themselves.

"Your precious Nighthawks can't find a sign of them," Leo replied, knowing damned well why. Honoria had left little trace, but what there was of it he'd buried long ago. "Patience, Vickers. They will come up for air. And when they do, I will be waiting for them."

A slight frown flickered through Vickers's pale gray eyes. There and then gone again. He examined his manicured nails, the lace dripping from his sleeves. "You'll fetch me first. Just locate them. I'll deal with the ungrateful brats."

"And the girl? Honoria?"

This time Vickers couldn't quite hide the flare of lust in his eyes. "Honoria." His voice caressed the word. "Honoria is mine. It's about time I broke that arrogant little bitch." He stood with a snap of his fingers. "Find them. Then send word." Without further ado, he strode past in a cloud of perfume. The strong scent couldn't quite hide the faint trace of rottenness that lingered about him.

Leo watched the door shut, chewing idly on his fingernail. He caught sight of his hand and paused. In the light the skin looked almost gray. The effects of injecting himself with colloidal silver were starting to show. He couldn't keep it up forever, or else the Echelon would recognize it for what it was—a desperate attempt to allay the virus.

He needed that diary. Before he too started to smell like rot. But if Honoria didn't have it, then where was it?

Chapter 6

Honoria rapped on the door, her stomach tying itself in knots. Around her, thick fog swirled. She cast a nervous glance over her shoulder, then tucked her new shawl tight around her arms.

She'd sold all of her dresses this morning and her mother's brooch. It was enough to see the doctor's outstanding bills paid and a handful of coins left over for the month's rent. She'd bought a pair of decent work-a-day dresses made of scratchy brown and gray wool and a pair of sturdy shoes. When Lena saw what she'd done, she'd cried.

Honoria had thought it would hurt more. The final cutting of ties with her former, privileged life. No going back now. But strangely enough, she'd felt nothing as she handed the dresses over. Nothing more than concern about how much she could get for them.

She could have waited. She had enough money now to see them through the month, but there was no point holding out, hoping for a miracle. If she didn't make this offer to Blade now, she feared she never would.

The door sprung open and the small boy who'd accosted her in the square peered out.

"You ain't s'posed to be out after dusk," the child said. "It's martial law."

"I need to see Blade."

"He ain't 'ere."

Still time to get away. She crushed the thought down ruthlessly. "What do you mean he's not here? Where is he?"

"The Pits," the child said. For a moment there was a softening of expression that gentled the child's heavy jaw.

"The Pits," she repeated. A blood-thirsty arena where men pitted themselves against each other or animals. The ultimate in blood sports in the city. And the last place a decent woman would go.

The child caught Honoria's arm as she turned. "'Ere now, where you goin'? You ain't s'posed to be out without an escort. Where's Will?"

"Will? I don't know. Why?"

"'E's s'posed to be watchin' you."

Honoria's eyes narrowed. "What do you mean?"

The child's mouth opened. Then shut. "Nothin'."

Honoria took the grimy wrist in her hand. "What did you mean, Will's watching me?"

"Watchin' your 'ouse!" The child pulled out of her grip, giving her an insolent look. "Keepin' you safe from the killer."

Keeping them safe? The only one who could have ordered that was Blade. But why? She was technically under his protection, but so were a lot of citizens, and none of *them* had a burly bodyguard.

"What is Blade up to?"

"'E protects what's 'is." The child gave a shrug that could have meant anything. As it did, its coat pulled tighter, revealing the slightest hint of curves. A girl.

"What's your name?" Honoria asked.

"Lark."

"Do you know how long he'll be gone, Lark?"

"Most o' the night, mebbe." Lark squinted up at her. "'Ere, now, you ain't still goin'."

Honoria took a step back into the fog. She had to do this tonight, before she lost her nerve. But there was a murderer out there, and she wasn't foolish enough to venture so far by herself. "Where is this Will? I might as well make use of him."

"Right behind you." A voice came out of nowhere, startling them both.

The big youth jumped off the rooftop, landing beside her with his fingertips touching the cobblestones. Leather braces rode over his massive chest and broad shoulders, and his once-white shirt had been hacked off at the shoulders, leaving his straining biceps bare.

Oh my. She'd seen her share of near-naked men in Whitechapel, but none of them had his…quality of muscle.

Honoria looked up as he straightened. And up. His yellow eyes met hers and she shivered. "I need to see your master."

"Tol' you not to open the door, Lark. Get back inside and stay there." Will's gaze swung to her again, his jaw stiffening. "You're bad for him, you know that?"

The cockney in his voice wasn't as pronounced as the others. Indeed, she could sense a vague Scottish burr within certain words. He took a step toward her and Honoria held her ground, though she was tempted to back away. "How?"

"He ain't thinkin' right with you. You're one o' 'em, all high in the instep. A fancy lass, who'll do his head in and not give a damn, 'cept what you can get from him."

Honoria took a step back. He was right. She had been thinking of what she could get from Blade. But then she remembered his words in the pub. *You'll beg me to take you in*...Any sense of guilt fled. This was purely a transaction between them. Nothing more.

"He wants blood. I'm prepared to provide it," she replied stiffly. "Are you going to escort me or not?"

Will's eyes narrowed, a thin slit of lambent gold. "Aye," he said. "But you hurt him and you'll have me to reckon with. Just you think on that."

Noise washed over him, a roar from the crowd as someone in the ring went down. Blade leaned back in his chair, boots kicked up on the rail of his private box in the Pits as he peered through the haze of smoke from his cheroot.

"That's Grady's bout!" O'Shay laughed, holding up his wager slip. "Told ye 'e'd win!"

Blade flicked the ash from the tip of his cheroot. "Scurvy's down. 'E ain't out yet. Watch."

O'Shay peered closer just as Jim Scurvy kicked out, his steel-plated boots striking Grady in the kneecap.

There was an audible crack and Grady went down, a look of shock and pain on his grimy face. Scurvy was on him in a second, drawing back his meaty fists and pounding the claret out of Grady. It splashed across the white sand, drawing another appreciative gasp from the crowd.

"Bleedin' useless cur!" O'Shay snarled, tearing up his ticket. He threw it out over the crowd like a handful of snowflakes.

Movement caught Blade's eye from the boxes across the arena. He ground out the cheroot, slinging his feet to the floor. "Themselves is 'ere. Watch me back."

O'Shay looked up, the purpose of the visit forgotten in the bloodlust. "Oh. Right." His gaze narrowed on the three men who were seating themselves across the arena. A pair of bodyguards stood behind the chairs, eyes roaming the crowd and hands held low, most likely on weapons.

Blade put a hand on the rail of his box and leapt over it, sinking into the sweating throng of heaving bodies. The heat of the crowd's lust surged through him, sending his heart racing. Blood everywhere. He could smell it. On the sand, on the men's knuckles, old blood lingering in men's clothes and even on some of the few women who joined the crowd.

He'd already fed tonight, but the hunger lingered near the surface, threatening to slide through the cracks in his control. Always present. Always keeping him alert. One slip and *he'd* be the monster carving up the crowd, raining more blood down on the arena than they could ever desire.

Yet they were oblivious to the threat among them.

He was too well known, a tiger in their midst that they no longer feared because of familiarity. Some cast a wary eye on him, but none backed away.

More gazes drifted toward the perfumed trio in the other box. Debney was there, a scented handkerchief held to his face as he peered toward the limp form being carried from the ring. At his side, the young, dashing Leo Barrons, heir to the duke of Caine, and the third…

The world narrowed as Blade stared at Alaric Colchester, a scion of the House of Lannister. Vickers's young cousin.

The world went gray. Then red. Blade fought it off, breathing hard through his nostrils.

"Blade?" O'Shay bumped against him.

A muscle in his jaw ticked. "Don't touch me."

O'Shay stepped back, wary of Blade's deadly soft tone. He knew what that meant and kept the crowd out of his way while Blade brought himself back under control.

It wasn't the time. Vickers would pay, and his House with him, but not yet. Not here.

The hunger clawed as Blade forced it down, swallowing hard. Plastering a mocking smile on his lips, he continued forward. The crowd parted around him, as though finally sensing some of the danger.

He bounded up, balancing on the edge of the rail. Barrons saw him, those unusual obsidian eyes sliding over him and away. He murmured something to his companions, and their heads swiveled toward him.

Blade walked along the rail, grabbing hold of the edge of their box. He swung over, giving a brief nod with his chin and leaning back against the box's rail with his arms crossed over his chest. "Evenin'."

Debney lifted his silk handkerchief again, as though Blade's scent offended him. It was a blue blood's way of saying you smelled like a vampire.

The bodyguards behind Debney stiffened, hovering on the edges of their toes. They were only human. The real danger lay in the three seated blue bloods who relaxed with feigned nonchalance in front of him. Debney he could take, and maybe Barrons, but Colchester was a vicious bastard, well trained in the use of the sword.

"Go away, you cur," Debney commanded. "And we'll forgive the insult. This once." His gaze remained on the fight, as though bored by Blade's intrusion. Thick white curls swept back from his high brow, heavily powdered in the Georgian style that most of the older blue bloods had not yet shaken. Sometimes he wondered if they did that to hide just how close they were to the Fade—those last few months when all color bleached out of their bodies and they became the blood-thirsty creatures they despised.

"You ain't in the city now, me lords."

"And you're alone." Debney's cold, gray gaze slithered to his. "Not even you could think to take on three of the Echelon."

Blade cocked his head. "'Cross the arena. See me man up there with the rifle? I told 'im to aim for the 'ead. You three can guess who 'e's aimin' for. I don't care, told 'im to pick."

O'Shay gave a little wave and a leer.

The bodyguards shifted.

"What do you want?" Barrons asked.

Ah. At least one of them had some sense.

"Wouldn't a bothered you fine gents," he said, "'cept I got a little problem in the rookery."

"Clean it up yourself," Debney sneered. "It's got nothing to do with us. Your messes are your messes."

"Aye. Only it ain't just *my* mess," he said, leaning closer to whisper. "I got a vampire problem. And mebbe I could take it by meself. Mebbe I can't."

That got their attention.

"That's impossible," Colchester said, his eyes narrowed. "There's been no word of anything in the city. Nobody's close to the Fade."

"That you know of," Blade replied, watching Barrons closely. The others were relaxing again, but Barrons held himself stiffly.

"I got two dead in the street. Me people think its war, 'tween you an' me. I'm keepin' it quiet before the whole city goes up in a panic."

"Perhaps a dog?" Debney suggested.

"Stinks o' rot," he replied. "I knows what a vampire smells like. I knows what it looks like when they goes for the throat."

Colchester examined his fingernails. "There's been no reports of any unregistered blue bloods or rogues."

Like Blade. Turned young and left in the gutters for someone's amusement. They were lucky if the blue bloods didn't simply kill them when they found them. Or maybe not so lucky at that. Blade could remember the heavy iron cage and the constant drip of water in the darkness. The hunger gnawing at him until he screamed with the pain of it. It had amused Vickers to keep him locked up, starving. The blood kept the hunger at bay, kept a man from turning into…something worse. Without it the Fade came quickly and a man could be a vampire within a month.

Blade had been Vickers's triumph. Three months with no blood, without turning. Somehow Blade had fought the hunger down, kept it caged. It was the only thing that saved his neck from the guillotine. Vickers wanted to know how he did it but wouldn't believe the answer. *I tore me own sister apart*, Blade had said. *I won't ever let it out again. I won't ever lose control again.*

Emily. The memory of her kept him strong.

He blinked the memories away. They were so vivid, as though they'd happened yesterday. Emily's smile, the sweet one she reserved just for him…

But it was Colchester's smile he watched now, tight and thin.

"Then someone's keepin' 'is cards close to 'is chest," Blade said. "Someone ain't reported a blue blood gone missin'. If it's a rogue unable to control 'imself, then who infected 'im?"

"There are rules against that," Debney bleated.

Blade never took his eyes off Colchester. "Are there?" he asked, silky soft. "And yet 'ere I stand. A living testament to the lie. No matter 'ow many times you lot tried to 'ave me killed."

Colchester shifted.

Barrons watched the interplay with a curious eye. "Vickers was reprimanded severely."

"It weren't enough," Blade said. "But 'e'll pay. One day."

Colchester jerked. Blade had the knife to his throat before he could move. "I wouldn't if I were you, ducky. Or I'll slit you ear to ear. A little present for me good friend Vickers. 'E's fond of you, ain't 'e? 'Is favorite little cousin."

"That's enough," Barrons said. "You've delivered your message. Now be gone. Before we take this as a trespass."

Blade looked up. Smiled. "Aye. But you're on my turf. I ain't the one trespassin'."

A roar went up from the crowd. The sounds of a dying gurgle came from the ring. Colchester was trying not to breathe. A thin line of blood sprang up against his collar.

Blade held Barrons's gaze for a moment longer, then stepped back.

Colchester sucked in a breath. "You son of a bitch," he spat, trying to rise.

Barrons caught his arm. Forced him back into his seat. "Sit down! People are watching."

"Then they can watch me kill this bloody cur!" Colchester retorted.

Debney looked around. "Not here," he said.

Colchester's eyes narrowed with hatred. "You'll pay for this."

Blade shrugged. "Mebbe. But it ain't goin' to be you."

Barrons's gaze suddenly caught on something in the crowd. His eyes widened, and then he looked away, far too swiftly.

Blade swung a leg out over the rail and glanced out to see what had caught his attention. There was nothing but a sea of people. And then he froze.

Honoria was making her way through the crowd, her face barely visible behind a charcoal wool shawl she'd draped over her head. She hurried along in Will's wake as he shouldered his way up toward Blade's box.

Barrons gave the crowd another seemingly disinterested sweep with his eyes, but his gaze lingered on her a second too long. He knew her, knew her well enough to identify her from the brief glimpse of her pale face. And he didn't want anyone to know.

How? Something vicious screamed through Blade for a moment, and his fingers dug into the rail. Something brutal and primal that wanted to go for Barrons's throat. Was she an old friend, a lover? Why would Barrons try to hide the connection between them? If he was any friend of Colchester's, he'd have pointed her out. Colchester could drag her before Vickers to collect the handsome reward.

Over my dead body.

Blade gave them a chilling smile. "Have a fine evenin' gents. Enjoy me 'ospitality for the night. I wouldn't recommend tryin' it again if I were you. I'll keep in touch." He touched his fingers to his hair in a mocking salute, then leapt off the rail.

Surging through the crowd, he shoved his hands deep into his pockets. He was going to wring her neck! And Will's, for daring to bring her here. What the bloody hell were they thinking?

Blade caught Honoria by the arm as they reached the stairs to his box. She gave a small shriek, covering her mouth with her hand when she saw who had grabbed her.

"Blade," she said in a breathy little voice.

Will turned quickly. Then eased back, reading the fury in Blade's tightly held frame. Blade pushed her toward him. "Get 'er out of 'ere. Now."

She staggered into Will's side. Blade continued on past them as though she were of no importance. He hissed under his breath, "Take 'er 'ome. And make sure you ain't followed."

"What's going on?" Honoria asked.

He shot her a dark sidelong look. "I got three of the Ech'lon 'ere, watchin' me every move. Go with Will and don't give 'im any trouble. I'll be 'ome shortly once I've slipped 'em."

Honoria's face drained of color. "What are they doing here?"

"They likes the blood sport. Now go."

At least if anyone was watching, they'd be hesitant to take Will on. Every blue blood alive knew what those yellow eyes meant and just what the burly youth could do. A single *verwulfen* could bring down a half dozen blue bloods when he was in a fit of berserker rage. That was why they'd been hunted to death in England, or caged as a curiosity for the Echelon to display.

Barrons was watching with his arms crossed over his chest. Just as he'd suspected. Blade gave him another chilling smile. "*Mine*," he mouthed silently, knowing Barrons could read his lips.

Honoria sat in the parlor, her hands pressed together. Will stirred the fire, and the one they called Tin Man rolled a ball of yarn across the floor beside Lark, trying to amuse the enormous thirty-pound tom that batted at it lazily. Despite Tin Man's grim appearance, the smile on his face was almost childlike. Lark leaned against his shoulder, her eyes blinking tiredly.

The door opened. Honoria stiffened as Blade stalked in.

The fury on his face had died, replaced by that cool look of nonchalance he often wore. He snapped his fingers and Lark and Tin Man looked up.

"Out," he said, including Will in the general sweep of his gaze. "Lark, you're fit for bed, and I want you two on the rooftops. The fog's thick enough to walk on tonight. I don't think I were followed, but you never know. Can't smell 'em comin', those bastards."

Will turned from his fire tending. "I tried to tell her not to go."

"Aye. I don't 'old you accountable. Can't argue with the devil."

They left the room without another word, or so much as a glance in her direction. Just her and him. Alone now.

Blade prowled toward the fireplace, resting a hand against the mantel. The light gleamed in a burnished sheen over his face and front, casting subtle shadows over his body. Tight, black leather pants molded faithfully over his thighs, and the flamboyant red waistcoat was made of touchable velvet. A pocket watch dangled from his well-cut black coat, the cuffs made of the same red velvet. Gray military-style frogging held his lapels open, and inches of black silk adorned his throat in an intricate cravat. Though his ensemble bore some similarity to the subdued wardrobe of the masses, he couldn't resist the exotic touches. Composed now, the only sign of his mood was in his disheveled dirty-blond hair.

"I didn't realize you were meeting with the Echelon tonight," Honoria said. She couldn't believe Leo had been there. With Colchester. He knew what a slimy cretin Colchester was, forever trying to emulate Vickers.

Blade crossed his arms over his chest. "Didn't think you'd want to see me tonight. Ain't your night for it."

"I…I…" The words died on her tongue as she stared at him. A flush of heat crept up her cheeks and she dropped her gaze.

"Honor?" His tongue curled around the word, sending a shiver over her skin. He took a step toward her. "Why did you come 'ere tonight?"

"Do you have anything to drink?"

"Whiskey? Rum? Gin?"

"Do you have any brandy?"

Blade crossed silently to the liquor cabinet. Honoria's knees trembled, so she sat down again, clasping her hands. The splash of liquid gurgled, and then he screwed the thin metal lid back onto the flask. "'Ere. Drink it slow like. She'll curl your toes."

She accepted the glass. For a moment their fingers touched and he refused to let it go. Their eyes met. She couldn't tell what he was thinking. His skin was cool, absorbing the feverish heat of her own body. What would it be like to have his hands on her? Those cool, callused hands that moved with such nimble grace. She'd rarely been touched by a man. Only Vickers, and his touch had always left her nauseous.

Blade's skin was cool too, yet when he touched her she burned.

"Thank you," she whispered and dropped her gaze.

He let go. Stepped back. "'Ere," he said, tugging a small package out of a drawer. "I bought you this."

Honoria's gaze narrowed on the small, paper-wrapped package. "What is it?"

"A gift."

She took it, though she shouldn't have. "You're not supposed to buy me things."

An ember of something hot flared in his eyes. "Are you goin' to open it?"

She tore the packaging apart. A pair of dark brown kid gloves tumbled into her lap, the leather so fine and luscious that they had to have cost him a small fortune. A little sinking feeling curled through her stomach. "Oh." She shook her head. "I can't. You cannot buy personal items for a lady."

"Who's to know?" His green eyes challenged her.

"I would know." And that made all the difference. He must have seen how worn her last pair was. The act was extremely considerate. She almost felt like crying. "I can't accept these." Especially not with the proposal she had come to put to him. She set them aside reluctantly.

A flat look came over his expression. "Why are you 'ere?"

The brandy burned all the way down. But it warmed her from within too. She was suddenly shivering, but not from the cold. "How much?"

The words were barely audible. But Blade froze as though she'd shouted at him. "How much what?"

"How much will you give me? For my blood?"

He could have been a statue. Honoria looked away and swiftly drank down the last of the brandy. Damn him. Bitterness burned in her throat. The words were hard to force out. "I no longer have employment. I need to pay the doctor's bills, to buy food for…for my brother and sister. I'm desperate."

And still he said nothing. A flare of heat burned in his eyes. He took a step away from her. Another. Turned and glared into the fireplace. "Bloody 'ell."

Fear ran through her. She'd thought he'd be eager for the opportunity to humble her. He'd made no secret of his intent to have her. But he didn't look eager at all. In fact, he looked almost as though she'd struck him a blow.

Honoria stood, her hands clinging to her skirts. He couldn't say no. If he did, then she had no other options. "I'm begging you," she whispered. It hurt everything she had in her to say it, but the sudden swamping wave of fear that he would reject her was stronger than her pride. Pride wouldn't see her fed. It wouldn't give Charlie his medication or Lena the new shawl she desperately needed.

Blade shot her a look over his shoulder, eyes ablaze with anger. She took a step back in surprise. "Damn you," he snarled.

Honoria didn't understand. "Do you want me to get down on my knees?" He'd liked the idea of her begging him after all. She swept her skirts out and bent down, the way she'd always done for one of the Echelon.

Blade moved so quickly she barely saw him. Then his hands were on her arms, forcing her back to her feet. Honoria sucked in a shocked gasp and looked up at him. He glared at her.

"No need to be so bleedin' dramatic!" he snapped and shook her a little.

Honoria clutched at his wrists. "I—I thought you wanted me to beg. Stop it. You're hurting me!"

He let her go and turned away with a snarl. Honoria staggered to the side, watching as he pressed the heels of his palms against his eyes.

Silence fell. She didn't dare move. She could feel his phantom touch on her arms where his fingers had gripped her. She rubbed at them. "Don't you want me?" she whispered. "I thought—"

"I want you." He lowered his hands, but he didn't turn to face her. A soft laugh escaped him. "Don't ever doubt it, luv." He shot her a look, and she saw that his eyes had bled to black.

Honoria stilled. She'd seen Vickers do that when he was angry or hungry. She'd learned to be very quiet when she recognized *that* look.

Blade sank into the armchair. "Don't you ever beg me again."

Of all the things! "You *wanted* me to!"

"Aye, well, I didn't mean it. I says things sometimes that's only me pride speakin'." His lips suddenly quirked. "You could say I've as much of a stiff neck as you at times."

She stared at him. The black was fading from his eyes, showing just a hint of hard emerald.

Blade crossed his arms over his middle. "How much do you want?"

She'd done the sums in her head. But it was best

to start higher and bargain her way lower. "Thirty pounds a month," she said boldly.

A high price for just her blood. A high price for the use of her body too. Perhaps her soul might cost as much.

"Done," Blade said. He stood and paced toward a painting. Behind it was a safe, with careless piles of coins. If it belonged to anyone else, they wouldn't dare keep so much money together, but nobody in Whitechapel was foolish enough to steal from the devil himself.

"That's all? I thought…" She trailed off. No need to invite him to lower the price. "How many times a week would you require my services?" A thought occurred. "*Only* my blood."

He counted out the money. Honoria licked her lips, trying not to stare at it. As soon as he put it in her hand she would owe him, but a part of her mind raced. *Thirty pounds*. Rent, medication, enough for a good doctor and food…So much food! New gloves for Lena, new thread for her stockings—goodness, perhaps even new stockings if she dared—and a thick, heavy coat for Charlie, not that he'd be going outside.

How quickly she had become so mercenary. A year ago she'd looked down upon such women as sold themselves on the streets. Now she was no better than they. Hunger and poverty could drive a person to abandon all of their morals.

"I know." Blade turned and held up the small pouch. It fell into her hands with a heavy jingle. He sank back into the armchair, tugging his gold cheroot case out of his pocket. "We'll discuss that later."

She jerked her gaze up from the pouch of money

in her hands. "No. I'd prefer to discuss it now. Or I'll leave this here and owe you nothing."

Blade ran a cheroot through his fingers, flipping it over and under like a sleight-of-hand artist. "Once every three weeks."

"So far apart?" Her eyebrows shot up. That was certainly reasonable. She put the heavy pouch down on the table and started tugging at her shawl. Her fingers wouldn't work properly.

"Takes the body awhile to renew the blood," he shrugged. "A lesson I learned o'er many years." His gaze narrowed on her hands. "What are you doin'?"

"I would prefer the marks not to be visible. I still intend to seek employment." She knew what that meant. There were very few veins that would give him what he needed. And neither her sleeves nor her neckline concealed her adequately enough. The shawl finally came free. She folded it neatly and put it down. Her hands were shaking.

"Honoria. Look at me."

To look at him would undo her. She slipped her shoes off and crossed toward him, her stockinged feet sinking into the thick carpets. *To have his mouth on her skin*…She shook the thought off with a shiver. Such an intimacy had never occurred to her. A hot little flush swept through her lower belly.

"What are you doin'?" he asked, voice low and rough.

His booted feet were crossed. Leather strained over his thighs, and his fingers dug into the armrests as though to restrain himself.

"We have a deal," she reminded him, lifting her skirts delicately and putting her foot up on the cushion. The hard muscle of his thigh rested against her ankle. His fingers went white with sudden strain.

"*Honoria.*"

She slid her skirts up. There was a lump in her throat. Her hands trembled but obeyed her will. The threadbare wool at her ankle was revealed. Then higher. Her calves. Her knee. She slid her skirts all the way up, revealing the faded pink ribbon of her garters. Heat flushed through her cheeks. What a shame that she couldn't be wearing better undergarments, like the fine painted silk stockings she'd once owned.

Blade sucked in a breath. "Put your skirts back down."

"I made a deal," she repeated firmly and started working on the ribbons that held her stocking in place.

His hand caught hers. Cool fingers against her own, the very fingertips touching her inner thigh.

Honoria couldn't help herself. She looked up. And nearly fell forward, into the burning depths of his black gaze. The hunger roared within him, a bottomless chasm that could never be fully sated.

Her breath hitched.

"You've been starvin' yourself for months. You ain't fit to lose any blood, let alone provide a decent feedin'. Put your bloody skirts down," he snarled.

"You want it," she whispered. "I can see it in you. And I won't owe you anything."

His fingers brushed against her thigh. For a moment he looked as though he was reconsidering. Then a steely expression settled on his face. "Damn your pride. It'll be the death of you." He moved in a blur of speed. Honoria found herself tumbled into the armchair as he streaked across the room.

"I'm not—" She fell silent as he turned, sweeping an arm out.

A vase smashed off the mantel. Blade spun and she froze, sinking back into the chair beneath his furious gaze.

"You ain't got a lick o' self-preservation. You're not strong enough for me to feed on. It'd do you in, quicker 'n the Drainers, but, no, you're more worried 'bout what you owe me. Do you know 'ow bleedin' stupid that is?"

It stung. Because he was right.

"You listen to me," he snapped, pointing a finger at her. "I take care of me thralls. I know 'ow much I can take, 'ow much they can afford to lose."

"An eighth of a pint a day," she said stiffly. "That's the base limit of what you need to survive."

"Where'd you 'ear a piece o' codswallop like that?"

"They've done studies," she protested.

"Aye. Studies on the newly infected. The more the virus takes a man over, the more blood it needs. I'm close on 'alf a pint most days, though it can be more or less. Ain't no rhyme nor reason to it."

"Half a pint?" she said faintly.

"You ain't the only thrall I got. I got ten I feed fresh from the vein off, and the rest I take cold, out o' the icebox."

"From the draining factories." Her thoughts on that flavored her tone.

"You think the Ech'lon'd let me 'ave any o' their precious blood supplies? I got me own stable o' donators. It's what it costs 'round 'ere for me protection. People is 'appy enough to bleed the odd 'alf pint for me."

The thought bothered Honoria somewhat. Ten thralls? That was practically a harem. And what a foolish thing to cause such prickling nausea. What did it matter if she were one of eleven? Or one of dozens even? It only meant that she would be spared the trials of feeding him more often. He could wallow in his blood whores for all she cared.

Pushing herself upright in the armchair, she tugged her skirts down so that they decently covered her ankles. Confusion reigned. She felt rather uncomfortable sitting there exposed, with one of her garter ribbons trailing loosely down her thigh.

"What are you thinkin'?" The fire crackled at Blade's back, shadowing his features once more.

"Would you turn your back while I tie my garter?" she blurted.

Green eyes locked on hers. A slight smile curled over his mouth. "As you wish." He turned slowly, facing the fire, leaning one hand against the mantel.

Honoria tugged her skirts up again and swiftly laced her garter back into place. The rustle of material seemed so loud in the still room. He couldn't see her, and yet his hearing was so superior that he had to hear each slither of material over her legs, each little tug of the garter ribbons into place.

Her cheeks burned and she tugged her skirts back down. "You can turn around now." She had to clear her throat twice to get the words out.

He pushed away from the fireplace, balancing on the balls of his feet. The way he moved was rather appealing. Blade was never clumsy, never unbalanced. He owned the space he moved through, whether it was on a rooftop, or roughened cobbles, or sitting in a rickshaw. That quiet confidence of body drew the eye. Frequently.

Her poor shoes rested forlornly on the rug. He fetched them and brought them toward her, his expression guarded. "You ain't ever this quiet," he observed.

She reached for the shoes, but he knelt at her feet and caught her ankle in his hand.

"That's quite unnecessary," she said.

He slipped her foot into the shoe and tugged it into place, moving with a smooth surety of action. Even here he thought he had the right to do as he willed with her body. Perhaps he did. She shivered a little at the thought.

"You were ready to offer me your vein a few moments ago," he said. "What's wrong with me touchin' your foot?"

"Nothing. I just...it's unnecessary."

He took her other foot, his fingers stroking over the fine wool of her stocking. There was a hole in the heel and she squirmed, trying to hide it. "Honor," he murmured, his fingers stroking her toes as he caught her gaze. "Bein' a blue blood's thrall...it's an intimate thing. You'll need to get used to it. To me."

"I know it's *intimate*." The word practically shriveled on her tongue. She almost felt like touching her cheeks to see if they were as hot as she imagined.

He dug his thumb into the arch of her foot. "I ain't talkin' 'bout just puttin' me mouth on you. About tastin' you."

Oh, goodness. She shut her eyes, but the image was burned there.

Again his fingers stroked her foot, tickling the soft

underside of her arch. "I look after me thralls. I know 'em. What goes on in their lives, what they need. They're like me family."

Honoria's eyes shot open and the words were out before she could stop them. "A harem."

His fingers stilled. "A harem? Christ, Honor. I wonder what Will'd say about bein' part of me harem? Or Mrs. Faggety down the road. Or Charlene and Mabel, the two Buckham spinsters." He chuckled. "Mrs. Faggety'd wash your mouth out for darin' to suggest such a thing."

"I've seen what happens when a blue blood feeds."

The laughter died. "It's an unfortunate side effect but rare. Will's a virile young lad, 'e feels it more 'an most. Mrs. Faggety don't feel it no more 'an a mild flush. The others…some do. Some don't. Some like it."

"I know," she said stiffly. "I've seen them. In the city, following the blue bloods around like addicts." He was still caressing her foot. She'd almost forgotten about it for a moment. "Are you going to put my shoe on?"

"As madam insists." He smiled and put her shoe on. Then he stood.

Her gaze drifted over the hard, muscled thighs directly in front of her. Blade had no inkling of the proper distance he ought to give a woman.

She stared at the hand he offered.

"You can't tell me that all of your thralls are old women and men," she said, taking it.

Blade drew her to her feet, but didn't back away or let her fingers go. "Do you want to know if some of them share me bed, Honor? Is that what you're askin'?"

"Of course not."

"The answer is yes. Sometimes they do. Some of 'em 'as needs. And so do I. There's two as I share a bed with on occasion."

Goodness. When she tried to tug her fingers from his, he tightened his hold reflexively. The back of her knees bumped the armchair. There was nowhere to go. She could only endure.

"But not for a while." He searched her face.

"That's none of my business anyway."

Blade took a step back. He looked almost disappointed, and she didn't know why she felt as if she'd failed at some test.

"Come. I'll walk you 'ome." He gave a pointed glance at the package by her feet. "And keep the gloves. That's an order."

Chapter 7

The streets were empty. Fog hung heavily over the 'Chapel, a silent blanket that trapped sound. Their footsteps echoed in the night and Honoria shivered, glancing around uneasily.

"Relax," Blade drawled. "Ain't nothin' gettin' close without me hearin' it."

He strolled beside her, hands shoved deep into his pockets. Despite the night's chill, he wore only his shirt, rolled up to the elbows. Practically indecent. A hint of his tattoo peeked out from the edge, ending in the hollow of his elbow. She couldn't quite get a good look at it. The heavy ink was vaguely tribal. Savage. It suited him.

"I know," she replied. "I'm simply not used to the…the silence."

He gave her a sidelong look. "You ain't lived through martial law before, luv." Even *his* words seemed quieter, as though he too felt the weight of the fog. "You ought 'ave been 'ere fifty years ago when the Ech'lon were fire-bombin' the 'Chapel with their metaljackets. Weren't no one allowed out for near on 'alf a year."

She wrapped her arms around her waist. "They were hunting for you?"

"Aye. They found me too."

She'd heard the stories, of course. Of how Blade had escaped the Ivory Tower and become lord and master of the 'Chapel, fighting off dozens of the metal-plated drones the Echelon sent after him. They'd nearly burned Whitechapel to the ground, until the mob rose against them, forcing them back behind the city walls.

"How did you rouse the people against them?" she asked.

"My debonair charm, 'andsome looks, and superior oratory skills."

She shot him a look.

He smiled and her breath caught. Such a wicked, devilish smile. If she had been a normal young woman, without the heavy burden she carried, she might have let her gaze linger. Or if he had been a man instead of a monster.

"I went straight to Rory O'Loughlan. He were leader o' the Sharks gang as run these parts. Told 'im I'd throw in with 'im if he kept 'em off me back."

"And he agreed?" A single rookery gang up against the Echelon?

"He were 'avin' problems with the Slashers. I 'elped 'im with 'is little problem. Then he 'elped me. Ole O'Loughlan were smart enough to see a use for me in 'is organization. Roused his men, they spread the word, said as 'ow the Ech'lon were comin' in to take their women and children as blood slaves. Rumors spread like wildfire. The mob rose up and started tearin' down the city walls, clawin' to get at 'em. The metaljackets coulda mowed 'em down like wheat, but the country were already up in arms over the latest hike in blood taxes. So the Ech'lon pulled back. Didn't want me that much."

"And you became a hero," she said. "For fighting off the metaljackets. They never knew why you did it."

Blade shrugged. "I takes good care of 'em. I don't ask for too much. Some few of 'em know the real story. They think I were clever, usin' 'em against the Ech'lon like that. And some good come out of it."

"Oh?" she asked.

"It taught the people that the Ech'lon were afraid of 'em too. Before that the blood taxes were gettin' 'igher and 'igher. The rulin' Council of Dukes were pushin' for the king to commit to more drainin' factories. But when Whitechapel rose up against the city, they didn't dare. The blood taxes 'ave been set at two pints a year for near on 'alf a century."

"The draining factories are still there," she said. "People still starve because they can't afford the regular taxes to pay for the prince consort's war against New Catalan."

"They make their own choices in goin' to the Drainers," he said. "They coulda come to me. And the war's one of the few things the prince consort and I agree on."

She shot him a startled look. The animosities between England and New Catalan had been going on for nearly twenty years. New Catalan had ceded from Spain under papal rule when the Inquisition drove the blue bloods out of Spain. A Catholic-dominated country, it had set its sights on cleansing England as the only remaining nation in Western Europe left under blue blood control.

"Of course you'd have a vested interest in it," she retorted. The war was familiar ground. Her father had followed the Humans First Party in that last year when his sentiments against the blue bloods worsened, and he spent most nights arguing the war into the ground.

"New Catalan's full o' righteous lunatics, frothin' at the mouth for blue blood 'eads. They're dangerous because they won't stop till we're all dead. And even then they'll find blue bloods in every corner, never mind whether it be true or not. Thousands 'ave burned at the stake in New Catalan and Spain, and many of 'em were only 'uman."

"They're a small country," she argued. "Hardly a threat."

"Aye. And if they drag France in, with their anti–blue blood stance, then we'll 'ave a horde of bleedin' fanatics on our doorstep armed with the finest airships France 'as got. The Germanic states won't 'elp us. They're overrun by bloody verwulfen and—"

"Maybe the Echelon shouldn't have slaughtered the Scottish *loupe* clans, then," she suggested. "They might have a few more allies rather than only the Russos."

"And the colonies," he muttered.

"Which are an entire ocean away."

Blade shot her a look. "Do you simply enjoy arguin', or is it just me?"

Honoria shut her mouth. Perhaps there was more of her father in her than she realized. She'd listened to Blade's arguments, of course, but she hadn't truly understood them until she lived in the rookeries, watching as people starved because of a war that didn't involve them.

"Ah, then, it's me."

"It's not you," she replied. "It's just—"

"So you admit to bein' argumentative?"

Honoria growled under her breath. "I do not. Stop interrupting. I was saying that I never understood the cost of war, until…well, until recently. Last month I watched a woman sell her children to the Echelon as blood slaves because she couldn't afford to feed them anymore. They'll be well fed and protected—until they're old enough to donate blood—and then they'll become nothing but cattle for the rest of their lives."

The woman hadn't lived much longer. A kind of despair had settled over her and she'd disappeared. Honoria added bitterly, "The Echelon take our money and they take our blood to feed themselves, and there's nothing we can do about it. There are too many of them, and they control the metaljackets and the Trojan cavalry. No mob could stand against them."

It would be slaughter. The armored mechanical horses would simply cut through a mob like a scythe, and then the legion would follow, restoring order with brutal precision.

Blade was looking at her in the gas-lit darkness. The faint bluish light played over his face, giving him an enigmatic expression. He saw her looking at him and took a deep breath, his gaze shifting away. "Would you prefer the New Catalans, with their Illumination and fanatics?"

"Of course not."

"Then the war's necessary," he said. "Ain't much we can do 'bout it. You'd be swappin' one despot for another."

"The *queen* is human," she replied. "If the people had some form of a voice, then—"

"The queen's doped up to 'er eyeballs and dancin' on the prince consort's strings. They parade 'er out regular for the people to see and pretend she's in charge." He shook his head. "Ain't mean shite, luv. Ain't nobody to stand against the prince consort. He's got the Council of Dukes on 'is side and the queen in 'is pocket. Who could take 'im on?"

Bitterness burned in her mouth. "What if there was a...a way to vaccinate against the craving? Or a cure?"

Vickers had been commissioned with finding a vaccine, a way to prevent the Echelon's servants, thralls, and women from accidental infections. It had been proposed that any boy denied the blood rites in his fifteenth year would also receive the vaccine. A way for the Echelon to control a man's place in the world, after several families had sought to elevate their sons' status by illegally infecting their children. To become a blue blood was to become an elite, and there would be no more mistakes tolerated.

It also served her father's purposes. Vaccinate enough of the uninfected aristocracy and their children, and the blue bloods would slowly die out, her father claimed. The Echelon would never stoop to offering the blood rites to anyone lowborn. It was a devious way to limit their numbers if a cure couldn't be found.

Blade shook his head. "Sounds like a pipe dream, luv. Sounds like somethin' the humanists and the

Humans First Party's been spreadin' in their propaganda pamphlets."

An icy chill ran down her spine. It wasn't a dream and it wasn't propaganda. She'd seen the notes, carefully detailed in her father's private journals. His work for Vickers at the Institute had brought untold wealth to the House of Lannister, but over the past two years Vickers had been focused on something else: a cure. It became his all-consuming desire, and her father's too.

Honoria and her father had worked on dozens of rogues who had been institutionalized because they couldn't control themselves. Or at least that was the reason Vickers gave them. It was a year before she witnessed the truth. Vickers was infecting them with his own blood to create test subjects. She'd been hiding from him in the servants' passage when the house drones brought in a young streetwalker. Vickers had held the girl down and forcibly injected her with his blood.

He had always been dangerous, but Honoria had never realized just how far he would go. It wasn't until the girl showed up at the Institute a month later, raving and frothing at the mouth in hunger, that she could no longer deny the truth.

Sometimes Honoria wished she'd never seen it, never told her father. It was the beginning of the end. In that last year he'd gone further than simply mouthing the phrases the legitimate Humans First Party believed in; he had joined the secretive humanist movement and started working long into the night on an experiment he wouldn't confide in her about. It was an experiment that had cost him his life.

Somehow Vickers found out. The next she knew, her father was shaking her awake and bundling the three of them into a steam cab with his diary.

Don't ever give this to them, he told her, looking over his shoulder in fear. *Don't ever let this fall into the wrong hands.*

Come with us!

I can't. He kissed her on the cheek and dragged her close. *I have to get this information to other people. They can use it!*

He'll kill you!

Her father smiled sadly. *This is more important than my life, Honor. And I'll be careful. I'll meet you at the coaching inn in Fulham. If...if I don't show up in three days, then go to your mother's cousin in Oxford. I've named Leo as executor in my will, but use him only as a last resort.* His lips thinned. *He's a good lad, but...he's still one of* them.

A day later her father's body was found in the Thames, his throat cut open.

"You all right?" Blade asked.

Honoria shook herself. What had she been thinking, to even voice such a thing to him? She couldn't trust anybody with that information. Not even Lena or Charlie knew about it. "I'm fine." She gave him a weak smile. "Just tired. And sick of watching people starving to death or taking drastic actions." Especially when she'd been so close herself.

The money felt heavy in her pocket. Perhaps she should have bent her neck weeks ago. But who would ever have thought that Blade would be so generous? Or so undemanding?

It won't last, a little voice whispered. *You escaped*

because you're weak. Sooner or later he'll cut a vein open, put his mouth on your skin, and drink.

A blue blood's thrall. Something she'd sworn she'd never be. It held a position of respectability at least, unlike the blood slaves who were simply anyone's for the taking.

Blade stalked along beside her in brooding silence.

"Nothing to say to that?" she asked lightly, forcing the thoughts from her mind. She had money now. That was all that mattered.

"You think I don't give a damn?"

Honoria missed a step, her ankle twisting on the rutted cobbles. Blade caught her effortlessly, a hand on her wrist. She swallowed the instinct to pull away. She'd have to get used to his touch. And it wasn't… unpleasant. Cool. Firm. A grip that no man—or woman—could break. Just a trifle possessive.

There was no hint of guile in his expression, just a sincere, burning truth shining in his wicked green eyes. But she'd been fooled before. Vickers had once been kind and persuasive, courting her father to his cause with gifts and a "shared" interest. Before there was no longer any need for it.

"I don't know," she replied honestly. "*Do* you care?"

He let her go. "I do me bit. But I can't do it for nothin'. They only respect the strong 'ere. Charity breeds nothin' but contempt." He cast a smile in her direction. "And people got their pride."

"Aye, well, I can under—"

She didn't get a chance to finish her words. Blade's head shot up, his gaze roving the rooftops.

"What is it?"

His eyelashes fluttered against his cheeks. He was listening to something. Honoria looked around. A heavy layer of soot stained the buildings. Crooked chimneys formed man-shaped shadows in the darkness, until she blinked to clear her vision.

A chain rattled. "Come on," Blade snarled, grabbing her by the hand and dragging her toward her home.

"The murderer?" she asked, running behind him and looking up. There *were* shadows moving now, running along the rooftops behind them and leaping between buildings.

"The fuckin' Slashers," he bit out, sliding to a halt in an intersection. He looked up and growled in frustration. "You can't outrun 'em." But he could.

Her heart leaped into her throat. The Slasher gangs were the terror of the East End, abducting families in their sleep or running down people who were foolish enough to be out at night. Maimed and enhanced with vicious hooks for hands or razor-sharp claws, they drained a person of their blood and fenced it in the slums. Or, some whispered, to the government's official draining factories.

"What are they doing here?" One of the reasons she'd chosen the Whitechapel rookery was because no Slasher dared enter Blade's turf.

"I'll 'ave to ask one of 'em," he said in a tone that told her exactly how he intended to get answers. Metal gleamed in his hands. "Stay behind me. Don't run. I'll keep you safe."

One, two, three, four…she counted six shapes in the darkness. No doubt there'd be more. They roamed in packs, like stray dogs.

"Are you certain you can handle them?"

He gave her a dirty look. "Just keep behind me."

Lifting a whistle to his lips, he blew. No sound erupted from it, but he seemed satisfied and dropped it back into his pocket.

Honoria fumbled in her skirts for the pistol. She cocked it and waited, her back to Blade, searching the darkness.

A laugh echoed out of the shadows, an eerie sound, like the hyena in Vickers's menagerie. A chain clanked and then three of the shapes sailed out of the air, landing in front of them.

Honoria swallowed a scream. A long, curved fisherman's hook drifted back and forth as the one in front of her grinned evilly.

"You get lost, boys?" Blade called. "Looks like you're in me turf."

"Looks like you're outnumbered," one of them called back, wielding a vicious hook.

"Oh?" Blade looked around. "But there's only nine o' you."

Which proved that there were more than she'd seen.

"And one o' you," the lead man said with a laugh. "Come on, you curs!" He leaped forward, brandishing his knife.

Honoria didn't have time to see what Blade was doing. She raised the pistol and aimed. The man charging her—with the fishing hook attached to his wrist instead of a hand—suddenly staggered back as the pistol retorted. A great, gaping hole appeared in the man's chest, and his mouth dropped open in surprise as he fell to his knees, then onto his face.

An automatic reloader, the pistol had six bullets. Now only five. She spun around quickly to shoot again, but Blade was too close to the three men attacking him. He was little more than a blur as he danced among them, the pair of razors in his hands gleaming like little scythes in the moonlight. The Slashers looked as though they moved through air thick as molasses in comparison.

Blade downed one, sweeping under a broad, awkward stroke of a short sword and flicking his razor across the man's throat. The Slasher went down with a bloody gurgle and Blade spun around, kicking another man in the throat as the other leaped for him.

Blade's gaze swept past, locating Honoria for a moment before he buried his razor in the man's gut. As the Slasher folded over the stroke, Blade whipped up with his other hand, neatly decapitating the man.

"Look out!" she yelled, seeing a pair of Slashers on the roof. A heavy net dropped down, and the man who'd been kicked in the face dove onto Blade.

"Get out of 'ere!" Blade bellowed, writhing on the ground beneath the net.

The man stabbed him with a needle-sharp poniard, and Blade grunted in pain. The two who had dropped the net jumped to the ground.

"This your little turtledove?" One of them advanced on her with a leer. A dirty eye patch obscured his right eye. "Maybe I'll let you watch when I drain 'er."

"Run, Honoria!" Blade had somehow cut through the net but was struggling to disentangle himself.

Honoria lifted the pistol. Her worst nightmare come to life, and she'd be damned if she would let them take her. Anger bit, sharp and hot. These men—these creatures—had terrorized innocent men and women. She'd had enough.

The man's head exploded like a rotten melon. The pair of Slashers struggling with Blade looked up in shock as his body hit the ground.

"Christ fuckin' Jaysus!" One of them muttered. His gaze went to the pistol in her hand. "What the 'ell is that?"

Honoria stared down the sight at him and he scrambled out of the way, ducking into the alley. *Damn it.* She turned just as the man still wrestling with Blade hurdled his body toward her.

He knocked her clean off her feet with a swoosh of rancid air. The pistol skittered across the cobbles and stopped several feet away.

The man drew back his arm with its deadly hooked blade. "You little bitch!"

Honoria screamed.

In the next moment his weight was gone. Blade staggered over her, blood welling all over his shirt. "What part o' *run* don't you bloody understand?"

She didn't hesitate to grab the hand he offered to her. He lifted her to her feet as though she weighed little more than a feather. The man who had attacked her was groaning, having been thrown face-first into a wall.

"You'd be dead if I had!" she retorted. She couldn't stop her gaze from dropping to his side. "You're bleeding."

"Aye. Get runnin'. There's five of 'em left."

"Are you coming?"

He pointed a finger at her. "If I tell you to run, you damned well better run! No more 'eroics, you bloody fool!"

"Stop cursing at me!"

A muscle in Blade's jaw ticked. He took a deep breath, his nostrils flaring. "Honoria..." he warned.

She dashed for her pistol and checked it. Four bullets remaining. Then she turned and tipped her chin up. "I'm not going without you. Come on. Or are you too injured to run?"

"Nothin' but a scratch, luv."

Four shadowy shapes shimmied down the drain-pipes. Blade pushed Honoria in the middle of the back and they broke into a run.

A low, whistling noise filled the air. Then something wrapped around her legs and she fell forward with a scream. The weighted ends of a rope wrapped themselves around her ankles.

"*Blade!*"

"I got you, luv." He hauled her up, tossing her over his shoulder.

When she looked up, she saw four men in pursuit, armed with an assortment of cruel hooks and pikes, and wearing a mish-mash of iron plating sewn together with leather togs. Weighed down as he was—and injured—Blade was barely keeping ahead of them.

She shot another man, but the jolting skewered her aim. He went down screaming, his right arm and shoulder blown away as though an enormous shark had taken a chunk out of him. The sound ricocheted in the night and dogs started barking.

"What the bloody 'ell are those things?" Blade yelled as the Slashers dropped back, wary now.

"Keep running!" She lifted the pistol again, but the Slasher darted around a corner and her shot went wide, exploding a shower of brick and mortar across the street.

"In me pocket," he said. "There's me whistle. Blow it."

She looked down at his breeches. "You want me to—?"

"Do it," he snarled.

Honoria reached down and felt in Blade's pocket. Hard, muscled thigh met her fingers, rippling with each stride he took. She swallowed hard and tugged the small whistle out. When she put it to her lips, nothing sounded.

"It doesn't make any noise!"

"Nothin' that you can 'ear," he replied. He put her down, panting hard. Honoria staggered back against the doorway he'd nestled her against. Sweat dampened his hair and the bloodstain on his shirt had spread.

She paled. "That's more than a scratch."

Sweat tracked rivulets through the soot that grimed his face. When he flashed her a smile, his teeth gleamed starkly. "Aye." Bending over, he rested his hands on his hips and breathed deep, an odd whistling sound. A bubble of blood broke on his lips.

"Oh, my goodness! You're hurt!" She reached for him, then nearly fell over. Grimacing, she tore the ropes off her legs, then tossed them aside.

"Hit a lung. Mebbe. Give me…the pistol…"

She handed it to him. Blade's dark gaze swept the

streets. He wiped his mouth with the back of his hand, leaving a bloodied smear across his pale skin.

Honoria touched the blood on his side. He knocked her hand away with a distracted growl.

"Ain't no time. They're…comin'…rooftops."

The first man who dropped into the street staggered back in a bloody mist.

"It reloads automatically," she said, taking refuge in the doorway. "There's one round left."

"Aye," he muttered. Ducking out into the street, he aimed up and pulled the trigger.

A scream filled the air and a man tumbled into the streets as Blade ducked back under the cover of the overhang next to Honoria. He shoved the pistol into the waistband of his breeches, hands trembling.

It seemed even a blue blood couldn't admit when he was hurt. Obviously a man was a man, regardless of what he drank to survive.

Leaning down, she gathered the rope with its weighted ends. She had no idea how to use it, but it was better than having nothing to use against the Slashers.

"Two more," he murmured, leaning his back against the bricks, his eyes closed as he tried to breathe. "They're cautious…now…"

"Don't waste your breath," she said quietly. "Maybe someone will have heard."

"Whistle."

She blew on it again, then tucked it back into her pocket. Useless thing. She looked at Blade and saw his teeth bared in pain and his hand clapped against the spreading pool of blood. A blue blood could heal from almost anything, but he needed blood to do it.

She swallowed. Hard. "Do you want my blood?"

"No," he said, shaking his head with a snarl. "Comin'."

"The Slashers?" she whispered, peering into the darkness. Her heart raced and she held the weighted end of the rope low.

A sudden scream tore the air. Honoria flinched. There came a horrible growling sound, almost like an animal, and then a body sailed into the streets. It was one of the Slashers, his head bent at an unnatural angle. She'd seen her share of blood from her Institute days, but something about the fact that the body lay on its front in the street, with its head facing upward, made saliva pool in her mouth. Her stomach heaved and she turned aside, pressing her hand to her mouth.

Blade slumped against the wall. "Will's 'ere."

There was another scream and then a tile smashed into the street. Honoria hurried to Blade's side. "Let me have a look."

He caught her fingers. "No."

Honoria pushed his hands away. "I do believe you called me foolish once, to risk my life for pride."

At that he looked at her. Then nodded curtly.

She peeled the wet shirt up, tugging it free of his waistband. A flush of heat burned in her cheeks. Blade leaned his head back against the wall, his throat bared to her. Corded muscles ran over his lean stomach, and the vee of his hips dipped into the low waist of his breeches.

"Goodness," she murmured. Then added with a blush, "The blood."

"O' course." Despite his pain, he smiled. Then grimaced. "Easy, luv."

"Your breathing sounds better."

Another scream arose in the darkness. She couldn't suppress a wince and looked over her shoulder. Rain was starting to spatter the street.

"It's healin'," he said.

One, two, three…four stab wounds, up under his ribs. "You're lucky he didn't hit your heart," she said.

There were two ways to kill a blue blood: severe damage to the heart or decapitation. And then, to be certain they were dead, it was best to burn the bodies.

Blade's gaze drifted over her shoulder. "Will. You took your time."

"Bloody hell," Will cursed. "What a friggin' mess. Couldn't you get out o' the way in time?"

Honoria glanced up. The tall youth glared at Blade. Blood dripped from a cut over his eyebrow, but he appeared otherwise undamaged. A dirty gray shirt clung to his massive shoulders, with leather straps holding a shoulder sheath in place. The hilt of a knife jutted over his shoulder, though it looked rather like a short sword. Strips of brown linen bandaged his wrists, like one of the fighters she'd seen at the Pits, and he held a shiv, low and bloody.

The two men grinned at each other. Unbelievable.

Honoria held her wrist up. "You need blood. Here."

Blade's smile died. "Need a lot. You ain't strong enough." He pushed off the wall, clapping a hand to his ribs and wincing. Honoria swiftly ducked under his shoulder. His weight nearly flattened her.

"Ease back. You ain't goin' nowhere," Will muttered, grabbing Blade's arm. "Here." The youth tilted his head, offering his throat.

Honoria got out of the way as Will wrapped his massive arms under Blade's shoulders, pinning him against the wall. Blade swept Will's shaggy hair out of the way, a fierce look of hunger crossing his face. A knife gleamed. One of Blade's razors. He met her gaze, making a small nick against Will's throat.

Honoria wrapped her arms around herself. The rain was starting to get heavier. She was trapped under the roof's overhang with the two men. Looking away didn't help matters. As Blade's mouth closed over Will's throat, the younger man sucked in a breath that sounded incredibly...*personal.*

She'd seen blue bloods feed before. Some of the Echelon filed their teeth into sharp points—to break the skin—but most simply relied on fléchettes or thin razors. She shivered, though she didn't feel cold. Indeed, an uncomfortable, prickly heat speared through her belly.

Will groaned again, and this time there was no mistaking the sound. He was *enjoying* this. Honoria glanced up. A mistake. For Blade was staring at her, his mouth locked against Will's throat, his hand fisted in the shaggy hair and the other arm wrapped around the man, clutching him hard.

Will's palms splayed over the pitted brick wall and his hips moved almost involuntarily. Small, harsh breaths broke the still night. She couldn't look away. It was horrible...and fascinating.

And for a moment she wanted it to be her.

Honoria tore her gaze away. Her nipples were hard against the abrasive canvas of her dress, her breath shallow. Behind her, Will groaned again. She clenched her eyes shut. That was worse. She could picture them, locked together, bodies straining, and Blade…watching her with a fierce hunger in his green eyes. The look on his face had been complex, as though he too wished it were her. She felt his gaze right between her shoulder blades. And other places. Lower. As though he stroked a finger down her spine, pausing at the indentation just above the smooth curve of her bottom. And lower still, brushing against the delicate inner flesh of her thighs.

"Enough." Will sucked in a ragged breath. "Enough, damn it!"

When she turned, Blade lifted his head, gasping. Will slumped against him, pressing him into the wall, his face buried in Blade's shoulder and his body shaking. Blade stroked his hair, his fingers tightening at the nape of Will's neck.

"Easy now," Blade murmured. Color flushed through his skin and there was blood on his lips. He looked remarkably…satisfied.

She would never have thought him particularly gentle. Yet he held Will in his arms as they slowly recovered, stroking his hair. Will made an inarticulate sound deep in his throat, then finally pushed away.

"Do you need anything?" she asked, clearing her own throat.

Will shook his head. Embarrassment burned in a fiery blush at the back of his neck. Blade leaned back against the wall, closing his eyes for a moment. Dark satisfaction curled over his face as he wiped his mouth.

She didn't dare look down, but it was quite evident

from her peripheral vision that he too had enjoyed the feeding.

Was it always like that?

The rain began to slacken. She decided to risk it. She couldn't stay here any longer, trapped in the steamy darkness with the two men, both of them trying to recompose themselves in the aftermath. Especially when she herself felt so unfulfilled.

Desire scratched against her skin like the heavy wool that she wore. It hurt. She dug her fingernails into her palms, took a deep breath, and stepped out into the rain. It pattered on her shoulders, little icy pinpricks against the bare skin of her décolletage and shoulders.

Something drifted past her nose, a rancid scent. Like rotten meat. Her nose screwed up in distaste as she gagged. "Goodness, what is that smell?" Covering her nose with her hand, she turned around.

Blade's head shot up, his eyes flaring wide. "Honoria!"

He didn't need to warn her. She looked up. A shadowy figure squatted on the edge of the roof tiles, sniffing the air. Claws gripped the edge of the gutter, its wiry, maggot-pale body leaning forward as it breathed in her scent.

Cold rushed through her, the hairs on the back of her neck standing up. An old primeval fear that burned away every last scrap of desire. She couldn't breathe, choking on the sudden urge to run and yet too afraid to move.

Then it scented her, its red-rimmed eyes widening in delight. It looked…almost like a blue blood, but horribly, horribly mutated. Bald, its white skin covered in flaky patches, and its mouth opening over a set of sharpened teeth.

Suddenly she knew what it was. And she screamed.

Chapter 8

The vampire landed in the street in a blur of movement. Blade leaped in front of Honoria and froze.

"Get back," he whispered, holding his arms wide as though to bar its path. His heart started ticking in his chest. Fear. Something he hadn't felt for a long time. But, then, any sane man would cower before this *thing*. He cleared his throat. "Will? You got your feet under you?"

"Aye," Will replied, taking a slow, cautious step into the street.

Blade didn't dare take his eyes off the creature. Days of hunting, and here it was, just when he was least prepared for it. It must have heard the whistle too. Blade's heart thundered with the adrenaline of his recent feed, his body primed to fight or flee. This was when he felt his strongest, especially after feeding on Will, but he wasn't alone. Will would be unsteady and Honoria was only human.

The vampire took a hopping step forward and crouched on all fours. It sniffed the air, its blind eyes covered in a filmy haze. Blade didn't dare mistake it for a weakness. The creature's hearing and sense of smell more than made up for its lack of sight. It made odd, high-pitched noises, and he remembered an odd fact he'd once heard years ago and thought he'd forgotten.

Vampires *saw* the world by using sound.

"Honoria. When it attacks," he said, "I want you to run. Don't look back. Go 'ome and lock the doors. And get more o' those bullets." He held the pistol out behind him.

"What about you?" she whispered, taking the weapon.

For a moment he admired her bravery. She should have been screaming in fear, but she stayed collected.

"Ain't the time to be brave," he reminded her. "We'll try to lead it off."

Will circled the thing, his feet crossing each other as he placed them carefully. Its head turned uncannily, tracking his movements. A forked tongue flickered over its teeth. Uncertain.

"That's right, you ugly bastard," Will muttered. "We ain't human. No easy feed here tonight." Slowly he reached for his blades. They flicked open, the razor edges still gleaming with Slasher blood.

The vampire's head shot back to him. Its lips curled back off its teeth in a silent snarl. Will made a feint toward it. "No!" he yelled.

The bloody thing moved quicker than he'd ever thought. It sprang and Will went down with a yell, bleeding hard. It bounded off the wall, bulleting back toward him, low and streamlined.

Blade clenched his jaw. He had a split second to act, but he didn't dare move out of the way. Honoria was behind him.

Choices. He hit the creature hard, raking in with his razors. Flesh parted like silk, spewing out a fetid stink like fish guts discarded on the wharves. Claws raked him, cutting across his arm with a branding-hot flash of pain. One caught the leather guard on his wrist and it dropped away, cleaved in half.

Honoria screamed behind him. Blade spun as he fell, grabbing out desperately. He caught a wiry ankle, and the creature twisted on itself with fluid grace, reaching for Blade's face.

"*Honoria! Go!*"

She took off in a flurry of skirts. Blade locked his arms around the vampire's body, trying to crush it with his strength. Its back claws hooked up between them, raking his guts like white fire. He ground his teeth together, keeping the thing away from his throat. *Bloody hell, it was strong!* His arms parted, fingers scraping over the knotted protrusion of its spine. He dug his nails in, barely slowing its progress.

Then suddenly it was free, lashing out with gnarled claws. They raked across Blade's throat. He touched the marks lightly. So close. A quarter inch to the right...

Will flew past, bellowing in rage, his pupils flared to thin slits.

Any other time Blade would have gotten out of the way and let Will tear it to pieces. But this was a *vampire*. Possibly the only thing alive that could stop a verwulfen in full berserker rage.

It ratcheted forward, after Honoria. Blade followed on Will's heels, his arms pumping at his sides and boots slapping the cobbles. Honoria came into view, the vampire loping after her.

She shot a look over her shoulder and saw it. The gap between them narrowed. Blade put on an extra burst of speed, passing Will. *No, you don't. She's mine.*

He wouldn't be fast enough. A split second to make the decision. Then his hand dipped, coming up with one of his throwing knives. He lost speed; the vampire was nearly upon her. With a flick of his wrist, he sent the dagger spinning.

The vampire squealed as it bit deep in its flank. Somehow Will got ahead of Blade, smashing his brutal strength into the creature with a roar. They went down, Will fighting simply to hold on. The knife was still buried deep. Blade grabbed it and ripped upward, tearing through tendons and muscle, trying to bury it deep in the vampire's gut. Sluggish black blood leaked out of the creature's wounds, which started closing almost as soon as Blade withdrew the knife. No use trying to bleed it out.

It screamed, a high-pitched squeal that made his teeth ache. Rotting stink clogged his nose. He could barely breathe through it. Then it tossed Will aside. A second to strike. The knife hit the creature's sternum, slipping between its ribs. Its red-rimmed eyes went wide with pain, and it jerked, kicking, clawing, fighting to get free. Blood splattered Blade's hands like acid. *Burning.*

He yelled and yanked his hands free, clenching them in pain. It swept through him in a nauseous wave. The vampire darted away, scrabbling up a drainpipe and vanishing across the rooftops.

Gone. With Blade's dagger still buried in its chest.

"Will?" His arms hurt. Blood leaked across his skin, a dark bluish-red that gave the blue bloods their name.

The vampire must have clawed him a few more times than he'd realized.

Will forced himself onto his hands and knees, head bowed. There was no sign of Honoria, but they were close to her home. Blade stared in the direction of her home, then looked back at Will. The vampire had gone in the other direction, and his lieutenant was hurt.

"You all right?" He squatted down.

Will bared his teeth. "Hurts. Son of a bitch almost disemboweled me."

Blade patted him on the shoulder. There was nothing to do but wait for the loupe virus to heal the torn flesh. Heat blazed beneath his cold hand. It was already working hard, spiking Will's body temperature up several notches. He'd be sweating with fever half the night as his skin reknit itself.

"Told you not to grapple with it," Blade said, rising to his feet and offering a hand. "They're stronger 'n we are. Quicker. This ain't like sparrin' with me."

Will clasped Blade's hand. "Thanks." He spat out a mouthful of blood and hauled himself to his feet. "I ain't figured that out."

Blade ran an eye over him. "You don't offer me blood again," he said, "till this is over."

"You weren't goin' to take it from 'er."

"She ain't strong enough. Yet."

Will held Blade's hand as he tried to disengage. "Don't get distracted," he said. "I ain't the only one who shouldn't go after the vampire alone. She's just a woman."

Blade shook him off. "Go 'ome. Get some sleep. You'll need it."

"Where are you goin'?"

"To make sure she got 'ome all right," he muttered, turning on his heel. The air smelled clean, the rain washing away the vampire's scent. It was injured; no doubt it would retreat to its hidey-hole to lick its wounds.

"Blade?"

"Aye?"

"You knifed it fair in the heart," Will said quietly.

He mulled it over. "I know. Keep your mouth shut. Don't let the others know. And go 'ome. I'll watch the Todd 'ouse tonight."

Chapter 9

Honoria slammed the door shut and leaned back against it, gasping for breath. *Sweet lord, have mercy*...She cringed, listening for any sign of pursuit. That thing—the vampire—had been right on her heels. She'd heard its odd, high-pitched pant. Then it was gone and Blade and Will were fighting for their lives.

Were they still alive? She couldn't believe that she'd left them there, but how could she have helped?

Her eyes shot to her bedroom. She pushed off from the door and dashed for it, tugging the pistol out of her pocket. Firebolts. They would tear a big enough hole through even a vampire.

Lena was sleeping on the cot. Honoria sneaked past.

She found the bullets in her drawer. Only twenty left now. She knew how to make more, but she didn't have the money to buy the compounds. Hands shaking, she opened the pistol's barrel and reloaded it.

Lena yawned. "Honor? What are you doing?" Rubbing sleep out of her eyes, she suddenly noticed the pistol. "Where are you going?"

"Outside," Honoria replied. "Stay here."

"What happened? There's blood on your skirts."

"It's not mine."

She unlocked the door and took a deep breath. This was insane. But, then, if the vampire wanted to get her, nothing—no doors or walls—would stop it.

Fog hung heavily in the street. She took a step outside, shutting the door behind her. Then another.

"Bloody 'ell, woman," Blade snapped. "What are you *doin'*?"

Honoria nearly shot the ground. Clapping a hand to her chest, she looked up. Blade peered over the edge of the roof as though he weren't perched on a twenty-foot drop.

"I was worried that you'd been injured," she said with a scowl, then added, "you and Will."

"You were frettin' over me." He jumped off the roof and landed beside her, his knees bending to absorb the shock.

"And Will." Despite the cool tone of her voice, she examined him for injuries. "What happened to your hands?" Then she saw his arms. They looked like he'd put his fist through a glass window.

"Vampire blood," he said, holding up his scalded hands.

"Does it hurt?" She couldn't actually see the virus healing the wounds, but each time she blinked, the raw flesh was slightly less inflamed.

"A little."

"What are you doing out here?"

"Watchin' the 'ouse. Will's in no state to be on guard."

"There's no need to do that. What happened? Did you kill it?"

Blade reached out. She didn't dare breathe. *Was he going to…?* His fingers caught one of the curls that framed her face, stroking it gently. "I gave you me word I'd protect you." Then he dropped his hand. "And no. We injured it and it run."

Honoria was almost disappointed. Her gaze flickered over his ruined shirt and the myriad cuts that smeared his skin with blood. "You may as well come in. I'll have a look at your arms."

She turned away before she could retract the invitation. Charlie was locked in his room. Blade wouldn't be able to smell him—her brother had started losing his distinctive boyish scent months ago.

And Blade had been sitting on her roof, bleeding and hurt, because he'd promised to protect her.

A little curl of warmth unfolded in her chest. *Don't be stupid*, she told herself. He might be more honorable than she'd have ever suspected, but he was still a blue blood.

Honoria snicked the three locks into place. Behind her, Blade prowled the room, his gaze flickering over the mismatched furniture and neatly scrubbed floors.

"Sit down," she said, crossing to the stove and putting the kettle on. The tiny stove was banked for the night, so she knelt down, stoking it. Anything to avoid looking at him.

The next step was worse. She shut her eyes and took a deep breath. "Take your shirt off. I'll wash the blood out of it."

"Ain't no point," he said. "It's nothin' but rags now, luv." But she heard him pulling it over his head.

Her mind flashed back to that intimate scene in

the sheltered doorway, before the vampire had found them. Heat stirred. That damned uncomfortable heat that she wanted nothing of.

Bracing herself, she stood and turned around. Even prepared, the sight of him stripped to the waist stole her breath. Firelight gleamed on his pale skin, highlighting the dips and curves of each long muscle. He was built lean, all smooth and fluid, lacking the broad strength of Will.

And yet she wanted to touch him. To stroke her hands over the mat of springy blond hair on his chest. Maybe let a finger trail down from his navel, following the arrowing path of hair that lost itself in his waistband...

He coughed under his breath, a smile tugging at his mouth. "Me 'ands, Honor." And she realized that he'd been holding them out for her inspection all along.

"Right," she said briskly, heat spilling into her cheeks. What was she doing? Bandages. She needed bandages.

She found an old shirt of Charlie's that she tore to strips. The water boiled and she poured it into a chipped basin, setting it to cool. She could move. Perform small actions. But not think. Or maybe she was thinking too much.

A thin line of blood ran across his abdomen. Soaking a piece of linen, she knelt at his feet. His thigh was hard muscle beneath her fingertips as she dabbed at the cut.

"It's closed over." Her voice was low and husky. Foolishness. She'd seen naked men before—some of the test subjects at the Institute, those who lost control and tore their clothes off, shaking at the bars that held them prisoner. Or some of the grooms at Caine House, swimming in the pond.

Blade was not a boy. Nor was he a raving lunatic.

"Aye," he said with a nod and leaned back in the chair. His hands rested on his thighs, and he watched her through narrowed, lazy eyes.

"You heal very quickly," she said.

"It's the virus."

No, it's not. She had treated injuries at the Institute. A blue blood healed fast, but not like this. Unless...The patients she'd treated had all been newly infected. Perhaps as the virus colonized the body, it also quickened healing times and responses. With the increased need for feeding, of course.

"Did you always heal this fast?" The scientific part of her wanted to know.

"Dunno. Depends 'ow much blood I've been drinkin'."

"I see." She rinsed the rag out. "The blood staves off the virus, giving it the iron and oxygen it needs. More blood provides..." What exactly? Did it hold the virus at bay? Promote healing? Or did the virus itself *need* more blood to survive and replicate? Did it therefore replicate in the stomach?

Silence had fallen. Blade was watching her. "You know a lot 'bout it."

She'd said too much. Very few people understood what the virus did, knowing only that it was spread by drinking or injecting a blue blood's blood. She had to think quickly. Blade's eyes were already narrowed with suspicion.

"I read Sir Nicodemus Banks's *Travels in the Orient*," she said, "when I was younger."

"The first blue blood."

"Technically he wasn't the first. Here, let me have a look at those arms." She dragged a chair closer and took his hand in hers. Her fingertips brushed over the calluses on his palms. He kept his nails short and neat. Working hands. Nothing like the cool, manicured hands of the Echelon. And yet she could picture them on her, his roughened skin abrading her own. "He was merely the one who spread the virus to Europe."

Dodging White Court assassins from the Orient the entire way. When she'd been a child, it had seemed an exhilarating adventure and she'd made her father read it again and again.

"Ain't ever 'eard of it," Blade said. "It tells 'bout the virus, does it?"

"He went as ambassador to the Forbidden City and the White Court. The Imperial family believed they were gods and that the virus was a gift. They passed it down through their family. Sir Nicodemus wrote of rumors that it came from a mysterious lost world hidden among the Himalayas many years before, and that the emperor had deliberately infected himself to gain power and terrify his enemies."

"So 'ow'd Banks get it?" Blade asked.

Honoria finished washing the cuts on his arms. They were almost healed. Only his hands bore traces of the scalding burn. "He was only allowed in certain areas of the palace, but Sir Nicodemus was…an explorer."

"A skirt chaser, you mean?"

"Apparently." Her own lips betrayed her, a smile sneaking over them. "He heard a girl singing and climbed the walls to see her. He wrote that her voice was as fine as a nightingale. He fell in love with her before he ever saw her."

Blade rolled his eyes. "A bloody poet too, by the sound of 'im."

"Somewhat poetical, yes."

"You like the story," he accused, a grin lighting up his face. "You're a romantic."

"I am not," she replied. "Sir Nicodemus took a terrible risk. The emperor considered it blasphemous for anyone in his family to spread the virus, let alone for it to be 'gifted' to a foreigner. When they realized what had happened, he barely escaped with his life."

"And the girl?"

"She was supposed to run away and meet with him. Instead they sent her hands. In a basket. And their finest assassins."

"So what 'appened then?"

"He escaped across the silk route and into the desert. He remembered very little of it; indeed, he believed he fell into a sort of melancholy. By the time he had regathered his senses, he was in Greece. And blood-thirsty."

"If 'e truly loved the girl, 'e shoulda taken revenge on 'er father."

"He did take revenge," she replied. "The Imperial family's power came from their secret and the fact that they alone were gifted. If the whole world knew of it, then they were no longer unique, no longer powerful. They were only human instead, cursed by a disease. So he started in Greece, spreading the virus to, ah, ladies of the night."

"Aye. I know the sort."

"By the time he reached England, he'd become more strategic in who he offered his blood to. In France he made a small fortune selling it to the French aristocracy. He was an extremely rich man by the time he'd spread it to England."

"Why would any man pay money for such a curse?"

Honoria glanced at Blade's expression, fighting the odd urge to reach out and stroke his face. "Increased speed, better vision, stamina, longevity. A guarantee that you would never become ill from anything else. They did not know then the course of the disease. The only negative was the fact that those who were infected needed to sustain themselves on blood. And once one of them was infected, the whole court wanted it."

"Now, that sounds like a plan I could approve," Blade said. "Sell your blood for your weight in gold and strike at your enemies at the same time. I could almost admire 'im if 'e didn't sound like such a bleedin' peacock."

"Typical," she muttered. "There. I've done what I can."

Blade held his arms up and inspected them. "They'll 'eal."

But how quickly? She needed her notebook, to scratch out the thoughts circling her mind. She'd have to test his reflexes too, but she suspected he was quicker and stronger than any of the newly infected test subjects. Was that why killing a vampire was reputedly harder than killing a blue blood? Because the virus was much stronger in them?

I wonder how quickly a vampire heals…She brushed

the thought away. Foolish even to wonder. She would never get a chance to study one. Except, perhaps, in the split second before it tore her apart. They were insane. Maddened by their thirst and unable to reason. In Georgian times, when excess had been *everything* to the Echelon, there'd been a rash of vampires. The city had burned twice, with vigilante mobs rising up to hunt them and even the blue bloods forming hunting parties.

Five vampires in a year. And it had cost the city more than ten thousand lives.

Since then, as soon as a blue blood even looked like he was approaching the Fade, he was swiftly beheaded. It was kept quiet, but she'd heard rumors. They called it mercy. She called it fear.

The city wouldn't stand for another spate of vampires. People were already muttering about the drones taking their jobs, and how perhaps the French had done the smart thing in executing all of their blue bloods. The Echelon's technology kept them under control, but the slightest provocation could set off the riots again.

"What are you thinkin'?" Blade asked.

Honoria blinked and looked up at him. He watched her face as though he could read every expression on it. But then he was *always* watching her, or so it seemed.

"I was thinking about the vampire." She gave a small shiver. "It was awful—"

"Aye. Stinks like a knackery in the hot sun for a week. Filthy, ugly brute."

She shook her head. "Of course it smelled and looked hideous, but the worst thing is that it was once a man, once a blue blood. Like you."

Brilliant green eyes met hers.

"Aren't you afraid?" she blurted. "They say it's inevitable."

"Ain't no cure. So I guess that's 'ow it ends." Blade shrugged as though he didn't give a damn. But his gaze dropped from hers. "I've given instructions to the lads. Will knows what 'e's got to do."

"That's a terrible burden for him. He's barely a man."

"'E's the only one as can."

She hadn't missed the burly man's eyes, or the way he moved, almost as quickly as Blade. "He's verwulfen, isn't he?"

A flash of green eyes, wondering if they could trust her. "Aye."

She sat very still. The Scandinavian countries were ruled by verwulfen, and the Germanic states leashed them and used them in the military. But blue bloods and verwulfen didn't mix well. When the Echelon came to power, the first thing they did was strike at the Scottish loupe clans and wipe out the majority of them at Culloden. The only verwulfen she'd ever seen was kept in a cage, at the prince consort's menagerie. A poor, maddened creature that paced constantly, its eyes gone wolfish in its human face.

"Where did he come from?" she asked.

"'E were sold by 'is mother when 'e first showed signs of loupe," Blade explained. "I found him on stage in the East End, locked in a cage. They were cuttin' 'im, tryin' to bring on a berserker fit to thrill the crowd. 'E were 'bout fourteen or fifteen, mebbe. Broke 'im out."

"I thought they were a blue blood's natural enemy."

"An enemy's what you make of it. Only reason

blue bloods and verwulfen don't get on is 'cos a verwulfen's the only one as can rip a blue blood apart—and do it easy. They're a threat," Blade said. Then he added softly, "And I guess I don't like cages. Couldn't leave 'im there, starin' up at me with those feral yellow eyes."

Honoria looked down at her hands. This conversation was veering into treacherous waters. She could admire a man who had broken a child out of a cage because he knew what it was like to be trapped in such a way himself. She didn't want to soften toward him. When she was stronger, she'd be nothing more than chattel. A thrall. Kept to feed himself with. Still...

"How old were you when the Echelon put you in the Ivory Tower?" she asked.

"Dunno," he said with a shrug. "Born in the rookeries. Weren't the sort of thing we kept count of. I 'ad a sister." Something about the way his voice softened made her look up. Blade stared at the wall, his mind a thousand miles away. "Vickers saw 'er sellin' flowers in Covent Garden. Took a shine to 'er when Emily were only sixteen. Young enough to buy what 'e were sellin'. Only problem was, she refused to go anywhere without me. If 'e wanted 'er, 'e 'ad to take me too.

"I think I amused 'im. 'E liked the way I spoke. Like I were a bleedin' novelty. Used to parade me out for all 'is friends. They 'ad fights, the blue bloods. Pittin' boys against each other. Or against beasts. 'E used to wager big on me. Said as 'ow if I won for 'im, 'e'd reward me. I weren't allowed to let Emily know, but by that point she were addicted to the feel o' the feedin'. I don't think she'd a protested too much."

"I'm sure she would have," Honoria said. If that were Charlie, she wouldn't care how good being a blue blood's thrall felt. One more reason to hate Vickers, as if she needed another one. The silence of the night felt as though it had grown, pressing in upon them. Her eyes were stinging with exhaustion, and yet she felt reluctant to take her leave of him.

Stupid. She'd done her best. She'd washed his cuts and tended his wounds. It was the least she could do. Now it should be time to see him out.

To sit on her roof in the cold, foggy London night. Alone.

"Stay here," she said, pushing her chair back. "I'll fetch you one of my father's shirts. And a blanket."

Something that might have been surprise reared in Blade's eyes. "You're invitin' me to stay?"

"Unless you'd prefer the roof. I gather you intend to remain the night, regardless of my protestations."

He was suddenly on his feet in front of her. Far too close, actually. She took a step back, but the wall was there.

"Honor," he murmured, reaching out, his movements deliberately slow, allowing her time to protest if she desired it. Her breath caught.

"I'll just fetch that shirt, then," she blurted, ducking beneath his outstretched arm. A low, husky laugh followed her.

Slipping into the bedroom, she caught sight of Lena diving for the bed. The small phosphorescent Glimmer they used for light cast a muted green shine across the room. It had cost two pounds, but it would never need replacing, unlike candles or gas lamps.

"Having trouble sleeping?" Honoria asked.

"He's staying here the night?" Lena said in reply. "What about Charlie?"

Honoria held a finger to her lips, glancing at the door. Opening the small chest at the foot of the bed, she dug through. Her father's shirt—the one he'd wrapped the diary in when he gave it to her—was buried in the bottom.

"That's father's!" Lena hissed.

"Well, he's not going to need it now, is he?"

Lena sucked in a sharp breath.

"I'm sorry. I shouldn't have said that. It was cruel."

Lena's dark eyes shone in the light. Her full mouth quivered. "You're giving it to *him*?"

The shirt still smelled like Artemus Todd. Like ink and chemicals. Honoria hesitated, rubbing the worn cotton. "His own is torn. He…he saved my life tonight. And I have my memories of father. I don't need his shirt to revere him by."

"It's all we have."

"No," Honoria whispered, sitting on the edge of Lena's small cot. Running a hand over her sister's shining, dark hair, she smiled. "He gave us each other. That's far more important than a shirt."

"You mean that?"

She hated that her sister had to ask her that. But it had been a tense couple of months. With exhaustion and hunger riding them both daily, it was hard to be tolerant. And Charlie's illness didn't help. Both of them had been on edge.

She leaned closer and pressed her lips against Lena's temple. "Of course I mean it. You and Charlie are the world to me. I would never wish otherwise."

A single tear slid down Lena's cheek. She was still a child, really, trying ever so hard to be brave. Of the three of them, she'd suffered the most these last six months. Honoria was used to working long hours at the Institute, and Charlie was young enough that she could make the transition into a form of adventure for him. But Lena remembered her pretty dresses and friends, the sweet cakes always on the table and the flirtatious young gentlemen who hovered around her like butterflies. On the cusp of making her debut—with all the excitement of what to wear, who she wished to make a thrall contract with—she'd been suddenly thrown into a grim, dreary world where she was always hungry and had to work her fingers to the bone just to eat.

Lena caught her hand. "I would never wish it otherwise either."

"I know. Move into my bed," she told Lena, picking up the shirt. "We'll have to share blankets."

Her own blanket was gray and dreary but warm. Honoria snatched it up and headed for the door.

Her stomach dropped as Blade looked up from where he'd been studying Charlie's door.

"My brother's room," she said unnecessarily.

"You lock 'im in?"

"He walks in his sleep. I'm afraid he'll leave the house one night." The lie came smoothly to her lips. So many lies she told now. Sometimes she felt as though she repeated them so often that a part of her started to believe them. "Here," she said, holding out the shirt and the blanket.

He crossed toward her, all lean, fluid grace. A man

comfortable in his own skin. And there was rather a lot of it at the moment.

"Thank you."

Blade took the blanket, placing it on the table behind him without looking. The shirt was another matter. He took it, letting the soft folds drift through his fingers. "I'll be gone in the mornin'. See if I can track the vampire to 'is lair."

"I'm sorry," Honoria said.

"For what?" One of his eyebrows arched up. They were thick and tawny, very strongly defined on his face. The look gave him a diabolical appeal.

"You could be hunting it now if it weren't for your promise to protect me."

"You don't 'unt a vampire at night. And not alone. I need Will at me back. 'E'll be dead asleep for most o' tonight and tomorrow. So I'm goin' to do some scoutin'."

At least the daylight would keep him safe. With their white, sensitive skins, vampires couldn't tolerate the sunlight. But if it was hiding in the tunnels of Undertown, where the rookery spilled under the ground for those families enterprising enough to live there, then Blade might go in after it.

"Be careful," she blurted.

"Worried about me, luv?"

"Who else will pay me what you do?" she replied. Then she added softly, "And I've no wish to see you hurt. Or any of your men."

A smile touched his lips, carving dimples in his cheeks. Blade was actually very handsome when he smiled. She couldn't help feeling just a little breathless.

"Of course," he said. "I'll pass your good wishes on to the lads. As for me..." He took a step closer, his voice roughening. "I'll thank you meself."

There was no time to step back. He moved with blurring speed, his lips brushing against her own. A cool, whispering touch, capturing the protest she opened her mouth to voice. The shirt still hung in his hands as he stepped back, his smile turning to something else...something almost wistful.

Honoria blinked, her hands hovering in front of her as if to ward him off. Or perhaps, if she were honest with herself, to touch him. "Why did you do that?"

That smile was driving her to madness. Her gaze roved his mouth, the imprint of his touch burning against her lips like a ghostly caress. She was afraid she'd never stop feeling it.

Blade shrugged, turning around and tugging the shirt over his back. "Just in case I die tomorrow. I'd 'ate to 'ave me regrets, and I've been wantin' to kiss you since we first met."

His brutal honesty shocked her. Somehow her fingers found her lips. She stared at him and said, "That wasn't part of the deal."

"No, it weren't." He shook the blanket out and looked at her. "Sweet dreams, luv." His smile suddenly blazed as though he knew what her dreams would be full of. "I know mine will be."

Chapter 10

The message came early the next morning. Blade was strapping on a knife sheath around his wrist when Lark hurtled in. "Whoa, kitten!" He snagged her into his arms, giving her a hug. "What's the 'urry?"

Her nose wrinkled at the smell of his body armor. "There's a blue blood," she said. "'E wants a word with you." She handed him a thick piece of folded parchment.

Blade put her down and ruffled her hair. "A blue blood, eh?" So his message the other night had been received. He looked at the parchment, but it meant nothing to him even if he sat and tried to focus on the jumble of letters.

"'E were comin' by steam carriage." Lark jerked the curtains aside and peered out.

Blade tugged his boots on, checking the knife tucked into the side. Its edges were serrated. Last night had only proven that he needed to cause as much damage as possible to the vampire before its wounds would heal. "Aye, I'm goin'. Get Rip on the rooftops with a rifle."

Lark bolted into the warren, searching for the big lieutenant.

Blade tucked a pistol in the small of his back, because he wasn't stupid, then tossed his knife kit aside. Time to go dance with the devil.

The horseless steam carriage was pulling up just as he crossed the threshold. A fancy coachman in blue livery sat on the high seat at the front, working the steering with impassive aplomb. The rest of the carriage gleamed in the weak sunlight, the inlaid panels covered in mother-of-pearl. Gilt curlicues scrolled over the surface, and as Blade watched, somebody twitched the blue velvet curtains aside.

Foolery to come here in such a bloody treasure when people were starving. That kind of idiocy caused riots.

Which explained the four metaljackets trotting alongside the carriage in perfect unison, their iron boots ringing on the cobbles. He saw the flamethrowers where their left hands ought to be and paused for a moment. Spitfires were the most dangerous models.

Blade leaned against the doorway. A liveried footman jumped down from the back, hurrying to produce a stool and open the door. He knelt beside the stool, head bowed, as an elegant, gloved hand rested on the door.

Well, well, well...a woman. Which meant they were either hoping to lull him into complacency, or perhaps sought to tempt him. Hell, it could mean anything.

There was only one woman this could be.

Blade stalked forward, tugging his gold cheroot case out of his pocket and fingering a slim cheroot. "Me Lady Aramina," he drawled, lighting it. "What an unexpected pleasure. I'd bow, but me knees ain't quite what they used to be."

Lady Aramina swept from the carriage, her full skirts held in one delicate hand. She glanced around with cool disinterest, the pale mounds of her breasts threatening to tumble from the olive green bodice of her dress. Black lace provided a fringe of modesty, and a scrap of exquisite lace covered her eyes. An intricate arrangement of black ostrich feathers and metal beads swept her auburn hair up into an elegant pile of curls, which she hadn't bothered to powder for the visit. The effect was erotic and mysterious, and he couldn't help enjoying the sight for a moment. He was only a man, after all, and this was, reputedly, the most beautiful woman in England.

He'd never seen her. The blue bloods of the Echelon were strictly male, except for this one shocking exception. They forbade the infecting of females in order to prevent the weaker species from the bloodlust and hysteria, but Lady Aramina had been the House of Casavian's only heir. When her father lay dying from some mysterious illness, he had done the unforgivable rather than see his House fade into obscurity. Some said he laughed as he lay on his deathbed. Others said the joke was on him, for Aramina had little real power. Somehow she'd survived the numerous assassination attempts following her father's death, but Casavian House was now the lowest of the seven Great Houses.

She started tugging off her gloves. Strangely enough, the action reminded him of Honoria, a troubling thought. He shouldn't be thinking of her so often, yet the damned woman never left his mind, it seemed.

And so it was that Lady Aramina's bountiful charms suddenly lost their effect. Her coppery hair wasn't dark enough, and her brown eyes were lighter, almost the same color as brandy. The eyes in his memory, Honoria's eyes, were dark and flashing with suppressed anger. They were the eyes he wanted to stare into as he buried himself deep within her body. Not these calculating ones that watched him now.

Troubling. He puffed in the sweet-scented smoke.

"You got my message?" she asked, handing her gloves to the footman without taking her eyes off Blade.

"I'd rather 'ear it from you. Come in. I'll send for tea and scones, and we'll 'ave a nice little tête-à-tête, ain't it called?"

Her brandy-brown eyes flattened, but she wasn't certain whether he was mocking her. "I have company."

Blade could smell the reek of bay rum in the carriage. "Aye." He glanced past, at the stockinged calf and muscled thigh within. "I seen 'im."

"We mean you no harm," Aramina said, sweeping toward him as though he would get out of the way.

Blade flicked the cheroot on the cobbles and ground it out. Aramina stopped in front of him, a little frown of displeasure on her pale, coldly beautiful face. He took a step forward, looking down at her. She didn't quite stiffen, but it was there in the firming of her lips.

Hands in his pockets, he walked a small circle around her as though examining her. "You're a swish dove," he said. "The prince consort sent you to sweeten me up?"

A little clenching in her fingers. Good.

She turned her head, glancing over her shoulder at

him. The look in her eyes could have flayed the skin off his back, and he suspected she was envisioning that very act. "You don't want to make an enemy of me," she said.

Pretty little viper. He moved. And caught her wrists from behind as she drew in a breath.

"Get your hands off me," she hissed.

"Listen 'ere, lovey," he said, his voice cold. "You're already the enemy. I ain't ever goin' to forget it. So let's cut all this mincin' 'round. I don't much like your little games."

He could hear the other blue blood stepping from the carriage, but the sound of clapping still shocked him.

A quick glimpse made his eyebrows shoot up. Leo Barrons, the last man he'd expected to see with her ladyship. The Houses of Caine and Casavian had been at each other's throats for years, just waiting for the other to take a misstep. Caine House had nearly destroyed Aramina.

Just what game was the prince consort playing? It was enough to give him a headache.

He let her go and danced out of the way as she spun on him, a little bejeweled dagger in her grip.

"Easy, now, princess. You don't wanna 'urt yourself with that little pig-sticker."

Aramina's lips peeled back from her teeth.

"That's enough," Barrons commanded. "I told you he doesn't like games."

"An interestin' assessment from a man who don't know me from Adam," Blade countered, sizing up the other man.

Barrons moved with an eerie grace he wasn't used to

seeing on a blue blood of the Echelon. A swordsman, then. The man who knew who Honoria was.

Blade jerked his head in the kind of acknowledgment one duelist gave to the other.

Barrons's gaze swept the roofline. "Snipers again?" he asked, taking a pinch of snuff.

"One never can be too careful," Blade replied, gesturing his visitors into the dark entrance of the warren. The metaljackets made as though to follow. "The drones can wait out 'ere."

"They're housetrained," Aramina said.

He held his arm out, barring her way. "Aye. But they ain't comin' into *my* 'ouse."

She opened her mouth to protest.

"Leave it," Barrons muttered. "We've more important things to discuss."

Blade lowered his arm. "Aye."

Aramina looked as though she might protest at having him at their backs, but Barrons stalked past, looking dangerous in his velvets and lace. The darkness of the warren swallowed him up.

"After you," Blade said silkily.

Aramina swept ahead of him in a swirl of jasmine-scented skirts. Blade gave the street and rooftops a swift glance and then followed.

O'Shay was waiting in what Blade liked to think of as his audience chamber. The room was dark and musty, the floorboards threatening to give way beneath their feet. Rotting curtains hung from the windows, and the fireplace was cold. The only hint that this was something more than a rookery slum was the trio of elegant Louis XVI chairs in the center of the room.

Even Barrons seemed taken aback as he prowled the empty chamber. Aramina screwed up her nose delicately. But Blade had long since learned that you didn't take a viper to your breast. This was for appearances only. Very few people ever saw his real chambers or the homey sprawl where his "family" lived. Honoria had been the only person in recent memory whom he had allowed within his inner sanctum.

"Wait outside," Blade muttered to O'Shay, then turned his attention to the two blue bloods. "'Ave a seat." Slinging out of his red coat, he tossed it over the back of his chair then sat. Lark darted out of the shadows with a footstool. After a moment's hesitation and a dark glare at her—he weren't no bleedin' lord—he cocked his boots up on it.

Barrons held Aramina's chair for her. Blade didn't miss the look she gave her companion. They might be playing at an alliance, but if one of them smelled poison in the other's cup, he was certain they wouldn't mention it until it was too late.

"You claim there's a vampire in the Whitechapel rookery," Aramina said, cutting straight to the point. Somehow, despite the circumstances, she made it seem as though he had come as supplicant to *her*. That took real talent, it did.

"Aye. Ugly brute too."

"You've seen it?" Barrons sat forward. "You said you'd only found the bodies."

"'Ad a little run-in with it last night. Seen it with me own eyes." He gave an incredulous shake of his head. "Never seen one before. 'Eard the stories, of course, but…to see it's somethin' else."

"You survived," Aramina said. *Unfortunately*, her eyes added.

"Barely," Blade replied. He gestured to Lark. "The blud-wein, please."

Lark nodded and darted out of the room.

"It's faster than I ever seen. Stronger." Blade leaned forward too. "I stabbed it right inna 'eart and it barely even blinked."

None of them were old enough to have been there during the Year of Blood. This was a new kind of horror for them, a myth come to nightmarish life.

"You're certain it was the heart?" Aramina asked.

Blade put a finger just under his sternum. "Right here. Didn't much like it, but it didn't cause it any undue concern."

"Have you located it?" Barrons asked. The man was deceptively at ease, yet there was an intensity in his dark eyes that belied his relaxed frame.

Blade shook his head. "It run off after I stabbed it, and I ain't had a chance to 'unt it down."

"You didn't follow?" Aramina asked.

"One o' me men were injured. And I ain't stupid enough to 'unt a vampire by meself. What I want to know is where it come from."

"We're still uncertain," Aramina replied. "The prince consort has requested an inquiry. This isn't the sort of thing we can allow to stand. Someone knew this was occurring. And someone allowed it to happen."

Barrons nodded, his gaze locked on a spot beside Blade's boot. Perhaps it was because he wanted to find the other man at fault for something, but Blade couldn't help feeling as though there was something the man was hiding.

Lark slipped in through the door, carefully balancing the tray with the blud-wein on it. She offered it to Blade first.

"We're willing to offer military support," Aramina continued. "The prince consort has—"

"Aye. A legion o' metaljackets sent in to cull the creature, and then what? They're just goin' to trot back out again and leave me the rookeries?" Blade laughed. "Ain't bloody likely. And what'll me people think, seein' the enemy comin' in? They'll riot."

"Perhaps you underestimate the strength of the people's intolerance for us," Aramina countered. "They've shown no sign of rioting in other quarters. Unless there's some other reason you don't want the legion coming in. Hmm?"

His eyes narrowed. "This ain't Kensington, milady. And maybe you ought take a look 'round. People is starvin' and the taxes just keep gettin' 'igher. Your prince consort ain't a popular name to say 'round 'ere. They see a horde o' metaljackets descendin' on the rookery, and they're goin' to think somethin's up." He leaned forward. "And if you're callin' me a coward, then just say it to me face."

Aramina actually colored. One thing he'd learned about the Echelon—they would smile ever so sweetly at you while they plotted to kill you, but calling them on it sent them into a dithering mess.

Barrons smothered a laugh with a cough. "Then what *will* you accept? The prince consort wants this mess cleaned up as swiftly as possible."

Blade pretended to consider it, but he'd already decided on the limits last night when he lay on Honoria's kitchen floor and listened to her breathing in the next room. "A score of Nighthawks."

Some of the Nighthawks were blue bloods like him, infected with the craving virus and then discarded once they had the hunger under control. With their enhanced senses, tracking down criminals was a perfect avenue for these people. And they worked similar streets to what they would work in the rookery.

"And you," Blade added, looking Barrons directly in the eye. "I'll work with you." Keep the man close, where he could keep an eye on him. And maybe, just maybe, find out what Honoria meant to him. Or more importantly what Barrons meant to her.

Aramina blinked. "Barrons? But why? He's a duelist, but he's no match for a vampire."

"Because 'e talks straight," Blade replied. "I like that. And if 'e's tryin' to play me, I can't see 'ow."

"Besides our mutual, shared acquaintance," Barrons murmured.

Their eyes met. Barrons knew precisely what Blade wanted of him. The hair on the back of his neck rose, but he managed a curt nod. "Aye. There's that."

"Acquaintance?" Aramina didn't like being in the shadows.

"An old friend." Barrons gave her a swift smile, then stood. "We accept the bargain. I'll work with you to coordinate the hunt. The prince consort will supply a score of Nighthawks. And I would urge you to accept a squad of metaljackets, despite your caution.

They can be useful at clearing tunnels when we don't want to risk lives."

A sensible thought. Blade chewed it over. "A squadron I'll accept. Some of 'em Spitfires and a couple o' Earthshakers. We can either burn 'im out or dig 'im out."

Blade handed his empty glass to Lark and swung to his feet, holding out his hand. Barrons eyed it for a moment, then clasped it with his own. Despite the froth of lace at his wrist, the man's grip was firm and there were calluses on his palms. And when Blade squeezed just a fraction more than necessary, Barrons smiled and squeezed back.

They broke the grip and nodded at each other.

"Done," Blade said.

"Done," Barrons agreed.

Aramina stood, smoothing out her skirts. "Well," she said. "I'm glad you've reached an agreement. I'll be in the carriage if you need me." Turning on her heel, she swept out, leaving behind the heady, exotic scent of jasmine.

"She's a beauty," Blade said. "But a man'd 'ave to be stark-ravin' to take such as 'er to 'is breast."

"She's not so bad," Barrons disagreed, "when her claws are clipped." He smiled and it wasn't nice.

Blade gestured toward the door. Silence welled up between them, an almost visible tension that crab-walked down his spine.

Barrons said nothing as his host saw him out, but paused in the entrance. "Do you know who she is?"

There was no mistaking who he was referring to. "Aye. What's she to you?"

"A very old acquaintance," Barrons replied.

"Acquaintance. I don't like that word. It tells me nothin'."

"Her father worked for the duke of Caine for many years, until Vickers lured him away. I grew up with her." Barrons's gaze turned sharp. "I won't claim that we're friends, for we're not, but I wouldn't like to see anything happen to her."

That eased Blade's mind somewhat, but not wholly. "*She* came to me," he replied. "I've given 'er me protection."

"As a thrall?" Barrons was insistent.

"Aye."

Barrons laughed under his breath, but there was no humor in it. "Gods. And I drove her to it."

"What the 'ell does that mean?"

"It means she came to me first. And I refused to help her. If I'd known what she intended, I might have been more tolerant." Barrons gave a little nod. "I'll refer the agreement on to the prince consort and return with my accompaniment on the morrow."

"Aye," Blade bit out, but the other man was already gone, striding toward the carriage with a loose-hipped grace.

She came to me first…What the hell did that mean?

Chapter 11

THE COLLOIDAL SILVER WAS THICK IN THE VIAL. Honoria pushed the syringe through the rubber seal, trying to ignore her brother's wince. The needle had to be large enough to draw the viscous liquid; hence it hurt like the devil. But the worst thing was when the colloidal silver interacted with the virus, sending Charlie into spasms of pain.

Sometimes the cure was worse than the disease. But, then, this was no cure at all. It simply held off the disease a little longer, buying more time for them.

"Here we go, Charlie," she murmured. "Which arm?"

"Right," he sighed, extending his scarecrow-esque arm. Little scar marks nestled in the groove of his elbow. With such frequent injections, the virus couldn't heal the wound site.

Honoria tugged the leather strap tight around his upper arm, then slid the needle into the vein with practiced ease. Charlie bit his lip and tried not to cry.

"It will pass, my little man," she murmured, eyeing the slowly depleting metal. "Won't be long. Few more moments." Then the colloidal silver would bind with the virus and he'd be trying not to scream. God, she hated this so much. There had to be a better way. The preventive vaccine had worked on both her and Lena. She didn't understand why it hadn't worked with Charlie.

There had always been a few people who didn't catch the virus when exposed to it. Her father had played with combinations of their blood, at a loss to explain it, but prepared to inject willing test subjects with the resistant blood. It worked in most cases. Perhaps one in several hundred exhibited signs of the disease. It was only cruel fate that had made Charlie one of them.

Or perhaps not. She'd always had her suspicions. Her father had scratched her once with a syringe he'd used on a patient at the Institute, claiming it was an accident. She couldn't help but wonder whether Charlie had a similar mishap. The thought made her ill, but, then, science had been everything to her father. The vaccine was everything.

"Here we go," she said, withdrawing the needle and pressing gauze padding to the injection site.

Charlie was trembling with the effort of keeping himself still. He made a sharp, animal-like sound of pain, then turned his face into the pillow. Honoria put the needle aside and rubbed his thin back. She felt each rib as she ran her fingers over his skin.

"Did you keep breakfast down?"

He shook his head, making strangled sounds. Honoria slipped into the bed beside him, wrapping her arms around his tiny body and holding him tight. "Hush, little Charlie, don't say a word," she started crooning, slipping into the lullaby their father had sung for each of them as children. "Papa's gonna buy you a mechanical bird. And if that mechanical bird won't sing, Papa's gonna buy you a clockwork king. And if that clockwork king breaks down..."

It was long minutes before he stopped crying. Longer still before the torturous shaking left him. Spent from the pain, he collapsed against the sheets.

Honoria slipped her fingers into his. "All over now, Charlie, for another day."

"I wish it were all over forever," he whispered.

A lump caught in her throat. "Don't say that. You don't mean that."

"I do." She heard the sound of tears in his voice. "You don't know what it's like."

"Shush." She rubbed his back, her mind white-hot with pain. *I promised you, Father, that I'd take care of him, but how do I protect him from this? From himself?* Then bitterly, *You promised it would work. That the preventive vaccine would work.*

But it hadn't and her father had never finished working on a cure. There were only his notes, in the diary and...

Her fingers froze. Her father had written most of the diary in code, but she knew the code. Maybe she could finish his work.

It was a desperate idea. But so was she. She'd been trying to fool herself for weeks, but the truth was that Charlie was getting worse.

Lifting up on one elbow, she peered at Charlie's face. His lashes fluttered against his cheeks. The pain had exhausted him. He often slept for hours following an injection.

Honoria slid off the bed and scratched a swift note for him, then tucked it on the pillow beside him. She paused just long enough to kiss his cool forehead, then gathered her shawl to keep her warm. It was a long walk to the Institute.

Nothing. A whole day spent canvassing the rest of the rookery and not even a single reek of vampire. Blade scowled to himself as he stalked along the rooftop, balancing on the capped tiles.

"It's got to be 'ere somewhere," Will muttered, following on his heels.

"It's in Undertown. It's the only place we ain't checked."

"Bloody 'ell."

It was a sentiment Blade shared. Undertown was a refuge for the homeless and poor, those who couldn't afford to pay the Echelon's taxes, and those who didn't want to be found. The desperate. The Slasher gangs ruled Undertown, hiding in the tunnels of what had once been the Eastern Link Underground Rail's project to connect to the district line, before it had collapsed and buried hundreds of railway workers alive. The resulting scandal drove the ELU Railway Company into dun territory, and the project had stalled for want of finances. Various attempts to clear the tunnels had resulted in toxic explosions as live gas deposits were hit, and rumors had spread of ghosts that tore the living apart. It hadn't taken long for the Echelon to declare the tunnel project a failure and board them up.

It was a bloomin' rabbit warren down there. The

perfect place for a vampire to hide. Blade had always suspected that was where it was, but a part of him had hoped he was wrong.

The breeze stirred, carrying a familiar scent with it. Blade's head shot up and he scanned the street. Dozens of people scurried home from work. He didn't recognize anyone…and yet he could smell Honoria, sure as it was day. Where?

Not that old woman near the corner. Or the gaudily dressed dollymop digging at her nails as she eyed the slim pickings in the crowd. The streets were a riot as a gang of rookery lads played tumbler in the alleys. They bolted in and out, chasing the clockwork tumbler ball that, once wound, careened off walls and carts and passers-by with equal abandon. The aim was to catch the tumbler before anyone else could, or before it got crushed beneath a passing cart.

The tumbler dashed past a dark-haired coal lass carrying a pair of pails balanced on a stick across her shoulders. Its clockwork whir was getting louder, a sure sign that the tumbler was winding out of energy. The girl staggered as the horde of boys swept past, whooping and carrying the long hooked sticks they used to net the ball—or to trip each other.

"I'll be damned," he muttered. Honoria had smothered her hair and cheeks in coal dust until she was barely recognizable. London was full of young women just like her, selling coal to get by. It was a bloody good disguise. Even his eye had skipped over her, so used to the sight.

Perhaps it helped that she moved with such diffidence, bobbing her head whenever anyone looked at her. The only thing that gave her away was the neat, clean fingernails. No coal lass had hands like that.

"Bloody hell," Will cursed as he narrowly avoided walking into him.

"Go 'ome. Get some rest. I'll be along shortly."

"She ain't worth it."

Blade knew why his lieutenant showed such dislike. Will despised most women or avoided them entirely. After his mother had sold him for five pounds, he'd vowed them all to the devil.

And then, of course, there'd been that confusion two years ago when the two men had agreed to the feedings. Will was a young male in his prime with few sexual escapades, if any. The feeding took him hard, stirring his body to feel things that he might otherwise not have been inclined to. It had taken Blade awhile to realize what was behind the sudden way his lieutenant couldn't meet his gaze anymore. And then that disastrous evening when Will had reached for him and broken all the rules.

They'd sorted it out. So it was with a gentle hand that he caught Will's grip and eased it off him.

"You'll get yourself killed. She's trouble. You ain't thinkin' clear on this," Will growled. "You got an itch, you get yourself down to one of the flash houses or find a bit of laced mutton on the street. There'd be plenty of lasses to give you a tumble."

"I want this one."

"Why?"

Blade shrugged. It wasn't something he wanted to share with Will, or even admit to himself, but Honoria intrigued him. "Let it alone, Will." He stepped onto the angled tiles of the roof and rode them down to the gutter. "I'll be back."

Ignoring his second's muttered curse about pigheaded fools—Will had to know he'd be heard—Blade landed with a jolt on the cobbles. His prey was just slipping through the narrow alley that led into Petticoat Lane. Where was she going?

He followed her through the foot traffic on Petticoat Lane and along Whitechapel High. She was heading for Aldgate. The city. And the heart of Echelon rule.

His gut twisted. A sudden vision of Barrons's face sprang into his mind and his fists clenched. If she was meeting up with Barrons, he wanted to know. He weren't no Brother Starling to lie with the same woman. She'd accepted his protection. That meant that any trespass on her person by another man was cause enough to kill.

As he followed her beneath the heavy brick edifice of Aldgate, people took one look at his face then darted out of the way.

It was a pity. He had almost liked Barrons.

Chapter 12

The Institute was an enormous stone building in Blackfriars, ringed by fifteen-foot walls topped with wires that conveyed charged lightning. Anyone touching those wires would be given an enormous shock.

From the outside it appeared a forbidding place, meant to keep people out, but Honoria knew what those walls and wires were really for: keeping the newly infected craving sufferers from escaping.

There were three ways to get inside. Carrying her pails around the back, past the ivy-covered walls, she looked around to see if anyone was watching.

There were two other options besides the main gate: over or under. Under meant holding her breath and swimming through the blackened waters that fed the Institute and squeezing through the iron bars at the bottom. Over meant climbing a tree, leaping the four feet between the branches and the wall, and then hoping that the western corner still had that tangle of wires that was just large enough for her to slip beneath.

It was a good thing she'd hardly been eating. She was slimmer now than she had been when she ran away—though putting on weight almost daily with the food that Blade's money had brought them—but not as slender as she had been at sixteen, when she was still young enough to race the other apprentices around the walled yards, or accepting the dares that most young people leveled at each other. Honoria had won them all. Most of the youths drew the line at crawling beneath a wire charged with artificial lightning, but she'd been determined even then. Carefree. A lot like Lena, actually.

She was twenty-four now, not so daring nor so foolish. And she was cold. Which meant she was going over the wall, not under.

She paused underneath the tree and knotted her skirts. The hairs on the back of her neck stood up. She felt almost as if someone were watching her, but a swift glance showed her nothing but empty streets.

Shimmying up the tree, Honoria paused for breath in the crook of the trunk. The last time she'd been here had been the night her father sent them away. With Lena and Charlie waiting in the steam cab a few blocks away, she'd broken into the Institute in the dead of night. Because her father wasn't the only one who had taken notes.

His diary was only as important as the information contained within it. Her own little notebook that she kept locked in her desk drawer in the Institute was at least half as dangerous as his. With it, Vickers could have re-created her father's discoveries.

All had been going smashingly well until the night watchman made his rounds with his guard dog. Honoria had been making her way to the exit with both diaries stashed in a small bag at her hip when the dog let up a rousing cry. She'd been forced to hide them and flee.

And sometimes the safest place to hide something was right under the very person's nose.

Crawling along the branch, she paused at the point where it began to dip beneath her weight and eyed the wall. Four feet away. And a fifteen-foot drop onto the grass.

Sweat dripped off her nose and she reorganized her grip, slowly gathering her feet underneath her. This had been much easier when she was a child and had no fear of such things. Holding on to the branch over her head, she eyed the wall again. Then she pushed off.

Honoria hadn't counted on her physical weakness, the result of months of starving herself. She hit the wall short of where she'd intended, her hands scrabbling for purchase. Ignoring the sharp pain as her nails tore, she hauled herself up. It took all of her strength, and she rested for a moment, panting sharply.

Dusk was falling, washing away the harsh signs of neglect and softening the heavy pall of soot that clung to everything. Honoria slithered along the wall. The wires were still tangled, leaving just enough space to crawl beneath.

Honoria started inching her way underneath them like a caterpillar. All was going well until she had crawled through as far as her hips. The knot of her skirt was going to scrape the wires.

"Come on," she whispered, reaching back awkwardly to shift it.

"Hey, now!" someone called.

Honoria froze.

A guard came around the corner in the gardens below, waving to someone in the distance. Thankfully he had no dog with him.

Don't move. Don't breathe. Maybe he won't notice you.

It was a long, tense moment. The guard called out something about his tea break, laughing at the reply. Then he disappeared around the corner of the west wing.

Letting out a shaky breath, Honoria started inching forward again.

She lowered herself over the inside of the wall and found rough footholds in the stone. The heavy undergrowth of the gardens hid her from the bleak arrow-slitted windows of the main building. Ivy clung to the forbidding bluestone walls, and the main doors were barred with a heavy portcullis, like grinning teeth.

The human guards would be taking their tea in the western guard tower. Honoria bent low and scurried toward the graveyard at the back of the main building. If the guards' routine had remained at all the same, she had fifteen minutes at most before they would begin their final rounds.

A low wall dissected the gardens from the graveyard. To reach the iron-barred gate, she would have to break from cover. Glancing at the building, she swept her gaze over the windows. There was no sign of occupancy, but, then, the inmates' cells would be along this side. The only ones watching would be the test subjects, most in deteriorating stages of the craving.

Taking a deep breath to calm her nerves, she ran for the stone arch that shielded the gate. Pressing her back against the wall, she peered around the corner. Nothing moved. The gate squealed as she eased it open, sending her nerves into a jumbling, panicking mess. There was no outcry. Slipping through the narrow gap she'd opened, she couldn't resist one last look behind her. That feeling of being watched intensified.

Or maybe it was the creeping cold of finding herself in the graveyard where the Institute interred the bodies of those craving victims who had succumbed to the virus's side effects. Some of them had been cut open and examined in the underground labs before being discarded. Others had been burned, with the body's cinders being ingested by voluntary test subjects—the poor—in order to discover if the virus lingered in the remains after fire. Horrific measures that she and her father had discovered in the last few weeks and had been powerless to stop.

The graves were simple granite headstones as a sop to human sensibilities. But set just a little farther back from them was a magnificent crypt with a marble angel soaring over it. The serene face tilted toward the sky. Inscribed on the brass plate was *Emily Anne Rathinger. Died 1821. Rest in peace, my love.* It was where she had hidden the diaries.

The gate wasn't locked, but the hinges were almost rusted shut. Honoria tugged gently at the bars, the grit of rust crumbling beneath her fingers.

It gave just enough to slip inside. The tomb was dark and cold. She didn't dare light the flare stick she'd bought on the way, for the phosphorescence would illuminate the crypt like Guy Fawkes Night. Easing the gate shut behind her, she felt her way down the stairs.

One. Two. Three bricks to the right. There. Her fingers found the loose brick she had discovered years ago. The mortar crumbled as she tugged it free.

The little bag with the diaries was tucked right in the back. Honoria grabbed it and knotted it to her belt, then hastily replaced the brick. The silence was growing on her. She didn't know why she felt so uneasy. The crypt had never bothered her before.

Time to get out. Before the guards came. And before this sudden dread overtook her nerves. She scurried for the entry, reached for the gate—

And froze.

A figure was crossing the unkempt grass and heading for the crypt. A crushed-velvet coat of Bleu de France framed his broad shoulders, with a gold breastplate gleaming over his chest. Armed with an ebony cane, he stalked across the grass, a distracted expression on his pale face.

Her very worst nightmare. The duke of Vickers was coming toward her.

Chapter 13

The hunger snarled and Blade took a half step forward from his place of concealment before forcing himself to stop. Vickers. In the flesh. He'd not had a chance like this in over fifty years.

Think, you idiot, he told himself. Vickers was within calling distance of a squadron of guards. And he was never vulnerable. He wore that damned breastplate everywhere. The only way to kill him would be to decapitate him, and with the narrow sword Vickers concealed in his ebony cane, getting close enough to do that was suicide.

And Honoria was in there. Damn the woman, what the bloody hell was she doing here? A sudden, horrific thought stole his breath. What if this was not coincidence? *No*. He refused to believe it.

Blade slipped from shadow to shadow, stalking the pair of them. Vickers paused by the tomb and jabbed his cane into the soft grass. It stayed upright and he started tugging on his gloves, draping them over the gold handle.

What was he doing? Blade crouched low in the

cover of an exuberant rose bush. Vickers bowed his powdered head, clasped his hands behind him and…simply stood there. As though paying homage to someone.

Grief? Or guilt? Blade's eyebrow shot up. He would have never suspected either emotion to inflict the deadly duke.

I 'ope it keeps you up nights.

At least it had become apparent that Honoria was not in league with him. There was no sign of movement within. If Vickers didn't drown himself in perfume, he might have smelled her.

So tempting. *What if you never get this chance again?* the devil on his shoulder whispered.

He swallowed. Hard. Fifty years for a shot like this. Days and days where he woke screaming, reliving the agony of coming out of the hunger and finding his sister lifeless and drained on the floor. Smelling her blood all over him. Feeling it slick and wet between his fingers. Tasting it in his mouth and—God damn him—wanting more of it.

And Vickers, standing there in shock, her blood splashed on his white brocaded coat, saying, *You killed her.*

The hunger—the demon inside—roared within Blade, desperate to unleash itself. It hated both itself and Vickers. The world muted to a harsh gray landscape. The color leeched out of the roses, and Vickers became a pale blot on the chiaroscuro landscape.

Fifty years.

Emily.

I love her, you know? Vickers had said in one of his

rarer, melancholic moments, when he'd been younger. *But she will never be wholly mine. Because of you. What I did to you…it was a gift. She doesn't understand.*

Distantly Blade felt his fingers clench into hard fists. Love didn't lock a girl in with her blood-starved brother. Vickers had never loved anyone except himself.

He shifted forward for the lunge—

"Your Grace!"

The animalistic hunger in him sent him for cover, searching for the new voice, the intruder into his killing fields. He smothered the vicious instinct that had him ready to tear the human servant apart as he came puffing through the gate.

Vickers spun around and snatched up his gloves. Anger flashed through his pale eyes, then he smoothed it over. "Abagnale. I told you I didn't wish to be interrupted."

"It's the girl! The girl Daisy!" Abagnale wheezed. "She's started showing remarkable signs of improvement. Her CV levels have dropped by three percent since last month."

Vickers went to attention like a hound. "Three percent?" he snapped. "You're sure of this? How?"

"I don't know yet, Your Grace."

"I want to see her." Vickers grabbed his cane.

Blade's chance—such as it had been—was lost. The demon inside him howled in frustration. Rage burned hotly in his stomach. Some part of him was saying, *No, you ain't an animal*, but it was a tiny part, locked away in the recess of his mind.

All of the dark thoughts he owned surfaced with a

vengeance. He wanted to kill, to drown the world in blood. His nails bit into his palms, and he realized they were clenched so hard they were shaking.

Emily. Oh God, Emily.

A whisper of movement came from within the crypt. The swish of skirts. Blade's head shot up like a hound on scent. A slow smile crept over his mouth.

Want, he thought to himself.

Then take, the demon inside him whispered.

Silence.

Oh, my goodness.

Honoria let out a shaky breath, dragging her hand away from her mouth. It felt like she'd been holding her breath for hours, waiting for Vickers to leave. Peering through the gate, she found no sign of him. She had to get out of here before he came back.

Sudden terror sent her scrambling for the gate. She slipped through it, darting around the corner and directly into a firm, hard chest. A scream tore its way up her throat, then a hand clapped over her mouth and an arm dragged her around, hauling her against a body as hard as steel.

"Here, now. What have we here?" Blade whispered. She nearly had an apoplectic seizure, her knees giving way beneath her. He caught her, dragging her back into his steel embrace.

Her eyes closed in relief. *Thank heavens. She was safe.* Or as safe as one could be in a blue blood's arms.

"A little kitten, all of my own," he purred. "Far from home."

Her eyes opened. That wasn't the voice she knew. His words dripped with haughty blue blood mockery. His voice had changed. It was rougher, smoother, like velvet over sand.

She pried at his fingers and he chuckled, an eerie sound that made every hair on her body stand on end.

"If I let you go, will you scream?" he said.

She shook her head.

"Pity."

The hand clamped across her mouth suddenly disappeared. But the arm holding her did not. Blade brushed his lips against her neck, sending a quiver through her stomach.

"Easy now, love. Easy." His whisper was almost hypnotic.

Strange how such a cold-blooded man could heat her so. Honoria flinched as the tip of his tongue darted out, tasting the sweat of her neck. She could feel the pulse thundering through her carotid artery and wondered if he felt it too.

"Blade," she whispered, glancing over her shoulder at him. His beautiful emerald eyes were dark chips of obsidian. Nothing human looked back at her.

His gaze dropped to her mouth. Something dark and hungry flickered through those depths. The demon inside. The hunger. It was ruling him and she would have to be very careful. One wrong step could send him tearing for her throat or thrusting her skirts up and taking her here, regardless of the consequences. What had sent him into such a state?

Don't ever show them fear, her father had warned. *It excites them.*

"Blade," she said, in a very quiet, firm voice. "We have to leave. There's no time for this."

Blade ignored her, his hand snaking into her hair and tilting her head back. Honoria gasped at his roughness, yet a part of her *burned*.

"*Blade.*"

His lips found her throat, and then his teeth grazed the tender skin there. It wasn't a nibble. He opened his mouth and bit her gently just above the collarbone. Honoria gasped, her knees dissolving as a surge of liquid heat went straight through her. His firm, callused hands found her breasts, cupping them through the scratchy wool. Her eyes nearly rolled back in her head.

"Stop," she whispered. But his hand was sliding down over the flat of her stomach, lower, bunching through the folds of material at her waist and lower…She caught it, her nipples aching through the constricting wool. "We can't do this. Please stop."

"You want it. I want it—"

"I don't want it," she shot back, then gasped as his fingers brushed teasingly against the juncture of her thighs.

"Don't you?" His other hand cupped the full weight of her breast. "There's no one here to see," he said in that dark, compelling voice. "I'd hear them coming." His fingers bunched in the folds of her skirt. "Honor. My Honor." It came out with his breath. "I want to taste you. I want to drink you all up."

Honoria shot a helpless look toward the building. She had to find some way to placate the hunger ruling him. "Later. If Vickers returns—"

"I'll kill him."

Then he had his hands on her, thrusting her back against the crypt. Her back met the stone wall, and Blade dragged her arms up, pinning her wrists over her head. Her head swam. She'd hit it on the wall.

"You're mine." His hand caught her chin, forcing her to look up at him. "You belong to me. *No one* else."

"Blade, please. Let me go." Those black eyes were starting to scare her. As he looked at her, she saw no emotion in his face, besides hunger.

Cold fingers wrapped around her throat. Honoria's heart pounded. He was in there somewhere. The man she knew—with his wicked smile and Cockney bluster—was still there. She just had to find him.

"Blade," she whispered. "You promised to protect me. If Vickers comes back, he won't be alone. They'll capture me. Not even you can take on Vickers and a complement of guards armed with stunners. They know how to deal with blue bloods here. They'll take you down and then they'll lock me up. Then Vickers will do whatever he likes with me."

Blade didn't like that idea. His black glare flattened. "No."

"You won't be able to stop it."

The hand on her throat eased.

"I want," he said, his gaze sliding down to where his hand rested, as though distracted.

"I know. I want too. I want...I want to touch you. Let my wrists go."

Blade thought about it for a long moment. Then released her.

Honoria moved slowly, sliding her hands down

his arm to his shoulder. She slipped them beneath the roughened leather of his long coat. His shirt hung open, revealing a pale slice of chest. Knowing that he watched her, she pressed her palms against his chest, feeling the slow, steady thud of his heartbeat.

His skin was so cool. Honoria wanted to press her lips to it, to open her mouth and taste him with her tongue. A shocking thought, much like the ones that played in her mind at night.

Honoria looked up. His face was closer, his breath whispering over her forehead. The throb of his heartbeat started to increase in tempo beneath her hand. She licked her lips, and he watched the movement with an absorption that sent a thrill racing through her.

"Slowly," she whispered.

His mouth drifted closer. Lips brushed against lips, and as she took a breath, she stole his.

Honoria's heart was pounding in earnest now, almost sounding like a voice yelling *trou-ble, trou-ble, trou-ble* in her ears. Blade pressed closer, his mouth opening over hers, tasting her, a faint hint of his tongue flickering over her lips. *Oh God.* Her eyes shot open and she felt the press of his chest against her palms as she held him at bay. It was all an illusion, of course. If he wanted to take more, he could, and there was nothing she could do or say to stop him. *If she even wanted to stop him.*

Her body throbbed with need, an alien sensation that she couldn't quite control. Her hands flexed against his chest, burrowing beneath his shirt, and an odd sound rose in her throat, almost a sigh. This was the enemy. And she was kissing him. But, oh, how good it felt…

It was almost as if he sensed the distance she held him at. Blade drew back, his dark gaze flickering to hers. Eyes narrowing, he caught her face in his hands, and then his mouth swooped across hers in a brutal claiming.

She couldn't help herself. Her traitorous hands were sliding beneath his shirt, over the smooth skin of his shoulders. Tentatively, she opened her mouth for him. The first full sweep of his tongue was a shock. Sensing victory, he pressed his body against hers, his hips grinding against the delicate vee between her thighs.

Too much. Honoria broke the kiss and came up for air, heat burning through her cheeks and lower, in unfamiliar places. "We can't do this."

He turned her face back to his and stole another breathless kiss. Honoria grabbed a handful of his hair and pulled his face back. She had to think. *Think, dash it!* But it was so hard with his mouth sliding down her throat, tongue licking the hollow in the middle. Her eyes rolled back and she shivered. "You promised. You promised to protect me."

His mouth paused on her skin. Honoria almost sobbed with relief. She couldn't fight this battle, not when her body wanted to lose so badly. The vulnerability scared her. Blade didn't move an inch when she pushed at him. Arms like steel caged her, his palms pressed flat against the stone wall. His head was bowed and he simply inhaled the scent of her, his breath harsh and ragged.

"You promised," she whispered.

His fist hit the wall. Despite herself, she jumped. Those eyes were as black as the devil's.

"Blade. Please, come back. I want to talk to you."

"You are." That cold, perfectly clipped accent. How much she longed to hear the rough cockney jargon she'd grown so familiar with. Who knew she would ever miss that drawl?

"Come back," she said, placing a trembling hand against his cheek. "Take me home."

"And if I do?" He turned his face and kissed her fingers. The wetness of his mouth made her gaze drift again, the words dying in her throat.

"If you do?" she repeated distractedly.

"What will you give me?"

"I'll…I'll…" Honoria gave him a helpless look. "I'll kiss *you*."

"You just did."

"No, I didn't. I let you kiss *me*."

His lips froze against her fingers. A rough purr rumbled through his throat. "Where?"

"Where?" The grounds were empty, but they wouldn't stay that way for long. The guards would begin their rounds soon, and if they happened across her hunger-crazed blue blood, she would never ease the strain from her conscience. Then she realized what he'd asked. "What do you mean, where? No. Stop. I don't want to know. I meant on the mouth."

It was a long, dangerous moment. His hand clenched and unclenched in the bunched folds of her skirt. He took a deep breath, and then the next moment he had stepped away and she staggered, almost collapsing against the wall of the crypt.

Blade had his back to her.

"Blade?" she whispered.

He took a long time to answer. Then he turned, eyes still black as spades. "Aye. I'll 'old you to it too, luv."

She almost breathed a sigh of relief. The danger wasn't over yet, but parts of his old self were starting to reappear. Pushing away from the wall, she said, "I think we'd best leave."

"When we get 'ome," he said suddenly, "you're goin' to owe me more than a kiss."

Her eyes shot up.

"You're goin' to tell me what the bloody blazes you were doin' 'ere." He pointed a finger at her. "And no more lies, Honoria." A growl sounded deep in his throat. "There ain't nothin' I 'ate more than bein' lied to."

Chapter 14

THE CARRIAGE RATTLED ALONG THROUGH THE DARKened tunnels, the steady hiss of the steam engines singing monotonously. The tunnels were lit sporadically by gaslights, and every so often they passed beneath one of the ventilation shafts that filtered the steam to the world above, where the faint slash of moonlight would flicker.

The carriages were nearly empty at this time of night. One by one the passengers got off, until it was just Honoria and Blade. Alone. Locked in silence. Neither of them willing to speak.

The harsh black had faded from his eyes at long last, but she wondered if the hot green flash that replaced it was any better. Occasionally he looked at her as though wondering what he was going to do to her, but she kept her gaze locked on the window, her fingers tight on the carriage strap.

You're goin' to tell me what the bloody blazes you were doin' 'ere.

The diaries seemed to burn a hole in her pocket.

There ain't nothin' I 'ate more than bein' lied to. What

had he meant by that? A little knot of dread tightened in her intestines. She had not lied to him very often—only about her origins, about which she'd been deliberately vague. So what was he referring to?

The carriage screamed to a halt, the engine giving one last, loud belch of steam. Honoria stood. Blade leaned his hip against the door, waiting for the conductor to open it for them.

The underground platform was empty. Honoria's dread intensified as she stepped onto it. Why wasn't he speaking to her?

They bypassed the elevation chamber and took the stairs. All 107 of them. Honoria was glad. She didn't think she could abide being trapped in the stuffy box with him while the cables hauled them to street level.

The last mile home was a miserable toil of silence, her mind going over every word she'd said, every action, trying to work out what she had done.

She was so distracted that she almost didn't notice when they reached the warren. Blade put his hand in the small of her back, and she looked up to see him holding the door open for her.

"Thank you."

His eyes narrowed and he stepped past, leading her into the dark hallway of the entrance.

They bypassed the parlor, which was her only point of reference. Honoria paused at the foot of the stairs as the darkness swallowed him up.

"Blade. Where are we going?"

His footsteps stopped on the stairs above her. "My chambers."

It sent a spurt of fear through her. She forced her

feet to start moving. *Don't think about it. Just don't think about it.*

But he wants an answer. And a kiss.

She didn't know which one frightened her more. If she thought about it for too long, she could almost feel the ghostly impression of his mouth on hers from earlier. Honoria stumbled.

The second floor was full of light. She stepped into a hallway with polished beeswax floors and elegant gas lamps on the walls. A Turkish-red runner cushioned her footsteps. Blade waited for her, holding open the door.

"This is…it could be a home in Mayfair," she said, looking around.

"I don't live like a rat," he replied. "But it ain't clever to advertise it."

Hands clenched in her skirts, she stepped through, into a lovely antechamber. Despite the elegant furnishings and curiosities, her gaze went straight to the opposite door, which was open. His bedchambers.

Oh my.

A woman swept through the door with a smile on her face, then stopped dead and blinked in surprise. "You're late. Nothing happened?" Her question was directed to Blade, but her gaze remained on Honoria. Though dressed in a work-a-day dress, her upswept chignon was thick with black hair, and the fine bones of her face spoke of a genteel upbringing.

"Esme. Weren't nothin' but a spot o' trouble." Where his voice and manner had been strained with Honoria, he crossed to the woman and gave her a relaxed kiss on the cheek.

"Perhaps…perhaps I should go," Honoria stammered.

Blade looked at her smokily. "Not until you've paid your debts."

The woman—Esme—shot him an exasperated look. Clucking under her tongue, she crossed the rich carpets and took Honoria by the hand. "Don't be a rotten beast, Blade. Look at her. What have you been doing to her? Rolling around in a coal bin? You ought to be ashamed." Turning toward Honoria, she gave a hesitant smile. "Come. I'll draw a bath, and I'm certain we can find you something clean to wear. You must be hungry. Blade, would you send for a tray from the kitchens?"

One of his eyebrows arched, but he nodded. "'Ow long?"

"Give me an hour with her," Esme replied. "I believe John made mutton stew. And there's bread in the larder."

The dismissal was clear. Despite a sardonic smile at Esme's back, Blade nodded and crossed to the door.

As soon as it was shut, Esme gave her a sharp look. "There. Now, let's get you tidied up before his lordship returns. You must be Honoria."

"Please, this is no bother. I should be getting back to my brother and sister. There's no need for…" They stepped into the bedchamber and she saw a hint of the enormous copper bath in the next room. "Oh."

"I believe Will is watching your house. Your brother and sister will be safe." Esme grinned. "The water's piped in. And sinfully hot. I keep some scented soaps as well, though Blade disdains to use them."

The idea of this woman's tall, curvaceous body

in Blade's bathtub stopped Honoria in her tracks. "You're his thrall," she said.

Esme's eyes widened. "He didn't explain?"

"I know he has them, but...you're certainly not Mrs. Faggety."

"You weren't expecting me to be here." Esme's tone softened. "I'm his housekeeper, dear. I look after them all, and yes, I...I provide blood for him."

There's only two as share me bed...

Honoria had the horrible, burning suspicion that the beautiful Esme was one of them.

Esme started the bath running, the hot water splashing into the copper tub. The floor was a checkerboard of black and white, and luxurious, fluffy white towels hung over a gold rack. In the corner was a music box with a large, curled horn.

"He doesn't strike me as someone who enjoys music."

Esme was sitting on the lip of the tub, swirling her fingers through the bubbles. "Or baths. Or cats. Or his family." Her smile deepened. "Keep your eyes and heart open, Honoria, and he may just surprise you. He doesn't very often allow a stranger in here. Especially one he's known for so short a time."

Honoria frowned. "He's spoken of me?"

"No. But the house is astir. Will's been in everybody's ear. Says Blade's got a lady-love."

"I'll bet that's not all he's been saying."

Esme laughed. "The boy's protective. Blade saved him from a horrible life when no one else gave a damn. And verwulfen tend to be very overzealous of their families—their packs."

"Will doesn't like me."

"If he didn't like you, then you wouldn't be here," Esme said. Her smile slowly died. "We're all protective of Blade. In our own ways."

The woman gave her a long, slow look. Honoria turned away, then gasped. There was a mirror in the corner. Staring back at her was a dirty ragamuffin with tangled hair, coal-streaked cheeks, and a dress that hung off her like a potato sack.

It had been a long time since she'd seen herself in a mirror. It wasn't an expense either she or Lena needed, and she'd been so busy at the academy that she'd rarely bothered to glance in the mirror that Mr. Macy made the girls practice their posture in front of.

She looked...awful.

"I'll fetch you a comb while you're soaking." Esme reached over and turned off the faucet. "There you are. If you'll disrobe, I'll see if I can find something clean for you to wear."

Though she'd been brought up in Caine House with various servants to see to her every whim, it had been a long time since she'd undressed in front of another woman. Especially one who shared a master with her.

At least the room was warm. And when she stepped into the steaming water, she nearly collapsed in relief. "Oh. My. Goodness." Sinking up to her throat, she couldn't prevent a sigh.

"This is one of Blade's finest ideas," Esme said. "A bathtub big enough for two."

Honoria splashed herself, trying not to think about where the other person would fit. Trying not to think, indeed, what that other person would be wearing, or just how much the bubbles wouldn't cover.

"How long have you been his thrall?" she asked, to distract herself.

Esme looked surprised as she swept up Honoria's dirty clothes. She blew a lock of hair out of her face. "Eight years. My Tom died in sixty-seven, and I lasted nearly a year before I was forced to accept Blade's thrall contract."

"He's kind to you?" It wasn't the question she wanted to ask, but it would do.

Esme thought for a moment, then put the clothes aside. "He's very careful with us. And he makes an effort to make it as painless and comfortable as possible."

"He doesn't insist upon flesh rights?"

Silence greeted her. Honoria looked up.

A flush of color swept over Esme's cheeks. "Not unless we want it too." She pressed a hand to her cheek. "I shouldn't say such a thing, but I suppose you have a right to ask. And I remember how frightened I was when I first agreed to it, knowing nothing of what it would be like."

"What is it like?" Honoria asked.

"Wonderful," Esme said. "It hurts, I won't lie. But it also feels…very good." She gave a helpless shrug. "Words cannot describe it, Honoria. But you shouldn't be afraid. He would never hurt any of us."

"Even when his eyes go dark?" she asked dubiously.

"Go dark? I don't know what you mean."

"When his hunger overtakes him," she said.

Esme slowly picked up the clothing again. "I'm afraid I've never seen his eyes go dark. He's always so very much in control. I'm fairly certain none of the others have seen him in such a state either." She nibbled on her lower lip. "Perhaps...perhaps Will's right. Perhaps you aren't very good for him."

Blade poured himself a tipple of blud-wein, listening to the brisk footsteps coming toward him. Esme. And in a mind to give him a lecture. He could tell from the distinctive swish of her skirts.

She peered into the room, in her hand a silk nightgown that had been spoils of war. Blade's crew did a brisk trade in the rookery, fencing stolen goods. Some of them he kept, like most of the furniture that filled the warren. Some of it—like the nightgown—was stored in the cellar for redistribution.

He eyed it warily. "You ain't givin' 'er that to wear, are you?" Honoria would have conniptions if she caught even a glimpse of that filmy scrap of lace. And he wouldn't be able to sleep for days without thinking about her in it.

"It's the only thing I could find that would fit her."

"She ain't stayin'."

Esme looked surprised. Then nodded sagely. "Not for lack of trying, I assume?"

He growled under his breath and swallowed a mouthful of blud-wein. "It ain't none o' your business."

"Of course it is. We're all concerned after the drivel Will's been filling our ears with over the last few days. I was almost expecting a lady of the Echelon crooking her finger at you."

"I don't dance to no one's tune." Bloody Will. The whole lot of them didn't have enough to do if they were earwigging over his private affairs.

Esme put the nightgown aside. He could hear the sudden nervous pounding of her heartbeat. Hell. Here came the lecture.

"She wanted to know what you were like as a master," Esme said. "And what I did when your eyes went dark. What did she mean by that?"

He drained the blud-wein. "It ain't nothin'."

"Blade." She caught his arm. "Is she a danger to you?"

"I lost control for a moment. It won't 'appen again."

Esme's eyes widened. "I see."

Blade cursed under his breath and put the glass down. He knew she would be straight in Will's ear with this. He sank down into his chair and scraped a hand over his face. "It ain't bad."

"Have you checked your blood levels?"

"Of course I 'ave," he snapped. He did a virus count daily, just to make sure he wasn't getting closer to the Fade. "First thing I did when I got 'ere. They're still 'oldin' out at seventy-eight percent. It ain't like I'm goin' to start tearin' the walls down anytime soon."

"They've been high for months." Esme knelt in front of him, resting her hand on his knee. "I've heard of these new colloidal silver injections—"

"Ain't worth a pinch o' frog shite. If they were, every bleedin' blue blood'd be on 'em." He shook her off and took a few steps away. "I'll let you know if they hit eighty. Then you can tell Will to keep an eye out."

"Blade—"

"'Adn't you better find that dress? She'll be all shriveled up like a prune."

Esme slowly gathered her feet underneath her.

"Well, we can't have that, now, can we? All that soft naked skin, shriveled up. It'd be a shame."

And that was for him. Esme always had had a bit of bite to her. His cock jumped at the thought, and he glowered at her. "That's plain mean."

"Stop looking like a drawn dog," she said, "and make yourself useful. She's afraid of you, especially after tonight. You need to be gentle with her, show her that you aren't the monster she's afraid you might be."

"Ain't my fault," he snarled. "I ain't the first blue blood she's known."

Esme gathered up the nightgown. "A word of advice, then. She's young and she's wary, but she's still a woman. Court her. Be charming. I know you have it in you when you want to be."

"I'm tryin'," he said through gritted teeth. "I've been bloody careful as kittens with 'er. It don't get me anywhere. She's still holdin' me at arm's reach."

"Answer me truthfully. Do you want her in bed, or do you want her to stay?"

"What's the difference?"

"All you need to do is lie to her and charm her if you want her in your bed. But if you want *something more*, then I would suggest other tactics. I would help you if you were sincere."

He knew she just wanted him to admit the depth of his interest in Honoria so that she could spread it over the house's gossipmongers. And yet it was apparent that Honoria had barely thawed toward him at all. The look on her face as he kissed her tonight had said it all. She would give him his kiss because she owed it to him. But only because of that.

"She don't want me," he said.

"Do you want her?"

He shot her another glower and tucked his hands in his pockets. "Aye."

A beatific smile spread over her face. "Then go and fetch my comb. You can play lady's maid."

Honoria shrugged into the silk Oriental robe that Esme had located from somewhere. It was far too large and the crimson-colored skirts dragged the floor, but it felt terribly nice on her skin. It had been a long time since she'd worn silk.

Don't get used to it. She sighed and wiggled her toes into the fur-lined slippers. Again they were too large, but if she crooked her toes she could walk in them.

The girl staring back at her in the mirror was a different creature from the one who'd been there before. Her brown hair tumbled over her shoulders, almost to her waist. She needed to cut it badly, for the ends were ragged, but she'd not given it any thought in months. There was no need.

A knock sounded at the door. "Come in," she called, turning in a swirl of Esme's rose-scented soap. Hopefully Esme had found her some undergarments, for she felt a little naked with nothing but the robe and nightgown to cover her skin.

It wasn't Esme. Blade stood in the doorway holding, of all things, a comb. He opened his mouth to speak and then seemed to see her for the first time.

"Bloody 'ell." It sounded like the reverent whisper of a man of worship.

Honoria froze and clutched at the neckline of the robe. "I wasn't expecting…you." She looked past him, but the room was empty.

"Aye." He hovered in the doorway, dressed in a clean white shirt that billowed at the sleeves and a tight leather vest that buttoned down his left breast. A red scarf was tucked into his neckline, and he'd washed the coal dust off his face. Dust, she was suddenly certain, that had come from her.

"Esme sent me," he said, holding up the comb. If she wasn't suddenly nervous herself, she'd almost have thought he looked anxious, standing there in the doorway. "She's tryin' to find you somethin' to wear."

"Then you're not here to claim your kiss?" The words were out of her mouth before she could think.

Blade scowled and stepped inside the bathroom. "You don't 'ave to kiss me if you don't want it. I weren't meself. I won't 'old you to it." He dragged a low chair in front of the mirror, then looked around. "Sit."

Honoria sat stiffly. What did he mean he wouldn't hold her to it? Just how long had Esme been gone from the room anyway?

"I made a promise," she said.

The mirror gleamed in the candlelight. Blade stepped behind her, his blond hair tousled. He picked up a piece of her hair and started combing it, carefully untangling the knots. Though he barely touched her, she shivered, her nipples tightening against the silk robe.

"I don't want you to kiss me because you owe me," he replied, concentrating on a knot. "I want you to kiss me because you want to."

Their eyes met in the mirror.

Honoria flushed. The backs of his fingers brushed against her shoulder as he scraped up another handful of hair. She didn't know how to answer him. And strangely enough, a part of her felt a little disappointed. Lazing in the bath, she had been prepared to kiss him, going over and over in her head how she would approach it. Just a light brush of her mouth, a hint of her lips, and then she could back away, owing him nothing once more.

Only now he was insisting that she didn't *have* to do it. Unless she wanted to. There was a hint of burning dissatisfaction within her. An odd sense of feeling *cheated*, but she didn't know why.

Blade's hands gently tugged the comb through her hair. It was quite pleasant. Indeed, almost hypnotic. She found her shoulders relaxing despite the nearness of his body. When he sat on the edge of her stool, his hip brushing against hers, her eyes shot open again, but he made no further move, simply concentrating on her hair.

"I guess," he said simply, "that answers the question."

Honoria looked at him. He'd almost finished with her hair, stroking his fingers over it as though reluctant to stop.

It took a moment to clear her throat. "I thought you were angry with me."

"Angry?" His hands froze.

"You wouldn't speak to me," she said. "On the way home. You barely looked at me."

Blade let out a long breath. "Ah, luv." His hands resumed their pleasant stroking. "I weren't angry with you."

"Then what…?" Her brow furrowed.

Reluctance radiated from him. He put the comb down in his lap. "I were angry with meself." He looked down, his words quietening. "It's been a long time since I lost control like that. I thought I 'ad it mastered, but one sight o' Vickers and I weren't meself."

"Vickers?" she whispered. "What does Vickers have to do with it?"

"He were the one that put me in the tower. The one that infected me." His fists clenched, almost obliterating the small comb. "The one that murdered me sister."

Honoria reached for him before she could stop herself, her hand sliding over his. "You'll break the comb."

He looked down in surprise. Then offered it to her. "Esme would 'ave me 'ead. It were 'er 'usband's."

Though she took the comb, she let her hand rest where it lay, stroking the roughened skin of his hands. Blade turned his fingers and caught hers in his grip, linking their hands together. Her palm pressed against his, her fingers laced through his thicker ones. So intimate. And yet she didn't tear out of his grip.

Her heartbeat started to pound in her ears. What was happening to her? She felt nervous. Or was it something else? Something she didn't understand?

"And 'ow do *you* know the duke o' Lannister?" Blade asked.

The question took her by surprise. Her wits were befuddled, muddied. Too busy dwelling on the feel of his cool hands and wondering what they would feel like on her skin.

"Vickers?" Her head lifted like a startled doe. When Blade's fingers tightened around hers, she realized she'd unconsciously sought to pull free. Her mind racing, she tried to sort out the previous conversation in her mind. Had she mentioned Vickers first? Or had he?

"Honoria." He gave her hand a warning squeeze. "No lies."

"I'm not…" She shut her mouth. She *had* been preparing to lie. Trying to find some way of explaining how she might have known Vickers. "I…I—"

Silence fell. She could feel those wicked green eyes on her, searching inexorably for the truth. But how could she tell it to him? A part of her wanted to, she suddenly realized. She wanted to confide in him—about Charlie, about the diaries and the never-ending watching over her shoulder for one of Vickers's assassins. But she barely knew this man.

Too many years spent watching the blue bloods play their games at court. Watching what she said. Keeping her father's secrets from even her own siblings. Tears pricked against her eyes suddenly, which was foolish. There was no point to it, and yet the swelling warmth spread until Blade's hand was a blur in the candlelight. God, how she wished for just one person to talk to. Someone to listen and hold her while she poured out all the weight sitting on her shoulders.

His hand brushed her cheek, stealing the trace of liquid warmth from her. "Honor," he said, stroking her face. "I won't 'urt you."

"How do I *know* that?" She looked up and met his gaze. "I barely know you. And you want something from me. How do I know I can trust you?"

His lips twisted. "Per'aps because I'm already keepin' your secrets. Miss *Todd*."

She almost missed the emphasis he placed on her name. Then her eyes widened. He had known her only as Miss Pryor.

Blade caught her by the shoulders as she stood. Honoria pushed at him, tumbling back against the dresser when he let her go, holding his hands up in a position of surrender. A flash of frustration crossed his face.

"How long have you known?" she whispered.

"All along."

She shook her head. "No. You couldn't have."

"I got eyes and ears in the Ech'lon, 'specially around Vickers. 'E put a price o' ten thousand pounds to the guild regardin' three people: Miss Honoria Todd, Miss Helena Todd, and Mr. Frederick Charles Todd. It ain't common knowledge, but it were enough for me to put two and two together."

Blade took a step toward her. Honoria backed away. The robe was tumbling open and she dragged it closed, feeling the lack of undergarments keenly.

"What do you want with me?"

"If I intended to 'urt you, I'd 'ave done it already," he said, then paused. "I wanted to know why Vickers wanted you. I want 'im dead, Honor. And I thought to use you as bait. At first."

The warmth drained out of her face.

"Not anymore," he assured her. His eyes narrowed. "I ain't lettin' that maggot anywhere near you."

The shock of it still hurt. He *had* been planning to use her. "Why?" she demanded. "Because you want me yourself?"

He took a step closer. "Ain't no secret. I want you in me bed, luv. But even if you don't want it, I won't let 'im near you."

Honoria circled the tub, keeping him on the other side. "I was going to *kiss* you," she said. "That's what I was thinking about before you happened to mention this. I can't believe I was so stupid!"

She might as well have struck him. His eyes narrowed as though cursing his own ill timing. "You were?"

"I *was*."

"That ain't fair." He moved and she moved too, dancing around the bath together. Blade could capture her in an instant if he wanted to, but he didn't use his speed. "I were only tryin' to clear the secrets between us."

"Why? It would have served your purpose better to keep me in the dark."

Blade stopped. "You don't know nothin' 'bout me purpose or what I want from you."

"Then what *do* you want?" She was so angry she wanted to throw something. Preferably at his head. Why did this hurt so much? For a moment it had been nice between them. There was no pressure, and she'd been relaxed, melting under his hands as he combed her hair. Then he'd ruined it.

Blade glared at her, his eyes narrowed.

"Well?" she asked. Anger was easier to deal with than tears.

"I don't know." The words were soft, spoken entirely without accent.

"Well, that's…honest." She leaned against the wall. Then slowly slid down it. The anger was starting to melt away in the face of his stricken expression. He didn't know what he was doing any more than she did.

Blade crossed toward her, his boots making no sound on the tiles. Her shoulders tensed, but she made no move to escape.

"Why does Vickers want you?" He knelt in front of her. "Why'd you go to the Institute?"

She stared at him. Her silence was answer enough. If it were only herself, she might have given in. But as much as she wanted to trust him, she was afraid she couldn't. Not with Charlie.

"I see." He pushed to his feet and took a step back. "I'll send Esme in with some clothes. Then I'll walk you back 'ome."

Honoria let out a breath of relief. He wasn't going to push her to divulge her secrets. She was safe. Charlie was safe.

But why did she feel so awful inside? As though she'd struck him another blow? And why should she even care?

Chapter 15

"Where have you been? I've been waiting for hours after I got your note. Are you insane? All I could think of was Vickers with his hands on you! I thought you were dead!" Lena scraped the chair back as she stood.

"Blade told me that he sent word." Exhaustion clung to Honoria, a result of the recent emotional upheaval. She put her bag on the table and crossed to the washbasin to splash water on her face.

"He did." Lena sniffed. "Is that a new dress?"

Honoria didn't know where the burgundy silk had come from, but she suspected either an actress or a merchant's mistress. Esme had pinned it at the back, where it was too large for her, and the front was a little too low for her liking. When she looked down, she saw a good couple of inches of pale flesh on display, and when Blade had walked her home, his occasional side-long glances told her that he too was very aware of it.

"It's borrowed," she said, sitting down.

"From who?" Lena dragged her own chair around, prepared to interrogate her.

"Blade."

There was a long moment of silence while she felt her sister's eyes boring into her. Honoria started unwrapping the bag, searching for the precious diaries.

"Honor, what were you doing that required disrobing?" Her hedonistic Lena sounded almost puritanical.

"I was taking a bath to wash the coal dust off me."

Lena's eyes went wide. "Honoria!"

"Alone," she added. "His housekeeper found the dress for me. It was entirely proper. Indeed, it might be the last we see of him for a while. We quarreled." She slid the first diary out of the bag then froze. A copy of *The Scarlet Letter* stared back at her. She tore the bag open and dragged out the other book, a slim edition of *The Taming of the Shrew*. Rifling through the pages changed nothing. These weren't her diaries.

"That...lying...scheming...bastard!"

"Honoria!"

She slapped the book down on the table and stood, biting on her knuckle to contain the sudden surge of emotion. This wasn't a game to her. She needed those diaries. "He must have swapped them while I was getting dressed. He must have thought I had no intention of returning." She swung toward the door in an angry sweep of skirts.

Lena grabbed her sister's arm. "Don't you dare! It's nearly midnight. There's a murderer on the loose."

"And a verwulfen on the roof," Honoria snapped. "I shall ask—no, demand—that he escort me."

Lena's mouth gaped. "A...a what on our roof?"

"A great big, hairy werewolf!" Honoria exclaimed, glaring upward. "A spy who listens to everything we say!" She was furious. How dare he? Blade had no right to take her diaries from her. She needed to start working on her father's notes. To try to find a cure for Charlie before it was too late. If it wasn't already. But she refused to think about that. She'd sworn an oath to her father that she would take care of them. She wasn't going to let this happen to Charlie.

"I don't think you should go tonight," Lena said, sweeping in front of the door and holding her arms out. "You're too vexed."

"I am not vexed. I am beyond vexed." Honoria held up her right hand, her steel ring glittering on her forefinger. "I am tempted to incapacitate him with the hemlock and then castrate him."

Lena paled. "I don't think that would be very wise," she said. "And the only knife we own is what I use for the cooking. You're not using that."

"I was planning on using a spoon," Honoria replied. She scraped her hands over her face, trying to drain away her tiredness.

"It's not as though you can do anything with the book tonight," Lena said. "Be reasonable. You'd be better off calming your temper and descending upon him in the morning. You'll have had a good night's sleep while he'll be just seeking his own bed. It will give you the advantage."

"Dash it," she muttered. She could barely keep her eyes open, let alone deal with that high-handed blue blood. And she knew she wasn't thinking at her most optimum when Lena, of all people, was offering a reasonable solution.

"You're right." Honoria's shoulders slumped. "I'll

deal with him in the morning." After she'd had a good, long night to brew her anger to the boiling point.

Bang. Bang. Bang.

Honoria stepped back. Her reticule hung off her arm, weighted down with the books. If worse came to worst, she could simply bash Blade over the head with it.

Thumping the door again, she heard footsteps coming. Esme opened the door with flushed cheeks as though she'd been running.

"Honoria." Esme brushed a black curl behind her ear. "We weren't expecting you."

"Blade is." Honoria swept inside. Stark morning light lit the hallway with little motes of dust swirling through the air around her swishing skirts. "He offered me an invitation last night."

"He did?" Esme was no fool. Her eyes narrowed with suspicion.

Esme's loyalties were quite clear, but surely as another woman, Honoria thought, she would understand. "He stole something of mine. I need it. Please, Esme."

"And just how do you plan to get it back?"

A little flush of heat crept into her cheeks. "By whatever means possible."

Esme mistook her meaning. A little smile played at the corners of her full mouth. "He's in his rooms. Most likely heading for bed for an hour or two. The men only just returned."

Despite herself, Honoria paused with one foot on the stairs. "There were no more murders?"

"Nothing last night," Esme answered. "They were keeping watch. Good luck."

"I thought you were in his corner."

"Perhaps." A hint of warm laughter came with Esme's words. "Or maybe I'm sending the lamb to the slaughter."

Ignoring the teasing, Honoria took a deep breath and started climbing the stairs. She was no lamb to the slaughter. Blade was going to pay for his deception. Esme's soap still lingered on her skin from the night before. Hopefully he wouldn't detect her presence.

She strode briskly to his door, then considered whether to knock. Esme wouldn't knock, and Honoria wanted the element of surprise for a few seconds longer. That decided, she pushed the door open and whisked inside. And stopped dead in her tracks—

Blade spun on his heel at her shocked gasp, swiftly wrapping a towel around his hips. It wasn't quite big enough and gaped over one heavily muscled thigh as he tucked the end into itself at his waist. His eyes widened in surprise when he saw her, then he scowled.

She couldn't stop herself from staring. Acres and acres of wide, muscled chest. The barbaric band of tattoo around his left arm and down his ribs. An arrow of hair trailing from his navel down into the edge of the towel. And the tented suggestion of what that towel was hiding, proving that Blade didn't find this intrusion entirely disagreeable.

Honoria turned away quickly. This wasn't what she'd planned at all, but how could she go about her revenge when he was practically naked?

"Well," he drawled. "I guess you ain't 'ere to tuck me in."

"Of course not," she threw over her shoulder. She caught a distracting glimpse of him in the mirror and turned her burning face back to the wall. "You know exactly why I'm here. Put some clothes on. This is indecent."

"I ain't the one as just barged into a gent's rooms without knockin'."

The sound of the towel hitting the floor made her mouth go dry. Oh, my goodness. He was naked. And her mind's eye was most enthusiastic about supplying her with a vision of what that might look like.

It would be very easy to confirm whether her vision was accurate. *Don't you dare*, she told herself.

"I'm afraid you've got me at a loss," he replied, leisurely moving around behind her. Sheets rustled and then she heard the unmistakable sound of leather sliding over skin.

"Are you decent?"

"Rarely," he said, with an ironic drawl.

"Are you clothed?"

"Aye."

He was going to play games with her. Her fists clenched and she turned to look him in the eye. At the edges of her peripheral vision, she could just see him tugging the leather breeches into place, but she didn't dare look lower.

"I need those diaries," she said firmly. "This isn't a game. You know how important they are to me."

"The diaries, eh?" He feigned surprise. "You're

'ere to fetch your diaries. I thought you took 'em 'ome last night."

"You swapped them while I was getting dressed! I opened the bag and found *The Scarlet Letter* and *The Taming of the Shrew*—no doubt you had a good laugh at that."

He crossed his arms over his chest and gave her a steady look. The muscles in his forearms bunched.

"Aye. I were so desperate for your company that I stole your precious diaries. What's in 'em that's so important, Honor?"

"That's none of your business."

"Then you ain't gettin' 'em back."

The ring on her finger seemed to burn. "Yes, I am." She started toward him.

"You goin' to turn me up sweet, luv? I got news for you—I'm tired o' playin' games." He took a step forward and glared down at her. "And you already owe me a kiss which you ain't paid."

He was in her space again, using his size and height to intimidate. A little flutter started, low in her stomach. "I thought you didn't want me to kiss you unless I wanted it too."

"Maybe I changed me mind."

A little flick of her fingernail opened the toxin-smothered needle. The thought of kissing him did horrible things to her willpower—and her knees—but it would also get her close enough to render him at her mercy. Honoria tilted her chin up and stared him directly in the eyes.

Go ahead, you bleeder. Force a kiss and it shall be the last thing you're capable of doing for some time.

His eyes widened imperceptibly, and his voice was low and husky when he said, "Is that a dare I see in your eyes?" He took another step closer, so close that her skirts brushed against his legs.

"I can't stop you," she said. "But I promise you shall regret this."

Blade reached up and slowly, slowly stroked her cheek, his gaze following the path of his fingers. They dipped over the lush pillow of her top lip. Tasted the wetness of her mouth. And then lingered at the center of her lower lip. She was shivering by the time he'd finished.

"Aye," Blade murmured, his lips curving in a satisfied little smile. "A bleedin' martyr till the end. I think not."

He stepped away, giving her his back. Honoria's jaw dropped as he turned and held up his shirt as though examining whether it suited him for the day or not.

"I beg your pardon?"

Blade knelt on the edge of the bed, with its rumpled sheets and mounded red cushions. His leather breeches molded faithfully to the lean curve of his buttocks, revealing a healthy amount of muscled thigh. He reached for his daggers, the thick black ink of his tattoo riding up over his ribs.

Her mouth went dry.

"You 'eard me." He straightened and slung the belt around his waist, pulling the buckle tight. Only then did he look up at her, with that mocking little smile playing over his lips, as though he knew precisely what was going through her mind at the moment. "If you think I'm goin' to steal a kiss just so as you can cry protest, you can think again. You want me, then you're goin' to 'ave to make the move yourself."

"I don't want you."

"Aye. That's why your scent changed. You smell all plump and lush, my little dove. I knows when a woman's got 'er eyes on a man. One of the advantages o' bein' a blue blood." He held his arms out, displaying his magnificent body to full effect. "Do you want to touch me? Is that what's got your heart poundin' in your ears and your breath thick in your throat?" A little smile touched his lips. "I'll let you, you know. You can run those pretty little fingers *all* over me if you want. Or that sweet little mouth, if you'd prefer." He took a step closer. "Do you want a taste o' me, Honor? Do you want to lick the sweat from me body, taste the salt o' me skin?"

He leaned closer, looming over her. It was only then that she realized she'd backed up against the wall, her gaze locked to his wicked mouth and all of the sinful things it was saying.

"I don't want to touch you. I don't want to taste you," she whispered and shut her eyes. It was no good. She could still see him, that lean body caging her in, the muscles in his arms rippling as he pressed both hands flat against the wall on either side of her hips.

"Liar."

A silky whisper. In her ear. A curious, whimpering sound came from her throat.

He took her hand. Pressed it against the ripple of his abdomen. Honoria's eyes shot open and locked on his.

It was the perfect opportunity. All she had to do was

turn her hand just so and press the tip of the needle into his body. But something stopped her. Perhaps the silky-cool feel of his skin beneath her hand. Or the look in his eyes as he stared down at her.

His mouth was close to hers. She barely felt his fingers trailing through her hair, tugging a soft curl over her shoulder. All she could see was that mouth, with its sensual lips, and the slight lopsided dimple as he smiled. A sinner's mouth. A demon's mouth. Tempting her with all manner of ungodly acts. His breath stirred over her face, caressing her cheeks.

Honoria could barely breathe for the pounding of her heart. This was madness. She'd never felt like this before, not even with the exquisite, practiced flirting of the blue bloods she'd encountered at Vickers's house. Blade was nothing like them. Rough. Raw. Virile. The kind of man who would steal a kiss and not take no for an answer. The kind of man who could capture her heart…and crush it in his fist.

This was dangerous. And yet for the first time in her life she wanted to throw caution to the wind and simply take what he offered. To just be a woman who wanted to forget about all of her burdens, her worries, and simply be young and carefree for once in her damned life.

I want to know what he tastes like. I want to be *kissed.*

She stared up at him. And all at once, the willful part of her nature erupted from its cage. Damn it. What harm could one kiss do?

Honoria rose up on her toes and pressed her lips against his hungrily. Oh, God. A mistake.

The taste of him curled through her, shooting

straight to her toes. Blade caught her arms in an iron grip, a muffled sound of surprise purring through his throat. Then he slammed his mouth over hers. No escape now.

It was too much. Not enough. She wanted to press herself into his body until she sank beneath his skin, and the feeling terrified her. She wanted more; she would *always* want more of this, of him, until she burned herself out or he wearied of her. This meant nothing to him, merely an urge he sought to satisfy. A contest he wanted to win.

And what does it mean to you, Honoria? she wondered. Her first thought was to deny it. But as he drew back, allowing her a chance to catch her breath, she realized to do so would only be to lie to herself.

Honoria turned her face away, struggling to gather her thoughts. Blade kissed her cheek, her brow bone, his tongue sliding to the delicate shell of her ear. Honoria clung to him, her heart and mind racing. What did she want of this? A moment of tumbled passion, a few nights of escape from the dreariness of her life? Or more?

Someone to love her. Someone to hold her in his arms, to tell her that she was the center of his world. That he would look after her. Someone to trust. Someone to love back.

Tears burned in her eyes. Foolishness. How could she even think of this with a blue blood, of all creatures?

"Stop thinkin' so much," he softly growled in her ear. "Just feel. You think too damn much, woman."

Yes. So easy to lose herself in this. To just feel and close off the part of her that was gingerly reaching out, longing for something more. Honoria shook her head and pushed at him. "I've given you your kiss. Let me go."

Blade raked a hand through her hair, gathering a knot of it in his fist. She couldn't move. The tender roughness froze her.

"A kiss? Is that what you call it?" His voice was dangerous.

"A kiss. For the diaries. You promised and I delivered."

"Ah, but there were two of 'em, weren't there? I promised *a* diary for a kiss." He was enjoying this too damned much. "And you know naught 'bout kissin' a man, luv."

Honoria's gaze shot to his, her eyes narrowing. *You didn't seem to mind.* "It seems fairly simple. I press my mouth to yours and you maul me."

His fist clenched in her hair then released. A hint of something dangerous flashed through his eyes. "Is that what you think, luv? You don't think I could seduce you? You think I'm just a bit o' flash who pumps a dove like a dog in 'eat?" He loomed over her, his hand sliding over her hair and down her throat. "Let me tell you somethin'. I'm more 'n 'alf a century old. That's a lot o' time to practice, Honor." A slow smile spread over his face. "Now you're in trouble."

Honoria gasped as he raked a hand through her hair, clutching a fist of it and tilting her head back. Her back hit the wall, his body pressed against her, each inch burning itself into her skin.

"I've been kind. And patient," Blade explained, his breath brushing against her heated cheek. "No more."

He took her mouth, his hips thrusting against her.

It was a complete domination, a claiming that should have frightened her more but didn't. She felt energized instead, her heart punching hard behind her ribs. Honoria clung to his shoulders to steady herself, but she might not have bothered. His hard body trapped her against the wall. There was no escape. Nothing but surrender.

Over her dead body.

She growled and pushed at him, but Blade was merciless. She caught just a glimpse of his burning green eyes, then he bit her lip, sucking it into his mouth. The sharp pain ricocheted through her, like a spark of lightning, soothed by the warm suckle of his mouth. His hand clenched harder in her hair, just a hint of pain, dragging her head back so that she couldn't fight him any longer.

"Submit," he told her.

"N-no." Her voice, broken and weak, more of a gasp, really.

Blade changed tactics. His mouth traced the slight edge of her ear, his teeth biting down on her lobe just firmly enough to make her draw breath. A shaft of heat speared through her stomach, lower, to the junction of her thighs. She shifted uncomfortably, very aware of the sudden slickness between them.

"Touch me," he ordered. He pressed her hands against his chest, forcing her palms flat against his skin. He stole traces of her warmth everywhere they touched, and suddenly she wondered what it would feel like to have the cool steel of his cock embedded between her thighs.

That way danger lay…

A whimper sounded, deep in her throat. She was uncertain now. The avalanche of feeling was starting to roll over her, threatening to steal her feet. "Let me go," she said. But she didn't mean it. And that was what scared her the most.

Blade stole a kiss. Another. Nipping at her mouth, pressing at her to open. She was helpless not to respond. He dragged her hands down, over the ripple of muscle at his abdomen. Through the tangle of hair that arrowed down, the sensation acutely new to her.

The taste of him. Oh, lord, the taste. His tongue met hers in a heated tangle, hot and hungry. His lips were cool, tracing hers, tempting her to kiss him back. And she did.

It started innocently. A curiosity, really. Just a little taste…But she grew hungry for more. Her blood was thick and warm, like molten honey pounding through her veins. She didn't know what was happening. His hands dragged hers lower, over the edge of his leather breeches, over the sudden, raging strength of his cock-stand.

Honoria's eyes went wide.

"This is what you do to me," he whispered. "Every god-damned time I see you." Heat flared in his eyes.

She tore her hands free, but he caught them, pressed them against the familiar, less-unsettling feel of his chest. A pulse pounded between her thighs, a tribal drumbeat of need. She found her hands sliding over his chest, learning the feel of him. And this time when their mouths met, she was the aggressor.

Blade shuddered, then flinched. Honoria followed

his mouth, taking a step forward. He drew back, avoiding her. "Easy now, luv." He frowned. A tiny smear of blood marred his pale skin.

For a moment she didn't understand. Did he not want her? Then she saw his eyes blink, as though to shake off something. He staggered. Honoria caught him under the shoulders, his weight almost driving her back into the wall.

"What'd you do to me?" he slurred.

Oh no. The ring. She glanced at the tiny needle. Somehow she'd scratched him with it.

He was too heavy for her. Honoria staggered toward the bed, hoping to get him on it. "One more step!"

They both went down. Honoria landed atop him, breathing hard, her arms caught beneath him. If he hadn't been incapacitated, she was certain he would have taken advantage, but one of the side effects of the toxin was partial paralysis for several minutes. He would be aware of everything that happened, but he wouldn't be able to move.

She leaned up on her elbows, tucking a stray strand of hair behind her ear. Blade glared up at her. He looked like there were a dozen things he wanted to say to her right now. It was probably for the best that he couldn't speak for a little while.

"This is your own fault," she said, sitting up and straddling him. Her eyes widened. It seemed there was one other part of his body that was currently paralyzed too.

Clearing her throat, she climbed off the bed and brushed her skirts down. "You won't be able to move for ten minutes or so. Then you'll recover completely.

You might feel a touch light-headed or nauseous, but that should pass."

"Grrhvf."

"There's no point trying to speak," she said nervously. "I didn't mean to do this." A slight frown. "Well, I did at first, but it was an accident how it occurred. Honestly, it was the last thing I was thinking of at the time..." With his hands and mouth doing wicked things to her body, it was amazing that she'd had any rational thoughts at all.

Blade was motionless, but his eyes tracked her. Honoria snatched a pillow from the bed and tucked it beneath his head.

"Don't give me that look. I've not injured you in the least. I simply want my diaries back."

His eyes were eloquent enough. When he could move—when he got his hands on her—there was going to be trouble. Far better for her not to be here when the paralysis wore off.

Honoria looked around. His armoire hung open, revealing his clothes. She rifled through them, disturbing an array of velvets and leathers. His tastes truly ran to the gaudy. Everything was almost...touchable. She couldn't help rubbing her fingers down the butter-soft leather of a pair of breeches. Imagine if he were wearing them.

She jerked her hand away, heat spearing through her cheeks. That was enough of that. She'd given him his kiss. There was nothing owed between them. Nothing except the consequences of this new set of actions.

The thought spurred her to haste. He'd been down for almost two minutes. The toxin's effects depended on a lot of things: the victim's body weight, how long since he'd drunk blood, his CV count, and myriad other factors. But in general it would knock a blue blood out for almost ten minutes. No time to spare.

She started hunting furiously for the diaries. Through his drawers, under discarded clothes, behind the curtains. Even in the bathroom, with the events of last night running fresh through her mind. The blackguard. Brushing her hair. Stroking the silk of her robe. Pretending he had nothing more on his mind than seduction. Probably plotting to steal her diaries the whole time.

She tugged a drawer open and frowned. It was full of little packets. Though they looked nothing like a diary, she couldn't stop herself from reaching for one curiously. But when she opened it, she almost dropped it. French letters. Dozens of them. Just how many bloody thralls did he take to his bed anyway? He must think her a fool.

Slamming the drawer shut, she stalked back out into the bedroom. Blade watched her, his eyes shouting their accusation.

"I know they're here somewhere." There were more drawers near the bed. She tugged one open and paused. A set of steel manacles gleamed within, with padded cuffs. "Really?" She dangled the cuff off her finger and shot him a look. "Only two thralls whom you take to bed? I think not. I wasn't born yesterday."

A growl sounded.

Honoria jumped, but Blade was still motionless. She discarded the manacles and reached for a leather roll. Slinging it open on top of the chest revealed a half dozen fléchettes. What he would use on her when he deemed her well enough to donate.

She was running out of places to look. Pausing, she closed her eyes and thought furiously. If she were a devious blue blood, where would she hide something?

A strangled sound came from the bed. He was starting to move. It shouldn't be possible. He'd barely been down for five minutes.

Blade managed to roll onto his side, glaring at her. Retribution gleamed in his green eyes. Oh God. If she wasn't gone by the time he recovered, she was going to have to pay the devil his dues. Unless…Honoria's gaze lit on the manacles.

His gaze locked on them at the same time with an expression like murder.

"Just until you catch your temper," she said nervously, scooping them up and crossing toward him.

His shoulders heaved. He was struggling to sit up. Honoria planted the palm of her hand against his chest and shoved. He tumbled back onto the bed, a warning growl erupting from his throat. Her mouth went dry. This was insane. Not only had she entered the ring with the bull, but now she was deliberately waving the red flag in his face.

"This is your fault," she told him, closing one steel cuff over his wrist. "You don't understand. I need those diaries. I nearly put myself into *Vickers's* hands for those diaries." The second cuff locked tight. The veins in Blade's wrists distended, his hands clenching. "Where are they?"

"*Pay*," he said.

Her face paled. "Aye. I suppose I will. But if you

just tell me where they are, I'll go away for the day and…and come back tonight. I'm certain we can come to some sort of agreement about my punishment." Her voice trailed off. "I could kiss you again."

Blade gave her a withering glance.

"Maybe…maybe more?"

He wrapped his fists around the chain, still ignoring her. Honoria licked her lips. "Don't hurt yourself. You won't be able to break them."

He gave a sudden wrench on the steel loops. Honoria squealed and grabbed for his hands. "You shouldn't exert yourself so soon! The toxin takes awhile to wear off!"

Another wrench. One of the steel chains looked almost as though it had stretched a little. Honoria scrambled off the bed. Damn him! Where were the diaries? She checked under the bed, even running her hand beneath the mattress. With 170 pounds of enraged, half-naked male atop it. If she didn't get out of here soon…

"Not even you can break steel links," she blurted, scurrying about.

Blade shuffled his grip on the chain, watching as she tossed clothes and furniture aside. She could feel his gaze on her back like a hot pinpoint of fury.

"Ain't…got…to."

Honoria stopped dead in her tracks. Her gaze shot to the timber slats she had linked the chain through. He hadn't been planning on breaking the cuffs at all. "Oh."

As she watched, he gave one final wrench. The slats splintered and the cuffs came free, though they were still around his wrists, thank heavens.

Blade rolled into a sitting position, slinging his legs off the bed. He swayed and caught himself.

Honoria took a step back. Then another. "Don't stand. You won't be able to control your body for… for a little while." How had he shaken off the toxin so swiftly?

All of her father's studies had been on the newly infected at the Institute. Oh, dear. Blade's age or his CV levels must have played a new hand into the deal. What would his CV levels be? He was over half a century old, more than enough time for the virus to colonize. For a moment fear curdled in her stomach.

"What poison did you give me?" He somehow found his feet.

Honoria didn't trust the look in his eye. She stepped back, her heels hitting the door. Her palms were sweaty. She brushed them on her skirts. "It's hemlock. A small dose has unusual effects on a blue blood. My father discovered it."

He took a lurching step toward her. "Feels like me 'ead's wrapped in wool."

Honoria felt around behind her for the door handle. She didn't dare take her eyes off him. "Yes, well. You'll feel strange for—well, I'm not quite sure. Studies show that it takes about ten minutes for the paralysis to wear off. But there you are, right as a trivet, and it's probably been only six minutes now." Her hand closed over the knob. "You should rest for a while. Let it wear off. I shouldn't want you to fall flat on your face."

"Ain't got time to bleedin' rest," he snarled. "Do you know what you done? I got the Ech'lon arrivin' within the 'our. I can't greet 'em like this."

Her hand paused on the doorknob. "The Echelon?"

"The duke of Caine's brat. Per'aps you 'eard of 'im? Leo Barrons? And a full score from the Guild o' Hunters."

The heat washed out of her face, down her throat, and lower, stealing her breath. For a moment she thought she was going to faint. "Guild of H-hunters?" The infamous Nighthawks who worked the city.

"We're 'eadin' out after the vampire. They're workin' with me on this. I can't take it by meself. Why? Got a problem with it, Honor? That's right. The guild's got a warrant with your name on it."

His hand hit the door beside her head. The manacle clinked. The door slammed shut.

"I just want my diaries back and then I'll go."

"I never 'ad 'em. I tole you that."

She shook her head. "Then who—?"

"Esme." Blade said. "She's the only one that reads 'ere. Stirrin' trouble between us. But she didn't force your hand. You were the one as poisoned me."

"I didn't…" She pressed her lips firmly together. "I'm sorry."

"Aye, well, an apology ain't enough." He held out his wrists. "This time you got to earn it, Honor. I need your blood to get me back on me feet."

Chapter 16

The key to the manacles was in Honoria's pocket, burning a hole through her skirts. "I thought you wished to wait."

"Circumstances bein' what they are," Blade replied. "I can't afford to."

"I could fetch Esme."

"Already fed from 'er this week. And Will. The only thrall within a 'alf hour is Mrs. Faggety, and I need more than she can afford to give." He pressed his finger between her breasts. "You're the only one as I can safely take, and there's a certain sense o' justice."

She swallowed, looking down at the firm finger pressed against her breastbone. She barely dared to breathe. But he was right. If he appeared before the Echelon—even Leo—looking like this, they'd be circling like sharks. And it had been her fault.

She let out a shuddering breath. "I'll do it."

It was only what she had agreed to anyway. Why not get it over and done with now rather than drag out the inevitable?

"Oh, I know, Honor. I weren't askin'." A hint of anger still stirred in his green eyes. "Come 'ere."

He gestured toward the bed.

"I don't think so," she said. The bed was entirely too intimate. And she was nervous enough as it was. "Why not the chair?"

"Honor." There was no disagreeing with that voice. "The bed. Lie down."

Her limbs were jerky as she crossed the room and sat down on the edge. Blade held out his hands in front of her with an imperious look.

"You want *me* to find the key?" he asked when she hesitated.

"No. That's quite all right." She dug it out. Her fingers were shaking. Damn him. It took her what seemed like ages to fit the key in the manacles and turn it. Blade could have taken over at any stage, but he merely held his hands still, as if forcing her to obey him was part of her punishment.

"Lie back." His voice was silky smooth.

She obeyed. He knelt on the edge of the bed, his weight dipping the mattress. Her hip rolled into his, and she caught at the sheets to prevent herself from tumbling into him.

Then his other knee came down, straddling her lower legs. Honoria wriggled backward, her back hitting the headboard. *Breathe*, she reminded herself. *Just breathe.*

But she couldn't stop her gaze from shooting to his mouth. That wicked, slightly lopsided mouth with its thin lips that often quirked in humor. A mouth that would soon be on her body, lapping at her blood.

Good God. She wasn't ready for this. Perhaps she never would be. *I made a deal*, she reminded herself.

Blade tossed the manacles beside her. There was no expression on his face, just a glint in his eye that she wasn't quite certain how to decipher. "Put 'em on."

"I'm sure that's not necessary. I'll lie still."

"Honor. Shut up." He reached over and dragged a small table closer then flung the leather roll of fléchettes open upon it. "I can't afford to 'ave you move. It excites me." His eyes met hers. "That's not a good idea right now."

"Could you please put your shirt on?" she blurted.

"Don't you like the look of me?" He pointed to his pale, chiseled torso as though she weren't well aware of it. Almost casually, he traced a line down the center of his chest, drawing lower, mingling with the tawny stubble of hair that arrowed toward his trousers.

Honoria ignored his question. "Please." A flush of discomfort swept through her. This wasn't easy. Though the role of a blue blood's thrall in society was a respectable one, she had always been somewhat old-fashioned. A thrall meant that one was owned. Cattle. She'd seen enough feedings at the Institute to know what lay ahead. He would hold her down and slash a vein, latching on greedily for the hot pump of her blood.

How could you respect something that was essentially food? An awful thought. It burned within her stomach, a nauseating curl.

He had been kind to her. Bought her dinner. Brushed her hair in an almost affectionate manner. But this changed. Now. Here. After this moment she would be nothing more to him than a meal.

Blade seemed to sense something amiss. His finger stopped its wicked path. He unstraddled her in silence, got off the bed, stepped away, and grabbed at his shirt, tugging it over his head. "Better?"

She nodded miserably. "Yes." The words were a hoarse whisper. She tried again. "Thank you."

"I won't 'urt you," he said abruptly then frowned. "Or I'll try to make it as easy as possible. It might sting a little."

He'd misunderstood her reluctance, though the thought of the knife blade on her flesh sent a shiver through her.

"If you would please get it over with. I'd prefer not to discuss it."

"Of course."

He knelt on the bed again, straddling her. Honoria closed one of the manacles over her wrist before she could change her mind. She was nervous enough that she wasn't entirely sure if she might fight him or not, and neither of them wanted that. It would only excite him, arouse the dangerous side of him. She'd seen enough feedings to know that. Still, the click of the latch sounded like a prison door closing.

"What should I attach it to? You've quite destroyed the bed." Strangely her voice was cool and composed now. She felt a little distant from it all.

"Let me." He knelt over her, his shadow obscuring the gaslights in the chandelier.

A shiver of anticipation swept through her. She lay on her back, feeling the oppressive weight of his body.

Blade focused on the manacles. He drew her wrist up, over her head. Then the other. Her nipples brushed against the stiffened linen of her stays. Strangely taut. Aching.

He latched the other manacle around the bedpost, then about her other wrist. Kneeling back, with his hands on his thighs, he stared at her, his weight heavy on her legs. "Where?"

"The femoral." Heat flushed through her cheeks, and she closed her eyes to avoid his penetrating gaze. "I would still prefer not to have the marks visible."

And no matter where he took from her, it would be intimate. At her throat, his mouth working on the delicate skin there. Or lips brushing against her wrist, but she already knew that the veins there weren't as generous as others.

A little tingle of awareness throbbed between her thighs. Anticipation. Fear. And something else, something that burned through her like wildfire.

Her breath hitched. Blade looked at her sharply, but she forced herself to stare at the ceiling, trying not to think about the heavy steel cuffs that bound her to the bed.

Every muscle in her body was rigid. She felt the brush of her skirts over her shins as he slid them up. Anticipation coiled in her womb, and she realized she was holding her breath and let it out. Then his fingers brushed against her garters. "*Wait.*"

He stilled. Patient. Waiting. Honoria tried to form some coherent thought behind the instinctive protest. There was none. Her mind seemed to have turned to mush.

And still he waited. It was that alone that gave her the strength to meet his eyes. He let her have the control in a situation that was clearly his.

"I'm ready," she whispered.

He picked up a tourniquet and tested the give in the leather. She recognized the style of it from the Institute. "I'll make it swift." One hand tugged her left knee up, pressing her stockinged foot into the mattress. The other looped the belt around her thigh.

She hadn't meant to watch. But somehow she couldn't tear her eyes off what he was doing. He moved with such efficiency she could almost forget that her skirts were up around her hips, her pale thigh naked to his gaze above the faded ribbons of her garter. Then he tugged the belt tight.

Pain. Constricting. A dull throb in her leg.

"'As to be tight," he apologized, his voice dropping to a growl.

She cried out softly as he tugged the belt tighter. Her upper thigh felt as though it were throbbing in time to the beat of her heart. She could suddenly hear it, loud and panicked in her ear. Wrapping her hands around the chain of the manacles, she ground her teeth and held on.

After a moment's wait, she tilted her head to look down. Blade was breathing hard, his jaw tight with strain. As if sensing her gaze, he looked up. Black eyes, the demon's eyes, met hers. And the world fell away.

She couldn't breathe again. She could only feel—the burning throb in her leg, the wet heat between her thighs, the aching tightness of her nipples. Danger screamed through her, sending her senses on alert.

Blade's hands dug into the soft, tender flesh of her thigh. He sucked in a sharp breath through his nose. "Don't move, luv."

She nodded then let her head slump back onto the pillow.

Shutting her eyes narrowed her world down to the feel of his hands on her thigh. Tugging her garter ribbons undone. Rolling down the top edge of her stocking. Each touch was a blistering scorch of sensation against her throbbing, heated flesh. She bit back a whimper, not quite of pain. An unusual feeling she'd never felt before. His thumb. Testing the artery. Then the sudden loss of touch as he reached for the razor.

She tracked everything with her peripheral senses. The shift of his weight on the bed. The rustle of sheets, an intimate sound. Then the smooth brush of his hand against her thigh.

The pain of the razor was sharp and sudden against the inside of her thigh. Honoria cried out, trying to hold herself still. Heart pounding. A drum in her ears. And then…his mouth. Shockingly wet. A burning, icy heat against her skin. Sucking. An answering tug deep in her womb, as though each mouthful of blood drew with it something of her essence.

He jerked on the belt and let it loose. Her hips arched off the bed at the sudden agony as blood rushed into her starved limb. The piercing ache of his mouth intensified until she could almost bear it no longer.

"Easy." A breath against her thigh, hoarse with need. An iron hand against the soft flesh of her lower abdomen, forcing her hips down.

She felt his touch keenly, the need burning through her with a fierce fury. She was barely aware of her wrists, tugging unconsciously at the manacles, or the way her skirts bunched around her hips, carelessly forgotten in the heat of the moment. Everything was his mouth on her skin—tugging, suckling, his tongue lapping at her sensitive flesh. Everything was the sudden surge of longing, so hot and wet between her thighs. Slick. An alien sensation so infinitely greedy that it swept her into this fury of need, giving no heed to consequences or rationale.

Need.

Her hips jerked. Blade's hand flattened on her stomach, forcing her down, but still she writhed. A soft cry tore from her lips as his teeth dug into her. He bit her. A sharp sensation that sent a shiver through her.

"Stay still." A warning growl.

As soon try to stop the tide. She was so on edge that the merest brush of his lips made her body jerk. Everything seemed too raw, too much. She wanted to tear her clothes from her body, to stop the incessant burning itch of the wool on too-sensitive flesh.

Blade cursed against her skin. Then licked her thigh. The hot swipe of his tongue nearly undid her.

She cried out.

"Honoria."

Perfectly pronounced. Edged with frustration and something else. Her eyes met his. The raw need she saw shocked her, and an answering echo of it tore through her.

He pressed his hand against her leg, forcing the blood flow to stop. Whipping the belt free, he tossed it aside then pressed a linen pad against her cut and bound it swiftly.

"Where?" he ground out.

She had no need to ask what he was talking about.

But not even the raw need flushing through her could force her to give voice to the desire she felt.

Their gazes locked.

Touch me. Please.

"Here?" He pressed his palm directly over the hot flush of her mons.

She should have protested the intimacy. Instead she ground her hips up so that her heated flesh pressed against him.

Harder.

"Like this?" His voice was low and strained as he tugged her skirts up.

Her cotton drawers were drenched. Cool air flushed against her liquid heat as he tugged at the buttons. And then she gasped, sensation streaking through her like stored lightning as his fingers brushed against her naked, throbbing flesh.

"*Damn you, Honor.*"

Blade's shirt hung open, his veins and sinews standing out in stark release as he rose over her. His fingers toyed with her, shooting sparks through her womb. Honoria bucked and writhed, feeling the edge of something building within her. A wave. An enormous tidal wave of need, threatening to drown her. She was helpless to resist.

"Please," she begged. "Faster."

His fingers stroked over the lush pearl of her clitoris. White-hot sparks shot through her. Her eyes shot open and she found him kneeling over her, his furious gaze locked on her face. The heavy weight of his thigh stretched over hers, and he rested on his shoulder on the bed beside her. His cock ground into her hip.

"Easy," he groaned. "Let it come easy."

A fingertip slid inside her. As if asking permission.

Don't think. She thrust her hips up. Felt him breach her further. A curious stretching. Her inner muscles clenched around his finger as if questioning this intruder.

He rubbed his wet thumb over her clit. Felt her shudder. A grim smile tore at his mouth. "Trust me."

Another fingertip, brushing at her entrance. Honoria's hips arched higher.

"Yes?" he asked.

She tossed her head from side to side, her entire being flushed with need. Another whimpering groan.

"Yes?" he demanded, sliding the tips of those two fingers inside her.

"*Yes.*"

His fingers filled her. Stretching. A throbbing ache. He coated them in her wetness, then dragged them out, tickling the very edges of her entrance before sliding them back to the hilt.

The edge built.

Somehow she turned her face into his shoulder. Shocked herself by sinking her teeth into the heavy muscle that ran from his neck to his shoulder. Blade growled low in his throat, his fingers thrusting faster within her. At another moment she might have cringed to find herself spread like this, her thighs tossed apart in desperate need, her hips moving wantonly. But all she could see was Blade. All she could feel was his touch and the aching build of tension within her.

He wrought delicious torture in her body. She couldn't move. Couldn't breathe. Her eyes shot open, a cry tearing itself from her throat.

"That's it." His whisper was dark and triumphant.

She felt his hand cup his cock-stand through his pants, rubbing hard against her thigh. The thought only made her burn hotter. Tighter. The wave loomed over her for one crushing, breathless second.

And then she was screaming, burying her face in his shoulder to hide the sound. Her greedy passage clutched at his fingers, milking them. Sensation suddenly became acute. Too much. Sweet God, it was too much.

"That's it." He thrust against her thigh, burying his fingers deep inside her. Something burned—a distant friction—but she didn't care. It felt too damned good.

Blade cried out, his fingers stilling within her. His breath stirred against her neck and then he bit her, his fingers tearing free of her body to dig into her thigh and drag her close. The sharp pain of his teeth made her eyes spring open.

It was long seconds before he collapsed against her, breathing hard. Her racing heart matched his. In the wake of the aftermath, strange thoughts suddenly started swarming over her. Good God. His fingers. Inside her. Bared to the day, her thighs slick and wet with her own pleasure.

"Don't think." The words were a raw sob wrung from his throat. How did he know what was going through her mind?

He tugged her skirts down a bit, fighting with the material, even as he buried his face against her throat. With every second a little of the pleasure faded, her senses coming back to her. What had she done? What had *they* done?

The violence of the outburst shocked her. *I let him touch me. I let him taste me. And sweet lord, I loved every second of it.* This was not the dry, dispassionate sex she had read about in books. This was a whirlwind of need and desire that swept away everything in its path.

She could feel her pins tumbling free in her hair. Her stocking loose and discarded around her ankle, much like her morals. The crumpled weight of her skirts, baring her legs to the world.

And Blade, a living, breathing weight. Collapsed against her, even now stirring her body to new wants.

Something burned within her. Some vague sense of dissatisfaction. *I want more.* A shocking thought. Five minutes it had taken, from respectable ignorance to aching, disheveled wantonness. Blade was far more dangerous than she had ever suspected.

"I think…I think you should let me go."

He wrenched his head off the pillow. Glowered at her. "Tol' you not to think." A flush of color lit his cheeks, and his mouth was swollen.

Don't look at it. She jerked her face away. The wetness between her thighs was an uncomfortable reminder of what had happened. She could smell her own musk, flavoring the air.

"I'm sorry," he murmured. "I ne'er meant to do that."

He was blaming himself. A little part of her might have been tempted to allow it, but she forced it down and turned her head back to look at him.

"I asked you to," she said.

His eyes widened.

"But it mustn't happen again."

They narrowed. "*No*," he argued.

"It mustn't happen," she insisted firmly. "Or I'll break our bargain. I can't…" A shiver went through her. "It's too much for me." It made her long for more. Even now her body throbbed restlessly.

How long before she begged him for more? Just the thought of losing herself in that whirlwind of need terrified her. Pleasure so intense she might do anything for it. Throw away all of her morals, beg him to take her. Lose herself in him. Lose her heart. *No.* It was too dangerous. She had too much to worry about. Charlie, Lena, Vickers's manhunt. Doctor Madison's dwindling month of relief before he reported Charlie's illness to the authorities. It didn't matter how much she wanted to curl into Blade's arms and wrap them around her. It was only selfish need. *I just want something for myself.*

Anger burned suddenly. Damn Lena. Damn Charlie. And most of all, damn her father. Hot on the heels of that emotion came wretched guilt. *I don't mean it. I just want…*What?

Blade waited, the silence dangerous.

"I can't do this. Please untie me," she said.

"Honor."

"Please," she repeated in a small voice. "I have to get home. My brother wasn't feeling well this morning. Would you fetch my diaries?"

Frustration danced across his face, but he reached for the manacles. A swift turn of the key and she was free, rubbing at her wrists. Sitting up, she tried to push her skirts down to a more modest length, but her head spun.

"Easy." Blade caught her against his shoulder. "You'd be best off lyin' still for a moment. That's why I prefer the bed."

"You do this with all of your thralls?" She pressed a hand to her temples as her vision blurred. His body was hard and solid against her. Some part of her longed to rest her cheek on his shoulder and curl into him. Let him shoulder her troubles. She quashed the desire ruthlessly.

"Not all of it. I don't usually confuse sex with blood thirst."

"How lucky for me."

"Mind you, most o' me thralls don't react the way you do," he growled, sliding off the bed with devilish grace. He looked as though he'd quite recovered his equilibrium.

"How long must I wait?" she asked. "I need to get home."

"I'll fetch your diaries. Then we'll see 'ow steady you are on your feet. Will'll walk you 'ome."

"Will will love that," she said sarcastically. Then she saw Blade's face. "I'm sorry. That was rude."

He shrugged. "'E's only protectin' me. It's the nature o' the verwulfen to guard their families from threat."

A curious insight. All of the men, and Esme, of course, were family to him. She felt a jolt of keen longing, swiftly quashed. Blade had his little family and she had hers. In a blinding moment of clarity, she realized that perhaps he would understand what she was trying to do.

And yet...she didn't have the courage to open her mouth and ask him for help. For what if he *didn't* understand? And what if he lost control of his inner demons—the way he had at times—and killed her brother?

"Honor?" He watched the emotion play over her face.

"I'll wait then. Until Will thinks I can manage," she said softly. *Coward.*

Blade stared at her a moment longer, as though waiting for her to say more. Then his gaze shuttered. "Aye. So be it."

Chapter 17

Blade leaned against the doorjamb. Esme hadn't heard him. She was folding pastry, sinking her knuckles into the wet dough and humming under her breath.

"Enjoyin' yourself?"

She started, slapping a pastry-covered hand to her chest. "My goodness, Blade. You could have given me some warning." As she raked an eye over him, a faint smile touched her lips. "You've fed. The question, I suppose, is did you enjoy yourself?"

Far too much. "I 'ad to. She disarmed me with some bloody poison she's got."

Esme's jaw dropped, then snapped shut. "You were careful with her?"

"Careful as kittens." He dragged a hand over his face, his stubble scratching his palm. It had cost him. He was still hungry, but for flesh now. The sweet taste of her blood had barely sated him. He could still taste it on his lips, and the scent of her arousal clung to him, a torture of its own.

Bloody hell. He knew what a feeding could do to some people. But Honoria had been almost clawing the sheets, her back arched and her hips thrusting. How the hell had he restrained himself?

Because you want her to trust you. He rubbed at his chest with another scowl. It was important to him, important enough to drag himself back from the edge when he knew he could have taken her...And destroyed her trust in him forever.

"You look thoughtful." Esme started kneading the dough again. "What's going through your mind, Blade?"

He slung a hip against the bench. Esme was possibly the only person who could ask that question and get an answer. "I nearly took 'er."

"Aye. But you obviously didn't. What stopped you?"

"I don't know. I'm tryin' to be patient. To win 'er over. Sometimes I doubt if she'll ever yield."

Esme scraped the pastry off her hands then wiped them on a cloth. She turned and slipped her arms around him. "She affects you, doesn't she?"

He looked into her serene face. "The 'unger's worse. With 'er. Even though I've just drank, it still wants. I'm afraid I'm goin' to lose control of it."

"You obviously managed to rein it in."

"This time." And his CV levels were only rising.

Esme pressed a kiss against his forehead. "Don't doubt yourself. You're a good man, Blade. I know how strong you are. And you'll have to wait a month before you take from her again. Perhaps in that time she'll have grown used to you."

"Maybe." If he could last the month without demanding more. He'd never before been tempted to break his own rule. "She wants 'er diaries back."

A guilty flush crept over Esme's cheeks. "I see. You figured it out."

"Well, it weren't Rip or Will readin' *The Tamin' o' the Shrew*."

Esme pushed away from him, leaving a heady cloud of her floral scent behind. "They're coded."

"You tried to read 'em?"

She reached up to the flour container and tugged it down, then pulled a pair of worn-looking diaries out of it. "I was curious to see if she'd mentioned you at all."

The leather of the spines was soft and creased when he took them. He scratched a nail over the gold lettering on the larger one. Why were they so important to her? Why risk her life—her freedom—just to fetch them from Vickers's Institute?

His hands tightened on the leather. Honoria. Cool, rational, guarded. An impenetrable tower he couldn't storm. At first the challenge had stirred his interest, but lately he'd begun to find it only frustrated him.

He wanted her to trust him. To share her secrets with him. He found himself curious, wanting to know more about who she was beneath the composed facade. *Let me in, damn you.*

He was lucky she'd believed him when he said he hadn't taken the diaries. That could have been one step back in the cautious dance they shared.

"Don't interfere again," he said, pushing off from the bench. "I mean it. Or *I'll* start interferin'."

Esme's gaze shot to his. "I don't know what you're referring to."

"Don't you? I wonder what Rip'd say 'bout it if I asked 'im?"

A flush of heat burned up her neck. She pounded both fists into the pastry. "You wouldn't dare."

He eyed the pastry. A wise man might not push a woman in this kind of mood, but, then, Esme had always been his confidante. "Wouldn't I?"

"If you mention anything of the sort to John, I'll box your ears."

"Well, someone oughta take the blinders off 'is eyes." Blade snagged a piece of pastry and danced past her as she swung out at him. "Man's got 'is 'ead buried deeper 'n an ostrich."

"John's been very kind to me." Her hands stilled. "Too kind. I'm not at all certain that how I feel..." She broke off and took a deep breath. "I don't believe my feelings are reciprocated."

"Aye. That's why 'e looks murder at me whenever it's your turn to come up to me rooms."

Esme shot him a sidelong glance. "He wouldn't dare. He worships you."

"Per'aps that's why 'e don't let on to you. Let me 'ave a chat with 'im, man to man." One little conversation ought to clear up this little mess that was developing in his home. Blade took his responsibilities seriously, and as far as he could see, Rip and Esme's future happiness was part of that responsibility.

"You're a regular matchmaker. Perhaps you ought to take your own advice. I'll let you deal with John if you allow me to have a little discussion with Honoria."

The smile on his face died. "No."

"Not so easy a solution when the shoe is on the other foot, is it?" Esme rolled her eyes. "You can't control everything, Blade. And you can't force her trust. Be patient."

He tapped the diaries against his thigh. "I been more 'n patient. She won't tell me a bleedin' thing."

"And of course you've been the soul of confession with her," Esme replied.

He paused.

"Why should she trust you when you haven't trusted her?"

"Not the kind of bedtime stories a lady wants to 'ear."

"Maybe her stories aren't either."

Blade scratched at his jaw. "I'll think 'bout it."

"Coward."

"Now, that's the pot callin' the kettle black, ain't it?"

Blade sauntered down the stairs, listening to the sounds of muted conversation in his audience chamber. Blue bloods. In his home. And one of them had some form of connection to Honoria.

He wore a scowl as he pushed the double doors wide with a bang. Both Barrons and a stranger turned to look at him, neither of them flinching in surprise. Barrons wore metal-plated body armor over his torso, with a pair of buff trousers, worn knee-high boots, and a short sword at his side. The hilt was unadorned and the grip had seen use. Once again Blade was forced to revise his opinion on the man. Barrons just might be dangerous with a sword. Blade's scowl deepened.

"Blade," Barrons said and nodded to his companion. "This is Sir Jasper Lynch, huntmaster of the guild."

Lynch was taller than both of them, his features

cool and calculating as he watched the byplay. The aquiline tilt of his nose and the deep-set gray eyes brought to mind the image of a falcon. He nodded courteously, though no deeper than one blue blood to another. "We have a vampire to hunt?"

"We do."

"Any idea of its location?" Lynch watched him intently. He wore the stiff black leather coat of the Guild of Hunters, with its white frogging down the middle and chrome epaulets on his broad shoulders.

Blade liked the fact that the man was straight to the point. None of them were friends, only wary allies. There was no need for formalities and polite backstabbing.

"It ain't aboveground in the rookery," Blade answered. "Me and me men 'ave covered every square inch. I think it's either in Undertown or 'idin' down in the factories by Brickbank."

Lynch nodded. "Where's the nearest entrance to Undertown from here?"

Blade crossed the floor toward the picture projector and lit the candle behind the pictograph. A grainy map of Whitechapel and its surrounding environs sprang up on the grimy wall.

"'Ere," he said, pointing toward the south end of the rookery. "There's an old broken drain someone covered o'er with mesh. Leads down into the sewers. One o' the Undertowner's cut a tunnel into it from the old, collapsed Eastern Link." The only way into the rookery without crossing the wall.

"I'll get the squadron ready." Lynch nodded curtly, then turned and strode for the door.

Blade scratched at his jaw. "Interestin' fellow. Abrupt."

"He believes only in getting the task done," Barrons replied absently, staring at the map.

"Blud-wein?" Blade asked, pouring himself a glass of it.

"Please."

The candle behind the projector guttered. He caught the slight hint of floral-scented soap and heard the whisk of skirts, soft-paced behind the door. Honoria. Sneaking out the back entrance with Will.

Barrons took his blud-wein and sipped. His eyes widened. "An excellent vintage."

"You were expectin' poison?"

"Rotgut, maybe."

They shared an uneasy smile, full of edges and raised hackles.

"I ain't the sort for poison," he said. "If I come at you, it'll be 'ead-on."

"That's a refreshing novelty," Barrons drawled. "They say you're nothing but a jumped-up alley rat. A mushroom. I could almost like you."

"Almost?"

Barrons drained his glass then put it down with a clank. "Interesting eau de toilette you're wearing."

Blade had come straight from the bedchamber, deliberately flaunting Honoria's scent. Some part of him wanted her mark on his skin, to show the world—or perhaps just Barrons—who she belonged to. "You got a problem with it?"

Barrons clasped his hands behind his back and studied him. "She hasn't told you about me."

That made his teeth grind together. Honoria's secretive nature was beginning to put him on edge. He didn't give a damn if she'd taken a lover in the past; he just wanted to know why she refused *him*. Unless she still had feelings for this man…The thought ran like ice water down his spine. Not that. God above, he didn't think he could be selfless enough to let her go to another man. "I'm curious. 'Er father worked for yours for many years?"

"Indeed."

"You were friends?"

Barrons's lips twitched. "No. Not friends. More than that. And less." He cocked his head to the side, as though considering Blade. "I have no claim on her, if that's what puts that look in your eye."

Blade stopped in his tracks. He was pacing the room like a caged tiger. Exhibiting a weakness. If Barrons wanted to bring him down, he would know just how to do it. Blade gave a loose shrug. "The girl's amusin'. But skittish." He gestured toward the door. "You ready to get those boots dirty?"

Barrons gave him a long, slow look, then nodded. "I have no claim on her, but I warn you. Be kind to her." He grabbed his hat from the hat stand by the door and fitted it with ridiculous care. They locked gazes. "Or I'll have to kill you."

Blade stared at his back as the man turned for the door. *Not the kind of thing a man with no claim on a woman would say*. "Son of a bitch," he muttered and followed.

Honoria rubbed at her eyes, trying to ease the tired strain. She knew her father's code, but deciphering it was still slow, tedious work. It didn't help that Lena had taken over the other side of the table with yards of yellow cotton and was blabbering excitedly as she stitched the seam.

Will had shoved a package into Honoria's hands with a grunt as he left her at her door. She'd been tempted to call after him and inform him to return it immediately. Then she'd read the note, carefully copied in an elegant hand—possibly Esme's—but obviously dictated by Blade: *For your sister. And your brother.*

If it had been anything else, she couldn't have accepted it and he knew it. Tugging open the brown paper, tears had welled in her eyes as she saw the carefully folded yellow cotton, threads, and a small sewing kit. There was a clockwork tumbler ball too, for Charlie.

He had outplayed her. She couldn't *not* accept the gifts, and the very thought that he had considered Charlie and Lena made her heart beat hard.

There was an awful knot of *something* in her chest. Honoria had stood in the street and cried with the two gifts clenched in her hands. It had been a long time before she could take them inside.

The letters in the diary were swimming before her eyes. She put her dip pen down and pushed away from the table. Weak afternoon sunlight streamed in through the window. Twitching aside the curtain showed the grimy cobblestones outside and the ragamuffin band of boys playing tumbler in the alley. One day maybe Charlie would be out there chasing the clockwork ball with the same ferocious energy.

A smile tugged at her lips then died. She was trying to be hopeful, but there was a lot of work for her to do before that scenario became reality. Her father had been on the verge of discovering a cure. It was all he spoke about in those final days, obsessing over the inoculations. But just because he was close to a cure didn't mean she could re-create his work. She understood it, but she had never owned the kind of genius Artemus Todd had. To make mad guesswork and leaps of logic before scrambling wildly for pen and parchment. What if she couldn't work it out?

Leaning her forehead against the chilled glass pane, she watched the boys rioting madly, upsetting the flow of traffic and nearly knocking a young woman over. Charlie deserved to have a life like that. Instead of confined to his bed, his arms marked with the track of numerous injections. Better that than the alternative… Or was it?

The craving was a slow death sentence. Worse. It turned men into blood-starved monsters who existed only for the thrill of the kill. But Blade was a blue blood. And although she might not be able to sort the jumble of her emotions regarding him, she could no longer despise him for his illness. Indeed, she could only admire the man. So close to the edge, and yet still he fought for control.

He'd be in Undertown now, hunting a vampire among the Slasher gangs and the humans who lived down there. Determined to do his duty to the people who relied on him, and to the little adopted family he'd gathered around himself. He was illegitimate, illiterate, and a self-professed scoundrel. And he had more honor in his little finger than half the so-called lords of the Echelon.

Honoria traced a pattern on the window with her finger. With Will recovering from the vampire attack, Blade had only O'Shay and Rip at his side. Humans. With a pack of blue bloods at his back and a squadron of metaljackets. All it would take would be one bullet and he'd cease to be a thorn in the side of the Echelon.

"What are you looking for?" Lena asked.

Honoria jerked her finger away from the window. "Nothing."

"You've been staring out the window all day," Lena noted, the needle and thread dipping between her fingers. "As though you're looking for something."

"My eyes are strained," Honoria replied, rubbing at her temples. "I just need to rest them every now and then."

Lena looked down, her fingers pausing on the fabric. "They're hunting something, aren't they? When I went to fetch water this morning, Lettie Hancott told me that a squadron of metaljackets was at the warren. Is it the murderer?"

What to tell her? Nobody could afford to have word of the vampire getting loose in the community, and Lena was the first to admit that she couldn't be trusted with vital information. "Yes," Honoria said after a moment's hesitation. "They think he's in Undertown."

"You're worried about him," Lena said, putting her sewing down.

"The murderer? Hardly."

Lena rolled her eyes. "I wasn't referring to the murderer and you know it." Her astute brown eyes seemed to see straight through Honoria. "At first I thought this was a business transaction between you. But it's not, is it?"

"If Blade dies, then we're back on the streets, without any way of fending for ourselves," Honoria retorted, her skirts swishing around her feet as she paced. "There's no money for food, for Charlie, for—"

"Honor."

"I don't have time for this…for him. I have too much to worry about—you, Charlie, the money to feed ourselves with."

"What are you afraid of?"

"I'm not afraid of anything."

"Yes, you are. You're hiding behind me and Charlie. Using us as a shield to protect yourself from him." Lena sighed. "I can't say I was thrilled when you first took up with him, but he's proven a man of his word. And he makes you smile. I haven't seen you smile for such a long time." Her voice trailed off into a wistful end.

Lena. Always searching for the fairy tale in every corner. Sometimes Honoria wished she could be as naïve.

"Its not as though he's bought you over completely with that cotton, is it?" Honoria sighed. "He's a good man. And he amuses me. Occasionally."

"Well," Lena said. "I suppose it could be worse. At least he seems to have money. Even if he is a bastard-born, rogue blue blood."

A little curl of anger warmed Honoria. "Blade is honest. And loyal. Far better traits to have than being born on the right side of the sheets."

"Perhaps. But if you were going to marry, I thought

that at least it would be someone with some kind of pedigree. Or someone who could at least read."

"He doesn't need book smarts to be intelligent," she retorted. Then she realized what else Lena had said. "And I'm his thrall, not his fiancée."

Lena took a sip of her tea, mocking her over the top of it with an arched brow. "I've seen the way he looks at you. And you at him. If you have no intentions of marrying him, then I'm not certain I quite approve of the relationship."

Honoria gaped. For a moment Lena had sounded exactly like…like her. And then the realization struck. Her eyes narrowed. "You little sneak."

"You *like* him. You do. You were all ready to jump down my throat." Lena grinned. "You're worried about him."

"Of course I'm worried about him," Honoria snapped. "He's hunting through Undertown, with the Echelon at his back. Any one of them could take the opportunity to dispose of him. Not to mention the vam—" She bit her lip. "The killer."

Lena got up and danced toward her. "You're so unromantic, Honor. And so stubborn!" Lena took her sister's hands and swung her around in a jig. "Have you kissed him yet?"

"That's none of your business," Honoria replied, tugging loose. Heat burned up her throat. They'd done infinitely more than that.

"You have! You flirt!"

"You don't have to sound so delighted."

"Was it good?" Lena's grin broadened. "It was. You liked it. How many times have you kissed him?"

Far too many times. It was becoming addictive. "This conversation is over."

"Don't be a spoilsport. Lord knows we have little else to find enjoyment in at the moment. One of us might as well have a little romance in her life."

It was all too heady a reminder. "I don't have time—"

"If it weren't for our circumstances, what would you do?" Lena gave her a serious look. "Take away me. And Charlie. And everything else. What would you do?"

Honoria hesitated. Then shook her head. "It's a purely hypothetical question, because you do exist. I can't pretend otherwise, and there's no point wondering 'what if.'"

"Honor."

She bit her lip. "I don't know. I haven't thought about it."

"Liar."

A little swell of heat burned behind Honoria's eyes, taking her by surprise. She turned away, stacking dishes in the sink. Anything to busy her hands. "I haven't."

"Honor." Lena caught her hand and stopped her.

Something wet trailed down her cheek. She dabbed awkwardly at it, turning her face away from her sister, but Lena knew. Her arms came up around Honoria's shoulder, and she tucked her chin against her sister's neck.

"I know you don't like to be impulsive," Lena said. "You think too much, you always have. But you should take this chance. You should go to him tonight. Don't think. Just follow what your heart is telling you."

"I don't know what my heart is telling me," Honoria replied, wiping her eyes with her sleeve. The damn tears kept coming. There was a sudden heavy weight rising through her chest, into her throat. "He's a blue blood. And a rogue. And he's got over a dozen thralls. He's nearly half a century older than me!"

"Weren't you the one telling me it didn't matter only moments ago? What's the real problem? What are you afraid of?"

Everything. She buried her face in her sister's shoulder as it all welled up within her, threatening to choke her. "I don't know what's wrong with me," she managed to gasp. "I don't *know* what I'm afraid of."

A smile dawned on Lena's lips as she wiped her sister's cheeks.

"It's not amusing," Honoria said.

"I know what's wrong. You can't control this. How you feel. Or how he feels. That's what you're scared of."

"It's not that simple...If I did feel something for him, what if he didn't return those feelings? What if—"

"I'm fairly certain he returns something," Lena answered. "For someone so logical, you're making such a mess of things."

"You're enjoying this far too much, Lena."

"Of course I am. It's not often that I get to see you in a dither."

"I'm not in a dither." Honoria's tears were starting to slow. Strangely enough, she felt as though some of the pressure had eased.

"Are too."

Honoria opened her mouth to deny it, then stopped. Lena was right. She was a mess. Over a man. And she didn't know why. *Because he's unsuitable. Because he might break your heart. Because you care for him*...She stopped herself there, closing her eyes and taking a deep breath.

"Let's look at this logically, then, since I know you're so fond of rational thought," Lena offered. "Firstly, the man has given you a small fortune to be his thrall when he only had to pay you a fraction of what he has. Secondly, he has his men guarding the house at night, and I know we're the only ones in the rookery, because I asked around."

"You didn't!" Honoria exclaimed.

"I did. Thirdly, we might presume that he is only interested in getting you into his bed. Any man might do these things and more for a tupping."

"Lena!"

"But he hasn't taken you to bed." Lena's eyebrow arched. "Or at least I presume he hasn't."

Honoria shook her head.

"So we must assume he is interested in something else. He likes you." At that Lena reverted to her normal tone of voice and rolled her eyes. "Though heavens knows why."

Honoria swatted her sister's arm. The skin of her cheeks felt tight and dry, as though scoured by her tears. "It's never that simple."

"You think too much. Stop thinking. Just do."

"Just do what?"

"Whatever pops into your mind when you see him next. If nothing else, it shall certainly shock him."

The thought of shoving him up against a wall and kissing him flashed through Honoria's mind. It would certainly shock him. She'd been holding him at bay for days. Despite the turmoil of emotion, she couldn't stop herself from laughing at the thought of his expression. "You're incorrigible," she said.

"But so much smarter than you when it comes to dealing with emotions," Lena countered.

Honoria could have throttled her sister. Or hugged her. Instead she smiled back. "Thank you."

"My pleasure. Goodness knows, it's pleasant to be the one doling out the advice for a change rather than receiving it." Lena turned with another laugh and a swish of her skirts. "I'll take Charlie his dinner."

The small bowl of soup would be barely enough to feed a soul, but Honoria knew her brother would never finish it. The thought sobered her. Her cheeks ached, as though unaccustomed to the laughter.

I used to laugh. I used to find so much to smile about. She trailed her fingertips sadly over the back of the chair as Lena prepared Charlie's soup.

Now there was no time for smiling. Time. She felt it heavily on her shoulders, as though she were trapped in the bottom of an hourglass and each grain of sand that tumbled through landed squarely upon her. It was a race now to see if she could hold all of that sand off before it buried her.

Honoria sighed and sat back down, dragging her father's diary in front of her. She could barely think for all of the revelations swirling through her head. When had Lena become so wise?

Concentrate, she told herself firmly. Think of the notes, of the disease. Blade would be dealt with tonight when she had time.

The code was hard to decipher. *Test subject twenty-seven shows remarkable signs of improvement, much like subjects nine and fifteen*, she scrawled onto the page. *He has been injected with the same antidote as the others in his subject group, so we must consider that it is not the antidote but something else—unless, of course, he is different himself from the other test subjects and therefore is reacting differently. Variables include diet, exercise, sleep, the amount of sunlight in his cell. I have examined these and conclude them all to be similar. Each subject is given exactly a quarter of a pint of blood a day, fifteen minutes of walking in the yard, and is strictly woken after eight hours of sleep. Sunlight appears to be the same. So what is different? What is the one thing those three subjects share that offsets them from the rest?*

Honoria scratched out the last word and stared through the paper, trying to remember the cell patterns and the number of faceless inmates who stared through the bars at her as she walked past.

And that was when Lena began screaming.

Chapter 18

The soup was splashed all over the floor. Lena stood frozen in the middle of the room. "Charlie?" she whispered.

Honoria sucked in a breath, her hand clutching the doorknob.

"I'm sorry," Charlie whispered. Tears streamed down his face, diluting the blood on his lips. "I'm sorry. I couldn't…I just couldn't stop myself."

Honoria's gaze darted, taking in the bloodstained sheets and the ruined mess of his wrists. She took a hesitant step into the room, feeling it start to spiral around her. Charlie's pupils were almost completely black.

"Oh, my God," Lena whispered.

"Lena. Fetch the washcloth."

Charlie shrank up closer against the headboard. "Don't come closer." His nostrils flared.

The vial of colloidal silver was sitting on the wooden crate that served as a bedside table. She bit her lip nervously, looking at it. "Charlie. You're bleeding everywhere. We have to stop it."

"I know." His pupils widened for a moment, and

then he groaned and banged his head against the head of the bed. "I can smell it."

"Stop it!" Honoria said firmly. She passed Lena, who scurried toward the kitchen. "Stop it, Charlie. Look at me. If we don't stop the bleeding, you might bleed out."

"Would that be so very bad?" he whispered.

Her heart felt as though it was being torn from her chest. "Don't speak like that."

"The worst thing was...I liked it. It tasted so good." His gaze drifted lower, to her throat. "I want more."

"Don't think about it. Think about...spinach. And smoked cod." Two of the foods he despised the most. It worked. He screwed up his nose. Honoria took another slow step forward.

Charlie bit his lip and shut his eyes. "I'm so tired."

The blood was welling from his veins sluggishly, as though they sought to reknit of their own accord. *Like a blue blood.*

Don't think like that, she told herself. It wasn't too late. It couldn't be. She'd been monitoring her brother's CV levels every day with the litmus paper. It was extremely crude, but she couldn't afford the brass spectrometers that the Echelon used.

Lena returned with the washcloth.

"Help me restrain him," Honoria said.

Charlie didn't resist. He simply stared at the ceiling as they bound his hands to the bed, looping the cotton around his fingers because they couldn't constrict his wrists. The bleeding had almost stopped, but Honoria dabbed at it anyway, forcing the gauze to soak up the vermilion splash of his blood.

"What are we going to do?" Lena asked, sitting back when they had finished tying his hands.

"I just need time," Honoria said automatically. "I can fix this. The vaccine that father gave him obviously didn't work, but if I can puzzle out the cure, then I can stop this. I can…"

"It's too late," Charlie interjected and turned his head toward the wall.

Honoria ran a hand through his tawny brown curls. Sweat slicked them to the base of his skull. "It's not—" she began.

"Honor." Lena caught her hand. "Don't do this to him anymore. It's too late."

It wasn't too late. It couldn't be. She just needed more time, needed to work out what that mysterious variable had been that started turning subject twenty-seven's blood results around. "Father knew he had it almost worked out. If I can translate his notes—"

"You're hurting him!" Lena yelled. Her eyes flooded with tears. "Stop it! Just stop it! I can't let you do this anymore. You're hurting him."

"I'm not," Honoria said, shaking her head in denial. "I know I'm close. I just need…" She saw the tears tracking down her sister's cheeks and faltered. Charlie lay limp and almost lifeless, staring blankly at the wall.

"I promised Father," she whispered, tears stinging her eyes and threatening to overwhelm her. "I promised him I'd look after you." A hiccup of pain burst up her throat. "*No*," she whispered, shaking her head. "No."

Charlie turned to look at her. "Please," he whispered.

The sobbing started deep within. She tried to hold it back, to force it down with knuckles to her lips, but it overtook her. Her shoulders shook from the force of it. Too late.

"We need a blue blood," Lena said, "to help him through the transition."

The words seemed to come from some great distance. She barely heard them. She had failed. Her gut twisted until she thought she might almost cast up her accounts.

"Do you think Blade would help us? Honor? Do you think he would help us?"

Lena's fingers dug into her sister's upper arm, and Lena's face swam into view, peering intently at her. "We need a blue blood," Lena repeated. "Do you trust Blade? Do you think he could help Charlie through the transition?"

Honoria bit her lip. She had to pull herself together. Charlie was still ill. Without someone to ease the transition for him, he might go on a rampage through the rookery. Could she trust Blade with him?

After months of trusting no one, it was hard to shake old habits. But the answer that came to her was surprisingly swift. He had been far kinder to her than she deserved when she had given him so little back.

"Yes," she whispered. "I'll fetch him."

It was the least she could do when it had been her own pride that had cost Charlie so much. And if Blade helped her, she swore she would find a way to balance the favor owed there too.

Blade strode into his rooms and shut the door firmly in Esme's face. She'd followed him up the stairs, demanding to talk to him, but he had not the time nor the inclination. It had been another long, frustrating day hunting through the edges of the tunnels with Barrons. His shoulders slumped in weariness. What he wouldn't give to be able to collapse onto his mattress and simply sleep. He needed just a few minutes of peace before he could face the household and deal with Esme's demands.

The day had been one gruesome find after another. The reason the vampire hadn't taken more victims from the rookery was soon clear: all of the people who lived in Undertown were gone. Some of the cavernous rooms showed signs that people had tried to snatch what they could of their belongings before fleeing. Others showed signs of vandalism or even splashes of blood. In some there had been bodies.

Blade tore his coat off his shoulders and threw it aside, the leather wrapping around the post of his bed with a wet slapping sound. Turning, he snatched a bottle of blud-wein off the table, lifted it to his lips, then froze—

Honoria stared at him solemnly from a chair, her feet bare except for her stockings and tucked up beneath her. As soon as he saw her he recognized the subtle feminine fragrance of her, mingling in the air. The stink of old blood and decay still filled his nostrils, but Honoria's scent was like a fresh breeze.

Heat stirred in his body and cock. He was filthy, covered in mud and other things too horrific to think about, but he wanted to press her up against the wall and shove aside those heavy skirts that she wore. His nostrils flared as his vision suddenly leeched of color. Blade clenched his fists.

"What are you doin' 'ere?"

She flinched at his harsh tone. For the first time he noticed the bruised circles beneath her eyes and the defeated way she stared at him. A fist tightened in his chest, just behind his ribs. He'd never seen that look in her eyes before.

"I need your help," she said quietly, not daring to move.

A soft laugh escaped him. "Of course." The only reason she would come to him. He turned and ripped at the leather cuffs around his wrists, carefully avoiding the razors sheathed there. The battered leather breastplate followed, leaving him in only a sweat-stained undershirt. Reaching over his shoulder, he hauled at the collar of his shirt, dragging it over his head.

Honoria looked down at her hands. She remained uncharacteristically quiet, nervously toying with her fingers. "I was worried about you."

Blade balled the shirt. "Why? Afraid 'is lordship'd take the chance to slip a shiv in me back? Thin out the competition a bit."

"I'm not quite sure I follow."

"Or mayhap," he said, throwing the shirt across the room, "you were worried it were I with the shiv in me 'and."

Color started to flood into her pale cheeks. "What the devil are you talking about?"

Blade stalked toward her. Leaning down, he rested both hands on the armrest for fear he'd put them on her body and not stop. Honoria stiffened and retreated into the chair.

"I think you know precisely what I'm talkin' 'bout," he said.

The plain gray dress was far too modest. His gaze roved the scalloped edges with a hunger he felt through his core, and he leaned forward. What he wouldn't give to put his hands on her and lick his way down that slender throat, discovering just how soft her skin could be.

Honoria looked up with a flinty gaze. "I don't know what you're referring to. I wish you'd stop speaking in riddles. And in case your nostrils have ceased to function, I should like to remind you that you stink. Like raw sewage, in fact."

She might as well have slapped him. His eyes narrowed, but he pushed away from her. "Aye. I need a bath."

"Possibly several," she countered.

She was certainly recovering her form well enough. Blade eyed her. "Come. You can wash me back."

"I don't *think* so."

Turning toward the bathroom, he threw over his shoulder, "You're the one as wants me 'elp with somethin'. So you can damn well wash me back."

"I don't have time."

"Make it."

Water splashed from the faucets as he turned them, steaming up the bathroom. Honoria hesitated in the doorway, examining it as if she'd never seen it. She looked everywhere but at him.

Blade's eyelids lowered lazily and he started working at his belt. *Just you try and ignore me now.* He tugged the belt open.

Honoria crossed to the stand and uncapped a bottle of scented oils, wafting it beneath her nose and closing her eyes to enhance the smell. Steam caused the soft curls at the base of her neck to tighten. Her skin grew flushed and dewy.

Behind the stiffened leather of his breeches, his cock raged for release.

Honoria finally chose one of the bottles of oils and poured a generous amount into the water. "You found no trouble today?"

Blade sat on the edge of the bath and kicked off his boots. They might have been a married couple, sitting down to discuss the day's events for the evenness of her tone. Except for the simmering tension lingering in her spine, or the wary glances she stole when she thought he wasn't looking.

"Nothin' but old bodies, drained o' blood. At least it cleared out the Slashers too. Found a drainin' laboratory down there, though the glass vats were smashed and empty. No doubt the vampire lingered there awhile." Other images flickered through his mind, some too horrible to dwell upon. The gurneys where the Slashers tied their victims down. The tourniquets. Rusted needles they used to drain the blood until the body was nothing but an empty husk. And those vats—five of them, big enough to hold the blood of hundreds of people.

Practically sitting beneath his turf and he'd never known. How many went missing that he'd never heard about? The furrow between his eyebrows deepened.

"Nobody was injured?" Honoria questioned. She was fussing with the towels, her back to him.

Blade watched her shoulders stiffen as his breeches hit the floor with a meaty slap. His cock sprang free, bobbing against his abdomen. He ached to take it in hand, but thought better of it. He was already on edge tonight. Best not to tempt fate, not with Honoria in the room.

"Is there anyone in particular you're askin' after?"

She hesitated. "No."

The hot water enveloped him in a steamy wave of scent as he sank into the bath. Honoria's head tilted to the side as though she were listening to gauge his level of nakedness from the echoes of the water's shifting.

"All covered up," Blade taunted, splashing water over his face. "You can look now."

The smell of something exotic wafted from the water, something lemony and slightly masculine, like rosewood. Water dripped off his lashes as he drew his cupped hands down. Honoria was staring at him as though he'd struck her. At least the sight of him still drew her eyes. Half the time he didn't think she even knew how often she watched him.

Blade deliberately hooked his feet up on the rim of the tub, sending water sloshing over the sides. Color rose in her cheeks and she gathered the washcloth and soap with her usual brisk efficiency.

"Lean forward," she muttered, "so I can wash your back."

"You could get in with me." He said the words lightly, leaving just a slight question at the end.

"No, thank you."

"You'll get wet."

"I'll be careful," she replied and dipped the washcloth in the bath to wet it.

Careful or not, she was going to get wet if he had anything to do with it.

Oil shimmered on the water between them, gleaming over his exposed flesh. Honoria scrubbed the bar of soap as though she wished it were lye and then pushed his shoulder. "Lean forward."

He did. Anything to get her to touch him. The coarse feel of the washcloth abraded his skin, but it felt delicious and Blade hooked his knees up, resting his head on his forearms as Honoria washed his back.

"You even have mud on your shoulders," she murmured. Angry scrubbing gave way to a gentler, more determined stroke as she tried to wash off a particularly stubborn spot.

He could imagine that washcloth, soaped up and wet, her hand clutched around it as she stroked him elsewhere. His jaw tightened with strain.

"You ought to see your friend Barrons," he replied, lifting his head. "Weren't watchin' where 'e were goin'. Ended up on 'is back like a turtle in 'bout four inches o'…we'll be generous and call it mud."

Honoria stopped running the cloth over him. Their eyes met and hers narrowed almost imperceptibly. "My friend Barrons," she repeated.

Blade leaned back against the tub, watching her through lazy eyes. He caught her wrist and dragged it to his chest, indicating for her to continue soaping him.

"It's a funny thing, keepin' secrets," he said. "You never know 'ow much the other person knows."

Her face drained of color, and Blade's heart

plummeted into his gut. His cock actually flagged at the sight. *Jaysus*. It had been a shot in the dark, but he'd hit the target. He felt as though the world staggered around him.

"If 'e's good enough for you, then why ain't I?" he growled. "Bloody 'ell. Do you love 'im?"

"*Love* him?" Honoria's jaw dropped. A certain look came into those luscious brown eyes—a look that spelled trouble. For a moment he thought maybe he'd made a terrible mistake.

"Love him?" she repeated. The washcloth dripped all over the floor, clenched in her fist. She seemed to consider the question for a moment. "Yes. I believe I do, though I sometimes wish otherwise." She threw the washcloth at him, but he caught it, soap suds flying everywhere.

"However, you asked the wrong question," she replied. "You should have asked whether I wanted to kiss him."

His head shot up, a hound scenting the fox. "What do you mean by that?"

"I'm very tempted not to tell you," she replied.

Blade caught her wrist. "Honoria," he warned. "Was 'e your lover?"

"Let me go."

"Answer the question."

Their gazes met in charged silence. Honoria tugged at her wrist, but there was no way in hell he was letting her go until she answered him.

"No," she whispered. "Nor do I want him to be." The fight seemed to drain out of her. "Though I should have made you suffer."

Relief flooded through him, leaving him breathless. "You ain't that cruel."

Sudden tears flooded her eyes. "Aren't I? Perhaps not intentionally." Two big fat tears slid down over her cheeks and her shoulders slumped. "I want to be so angry with you right now, but I haven't the strength for it."

A tear dripped from her chin into the bath. He stared at the ripples and then remembered the bruises beneath her eyes. Bruises he'd overlooked in the face of his sudden, leering jealousy. "You were cryin'. Before you come 'ere."

"Yes."

Blade reached up, stroking her cheek. A fat, salty tear slid over his thumb. "And you needed me 'elp." Guilt burned in his throat. "Before I started actin' like a great, bleedin' lummox."

She pressed her cheek into the palm of his hand like a cat seeking a pat. Her hand came up, holding his in place. "I've done something very wrong. I thought…I thought I could stop it. I thought I could help Charlie, but all I've done is hurt him."

Light shimmered off the sudden flood of liquid in her eyes. She closed them and the tears streaked down her cheeks.

Blade couldn't help himself. He leaned up and kissed her cheek, pressing his lips against the salty rime. "You ain't got a mean bone in your body. Whatever you done, it were done with the best of intentions."

"Was it? Or was it something else? Pride? Or the desire to…to control the situation? I've been so bloody blind. It's been too late—" A sob caught in her throat, but she bit it down. "Too late for a while."

He slid his arms around her, trapping her tightly against his chest. Curse him, but it felt good to hold her like this, without any of her usual customary stiffness. "Hush, luv," he murmured, stroking her hair.

Tentatively her arms slid around him, and she burrowed her face into the crook of his neck. "I'm so scared. But you've been so good to me. I never expected it. Not from a blue blood. It makes me think—hope—that maybe it isn't so bad after all."

"Now *I* don't know what you're talkin' 'bout, luv."

She drew back, eyes serious. She wasn't the type of woman made for crying, and yet something punched him in the chest at the sight.

"Can I trust you?" she asked.

There was a weight of seriousness to the words that stopped him from simply replying. He gave it some thought. "I would never 'urt you. Or anyone you cared for."

"Promise?"

"Promise," he repeated.

She gave him a sad little smile. "I think you should get out of the bath, then. There's something you need to see."

Chapter 19

The walk home was silent. No matter what questions Blade asked, Honoria refused to answer him. Indeed, the brief spurt of willfulness she'd shown in his rooms had faded under the weight of her weariness. She was quiet now, mostly withdrawn into herself, her arms wrapped around her body as though she were cold.

Blade paused in front of the house. "We're 'ere."

Honoria looked up, blinking.

"Are you goin' to invite me in?" he asked, his curiosity rampant. This was the most she'd ever allowed him to see into her life. The walls that she held up against him were slowly crumbling, and he was intent on seizing this chance to tear them down.

Honoria drew her shawl tighter. "Do you ever think that maybe if you'd done things differently, you might not have failed?"

He gave a bitter laugh. "Aye. But we ain't ever given those choices. That's the joy o' hindsight."

"Is it…is it bad?"

"Is what bad?"

"Becoming a blue blood?" She gave him an earnest look as though she desperately needed to hear his answer.

A chill ran down his spine as little connections started forming in his mind: the brother who was always ill, the locked door. "Honoria, what exactly is the problem you need 'elp with?"

She gave him a heartbroken look. Then opened the door. "Inside."

Blade pushed his way inside, taking in the room. The sister looked up from the table, where she was toying with a variety of springs and cogs, trying to put some form of clockwork toy back together. Her eyes widened when she saw him, and she sprang to her feet.

"Has there been any change?" Honoria asked in that quiet voice she'd taken to using.

The sister shook her head. "He's asleep."

Honoria crossed to the door and unsnapped the lock. She hesitated once more, then slowly pushed the door open. Reluctance showed in the curve of her spine. She didn't want to do this, but he suspected she had no choice.

The door swung open. Blade caught a glimpse of a narrow bed, an empty jar of colloidal silver, a syringe, and a young boy turning listless eyes toward them. The boy's hands were tied to the bed and thick bandages swathed his lower arms. Blade felt a chill at the sight. Bloody hell. The boy had gone for his own wrists.

Better that than the alternative.

White-hot anger speared through him at the thought. It could just as easily have been Honoria or her sister lying there with her throat torn out. And Blade wouldn't have been able to blame the boy. He knew how harshly the hunger bit when a boy was starved for blood. People ceased to be relatives or friends and became nothing more than a source of food. Vision fled. Sound fled, leaving a roaring rush in the ears. And then the smell of it. Coppery. Warm. The taste of it, so fresh. Like water to a man dying of thirst, finally satisfying an ache that nothing else could assuage.

A moment of sheer ecstasy. But that wasn't the best part. The best part was that the hunger no longer hurt so much. Burning relief that almost made him sob. And then the gradual returning to his self, crouched on the floor, licking the blood from his fingers. Emily's blood.

No.

Pain speared through him—a wound that would never heal, no matter how much time passed. He'd spare anyone that pain if he could.

Blade's throat went dry. He could barely speak for fear he'd say something irreversible. Honoria couldn't have known. She'd never felt the violent, all-consuming *need*. He wanted to wring her neck. "'Ow long's 'e been like this?"

"Six months since it started," she whispered. "Charlie? Are you awake?"

"Go 'way," the boy murmured tonelessly. "Don't come close."

Honoria hovered near the bed. "We need to speak. No more needles. I promise."

Charlie rolled his head toward them. His gaze focused on Blade—and then sharpened. He jerked on the bed linen tying him to the bed, an almost unconscious move. "He's a blue blood," he said.

"This is Blade. He's here to help you."

Blade moved forward and knelt on the edge of the bed. "I'm goin' to untie you," he said, holding the boy's gaze.

"No!" Charlie went rigid. "No, please. It's best like this." His gaze drifted past, toward where Honoria hovered. "Please don't."

"Look at me," Blade commanded. "Charlie, look at me." The boy met Blade's eyes, his own wide and frightened. Bloody hell, it was like looking into a mirror of himself at that age, lost and alone and so terribly afraid that he would hurt someone. Blade had had no one to help him through the ordeal and teach him control. Only an object lesson that would haunt him to the day he died. "I won't let you 'urt 'em. I'm stronger 'n you. Faster. You can't get to 'em without goin' through me."

Honoria gasped. "Oh, Charlie, don't be silly. You wouldn't."

Tears glimmered in the boy's eyes as he stared desperately at Blade. "Promise?"

"Promise," Blade replied firmly.

Wetness spilled down Charlie's cheeks. A sob tore from his throat. "Thank you. Oh, God, thank you. It's all I can think about. I dream about it—" He broke into a storm of weeping. "They don't understand. Nobody understands."

There was a swish of skirts. Blade held his hand out, stopping Honoria in her tracks. "*I* understand." Anger filled him again and he tore the bed ties off, flinging them aside.

Honoria flinched.

"You shoulda come to me," Blade said, unable to help himself.

She swallowed. "I thought…"

"Don't you even bloody finish that sentence," he warned. "I ain't like the Ech'lon."

A little quiver of anger trembled in her clenched fists. "How was I to know that you wouldn't simply kill him? You have a certain reputation for it."

"I don't 'urt the innocent."

"Of course. The Devil of Whitechapel doesn't hurt the innocent." Sarcasm laced her tone. "Do you know that where I come from they use your name to frighten children into obeying?"

He shot her a heated look. "'Ave I ever, by word or deed, caused you to fear me?"

Honoria glared back, just as stubborn. Her eyes dropped first, seeking out her brother's figure on the bed. "No."

He stared at her a moment longer. How he wished to shake her, not for her brother's misery but for the blatant fact that she had not trusted him. Indeed, if Charlie's outbreak had not become so bad, she most likely wouldn't have come to him at all. Only desperation had driven her to reveal her secrets. For a moment he had thought that something had grown between them, a secret little affinity. But now it seemed that he was the only one who thought that.

Blade turned back to the boy. "I'm goin' to offer you me blood. There's enough o' the virus in it to tip you over. You'll feel better for the moment, then it'll 'urt—worse than you ever suffered—while the virus makes certain changes in your body. One or two days and then it'll clear and you'll be...different." He settled on the edge of the bed. "'As to be your choice, though, lad. It weren't mine and I'd not force you to it."

Charlie considered him and then asked quietly, "Does the hunger ever go away?"

"No. But I can teach you to control it."

Not the answer Charlie wanted to hear. He looked at Honoria nervously. "If I don't take your blood? What then?"

"The 'unger'll get worse," he said. "You'll lose control and go after someone, sooner or later. I'd 'ave to put you out o' your misery before you tore through the rookery. Or worse, turned vampire."

"What if I asked you to do it now? To spare me this?" Charlie's burning blue eyes met his.

Honoria gasped, but again Blade held his hand out. "I don't deal with murder."

Charlie's stubborn mouth thinned. Though the boy was fairer than Honoria, he bore a great deal of resemblance to her in expression and mannerism. "That's not fair. You said it was my choice. Then this is what I want: I want to die."

"That's a noble sentiment, boy-o, but ultimately it ain't necessary." Blade deliberately shrugged. "And rather dramatic too. Seems it's an in'erited trait."

Charlie's eyes flared with anger. "You said you knew what it was like. Then how can you ask me to accept this?"

"I know more 'n you'll ever guess," Blade replied.

Charlie's lip curled. "You understand nothing," he choked out, spitting with fury. "What is there to live for?"

"The same as any man," Blade answered. "To work, to marry, to build a family. A home." He kept his voice cool and calm. Charlie was already overwrought, the hunger winding him to an anger fit. "Whatever you want to do with your life."

"*I want to kill my own sisters!*" Charlie yelled. "Tell me you understand *that*!"

He launched off the bed, but Blade was ready for him. Wrenching him back against his chest, he hooked a forearm around the boy's throat and held him immobile, waiting for Charlie's struggles to cease.

Honoria was backed against the wall, her face pale as she stared at her brother. Finally she understood. Tears gleamed in her eyes.

Blade kept his gaze on her. "You want 'er blood? You think I don't understand that?" He spun the boy around, tossing him on the bed. Charlie bounced and came up onto all fours, prepared to defend himself, his instincts working against his logic.

"I 'ad a sister once," he said. "'Er name was Emily. And when she took up with a blue blood lord, 'e took me in too. Decided to give me 'is 'little gift' and then locked me up when I wouldn't do what 'e wanted. 'E swore 'e'd give me blood when I obeyed and not before. And I swore I'd never give in."

Pride. That was the cost of Emily's life. Foolish, bloody pride. If he'd done as Vickers commanded, maybe Emily would still be alive. *Do you ever wish you'd done something differently?* Oh yes. God, yes.

And just as easily as that, Blade's anger against Honoria abated. She had made a mistake and she knew it. But she'd done so with the best of intentions and with all of the resources she owned. If she'd feared him and distrusted him, then God knew he'd earned that reputation over the years.

"What happened?" Charlie asked.

"'E starved me till I weren't meself," Blade replied. "Emily demanded to see me and Vickers gave in." Charlie's eyes met his and he saw in them the horror reflected from his own face.

"So don't tell me I don't understand," he said softly. "'Cos I understand better 'n any other poor blighter in London. You don't want to 'urt your sisters? Well, that's good. That's 'ow we does it, then. Every time you feel the 'unger threatenin' to overtake you, you remember your sisters. Picture 'em. Use that to control yourself."

"Is that how you do it?" Charlie asked.

"No," Blade replied grimly. "I use the memories instead. Somethin' I swear you'll never 'ave to resort to."

He could see the boy thinking it over. Charlie might be only fourteen or so, but there was a wealth of pain and fear in those eyes, turning them old before their time.

"All right, then," Charlie finally whispered. "Do it."

Honoria couldn't watch. She had her arms buried up to the elbows in soapy water, her mind as blank as a slate as she moved with purposeful intent.

I want to kill my own sisters! The memory of Charlie's expression was like a knife through the heart. Wrong. She'd been so wrong. All of his pain was her fault, because she could see no other way through her wrong-headed pride.

Who was she to find a cure when her father couldn't? Who was she to make Charlie's choices when she had no concept of his pain?

She felt at such a loss. For months she'd had purpose. To work from dawn till dusk, to scratch together every coin for the doctor, for the colloidal silver…None of it was necessary now. Blade had given her far more money than she could ever hope to spend, and now he was taking Charlie away from her too.

That wasn't fair.

He was helping Charlie when she could not, and a part of her resented that. Pride again. She looked at her feelings, all of her ugly feelings, and pushed them away.

Right now he'd be giving Charlie his blood. Helping them again when she had given him so little in return.

She'd never met a blue blood like him. For too long all she'd seen when she looked at him was the Echelon, flavored with her own prejudices and her father's as well. She'd not allowed herself to see more. She'd held him at arm's length, erecting walls around her heart for fear he'd find his way through.

And now he was angry with her and justifiably so.

What a mess she had made of everything. A tear slid down her cheek. Then another. She dashed them away. She was sick of crying. It solved *nothing*. And yet she couldn't stop the silent slide of wetness down her cheeks.

In her distraction, Honoria didn't notice the floorboard squeak behind her.

"'E's restin' up now."

She jumped and then started wiping furiously at her eyes. Soap clung to her hands.

Blade caught her wrists, his chest a solid presence against her back. "Easy now, luv. Easy. You'll get soap in your pretty eyes."

Honoria slumped in his grasp. Blade held her up like a puppet-master with a marionette. He slid her hands down, circling her stomach and drawing her back into the sanctuary of his arms.

"Lean on me," he said.

Her nipples were uncomfortably tight. A different kind of tension began to wind its way through her. Honoria looked up and met his obsidian gaze in the reflection of the window.

"Is it done?" she asked.

His lashes fluttered against his cheeks as he reached out with his tongue and traced the tantalizing rim of her ear. "Aye."

A stab of grief and failure shafted through her, but she nodded. Heat stirred behind her eyes again, and she shut them, trying to force it back. "Is Charlie all right? Does he want to see me?"

Blade hesitated, then pressed his mouth against her throat. "No."

No. Honoria clutched at his hands across her midriff.

"'E ain't angry at you, luv. 'E's afraid o' what 'e might do. It'll take time for 'im to trust 'imself when you or Lena are there. And I won't push 'im to forget—it might be all as keeps 'im from killin' someone."

"I'm so sorry."

"For what?"

"I should have come to you earlier."

He pressed his mouth against her neck again. "Aye." The word whispered over her skin. "But I can understand why you did as you did. It don't matter. Nobody were 'urt or killed, and the boy's goin' to survive."

Honoria turned and looked up at him, pressing her back against the sink. She wanted to make him understand. "All my life I've lived among the Echelon. I've seen how they treat their thralls, how they treat their servants. And then when I lived under Vickers's roof…it was awful. He developed some sort of obsession with me, perhaps because he knew how much I despised him."

Blade stroked the back of his hand down her cheek. "Aye. That'd do it. 'E's rotten to the core."

"He used to hunt me. Like I was prey. I was so afraid to go anywhere alone. He would never do or say anything when there were people around, but when we were alone…he used to pin me to the wall and whisper in my ear what he was going to do to me. I didn't dare tell my father. And when we finally escaped, it felt like I was done with them for good. Until you sent for me that night."

"And you thought you were 'bout to be toyed with again."

"It's all I knew of them. And with your reputation…They hate you in the city. You're the monster hiding under the bed, Blade."

He took a step toward her, his legs brushing against her skirts. "And you. What am I to you?"

She looked up into his face helplessly. His hands came to rest on the sink on either side of her hips.

"I don't know," she whispered. "I'm still trying to work out what I feel." She saw his face and grabbed his sleeve as he moved to step back. "You wanted the truth between us? I'm sorry, then, but this is how I feel. I'm so confused. There's been so much going on with Charlie, and losing my employment and then...you. You're not who I thought you were."

Blade didn't like that, she saw. Her fingers tightened on his sleeve, the only thing keeping him from stepping away.

"I do know this, though..." She swallowed, toying with the lapel of his shirt. "I would like to kiss you. Again." The words were a bare whisper, breathed into the heated atmosphere between them.

His gaze shot to hers. "I ain't stoppin' you."

She'd hurt him with her revelation. Slowly she stroked the edge of his sleeve, drawing closer. Pressing both hands against his chest, she reached up and brushed her mouth against his.

Blade held himself stiffly, his arms straight and his fists clenched. Honoria trailed her tongue across his closed mouth, tasting him the way he had done to her in the past. He didn't fight her. Nor did he help her. She drew back. Blade's eyelashes flickered against his cheeks and then he met her gaze. His eyes were as black as Hades and twice as hot. In them she saw everything that he refused to tell her. Her heart thumped hard in her chest, and this time it was her who almost stepped away.

Blade's hands came up and cupped her face, the thumbs stroking across her cheeks. His gaze followed the movement as though he were captivated by the silky feel of her skin. "I can't control meself with you," he said hoarsely.

A muffled groan came from his throat. His hands were shaking as though he fought to contain himself. She pressed closer, rubbing her sensitive breasts against his chest and sucking his bottom lip between hers.

His hands came up and captured her face between them. "Damn you," he cursed. And then he took her mouth in a blistering kiss.

Chapter 20

Fog clung to the chimneys of London like a heavy skirt, obscuring the world and drawing silence down upon her like a weight. The moon was a thin sliver, like a blue blood's smile. Lena pushed open the window and slipped out onto the edge of the roof. This was her private place, the only place in their cramped quarters where she could go without stumbling over somebody else.

A faint whisper sounded above. Lena froze. The hair on the back of her neck rose, and she slowly looked over her shoulder.

The man kneeling on the roof above was enormous. His shaggy hair brushed against his collar, and his eyes gleamed an odd amber color in the moonlight. Dark, coarse stubble covered his jaw, highlighting the blade-sharp cheekbones. Certainly not a handsome man, by her standards, and yet a heated flush went through her at the sight of him. So big, so coarsely put together, all heavy muscles and thick sinew. His shirt could barely contain the thick bulk of his trapezius or the breadth of his forearms. A glint of silver shone at his throat, a winking piece of silver shaped like a tooth or a claw. The verwulfen.

Lena found her feet, measuring the distance between the windowsill and herself. Her heartbeat pulsed in her throat like the rapid tick of the clockwork soldier she'd made for Charlie.

"You wouldn't make it in time," he said and jumped down to the edge of the gable, barely three feet from her. As he straightened, his eyes narrowed. "And if you couldn't avoid *me*, then you couldn't avoid *it* either. Are you stupid, girl, to come out here with the creature on the loose? Or just wantin' to die?"

Lena gaped at him. How dare he? Before she opened her mouth to retort, however, his words penetrated. "Creature? What creature?"

Two bodies, lying in the streets. The chill at her spine grew, spreading across her lower back, and she looked around as though sudden eyes had settled on her from the shadows.

The man stared at her. His gaze was bold, as though he had no inkling of the rules of polite society. "You didn't know. The bloody fool didn't tell you."

He could only be speaking of Honoria. Lena bristled. Though she might fight with her sister at times, she'd be damned if anyone else could disparage her. "If she didn't tell me, she must have had good reason for it. And both of us have had a lot on our minds these last few days." She actually took a step forward, glaring at him. "What creature are you referring to, wolf-boy? The one that killed those two men?"

His shoulders stiffened. "Me name's Will. Not wolf-boy. And I were talkin' 'bout a vampire."

Lena froze. All thoughts of taunting him faded. "A vampire? That's impossible."

"Believe me, it ain't," he said in a dry voice. "'Alf tore me apart just a night ago."

"But…" How? The Echelon strictly monitored its members. "It must be an unregistered rogue."

He rested his hand against the side of the building. The loose sleeve of his shirt slid down, revealing a heavily muscled forearm. For a moment Lena was distracted by his bronzed skin. Then she flushed. He was obviously uncouth, with his loose, dirt-grimed shirt and the ragged mess of his hair. She'd grown up among the vibrant, butterfly-like colors of the Echelon, where every man wore his nails short and manicured and his boots buffed within an inch of his life. She was used to pale skin and padded shoulders, not this raw, virile youth whose body was almost obscenely rippling with muscle. A hulking farm boy. Or a Viking in disguise.

"You ought to stay inside till it's caught," Will said.

Lena looked around. There were two men in the distance, watching the rookery.

"But I have you fine fellows to protect me," she said lightly, sending him a flirtatious smile. It never hurt to have a man in the palm of her hand. "Whatever harm could befall me?"

"I could wring your neck," he muttered, almost too low to be heard.

"I daresay that's not the only place you wish to put your hands." Lena let her smile deepen and stepped past. Her lips curved at the dark look on his face. He didn't like that. "I believe I should like to take some air. If you would just go that way a little bit..." She wrinkled up her nose as if he smelled bad. "You can still keep watch and I can get some *fresh* air."

Will stepped forward to grab her, his nostrils flaring. His hand locked around her wrist. "That's not me..." He barely had time to turn his head before something pale and streamlined flew out of the shadows and smashed him up against the wall.

A wretched scent filled the air, and Lena gagged as she sought to make sense of the blur of movement. An arm slashed and blood flicked across her face, warm and salty. Lena gasped, patting at it in shock. Will cried out, and her vision finally caught up with the fight. The stranger—a pale, balding creature—had its teeth in Will's throat and an arm buried up to the elbow in the man's stomach.

"Blade!" the Irishman yelled, leaping over the rooftops with a pistol flashing in his hand. "Blade!"

Will turned and with great effort smashed the creature up against the building. Its back legs raked up between them, forcing him back, and he fell, his knees giving way beneath him as though he'd lost the strength to use them. With her back pressed up against the wall, Lena could do nothing but watch and scream as the two rolled toward the edge of the rooftop, blood spraying everywhere as the creature—the vampire—tore its way through the burly youth as though Will was merely human and not superhumanly strong.

Somehow Will grabbed it by the throat, his teeth clenched in pain. Blood dribbled from his lips, but he met Lena's eyes. "Run," he said with a weak gasp. Holding it away from her so that she could get away.

Lena wasn't a brave girl. People had told her that time and time again. But they'd also told her that she was foolish enough to have some form of courage. Perhaps it was that, then, that made her launch herself at the monster, tearing futilely at its face with her nails. Her finger sank into something soft and squishy, and the creature screamed, a high-pitched ache in her ears almost at the edge of hearing.

Reflex had it arching backward, away from Will. It hit Lena in the chest and she stepped back, her foot finding nothing but air. With her arms windmilling, she screamed again, grabbing frantically for anything—even the vampire—to keep from falling.

For a moment she clung to its filthy shoulders, staring into the sightless, filmy eyes. She almost thought that it grabbed for her, its claws raking through her skirts and tearing through the cotton. Then she was falling, and the vampire was coming too.

A scream tore through the air.

Inside the flat Blade pushed away from Honoria, his head cocked as though he was listening to something she couldn't hear.

"Blade?" she asked, licking her lips and struggling to find her feet. Her knees shook. If there'd been an inch of privacy, she would have done something reckless, she was sure of it.

His nostrils flared and he held a hand out toward her. "Stay here."

"What's happening?"

He shot her an intense look. "Stay here. And fetch your pistol. I can smell the vampire."

Honoria's blood went cold. Blade started toward the door, but she grabbed him, a horrible feeling of dread running down her spine. "Be careful." She grabbed his face in her hands and kissed him, a brief, furious press of her mouth to his, trying to tell him everything that she didn't have time to put into words.

Blade stepped back and nodded. "I've got to go." And then he was gone.

Ducking into the bedroom, she hurriedly loaded the pistol, her hands shaking. She'd seen Blade fight the vampire before. It was quicker than him. Stronger. "Damn it," she swore, dropping one of the firebolt rounds. It rolled beneath the bed and she ducked down to search for it. Shoving the round into the chamber, she cocked the pistol and then hurried to the window. It was half open, a cool breeze stirring the curtains.

Outside, Will lay on the slope of roof near the window, trying to sit up. Black shadows stained his shirt and pants, and he was trying to stuff something back inside his stomach. His throat was a mess. Beyond him, Blade grappled with the vampire, trying to force it off a prone shape on the rooftop below. It was tearing at the throat of someone on the roof, but she couldn't see who it was. Another man lay nearby. Too late.

At least Charlie was safe in bed, Honoria thought, and Lena…Where the hell was Lena? The warmth drained from Honoria's face. Her gaze traveled unerringly to the half-opened window. Lena always liked to sit on the roof.

Yanking the windowpane up, Honoria hooked her leg over the edge. Will had managed to drag himself into a sitting position, panting hard as he held his arms over his abdomen.

His eyes met hers, then his lips peeled back from his mouth. "Don't."

Honoria knelt beside him, her shoes slipping on the tiles. "Where's Lena?"

He nodded toward the tableau below, sweat dampening his hair. His body was starting to tremble, and when she pressed a hand against his cheek, his skin was burning hot.

"Will you be all right?" she asked. So much blood. And worse...his exposed intestines gleamed in the pale moonlight. She glanced nervously around for Lena, but she couldn't just leave him here.

"Go. I'll live." Will flashed a grim smile at her, his teeth stained with blood. "Ain't the worst I e'er got."

Honoria handed him her shawl and helped him to put it in place against his stomach. "Hold here. Tightly. I'll be back."

She peered over the edge. The other rooftop angled in sharply beneath hers, almost touching the sides of the wall. That was how they built houses here, pressed up against each other like bodies seeking warmth on a cold night. She saw Lena huddled on the edge of the rooftop, blood splashed across her pale face and her wrist bent at an unnatural angle.

"Lena!" she hissed and glanced toward the vampire. Blade had thrown it off, but it was clear that it was too late for his man. The curly-haired Irishman, she noted with a stab of sorrow. O'Shay. His throat had been ripped open, the bone inside gleaming like teeth in the mangled flesh.

Blade circled the vampire. He shot her a dark look, then turned all his attention to the creature. It paced the rooftop on all fours, snarling at him silently. Blood dripped from Blade's side.

The pistol was a heavy weight in Honoria's hand. She slipped her legs over the edge of the roof and then dangled, trying to soften the fall. She landed with a jarring thud and tumbled onto her back. The pistol slid across the roof tiles, stopping a few feet away.

The creature screamed in rage, a high-pitched whine that shot through her ears like a knife. Blade cried out and clamped his hands over his ears, his knife dropping from his hands.

"No!" she screamed as it attacked him. They went down together in a vicious whirl of action, blood flying.

Honoria scrambled for the pistol then stopped when she saw the vampire bulleting toward Lena. She would never reach it in time. "*No!*"

Somehow she caught its ankle as it leapt past. The vampire spun with blurring speed, its claws raking across her arm like white fire. Honoria cried out and it stopped, hissing in her face. She couldn't move, every muscle in her body paralyzed in fear as she stared into its sightless eyes.

Its breath stirred across her face, thick with the coppery scent of blood. With Lena forgotten, it hopped toward her, reaching out with its claws as though to touch her face.

Honoria couldn't take her eyes off its gnarled hand, coming closer and closer. Oh, God, what was it doing? Would it go for her throat too? Fear curdled in her stomach, freezing her lungs. Her breath came in short, sharp, painful gasps.

"Lena," she whispered, trying not to draw its attention. "Lena, you have to move."

"What about you?"

"I'll be..." The creature stopped in front of her, and she felt the first stroke of its claw against her cheek, strangely gentle, and shuddered. "I'll manage."

"Don't move," Blade called. "It's attracted to movement."

Beyond the vampire's shoulder, she could sense a shadow dissolving in the moonlight. Blade. Daring to take her eyes off the creature for a moment, she saw him easing his way across the roof toward the pistol with a grim expression on his face. Their eyes met. Fear turned her spine to ice.

The vampire's hand curved around her face, its claws scraping along the soft underside of her jaw. Honoria swallowed. It lowered itself toward her, face-to-face, until she had no choice but to look at it.

Thick, ropy scar covered its throat. This close she could see the sloughing scales that covered its cheeks and its coarse white eyelashes. Its eyes were clouded with film. As she watched, it leaned closer until she could almost taste its breath on her tongue.

Its mouth opened. Wicked, needle-sharp teeth gleamed, the canines predominant. A scream curdled in her throat. The vampire's jaw worked, a faint hiss coming through its teeth. Heart thundering, she stared at it, a frown growing between her brows.

"Stay still," Blade hissed with urgency. "I've nearly got the pistol."

Honoria barely heard him. All she could see was the vampire's mouth, its jaw working awkwardly.

"Got it," he said. "Don't move, Honor."

She could barely hear for the pounding of her heart, but somehow she managed to hold up a hand. "Wait," she whispered, knowing that she was taking a deadly chance. And yet it seemed that if she watched the creature's lips moving, she could almost make out the shape of words. The vampire was trying to talk to her.

"Honor," Blade growled in frustration.

"If it had wanted to kill me, it would have done so already."

Its lips curled back off its teeth, and it snarled over its shoulder at Blade. He aimed the pistol, but the vampire was directly between him and Honoria. If he missed, he would hit her and he knew it. Frustration flickered over his face, and he paced to the side, trying to draw the vampire away. It followed, keeping its body between them at all times. Blade thumbed back the hammer.

The vampire gave one last snarl and then fled, blurring over the rooftops and vanishing toward the tunnel into Undertown. Honoria stared after it, confusion flooding through her. If she had understood that right…Finding her feet, she realized that her hands were trembling. Everything she knew was spinning through her head like a whirlpool.

"Are you insane?" Blade yelled, grabbing her by the

arms and shaking her. His eyes were wild but hadn't descended to the demon-dark pools of his hunger. This was entirely human—furious and frustrated and, most of all, afraid. "It could 'ave killed you."

"I don't think it wanted to," she blurted.

"They don't think, Honor. They ain't rational. It's only 'unger, constant and maddening. The only thing they can think 'bout is blood."

She opened her mouth, saw Blade's face, and shut it again. He was in no mood to listen to her explanations. Cupping her face, muttering under his breath, he stroked his thumbs across the plane of cheek beneath her eyes.

"Bloody 'ell," he muttered. And then he kissed her, his mouth slashing across hers with an almost violent need. It wasn't lust. It wasn't hunger. It was fear, driving them together.

Honoria sank her hands into his hair, wrapping herself around him. Seeing him there, over O'Shay's body, the vampire ripping into him…

She pushed at Blade's shoulders, breaking the embrace, and tore his coat open. "You were bleeding. Are you all right?"

He caught her hands, an odd, purring rumble deep in his throat. "Torn up a bit. It'll 'eal. What 'bout you? It didn't scratch you?"

"No. It…it wasn't trying to hurt me."

His face darkened. "Aye, it were tryin' to talk to you, that's all. A creature as ripped O'Shay apart like 'e were made o' cotton stuffin'."

But it was. She turned without saying anything, to where Lena was crying by the wall, limply holding her wrist in her other hand. Honoria would think of it later when she was alone with her thoughts. "Will was injured. Badly."

Blade blew out a deep breath. "Aye," he said, and jumped up, grabbing the edge of her roof with his hands and dragging himself up.

As she knelt by Lena and examined her for injuries, she couldn't help seeing the vampire's face in her mind, silently trying to mouth words it could no longer give voice to. It would haunt her dreams at night. *Please. Help me.*

Chapter 21

Blade knelt by O'Shay's body, a rush of warmth swimming behind his eyes. No tears, though. Never any damned tears.

He'd known it might come to this when they set out to hunt the vampire, which was why he'd always kept O'Shay, Tin Man, and Rip in the background. They were only human. He hated even having Will at his side, but at least the verwulfen could heal almost any damage—and Blade could not do this alone.

Something rattled nearby, breath through a man's torn throat. Blade's head shot up and he stared at Rip and the spreading pool of blood beneath the man's body. Placing O'Shay's head on the ground as gently as he could, he scuttled on hands and knees toward Rip.

"Rip?" He slid his fingers behind the man's jaw, feeling for a pulse. The gurgling whisper of Rip's breath came again, harsh and strained. And his heartbeat pulsed against Blade's fingertips. It was weak, but it was there.

"Sweet Jaysus." Blade gently eased Rip onto his

back. The man's abdomen was torn open and his throat slashed, but the vampire had missed his carotid artery. A miracle. A bloody miracle. And yet as soon as Blade thought it, his eyes assessed the damage. It was a gut wound, a mortal wound. There was no way a human could heal this.

"Shit." Tears swam in his eyes. Rip had been with him the longest. Lark would be devastated. And Esme...His fingers grasped Rip's coat. Esme's heart would break. She had already buried one husband.

Rip's eyes widened with pain and panic. His fingers clutched at Blade's coat sleeve as blood bubbled on his lips.

Such was Blade's grief that he didn't hear the soft footsteps on the rooftop behind him until Honoria laid a hand on his shoulder. "Oh, Blade," she murmured. "I'm so sorry."

Blade nodded curtly, unable to reply. The lump in his throat was sharp with guilt. He'd been inside with Charlie too long. If only he had come out earlier, he would have been there when the vampire first attacked. The two men had had no chance against the creature once Will was down.

Honoria knelt at Rip's head and eased her knees underneath it to form a pillow. His eyes rolled back to see what was happening, then another bubble broke on his lips. His breathing came easier, though. What was left of it.

"Is there nothing you can do?" she asked.

Blade stared at the mess of exposed viscera. "Me blood can 'eal a wound, but not like this. And not before 'e chokes to death."

Honoria stroked her hand over Rip's shaved head. "So it's his lungs that will kill him?"

Blade nodded.

It was a long moment before she spoke again. "You couldn't…you couldn't do what you did to Charlie?"

Blade's gaze shot to hers. A wild hope. Virtually impossible. But Esme…If there was a chance, no matter how slim, he had to take it.

"Ain't ever infected someone so badly injured."

She laid her hand over his, her warmth taking away some of the awful cold that seemed to fill him up. "The older the blue blood, the stronger the virus." Her hand stilled on Rip's forehead. "It might work. All of your other data overshoots the expected outcomes."

Blade looked down at his friend again. Rip's gaze found his. "We're goin' to give you me blood," he said, squeezing the big man's metal hand. Rip probably didn't feel it, but Blade needed to hold something. "The virus might keep you 'live long enough to 'eal your wounds."

He pushed past the lump in his throat. He knew how Rip felt about becoming a blue blood; he'd offered once, only to have the man soundly reject him. "If you don't want it, blink. If you do, squeeze me fingers." Before the man had a chance to reply, Blade leaned low, cupping Rip's hand in both of his. "But know that this'll devastate Esme." A cruel move. But worth it if his friend chose life.

Rip froze, staring up at him. Thought flickered behind his eyes, and then slowly he squeezed Blade's fingers.

Relief flooded through Blade's mind, followed by

bleak despair. This was a desperate last attempt to save a life. The Echelon had laws that forbade infecting a sick or injured person. With so little strength, the virus could overtake them far swifter than it could a healthy adult male. And it was harder to fight the bloodlust without all of a man's strength behind him. If it succeeded, he would have to watch Rip carefully. If...

"'Old 'is 'ead," he told Honoria firmly. "Whatever you do, don't let 'im move."

Then he withdrew one of his razors and slashed it lengthwise down the vein in his own wrist.

Blade had decided that it wasn't safe for them to stay at Honoria's house for the night with the vampire on the loose and its odd interest in the Todd family. Besides, Honoria didn't think she could stay away from him. The look in his eyes was bleak. She wanted to press her hand against his cheek, her lips to his forehead. Anything to ease his pain. But when she'd tried to take his hand in hers, he'd snapped at her and shaken loose. *Distracted*, she told herself.

Lena's wrist was swollen but not broken, and Charlie's eyelids were starting to droop sleepily. Will was on his feet, but only through sheer willpower. Bruises marred the skin beneath his eyes, and he could barely manage to keep his eyelids open. The loupe virus had closed the wound across his abdomen. Now it was trying to heal the rest of him. Though insanely strong in battle, verwulfen were vulnerable following injury, when the virus knocked them unconscious in order to heal.

Lena hovered at his side, her face pale and strained. It had been a nasty shock for her tonight. Honoria hadn't had a chance to ask her what happened, but Will had mentioned that "bloody, stupid girl" launching herself at the vampire when it attacked him. Honoria couldn't have been prouder, and yet she wanted to shake some sense into her sister. What had she been thinking?

Blade carried Rip carefully, his body staggering with weariness. He'd lost too much blood today, both in donating it to Charlie and Rip and in the healing slash the vampire's claws had gouged in his side. Honoria kept a careful eye on him. It was a weary, battle-stained little group.

The warren came into view, cheery lights gleaming in the upstairs windows. Esme, no doubt, trying to make a home for the men.

Honoria pushed past Blade, opening the door.

"Thanks," he murmured, swinging Rip through. It looked ridiculous, one man carrying a giant like a child balancing an adult in his arms.

They were almost to the stairs when Esme came down, a candlestick in her hand and a gentle smile on her lips. "Honoria," she said, greeting them warmly, and then her gaze took in Honoria's bloodstained skirts. "What happened? What..." And then she looked past to where Blade stepped into view. The color drained from her face as she saw who was in his arms. Another woman might have screamed or gasped, but Esme went white as a ghost and staggered against the wall. "John," she whispered.

Blade's face was grim. "I give 'im me blood. I 'ad to. 'E's still breathin', but I can't promise you anythin'."

Esme nodded, her hand sliding along the wall as though she couldn't quite keep herself upright. Honoria leaped up the stairs and caught her before she fell.

"I'm so sorry," Esme murmured in shock. "I don't know what came over me." She looked at Rip again in disbelief.

All of the remaining questions regarding Esme and Blade's precise relationship shriveled. *Oh.* Honoria looked at the villainous-looking giant dubiously.

"'E needs blood, Esme," Blade said.

"Aye," Esme whispered. "Bring him to his room."

"Are you sure?" Blade asked. "It ain't been long since you offered to me."

A firm look came into the woman's eyes. "I'm strong enough. And you'll be there to contain him if necessary."

They turned and made their way up the stairs. Blade swung Rip through the doorway, easing him onto the bed. He knelt for a moment on the edge of the mattress, a hand pressed against his side as he breathed hard.

Honoria pressed her palm against the small of his back and raised a questioning eyebrow when he looked at her.

His lips thinned. "I'm right as rain. Just let me catch me breath."

Esme plumped the pillows. The jagged wound at Rip's throat had closed almost completely, courtesy of a splash of Blade's blood. Just what precisely was Blade's CV count coming in at? He had to be close to seventy or eighty percent for Rip's wound to heal so swiftly. A troubling thought, for it meant Blade was also standing on the verge of the Fade.

Esme knelt on the bed and started to unbutton her collar. Rip focused on her so intensely that Honoria almost felt as though she was intruding on something private. A strangled noise came from his throat. "No," he managed to spit out. "Not 'er."

His hand rose to push Esme away, but Blade caught it, forcing it back to the bed. The iron fingers closed around his and Blade squeezed back, his teeth clenched. "This is what you agreed to," he said. "And there ain't nobody else. Unless you'd prefer it to be Lark?"

Rip's green eyes rolled wildly, searching for escape. He shook his head.

Esme took matters into her own hands, straddling Rip's hips and leaning over him. Her collar gaped, revealing a slim throat marred by tiny, silvery scars. "John Doolan," she said in a firm, no-nonsense voice and grabbed his face in both hands. "My blood's as good as any other, and you'll damned well drink it or I'll box your ears. You can choose your own thralls when you're well again."

Rip's eyes blazed as they focused on Esme's face. His mouth thinned, and then suddenly his right hand jerked up, the fingers clenching her skirts. Esme gasped, but Blade was there to ease the big man back onto the bed as he jerked Esme toward him.

"Easy now, lad," Blade murmured. "I'll 'elp you through it, but you 'as to remember to be gentle. You don't want to frighten 'er, do you?"

Movement danced at the corner of her vision. Honoria turned and saw Will watching the scene, his golden eyes burning and his nostrils flaring with an emotion she couldn't quite name. He should have been in bed, but somehow he had dragged himself up here to watch.

Will's eyes met hers and then he turned on his heel and strode away. Behind her, Honoria heard Esme's gasp and Blade murmuring, "That's it, big man. Be easy with 'er."

They had the injured man well in hand. There was no need for her to be here. She strode for the door, startling Charlie in the hallway. In her haste she almost walked directly into him, but he jerked back with a horrified expression on his face, as though he was afraid to touch her.

"Where's Lena?" she asked, fighting the urge to reach out to him.

"She went with Lark to the kitchens to boil water and fetch bandages," he said, staring at the ground.

Honoria took a step back, giving him the distance he desired. It tore through her, a spear to the heart, but she did it. A part of her would never forget the look in his eyes as he admitted to Blade how much he'd thought about drinking their blood. *He just needs time*, she thought and then prayed that it was true.

"Do you want me to find you a bed—"

Charlie pressed his back against the wall. "No. No, it's fine. I'll wait here. In case they need me."

Another knife to the heart. He was afraid to be alone with her. Honoria's voice softened. "I'll be back. I'm just going to see how Will is."

She went to Will's room at the back of the house. The door was shut, but light spilled beneath it. Knocking, she pressed an ear against the thick wood to listen.

"Go 'way," he growled.

"You're still bleeding. Would you like me to see to it? I have some skill at tending patients."

"No."

"May I come in?" She didn't wait for him to answer, instead pushing the door open.

The room was smaller than she would have expected. Her eyes darted around, surprised by the accumulation of belongings. The bed was narrow and better suited for a child, with a faded patchwork quilt over the threadbare sheets. Simple shelves held dozens and dozens of children's books, all of them well read and their spines cracked. There were bits of feathers and rocks scattered in a collection of polished mahogany boxes laid open upon a small desk, and a curl of dark hair, carefully bound with a pink silk ribbon. Esme's hair.

Will growled and slammed the box shut over the hair, obscuring her view. He was shirtless and radiating displeasure. From the bandages on the bed, his intentions were evident.

"You should wash the wound," she said. "Before you bandage it."

He scowled and turned toward the bed, limping slightly. The broad plane of his back was heavy with thick muscle.

"I'm not going to go away," she said.

"It'll heal. Your help ain't needed."

"You mean you don't want it. You do, in fact, need it." She took a hesitant step forward. He was so big and surly that if he made a move toward her, she probably couldn't stop him. And yet with Blade preoccupied, Will needed someone to care for him.

He ignored her, swiping at his bloodied stomach with a wet swatch of linen. The cloth looked relatively clean, but Honoria couldn't help pursing her lips as she peered at the bowl of water.

"You don't like me," she said, taking another stealthy step toward him. "Since I don't believe I've ever done anything to harm you, I can only assume you don't approve of my association with Blade."

Again silence. But his head tilted as if he was listening to her. Water dripped into the bowl, filling it with vibrant red. She'd thought the wound to be closed, but parts of it still gaped like a badly sewn hem.

Tremors started in his hands as he kept cleaning the wound.

"Here," she said, closing her fingers over his. "Let me. Please."

A growl vibrated through his throat. A warning.

Honoria put her hand in the small of his back and pushed him toward the sturdy rocking chair by the window. "Yes, yes. I know you're not happy about it, but let us pretend for a moment that neither of us finds the other rude, surly, or obnoxious."

His legs chose that moment to give out, and he found himself staring up at her, his nostrils flaring with pain.

Honoria collected the bowl of water, pleasantly surprised to find that it was still hot. It had been boiled after all. She knelt at his feet and wrung the cloth out. "Do you need stitches? Or will it heal naturally? Or supernaturally, as it may be?"

"It'll heal."

Honoria rolled her eyes. "Honestly, would it hurt you to be polite?"

Will met her gaze. "I don't like you 'cos you ain't good for him."

"Blade seems to think otherwise."

"Aye. When a man's dog-drawn, he ain't thinkin' with the best of his faculties."

Honoria patted gently at the fleshy wound. "I'm not entirely certain what you mean, but I assume it isn't flattering." Silence lingered as she cleaned the wound. She sat back and discarded the rag in the water, reaching for the clean linen bandages. "I don't intend to hurt him," she said. "Never that. He's been so terribly good to me."

"You aren't part of this world." He sneered down at her work-a-day dress. "How long before you head back where you belong?"

Honoria drew the bandage around his waist, gesturing for him to sit upright. "You're mistaking me for someone who cares for the fancy silks and fine steam carriages of the Echelon. That's Lena's style, not mine. It never has been." She gave a tug and drew the bandage tight, causing his breath to hiss between his teeth. "And you'll have to come to some sort of accommodation with your dislike of me, for I'm not going anywhere."

As soon as she said it, she realized it was true. She had never had a home, not truly. Caine House was a distant memory, and Lannister House was nothing but a nightmare dreamscape to her. Her present little flat, while shabby and barely habitable, had become the first place she'd ever had for herself. And the thought of leaving Blade behind made her sick to her stomach.

The rookery was a dangerous place, and he was

reckless with his own life, placing himself between his own men and danger. A blue blood was not indestructible. She couldn't bear the thought of leaving him behind, never knowing if he was alive or hurt. Never being able to hold him in her arms. To kiss him.

She blinked and realized that she'd frozen in thought. Will watched her, his expression unfriendly. Honoria leaned forward to wrap the bandage around his waist again.

"He's mine, you big brute," she said fiercely and tugged the linen tight. How curious to realize that she meant every word. "And you shall simply have to reconcile yourself to that fact. Now, may I fetch you anything?"

"Raw meat," he said sullenly. "From the larder."

Chapter 22

Silence echoed through the warren. Honoria found herself at loose ends, having seen Lena and Charlie to their beds. Esme was sitting by Rip's side, and Honoria couldn't find Blade anywhere.

Nervousness settled down her spine, like ants tracking across her skin, as she climbed the stairs to his chambers. There were plenty of spare beds for the night, but she knew she'd find no rest until she'd seen if he was all right. Grief had etched itself into the hard lines of his face, and though his tone had been light as he talked Rip through his first feeding, a line of tension lingered in his shoulders.

It was frightening how much she had begun to think of him. He haunted her every thought, every action. She found herself looking for him when she entered rooms, and when he was not there the flare of excitement in her stomach died a little death. Worry ate at her, her heart opening just wide enough to reach out tentatively toward him. Once, only Lena and Charlie had owned pieces of her worry, her care. Now there was another claim on her emotions.

A blue blood. A creature Honoria had always despised, and yet he'd managed to force her eyes open, to make her question everything her father had always told her about them, to question everything she'd seen herself. She was so confused.

Perhaps she had been hasty in declaring her hatred. And perhaps, she was embarrassed to admit, a trifle prejudiced. After all, had it not been her own voice that said, "*Manipulation is not a symptom of the disease…*"?

Light shone beneath his door. Honoria took an unsteady breath and eased it open. "Blade?" There was no answer.

His bedroom was dark, but light beckoned from the bathroom. Honoria paused in the doorway, the warm candlelight illuminating the room with an ambient glow. Something in her chest tightened as she saw him, naked except for a towel around his hips, his head sunk into his hands as he sat on the stool by the mirror. He didn't move when she entered. There was a half-empty bottle of blud-wein by his feet.

Honoria took a hesitant step forward and drew breath to call his name again.

"You shouldn't be 'ere."

Her lips parted in surprise. "I wanted to see if you needed anything."

Black eyes met hers in the mirror, stealing her breath. The look on his face was expressionless. "Do I look like I need anythin'?"

A lump formed in her throat. "Yes."

His gaze darkened. "Get out."

"No."

Suddenly he was on his feet in front of her. She had

barely taken a step back in surprise before his hand tightened on her arm.

"I ain't fit company tonight."

Honoria stared up at him. Her heart was pounding madly in her ears. He was giving her a chance to leave. A chance to escape before...before things changed between them. This was not the man she knew. This was a man driven by his demons tonight. Crushed by grief, by hopelessness, by failure. She wanted to wrap her arms around him and hold him tight but knew immediately that such was not the comfort he would take tonight. The look in his eyes was too heated. Blistering.

His gaze lowered at her hesitation. Settled on her breasts. There was just the slightest hitch in his breathing. "Last chance, damn you," he said.

Her hands curled into fists. The very thought of it left her breathless. And yet when her mouth opened, the words that came out were not quite the ones she'd expected. "I'm not going anywhere."

A stunning realization. She wanted this man, wanted what was to come between them. The very thought tightened her nipples. Wet heat pooled in her stomach and lower, in places she tried not to think about very often.

If she had expected him to be pleased with her response, she'd thought wrong. Blade turned and swept his shaving kit off the vanity. His little mirror shattered across the floor into a million shards. The soap skittered under the claw-foot bath, and his shaving brush rocked slowly to silence beside the razor. Blade leaned on the vanity, his head lowered as though he sought some measure of control. His back, his spine, his shoulders—all tight with rippling tension.

It should have frightened her. His passions were wild and animalistic, his fury sharp-edged. But he would never hurt her. She knew it with a certainty she'd never felt before.

It encouraged her to step forward, her shoes crunching on the glass shards. Nervousness faded. "You don't scare me," she whispered. "You would never hurt me. So if you're trying to make me run away…then you've failed."

His head lifted. Black eyes met hers in the mirror. Honoria's breath caught, but not in fear. A pulse of desire throbbed between her thighs at the look.

"I am dangerous," he said through tightly clenched teeth. His nails dug into the vanity. "Damn it, Honor. Are you so foolish? These 'ands 'ave known blood before."

"I trust you." She reached out to stroke his trembling back. She'd seen him in this state before, knew how hard he fought to control himself. And hearing what he'd admitted about his sister, Emily, only strengthened her resolve. This was a man who knew the cost of failure. She trusted him more than he trusted himself.

Blade flinched. His nostrils flared as he squeezed his eyes shut. "I need to be alone tonight."

"I want to be with you."

Silence fell, broken not even by the sound of his breath. His head lifted, the predator staring at her once again in the glistening facet of the mirror. "You've only ever seen me at me best." He did not want her to see him like this. There was a faint self-loathing undertone to his voice. "'Ow can you forget what I've done?" He spoke of his sister.

"Does a pistol murder a man? Or is it the man who pulls the trigger? Can we blame a rabid dog who tears apart a child? Or should we blame the one who kicked and starved and tortured it?" Her heart ached at the look on his face. "I *don't* forget what you've done. For me, for Charlie, for Lena even. I don't forget my gloves. I don't forget all the times you bought me food when I was so hungry I could cry. The people you look after." Tears flooded her eyes. "I'm sorry. You can never bring her back. A part of you will probably never forgive yourself. But when I look at you I don't see a man who murdered his sister. I see a man who clawed his way out of the gutters and took control of his life. I see a man who made a family of his own. Who loved. And is loved. I see a man I want to kiss." Her hand stroked down his back. "I see a man I want to...to give myself to."

A sound erupted from his throat. Half groan, half cry. Then his hands were on her, shoving her back against the vanity, her back pressed against the mirror. There was no time to protest. No time to halt the invasion. His mouth was on hers, brutal, claiming, and his hands shoved her skirts up in thick bunches.

Glass bottles of scented oil smashed to the floor as he grabbed her under her knees and dragged her body against his. Her thighs caressed his hips and he settled into place as though he belonged there.

"I want you more 'n I've ever wanted anythin'." His hands came up and cupped her face. The thumbs began a gentle stroke against her cheeks as he stared at her mouth. His hands shook. "But I'm 'fraid I'll 'urt you."

Honoria took his hand and dragged it lower. She slid it under her skirts, against the heated skin of her thigh. "That fear is why I know you won't," she whispered. Her other hand went to his nape and she dragged his mouth back to hers. "Make love to me, Blade. And don't stop."

The words stole the last ounce of his control. He groaned and buried his face against her neck. Cool breath brushed against her heated skin, stirring a shiver down her entire body.

The hand on her thigh tightened. "So be it."

His mouth took hers in a punishing kiss. She could taste the hunger on him and the reckless passion. It swept her along into a torrent of need until she was shaking and trembling. Her hands found his chest and slid over the silky-smooth muscle, exploring the hard planes of his flesh. His nipple abraded her palm and she dragged her hand lower, tracing the ripple of his abdomen. It was all so new, so unexpected. The thought that came to mind was *hard*. His body was the very opposite of hers.

Only his mouth was soft. His tongue traced hers with a hungry touch, any attempt at civilized conduct flying out the window. The hand on her thigh slid higher, cupping her buttock. He rocked her against his hips, the towel abrading the delicate flesh of her inner thigh. His cock, proud and erect, butted against the wet fabric of her drawers.

"Oh, *God*," she groaned, stealing a breath. She

couldn't stop her nails from curling into little claws in his shoulders.

His tongue pushed inside her mouth, a sweeping caress against her own. Hand cupping the back of her neck, he dragged her closer, rubbing his hips harder against her. Honoria fell backward, thrusting a hand out to support herself. Another bottle of cologne tumbled and hit the floor. The very hand that had stroked her nape became an anchor in her hair, fisting in the thick strands. Blade tilted her head back, leaving her vulnerable and exposed to his mouth.

Hot. Wet. His teeth gently scraped the column of her windpipe, reminding her just how precarious her position was.

Her other hand clutched his shoulder. She had to trust him. But as his lips traced a blazing path across her collarbone, a little flicker of fear pulled in her womb. Honoria gasped as her body went liquid.

Blade nuzzled her neck, his tongue darting out to trace the vein that throbbed so hungrily. With his other hand, he brushed against the cotton of her drawers. The sensation made her jump. The pressure was so light it stirred the material against her skin, a teasing whisper of sensation.

A finger slipped through the opening in her drawers. A faint brush against the wetness of her quim and then a stronger, less tentative touch. Honoria trembled. She wanted…ached…It was too much. And not enough.

"Open for me," he demanded, pressing his hips into the vee of her thighs. "Spread your sweet thighs, Honor."

Cool air traced the skin of her inner thighs. Her skirts were heaped around her waist in disarray. No doubt she looked like a blowsy wench about to be tumbled. And for once she didn't give a damn.

"That's it," he breathed. The tip of his finger parted the delicate folds of her flesh, stroking the lush pearl deep within.

Honoria's mouth widened in a silent gasp. She clutched at his neck with both hands, her hips jerking. "Oh, God. Oh, don't stop."

"I ain't goin' to." He found the precise spot that sent a spear of lightning through her.

Her vision went blank. She cried out, throwing her head back.

"Like that?" he whispered. His other hand was furtively tugging at her drawers.

For a moment the feather-light touch was gone as he dragged them down. He pressed her thighs wide, leaving her exposed and vulnerable. A dashing kiss against her lips and then he was working his way lower, scattering little kisses down her throat, over the flushed skin of her breasts as they heaved over the top of her bodice and then lower…a wet, open-mouthed kiss against her inner thigh. His tongue darted out. Tasted. Honoria's hands sank into the guinea-gold silk of his hair, and she stared in shocked fascination as he glanced up at her.

The next kiss was directly between her legs. The soft dark curls hid the sight of his mouth, but she felt it through her entire body as his tongue darted out.

"What are you doing?" she gasped. Her eyes nearly rolled back in her head as he nuzzled at her tender flesh. It was indescribable. Horrifically embarrassing. But she couldn't have asked him to stop if she'd wanted to.

Blade slung her knees over his shoulders as he knelt in front of her and tongued her tender flesh. Cupping her buttocks in both hands he pressed his face deep between her thighs and drank in the wetness that drenched her.

She couldn't breathe. Her stays, no doubt, digging into her ribs. Another soft cry left her lips and she shuddered as that strange, restless feeling began to build within her. It felt exactly as it had when his mouth had been on her thigh, drinking her blood.

Blade looked up and wiped his mouth on his wrist.

"Don't stop," she gasped.

"I want to be inside you," he growled. "I want to feel you come 'round me." Standing, he dragged her hips to the edge of the dresser. The towel hit the floor. "I want to *own* you."

"You do." She gasped as he rubbed his erection between her thighs. It was exquisite torture against her heated flesh. She writhed helplessly, tormented by the brooding storm beneath her skin. It hurt to keep it contained.

"Only me," he demanded.

"Only you." She sobbed the words, trying to draw him closer.

The head of his cock brushed against her, dipping into the molten recesses of her body. Honoria sucked in a quick breath, her nails digging into his skin. "Oh." Stretching wider. Almost uncomfortable. She scrabbled at the vanity, her hips shifting to ease the sudden hot ache.

Cradling her in his arms, Blade thrust and buried himself to the hilt.

Honoria's shocked cry echoed in the room. Blade stroked her face, her lips, her eyebrows. A kiss to steal her breath. Without any feminine figures in her life to explain this, all her knowledge had been gleaned from textbooks. But they had never described anything like *this*.

It burned. Honoria clung to his shoulders, her mouth and eyes wide with shock. Blade trembled, his forehead resting against hers as though he fought to restrain himself. His thick, gold lashes fluttered against his cheeks. Stroking her face, her lips, trailing tender fingers across her cheeks, he looked up. Black eyes met hers.

"Mine," he whispered. A shudder went through him, his hands raking down her back to cup her bottom. "*Mine.*" The second word could have belonged to a different voice.

His hips moved. The sensation was raw; for a moment she was not entirely certain if it was pain or pleasure or a curious blending of both. Another thrust, the odd pleasure-pain shooting through her. It was too much for her. Too much. The restless storm within her began a slow burn, fingers of lightning licking along her nerves.

Candlelight gleamed on his skin as he pumped inside her, slowly at first, then faster, his hips meeting hers with the sound of flesh slapping against flesh. She wanted to taste him, she realized. Wanted to lick. To bite. Kissing his throat, she nuzzled up beneath his chin and drew his lower lip between her teeth.

Blade wrapped a hand in her hair. "No." The next thrust earned a gasp. "God, don't kiss me."

His words sent a shaft of hurt through her. Rejection. And then she realized what he meant. He wasn't thinking only of sex right now. Both of his needs had collided and he was fighting hard not to succumb.

Honoria's hand swept back to support herself and brushed against the razor he used to shave with. Eyes widening, she clung to him with the other hand, her back hitting against the mirror. His hand slid over hers, cool fingers pressing her palm down until the handle of the razor imprinted itself in her skin.

Their eyes met. "Do it," she whispered, and kissed his lips. Slowly she withdrew her own hand, leaving the razor beneath his.

A shudder ran through him. The next thrust was forceful, rocking her back. And then he had the razor at her throat.

Honoria cried out at its sweet pierce. His mouth latched onto her neck, hot and greedy, seeming to draw straight from the lush button between her thighs. The edge of the storm curled over her. She could barely think for the rush of sensation.

Teeth grazed her throat. A hint of warning. Her body clamped around his, greedily clutching at his cock. Honoria gasped, her eyes widening sightlessly as the climax took her. She was drowning in a sea of need, barely aware of the feel of his hands on her, stroking her back, or the sudden, stiffening shudder as he collapsed against her.

Sweat gleamed on her skin. She felt lush and weak, her body throbbing in the aftermath. If *that* was why women fell into sin, then she could not blame them.

With a shuddering gasp, Blade lifted his head to

stare at her. He looked as though he'd never seen her before, or her like. "Bloody 'ell," he whispered in a tone not unlike awe.

Chapter 23

Blade stepped into the tub with Honoria in his arms and sank into the scented heat. The candles had burned low, and the light was muted. Little licks of steam curled off the surface of the water.

He felt whole. Renewed. And nowhere near sated. He wanted to take her again, to rut over her like a bloody selfish bastard, when she had never done this before.

Adjusting her in his arms, he frowned at the vanity that he'd just fucked her upon. Her dress, chemise, and stays were puddled in a heap on the floor. It had been all he could do not to take her again as he caught a glimpse of the rosy-tipped curve of her breasts, or the smooth plane of her stomach. Mastering the impulse, he'd picked her up and stepped into the tub before he could do something he'd regret.

Honoria snuggled against his chest, the long strands of her hair floating on the water. She seemed relaxed, but the previous scene between them was only a vignette of memories in his mind as the hunger overruled him. Had he hurt her? He'd given her pleasure, he knew that, but did she regret it?

"You shouldn't 'ave come to me tonight," he said gruffly.

She looked up. Water spiked her eyelashes together. "Why not?" A sudden smile darted across her lips. "I should have come to you a long time ago."

His breath caught. "You ain't sore?"

At that she looked down as though mentally cataloging the feel of her own body. The neat little slash at her throat had closed over, but his eyes dropped to the mark and stayed there.

"Yes. And no." She settled back into his arms, her back cradled against his chest. Blade shifted at the stir of desire that flushed through him. Her skin was slick against his. She had to feel the firmness of his cock against her buttocks.

"It was like nothing I've ever felt before."

"Aye," he murmured. *Me too.*

Taking up the washcloth, he suddenly busied himself with the soap. Honoria watched with lazy abandon, seemingly content to lie in his arms.

"You want to do it again, don't you?" she whispered.

He almost dropped the soap. "Not tonight."

"Liar." Christ, when had her voice turned to smoke? It liquefied his insides, his cock throbbing at the sound.

Fingers brushed against his thigh. "I don't think I would mind," she said tentatively.

Blade stroked the washcloth down her arm. He kissed her shoulder. "Do you want me to touch you?"

She stirred restlessly. Still innocent enough to feel embarrassment at her needs and desires.

He could do this, he thought. Give her pleasure

without the taking of it. Slowly he dragged the cloth across her chest, over the swell of her breast.

Honoria sucked in a gasp.

"Where do you want me to touch you?" he murmured, circling the rosy pucker of her nipple. "Here?" Soap gleamed on her skin. He dragged the cloth lower, into the depths of the water. Oil stirred on the surface, leaving shimmering little marks against her flushed skin. He slid the cloth between her thighs, burying a kiss in her hair as she arched her hips.

"*Oh*," she breathed.

"Or 'ere?" He dragged the cloth back up, rasping over the sweet flesh between her thighs.

Honoria stiffened, her breath coming in harsh little pants. "There."

Blade smiled. "But I ain't seen your lovely tits before." He abandoned the washcloth and reached for the small vial of scented oil that sat on the bath rim. "You're too impatient, luv. You don't know 'ow good it can be."

Easing the stopper out, he tipped the vial and splashed oil over her breasts. With his other arm, he dragged her higher so that she was exposed, the water sitting just beneath them.

Her hand caught his, fluttering, trying to decide whether to cover herself or not.

"There ain't no shame. Not 'tween us," he murmured into her ear, and put the vial down. Oil gleamed on her skin, the light refracting a thousand different colors. Blade smeared it across her gleaming chest, his hands cupping the slight swell of her breasts. Just a handful. Just enough. A purr started in his throat.

Her nipples were erect, practically begging for his mouth. He pinched them between his thumb and forefinger, the oil making them slip. Honoria's fingers dug into his thigh.

"Sweet lord," she whispered.

One hand sank into the wet curls between her legs. He wanted to feel her. The oil staining his fingers made it easy to slip within her, nestled in the burning heat. A cry tore from her throat. She was hopelessly vocal, ungiven to any thoughts of disguising her pleasure.

Every gasp, every writhing wriggle was bliss to him. He brought her to the edge with his fingertips and took her over, listening to her scream. The darkness stirred its hungry head, but Blade forced his eyes shut and curled her up in his arms.

"Shush," he whispered, pressing a kiss against the top of her head.

The sound from her lips was halfway between a sob and a pant. She melted against him in a boneless heap, the silk of her skin driving him to distraction.

A sudden rush of tenderness flooded through him, bittersweet with regret. He'd never given much thought to a wife. Though there had been many women through his bed over the years, and even friendships with quite a few, none had tempted him to dream of anything else. Until now.

When it was too late.

"I wish I'd found you earlier," he said. Before his CV levels became so high. How long did he have before the Fade took him? Months? A year? He could not subject her to that.

Honoria glanced over her shoulder at him, her skin

flushed with the heat of the water. A blush stained her cheeks. "I wish…I hadn't been such a fool," she replied. "I wish I'd come to you earlier. So much could have been avoided."

"Trust is somethin' as must be earned," he admitted.

Honoria turned her body in the tub and straddled his hips. Oil gleamed across her breasts as she rested her palms on his chest. Leaning forward, she nibbled at his mouth. "I was wrong," she admitted. "You're a good man."

Blade caught her wrists and smiled darkly. "Don't cast all your prejudices aside," he murmured. "I ain't good."

She smiled. "You're terribly wicked, of course."

"Sometimes." He drew her closer, then slid his hands down her body. His gaze followed, darkening. "And sometimes I'm just a bastard." To be thinking of taking her again, so soon.

Honoria sucked in a breath and flexed her hips. Blade stilled, his gaze meeting hers.

"Easy, luv. Don't stir the devil, or you'll 'ave to pay the consequences."

"I'm not sure I have any coin on me," she said, leaning closer and kissing the stubbled roughness of his jaw. "Do you think he would accept my favors instead?" A sultry whisper in his ear.

Blade groaned. "Bloody 'ell, Honor. Don't tease a man so."

"But it's so very exciting."

His cock grazed her tender flesh. Desire swept through him like a flood of heat. Christ, she made him feel warm all the way through, as though his blood weren't cold.

"Well, damn me, if you ain't got a touch o' the devil yourself," he muttered.

Another kiss. Against his throat. Her tongue sliding over the hollow of his collarbone. "I've been so tired and scared for so long. It's nice to feel safe." Her hands slid down his body. "To laugh. To tease you. When I'm with you, I don't think of anything else. I don't think I've felt this happy since before my father died."

He shifted uncomfortably. "Honoria." A husky warning. "You're 'bout three seconds away from bein' bent over that vanity and pumped."

She sat up, water streaming off her. Wide, innocent eyes met his and she brushed her hair behind her ears. The action thrust her breasts forward, her hips rocking against his. As he dug his hands into her thighs with a hiss, he saw the wicked little gleam in her eyes.

"So be it," Blade said, his voice harsh with need.

He dragged her out of the tub. Water poured off them, splashing across the tiles. Honoria's eyes widened as he started toward the doorway.

"Where are you going?" she asked, clinging to his shoulders.

"The bed," he replied curtly. "As I shoulda done weeks ago."

Chapter 24

A knock sounded at the door. Honoria lifted her head off the pillow, but Blade's hips and legs were thrown over her carelessly and she couldn't move.

"Wake up," she whispered, stroking his jaw. The prickle of his stubble tickled her fingers. He gave a rather inelegant snore.

A smile curled over her lips. He was exhausted. A fierce little part of her wanted to tell whoever was at the door to go away and leave him alone for the day, but she didn't dare. Who knew what news they brought?

Wriggling out from under him, she left him snoring on the bed and slipped into one of his robes before answering the door.

"Esme." Honoria slipped through the door, shutting it behind her. "Is it Rip? Is he well?"

Esme's chignon dangled from its pins and her eyes were bloodshot with weariness. "He's still sleeping. There's been no change."

"What is it, then?"

"There's an Echelon lord here. That man Barrons whom Blade is working with. He's got a company of metaljackets with him."

"I won't let him go out today. He's exhausted and there's nobody to watch his back."

Esme arched a brow. "You don't know Blade if you think he's going to stay abed and not do his duty."

"If he doesn't know about it, then he can't do it, can he?"

"And what about the Echelon lord?"

"Let me deal with him," she replied. "Is there anything that I can wear? My dress…it's wet."

A smile flickered over Esme's lips. "I won't ask how that happened. Stay here, I'll fetch you one of mine. It might fit if we pin it in."

Twenty minutes later Honoria was dressed, her hair pinned into a tight chignon. She descended the stairs toward the front parlor, where Leo was waiting.

The room was full of cobwebs and dust. Leo paced by the fireplace, his hands clasped behind his back. He wore unrelieved black—a leather carapace over his chest with obscenely carved muscles, and a pair of tight, black wool breeches thrust into his knee-high boots. The only sign of adornment was the heavy gold signet ring on his finger.

His eyes lit on her and he stopped in his tracks. "Honoria."

"Leo."

"You're well?"

"I shouldn't see why you care," she replied.

His eyes narrowed. "I don't. Particularly. But it's considered polite to start a conversation with such trivialities. How are Helena and Frederick?"

She stared at him, her fists clenching. "Charlie," she insisted. "We call him *Charlie*. And they're both well."

How she longed to simply tell him, but she didn't dare. Leo had never looked more like one of the Echelon, and if he betrayed Charlie's condition to the authorities, both she and Blade would be in trouble. It might be an excuse for the prince consort to send his metaljackets down upon the rookery, and this time he would have the law on his side.

"May I ask whether you are Blade's emissary, or whether he will be along shortly?"

"He's asleep," she replied. "The vampire attacked last night and killed one of his men, injuring another two."

Leo stilled. "And the vampire?"

"Got away," she replied.

"Where was it?" he asked. "If we can pinpoint its location or discover what's drawing it to the rookery, we might be able to set a trap."

An icy flush ran through her, tingling in her veins. "What do you mean, 'drawing it to the rookery'? Isn't that where the tunnels come out?"

"The tunnels run through this half of London," he replied. "It's unusual for it to keep coming here."

She rested her hands along the back of a chair, her fingers tapping. There had been one thing that was common in all of the attacks: her. That time in the street, it had tried to chase after her, practically ignoring Will and Blade, who were both bleeding. And then it had been near her home.

"Honey?" he asked, in the quiet voice he used to use when they were children and had signed a temporary truce.

"Don't call me that. That was Father's name for me. Don't you dare use it."

"You know something."

She met his gaze. "Perhaps."

"Share it with me," he said. "It might be a way to trap it before anyone else gets hurt."

Still she hesitated. How much could she trust Leo? Not very much, she concluded. "Why are you hunting it? Why you?"

"The prince consort sent me." His tone was abruptly curt, and he looked at her hair rather than meeting her eyes.

Honoria's fingers stilled on the chair. "You're lying. You never could look me in the eye when you lied."

His gaze shot to hers then. "And you know me so well?"

"Not at all," she admitted. "I used to think you were someone I could trust."

"You hated me as a child," he said incredulously. "And with good reason."

"I pitied you." Her voice softened. "I never hated you." A rueful twist of the lips. "Perhaps once or twice, when you put those mechanical spiders in my bed or cut off my doll's head and buried her."

Silence crackled in the room.

"Pitied me?"

Honoria looked at him. If things had been different, she would have accepted him as her half brother. But both her father and the duke of Caine had destroyed any chance of that.

"Because the duke despised you, and Father…Father was indifferent." It hurt to admit that anything her father had done was wrong. But she could not deny that he had not done his best by Leo. Memory flashed through her mind of a little boy with angelic blond curls—a little boy who looked a lot like Charlie at that age—watching her with hate in his eyes as she drew back from her father's hug. The boy had turned and run off, and that night little mechanical spiders were crawling through her sheets.

Only as she matured did she come to understand why she was being so persecuted. The boy who claimed he didn't care cared far too much.

"I don't know whether I preferred your dislike of me to your pity." He gave a bitter laugh. "Pity makes one sound so weak. But you haven't managed to divert me, alas. You know something about the vampire."

"I also haven't been diverted," she replied. "You lied to me about your reasons for hunting it. You have some personal investment in this, which leads me to believe that you know who it used to be."

Leo stared at her with considering eyes. "And now you ask me to trust *you*?"

"I wouldn't betray you," she replied.

"How refreshing. Forgive me if I can't quite trust the sentiment." Cynicism curled across his mouth. "I think, in this circumstance, that you might."

"Then we're at a quandary. Your information for mine."

"People might die, Honoria." .He took a step forward, looming over her. "Don't you give a damn?"

"They might either way. I don't know yet."

A frustrated sound rumbled in his throat, and he grabbed her arm. "Are you always this bloody argumentative?"

"The answer to that would be 'aye'." The words were softly spoken and came from behind.

Honoria turned to the voice. "Blade."

Blade took a step into the room, slowly surveying it. His dark gaze—blackened to that demonic obsidian—swept over Leo and her. She had the feeling that he noted precisely how closely the two of them stood to each other.

"You should be in bed," she said. She felt guilty, and she had not a damned reason in the world to feel so.

"Sorry to spoil your plans, sweet'eart."

"Plans?" Honoria took a step toward him. "And what, precisely, do you mean by that?"

"I don't know, exactly."

Blade pushed the door shut behind him using just his fingertips. His gaze narrowed on the hand Barrons held her with, and the ease of familiarity it showed. She had asked him to trust her, and after last night he'd finally felt as though she'd made some form of commitment to him. There was just one anomaly. Barrons.

"This isn't what it looks like," she murmured.

He assessed the situation again, taking a slow step forward. Every hair along the back of his neck rose as he caught the scent of Barrons's bay rum aftershave. The demon in him, the dark, hungry part he could never quite excise, wanted to go for Barrons, blades swinging. But...last night. It had to mean something.

Light streamed into the room, highlighting the pair of them within the golden rectangle of the window's sphere. It gleamed off Barrons's gilt-colored hair and the vibrant crimson of the dress that Honoria wore.

They made a handsome couple. Both young and slim, with creamy skin and dark brown eyes. He felt incredibly old all of a sudden, relegated to the shadows.

"I know what it looks like," he said, hurt burning within him. "And I want to trust you. But...bloody 'ell, Honoria...Would it kill you to give me one damned scrap of explanation?"

"You were sleeping. I thought it best to see to Leo myself. And I had questions for him regarding the vampire."

All of which he'd overheard before he entered. "I'm not askin' 'bout why you're 'ere."

Barrons took a careful step away from her. "I'm not poaching."

"I ain't askin' *you*."

Her fists were clenched, her lips thinned. And yet it wasn't anger that shone in her dark eyes but hurt. "You claim to trust me."

"I do. But Barrons just seems to keep comin' between us, and you won't tell me what 'e means to you." He couldn't help himself from giving way to frustration. Taking another step forward, he almost reached for her, almost grabbed her by the arm, but that was the angry, hungry part of himself. *No. She'll take fright.* His nostrils flared and he drank in the scent of her, still warm from his bed. She had cleansed with rose water, but the faint underlying tang of sex and blood stained her skin. "I'm tryin' very 'ard to trust you."

A little quiver went through her. "I wish that you could." Her voice was soft with hurt. "Leo?"

Barrons stiffened. "No."

Honoria turned on him. "I've had enough of

secrets. And I'm tired of protecting you when you don't seem to give a damn about any of us. Perhaps you've been too long in the Echelon not to recognize when a man doesn't give a damn about all of your little games. Blade won't use this information to harm you."

That depends.

"I don't trust anybody, and with good reason. Or have you forgotten who infected me in the first place?" Barrons glared at her.

She blanched. "He didn't mean it. He was trying to prevent you from succumbing to the disease."

"He was trying to test his bloody vaccine," Barrons snapped. "He didn't care whether I succumbed or not. I was never anything but another test subject to him."

"Who the 'ell are you talkin' 'bout?" Blade demanded.

Both of them looked at him with thick-lashed dark eyes. The expression in them was almost identical. Just a moment, and then she turned away, the angle of her face changing the perspective. Yet he couldn't forget what he'd seen. *Christ Jaysus*. He froze in his tracks.

"You're 'is sister," he said in an incredulous tone. "You're 'is bloody sister."

The blood drained out of Barrons's face, but Honoria slumped in relief. "Yes," she whispered. "Half sister. Leo and I share a father but little else. I'm the only one who knows. Lena and Charlie have never met him."

Blade's mind was racing. There was little similarity between their features, only a certain look about the eyes. No wonder he'd missed it. Charlie shared more in resemblance to Barrons, which would probably strengthen as he matured. "Who's Barrons's father?

The duke or Artemus Todd?" Then he answered his own question. There was no other reason to hide this. "It's Todd, ain't it?"

That's why she'd gone to Barrons for help before she came to him. The thought almost brought a smile to his lips. He had been worried about nothing.

Barrons shot Honoria a dark look. "What are you going to do with the information?" he asked Blade.

Blade rocked back on his heels. A little bubble of euphoria burned within him. He felt like sweeping her up and swinging her around in his arms. She was his. All his.

"Nothin', most like," he shrugged. "After we catch the vampire, I don't reckon I'll see much o' you. Or give a damn."

"I find that hard to believe," Barrons replied flatly.

"You would, wouldn't you?" Barrons was a blue blood to his soles. He would never understand that Blade simply wanted to be left alone with his little family…and Honoria.

As if uncertain how to take the words, Barrons glanced between them. "I do have a confession to make. But I'll tell you. Only you," he said, his gaze locking on Blade's.

Honoria stiffened, but Blade held up a hand, stalling her. "Wait for me in me rooms."

"Don't think you can order me about like one of your…your…"

"Thralls?" he suggested, with a slight arch of the brow. Color flooded through her cheeks, but he wasn't about to let her off the hook that easy. They needed to talk. Last night had done a great deal, but it was evident that they needed to have words as well.

He could sense her stiffening, putting up those walls that she protected herself with. Hell, after hearing Barrons's confession, he could almost understand why she had those walls in the first place. Her own brother barely gave a damn about her circumstances.

Blade stroked his hand across the small of her back, trying to soothe her. He leaned close and whispered in her ear. "Please." A slight bending of the pride to ease her own. She would have to learn to yield too, but he could do this for her.

Honoria's eyes softened and she put a hand on his wrist tentatively. He could almost see the thoughts spinning behind those liquid, dark eyes. She would never be easy to manage, but he found that he liked that. A man could weary of a woman who never challenged him. Honoria would be a constant puzzle.

"I'll wait for you," she said quietly.

He brushed his lips across hers, startling her. "Thank you."

She turned and started for the door, yet something stopped her from leaving without saying a word to her half brother.

"Be careful," she said. "I know Father would never accept you as his, but you were a fool not to realize that I would have opened my arms to you. If you'd ever let me."

Then she left the room, leaving Barrons staring after her with a slightly stunned expression on his face.

Chapter 25

BLADE CLIMBED THE STAIRS WITH A HEAVY TREAD. Damn the man. His mind was reeling with the depths of the confession that Barrons had just shared with him.

Far too quickly, Blade found himself in front of his own door. Barrons and his men could wait in the yard. This was nothing to rush, and it was the least the bloody bastard could do.

"I know who the vampire is," the other man had said with quiet conviction. "You have to understand, I thought it was justice. Todd was preparing to vaccinate himself with the specimen he'd found that worked. He'd waited all those years to make sure it was effective when he'd bloody injected me with a trial. And so I switched the samples. He injected himself with the same vaccine he'd trialed on me."

Blade's breath had caught. "Sounds more like revenge than justice."

Barrons's composure had broken down, his eyes wild with anger and pride—and strangely enough, grief. "I never wanted this. He promised that it would prevent me from turning when I reached my fifteenth year and the blood rites. He promised."

A part of Blade understood. He wouldn't have chosen this life with the craving virus either. A lifetime of hunger, of watchfulness. And at the very end, the inevitable spiral toward madness as the vampiric part of his nature took over. "You're the duke of Caine's 'eir. Surely he'd 'ave demanded that you become a blue blood." In the world of the Echelon it was considered not a curse but a blessing. Power, strength, invulnerability toward mortal concerns. The cost of it was minute compared to the power to be gained.

"I am nothing more than my father's pawn." Barrons gave a bitter laugh. "Both of them."

Blade considered it. "You know she'll never forgive you for this."

A nonchalant shrug, as if the man didn't care. But why, then, had he threatened Blade with death if he didn't treat Honoria well? A liar, both to himself and others.

"You poor bastard," he'd murmured. What a bloody mess. And there was worse to consider. "The boy. Charlie. He's got the cravin'. Honoria couldn't understand..." Blade raked a fist through his hair, knotting it in frustration. "The vaccine worked for 'er and Lena." He'd met Barrons's eyes then. "But not for the boy. Or the father, so it seems. Guess the boy got the wrong vaccine too."

The words had taken Barrons like a punch to the throat. He'd ground his teeth and turned away. "Fuck." Slamming a fist against the wall, he had ignored the plaster dust that rained over his shoulders. "Fuck!" Shoulders shaking with fury—or perhaps something else—he'd pounded the wall until his fists were thick with the scent of blood.

Honoria might have forgiven Barrons for what he'd done to her father, Blade now thought, but she would never forgive him for doing the same thing to Charlie.

How to tell her? Or *should* he tell her?

"Curse 'im to 'ell," Blade muttered, pushing open the door to his room.

Light streamed in, gilding Honoria with gold. It picked out faint mahogany highlights in her coffee-brown hair and kissed the creamy curve of her cheek as she lifted worried eyes to his. Clasping her hands in her lap, she composed herself, but the scent of fear lingered.

"It wasn't my secret to tell," she blurted. "I've never breathed a word of it. Not to anyone. If they found out, they'd destroy him. And I didn't realize you were jealous of him." Color washed through her cheeks and she dropped her gaze to his feet. "I told you he meant nothing to me." There was a faintly accusing edge to her voice.

Blade took a step toward her. "Aye. I know what you tole me." He paused in front of her, reaching out to stroke her hair. He couldn't help himself. Honoria looked up, her breath in her throat. She was so beautiful. And his heart was hers. Had been from the moment he started chipping away at that damn wall of ice she hid behind. But was she his?

Blade traced the curve of her jaw, a sigh easing through his throat. Honoria cupped her hand over his, pressing his palm against her cheek. She turned her face to press her lips to his skin, looking up at him as if to gauge his reaction.

"I thought you would be angry," she admitted.

"You were tryin' to protect your family—"

A scowl twisted her eyebrows. "He's not—"

"'E is," he corrected. "You can tell yourself what you want, but your first instinct is to protect 'im." He knelt on the bed, pushing her onto her back.

Honoria tumbled onto the mattress, staring up at him. Blade straddled her hips. Sinking his face into the curve of her throat, he clenched his fist in a handful of her hair and breathed in, filling his nose with the scent of her body. A little gasp caught in her throat, and she pressed hesitant hands to his shoulders.

Blade kissed her neck, sliding his fingertips down over the silk of her bodice. He found her nipple and stroked concentric circles around it, slowly tightening the circles until his fingertips barely circled it. Honoria arched beneath him, catlike.

"It's one of the things I love about you," he said, burrowing his face in her hair. "You're proud and stubborn, but you're so fierce when it comes to your family." Looking up, he met her startled gaze. "Let down your guard, Honor. Let me in. Let me love you." He kissed her lips, tasted the sweetness of her breath. "Trust me. I won't ever 'urt you."

A part of him waited, holding his breath for her reply, but it never came. She captured his face in her hands and dragged his mouth to hers hungrily. The taste of her was intoxicating. Her tongue met his—a slow, sensual slide that mimicked the movement of their hips.

His cock ached. Honoria rocked against him, her molten core shielded from him by layers and layers of silk and crinoline. He could feel the press of her stays and the hoop of her pannier crushed between their bodies. Sinking his hand into the wealth of fabric, he yanked her skirts up, seeking soft, smooth skin.

Her thighs trembled beneath his touch. Little gasps punctuated the air until he was whispering, "Easy now, luv, easy." Fingers sliding over her garters, over the smooth, naked skin of her inner thighs, he found her heat through the silk of her undergarments. It clung to her, wet and dewy as he took her mouth in another blistering kiss.

Honoria's hands came up, sinking into his hair. He felt her thighs part, felt her give in to the teasing tickle of his fingers. Sneaking between the slit of her drawers, he groaned hard and flexed his hips at the feel of wet-slick flesh.

She wanted him. God help him, he was lost. It didn't matter if she could never feel the same way he did, but he was too damned selfish to let her go.

She tore her mouth away. "What about…about Leo?" Breathless. "Won't he be waiting?"

"'E can damn well wait." Blade stroked his fingers through her lush wetness. Honoria shuddered, burying her face against his throat. She licked him, tasting the sweat of his flesh, and he turned and bit her ear, grinding his teeth against the smooth skin of her lobe.

Honoria cried out and he stiffened.

Too much. She was only new to this. He would scare her if he unleashed his full passion upon her. Blade froze, trying to rein in his growing hunger. His vision dipped to gray—then back again—but Honoria was grasping, grinding her body against his fingers.

"Easy." He stilled his touch. The vein in his temple throbbed. "Damn it, Honor. Give me a moment, or I'll be ruttin' on you like a beast."

Their eyes met. He was surprised at the determined gleam in hers. "I'm not fragile. As I believe last night proved."

He withdrew his fingers from between her legs, earning a sigh of frustration. "Compared to me you are." He pressed his forehead against hers, trying to regain some control. He was damnably close to taking her.

Grasping her hips, he rolled them until she was straddling him. Her eyes opened wide and she rested her hands on his chest. In this position he could touch, but he couldn't get at her throat without lifting off the bed. It might be enough to remind himself.

"I trust you," she said, that determined glint darkening her eyes. A rumble of satisfaction sounded in his throat as she slid her hands over his shirt.

"I don't," he countered, lying flat and still as her hands explored his chest. She started plucking at the buttons, starting with the ones near his throat. Blade lay still, expectant, his body quivering as she went lower, and lower…

When she had finished, she pulled each edge apart roughly, pinning his arms within the sleeves. Desire fueled her expression as she placed a hesitant hand on his chest. "I like to look at you. At your body. I've often wondered what it would feel like to touch it." A hint of color bloomed in her cheeks. "I've wondered what you would taste like."

It nearly undid him. He stopped breathing. Perhaps this hadn't been a good idea. His emotions were too raw. And hearing her say that shot his control all to hell. His vision flickered again, and he knew his eyes were darkening, turning black with hunger. He gripped her thighs in his hands. "We 'ave to stop."

"Whatever for?"

He forced her to meet his gaze and see what she was doing to him. "I can't control meself this mornin'. I'm on edge. It's dangerous."

"You wouldn't hurt me."

"I wouldn't be gentle," he snapped. "Or kind."

Honoria slowly lowered her head, her tongue darting out to flicker over his nipple. "Yes, you would," she replied, and then, incredibly, she bit him.

Blade sucked in a breath. The look in her eyes was curious. Experimental. Dangerous.

"We 'ave to talk." He caught her wrists, restraining her.

"Later." She nibbled her way across his chest to his other nipple, nuzzling it with the warmth of her tongue.

His cock ached. Blade couldn't stop himself from thrusting his hips against her. Acres of skirts covered him, and he slid his hands up underneath, through the layers of hoops and petticoats.

There was something sensual about being fully dressed. With buttons to her chin and wrists, Honoria looked like the most modest of women. Even as she licked her way down his stomach, her tongue dipping into his navel.

Her gaze dropped shyly as she reached the edge of his waistband. Blade smiled. "Aye, lass. You ain't stoppin' now, are you?"

She shot a look of challenge at him. Then her shoulders deflated. "I'm not quite sure…what to do."

Blade took her hands and guided them to the buttons on his breeches. Her nimble fingers darted over them and his cock sprang free, proud and jutting slightly to the left.

"Just do as you was," he purred.

"You mean…" She stared at his cock, her eyes wide.

Blade took her hands again and wrapped them around him. "Aye."

A part of it was challenge. A dare. Wondering if she would take him up on it. Thought ticked behind her dark eyes. And then she lowered her face and pressed a kiss to the patch of smooth skin just above.

"You're a wicked man," she whispered, her hands growing bolder.

Blade slid a hand through her hair. "I want your mouth on me." His voice was edged with just the slightest touch of frustration. Hell, he wanted more than that. He wanted to thrust deep into her throat, to feel the satiny slide of her tongue on him.

And then it was on him. His eyes shot open. Honoria's tongue darted out and tasted him, her eyes filled with a kind of wondering curiosity. "You like this?"

He groaned, head flung back as her hot little mouth worked over the crown of him. "God. *Yes.*"

The tentativeness of her touch grew stronger. A little smile toyed around her lips as she learned what pleased him. "Whoever would have thought?" she murmured. And then her mouth swallowed him whole.

It was sheer, blinding ecstasy. He slid his hands through her hair, guiding her to take more of him. His balls tightened and he ground his teeth together. As much as he wanted to come in her mouth, he wanted to be inside her body more.

"Come." He hauled her up abruptly, her spill of skirts tumbling all over him.

Honoria fell forward, onto her hands. "What are you doing?"

He rifled beneath her skirts, tearing her drawers clean off her. Honoria gasped. "Blade!"

She was wet. And hot. And luscious.

Blade shifted and then impaled himself inside her.

The look on her face was almost comical. A hint of shock. Eyes widening as she tried this new sensation and found it pleasing. He growled under his breath and caught her hips. "Like this."

It took her a moment to realize what he wanted. And then she was rocking heartily. He loved watching her face, her expression, so open and full of sensual curiosity. He kissed her fingertips and started unbuttoning the strict silk of her bodice.

Layers upon layers. He tugged them all down until her stays and chemise sat beneath her breasts, thrusting them high. Color stained her throat.

"You are so terribly wicked," she said breathlessly.

"I think you like it." He scooped her skirts back, until he could see the thick, dark curls of her quim. "Do you want to be naughtier?"

Her color deepened. But she didn't say no.

He took her right hand in his and licked her fingers. Then lowered them to the swollen, blush-pink slickness of her clitoris.

Honoria gasped, throwing her head back in wicked abandon. Her hot little body clenched around him and

Blade felt himself tighten. He was close. Incredibly, bloody close. A prickle of excitement flushed his entire body. God, it was excruciatingly delicious. And it was with the woman he loved.

The thought stirred him to frantic movement. Showing her how to ride her own fingers, he tugged her hips closer, thrusting up to meet her. He longed to simply close his eyes and throw his head back in pleasure, but he couldn't take his eyes from her. He wanted each moment, each image of her, captured forever in his memory. From the flushed pink of her cheeks, to her slightly unfocused eyes, or the way she caught her lip between her teeth in unself-conscious abandon. In this moment he saw what might have been between them if his CV levels weren't so bloody high.

The pressure of time weighed heavily upon him. He dragged her closer, kissing her, capturing her whole body to his and holding her there, as though afraid something would tear her away.

Sobs shook her and her body clenched his hungrily. He felt the moment the climax took her and gave himself up to the hot pulsing of her sex.

It took minutes, hours, years, to come back to himself. Honoria shuddered against his shoulder, her entire body boneless and collapsed over his like a wilted flower. He was so breathless he couldn't speak. He let his hands communicate his feelings, stroking her damp back and clutching her tight.

Slowly, Honoria lifted her head. Her eyes were dazed and shadowed with lush pleasure. "Wicked, wicked man," she whispered, and pressed her lips against his throat, a gentle, affectionate caress that made him slightly uncomfortable.

Blade rolled her onto her back, spilling from her body. Honoria laughed softly, half drunk on pleasure as she stretched, careless of the fact that her breasts and legs were exposed to the world.

He tugged his breeches closed and knelt over her. A certain seriousness settled upon him. "We need to talk."

Her eyes sobered. "About what Leo told you?"

Blade opened his mouth to speak...How to tell her? *I think I only have months...at most...*before the color started leeching from his body. A guttural groan died in his throat. He couldn't. Instead he drew her hand to his mouth and kissed her palm.

"Yes," he lied. "It's 'bout your brother's confession."

Honoria tugged her bodice up and straightened her skirts. "Well?"

"It's 'bout...it's 'bout your father," he said nervously, and then he told her everything.

Chapter 26

Blade opened the pressurized air dart rifle and stared down the barrel. "You use these to hunt blue bloods?"

"Only rogues," Barrons admitted, resting one foot on the step and leaning on it. "The dart has some sort of toxin in it that partially paralyzes a blue blood for nearly ten minutes. We've managed to refine it so that the steam buildup doesn't alter the chemical state of the toxin. It's highly accurate at fifty feet."

"Aye." Blade shoved the dart back into the chamber. "Don't expect this to 'old the vampire long."

One of Barrons's eyebrows disappeared under the tumbled curls across his forehead. "You've heard of the toxin?"

"Your sister knocked me on me arse with it. Lasted 'bout five, six minutes. She thinks the time you're down's got somethin' to do with the level o' CV in your blood. If so, you might get a minute or less with a vampire."

Laughter broke from Barrons's lips. "Good God, I should have liked to have seen that."

"Stick 'round," Blade said as he shot him a filthy look. "She gets wind o' you at the moment, and you might get some first'and experience with it."

Barrons sobered.

A head popped around the door of the audience chamber. Jasper Lynch examined them coolly. "Are we ready?"

Blade patted the air dart rifle. "Let's get to it, then."

The score of metaljackets stood motionless in the street, an eerie sight. Beside them, snorting steam like truffle pigs, was a pair of Earthshakers. With the heavy armadillo plates that overlapped their bodies and a spade-like appendage at their snouts that could clear a tunnel in minutes, they'd been invaluable so far. Their handler was sitting on the step beside them, fiddling with the frequency device that controlled them.

The cadre of Nighthawks stood almost as silent. They obeyed Jasper Lynch with an alacrity Blade might have almost envied and spoke rarely to either him or Barrons. Blade had watched them move like liquid through the tunnels and concluded that if it ever came to war, he'd rather have them on his side than as his enemy.

The sound of pattering feet on the stairs made him glance back at the warren. The next second a small, ragged shape barreled out, dressed in an assortment of Lark's body armor and breeches. Honoria's dark hair had been shoved up under a cockney lad's cap, and soot was smeared across her cheeks. Her dark eyes met Blade's, and her chin lifted slightly in challenge.

On her heels was Tin Man, wearing a slightly guilty expression. He shrugged helplessly.

"No," Blade snapped, glancing around at the blue bloods around them. Was she bloody insane? The guild had her friggin' poster splayed all over their quarters with a hefty price on it.

Barrons stopped to see what the commotion was then blinked. "Hon..." He shut his mouth abruptly. "Your servant?" he asked Blade in a nonchalant tone.

"Who's goin' to get a good whippin' in a moment," Blade growled under his breath and strode toward her. Grabbing her by the arms, he glared down into her dirty face. "Are you bleedin' mad?"

"Will and Rip're injured," Honoria replied. "I ain't allowin' you to go alone." The accuracy with which she mimicked his speech was almost eerie.

Aware that there were too many ears around them, Blade dragged her into the shadows of the doorway. "This ain't the rookery, luv. This is Undertown we're enterin'. And we're huntin' a vampire."

"I ain't lettin' you go alone."

He looked around. "This isn't safe for you."

Honoria leaned closer, her body pressing against his and her lips to his ear. Damn his soul if he couldn't help reacting.

"You're not the only reason I'm here," she whispered. "He was my father, damn it." Tears glistened in her eyes. "I know you think I'm mad, but the last time we met, he begged for my help. I asked Lena about the incident. She said the vampire only attacked when Will grabbed her. It never tried to hurt her. Or me."

"Maybe it 'ad other things to worry 'bout," he snarled. "Maybe it were more concerned with killin' me men before it could rip you apart." Yet an image rose unbidden of that night on the rooftops, when he faced the vampire with Honoria's gun in his hand and didn't dare shoot. There had been plenty of chance for it to kill her if it had wanted to.

Her argument was rational. And he did need someone to watch his back. But not her. The very thought of putting her into danger made his gut curl.

"No," he repeated. "You ain't goin', and that's final."

Undertown was nothing like what she'd expected. Splashing along in Blade's wake, Honoria couldn't help a shudder. There'd been a number of gruesome discoveries today, most of them shielded by Blade. Yet even as he shielded her, she could see the faint horror on the men's faces and hear their swift intake of breath.

Blade was angry with her, but at least she'd won the argument. If he wouldn't take her with him, she would simply follow. Threatening to tie her down, he'd been very nearly speechless when she shrugged and asked him how long he thought that would hold her. If the situation weren't so dire, she'd have been given to laughter at the look on his face.

Blade's long strides ate up the ground, despite the foot-deep water they waded through. Fingering her father's pistol, she scurried in his wake.

A steady *thrum-thrum-thrum* started to drone overhead. Honoria glanced up. "What's that noise?"

"The draining factories," Leo muttered. "We're directly beneath them. That noise is probably the steam engines on the filtration machines."

The tall, grim man who led the Nighthawks held up his hand with a closed fist. They all stopped in their tracks, and Honoria peered over Blade's shoulder.

"What is it?" she whispered.

The guild master shot her a hawkish glare, his eyes hunting the shadows.

Blade grabbed her by the wrist and shoved her to the side, hovering over her protectively. "Be still, luv," he murmured. "It's too quiet in 'ere. And somethin' stinks."

You mean, apart from the usual? Her nostrils had shut down long ago.

Someone lit a flare stick. It hissed to life with a phosphorescent glow, and curses lit the tunnel as they all tried to adjust to the glare.

Suddenly Blade clapped a hand to his ears, his teeth bared in pain. The other men around them echoed his motions.

"What's wrong?" she shouted.

Tin Man stared at her over Blade's bent back. And then the path of his gaze drifted over her shoulder and his eyes widened.

Honoria spun on her heel. There was a flash of corpse white, and then one of the Nighthawks went down with a scream, the one holding the flare stick. The stick splashed into the water, still burning beneath the dirty sludge. The immediate phosphorescence dimmed.

"Get 'er out of 'ere," Blade snapped to Tin Man, shoving her roughly into his arms.

The scream cut off abruptly, and then several pistols retorted with brief, spitting flares of light.

Honoria's hand was shaking as she drew her pistol.

Tin Man hauled her into a side tunnel, the hook on his hand held defensively.

"Blade!" she screamed.

He was lost in the shadows and the melee. Pistol fire barked in the main tunnel, and men shouted in confusion.

"It's too narrow in 'ere! Stop firin'!"

Honoria stilled. That was Blade's voice. She pushed forward, evading Tin Man's grip as she peeked around the corner. There were floating corpses everywhere. Blade's pale hair came into view, dragging a screaming, mangled body back to safety. Leo was at his side, holding a hand against his thigh and limping.

The tunnels ahead intersected. The vampire had lain in wait for them, using the narrow depths to its advantage. Where was the metaljackets' handler? They stood still and silent, the bluish glow in the empty sockets of their eyes powered down to a mute flicker of light.

With the shadows and the slowly dying flame of the flare stick, she could barely see. Only by following the sounds of screaming could she track the vampire.

She saw Blade's body stiffen as he looked up, and then he was dropping the body he was dragging and reaching for his knife. Leo moved to grapple the white blur streaking toward them but stumbled in the knee-deep water.

Before Honoria knew what she was doing, she was running forward and screaming, "No!"

The creature hit Blade, who staggered backward, his serrated knife punching into his attacker's side. A high-pitched squeal echoed at the edge of hearing, and

Blade flinched as the sound cut through him. He went down with a splash.

She couldn't use the pistol without hitting him. Tucking it at her belt, she threw herself at the creature and screamed in its face. Somehow she managed to halt the deadly strike of its slashing claws.

Filmy white eyes met hers. The stink of it was strong enough to cut through the stench of the tunnels. She could taste it in her mouth, thick and rancid, like old grease.

A backhand caught her by surprise. She went sailing through the air, her body crumpling against the wall of the tunnel. A shaft of pain went through her shoulder, and her head rocked at the impact. In the dim light she could see the creature's hand strike down into the body beneath it. *Blade.*

"Father! No!" Stumbling forward once more, she caught at the rigid tendons in the vampire's wrist and pulled futilely.

Blade's face came out of the water with a gasp, blood spreading through the swampy muck.

"I can help you! I can help you!" Honoria yelled, tears streaming down her face. The hand beneath hers suddenly shifted.

Blade dragged himself against the wall, cradling his side. Their eyes met and Honoria deliberately put herself between him and the vampire.

"Don't," he gasped. "Run, you bloody fool woman."

So close. The vampire's nostrils sniffed the air as it turned to face her. She let its arm go, drawing the pistol from her belt. "I can help you." A whisper.

Honoria stared at the creature who had once been

her father. There was no resemblance now, though she looked for it. The irony was cruel: Her proud, anti–blue blood father would have hated this end of his existence.

Honoria's hand shook as she lifted the pistol. The vampire quivered as it stared at her, head drifting side to side as it fought the base hunger of its nature.

The vampire tried to say something. Its lips stretched over vicious, needle-sharp teeth stained with blood. *Please.*

Its hand caught hers and dragged the pistol to its forehead.

"Lena and Charlie miss you," she sobbed. "And so do I."

Gritting her teeth, her eyes hot with tears, Honoria leaned forward and pressed her lips against its cheek. "I love you," she whispered. And then leaned back and pulled the trigger.

Explosive sound ricocheted through the tunnel. Blood sprayed, splattering across Leo's face, and then the headless body slumped into the water, twitching.

Honoria's hand dropped to her side. She could barely hold the pistol, she was trembling so hard. A glimmer of maggot-pale flesh gleamed in the dim light and then slowly sank beneath the surface of the water. He was gone. Again.

Don't think. Just don't think. Tears spilled down her cheeks as she stared. *Father…*

"He's at peace, Honor," Leo said.

"No thanks to you!" she spat, then gave him her back.

Blade leaned against the tunnel wall, struggling to sit up, his hand clapped to his side. There was blood all over him, some of it the viscous black of her father's, the rest thick and blue.

Struggling to his side, she went to her knees. She could barely see for the tears that blinded her, but she managed to wipe them with her grimy sleeve. This was no time to fall apart. Blade needed her. "Let me have a look," she said.

"She'll 'eal," Blade said. The look in his eyes suddenly darkened. "You bloody fool. What the 'ell did you think you were doin'?"

"Saving you," she replied, rocking back on her heels at the sudden vehemence in his voice.

"I told you to—"

"I don't give a damn!" she yelled. "I don't care how many times you tell me to run, I won't leave you behind!"

"Yes, *you will*," he hissed. A grimace flickered over his face as he tried to sit up. "Damn you, Honoria. Seein' you like that…in danger…it kills me."

"He wasn't going to hurt me."

"'Ow do you know?"

"He was my father."

Blade's face darkened. "And Charlie's your brother. And me? I'm your lover. You don't think either of us could kill you? You don't think there's an 'ungry part of us that ain't seen you as nothin' more 'n blood? That's wanted to 'urt you?" To her surprise, pain twisted his expression. "I would die a thousand times over to see you safe. Even from meself."

"And I will never walk away," she whispered, reaching out to press her palm against his cheek. There was a sudden thickness in her throat. "Maybe I'm wrong. Maybe it's foolish. But I can't help how I feel."

A strangled sound came from Blade's throat. He pressed her hand against his mouth and kissed it, his cool lips gliding over the palm.

A hydraulic hiss suddenly swept through the tunnel. Both of them looked up as the squad of metal-jackets took a sudden step forward in eerie formation. Honoria held Blade's hand, hovering protectively over him.

"What the hell…?" Leo broke off as the first metaljacket engaged its firing arm, pointing it directly at him. He froze, the blood burns from the vampire's blood on his face standing out in stark relief.

Honoria's breath caught as another metaljacket aimed at them. Leaning forward, she tried to cover as much of Blade's body as she could, though the Spitfire's fireball could consume them both easily.

Blade caught at her arm. "Don't."

A man stepped out of the shadows. The metal-jackets' handler. "I thought I recognized your face," he said. "You're the girl from the bounty sheet. The ten-thousand-pound girl." Avarice gleamed in his pale eyes as he examined the scene. "Nobody move. You." He gestured toward Honoria. "Come here."

"Sterne." A cool voice came out of the shadows, and Jasper Lynch stepped forward, bleeding heavily. "What are you about? Why didn't you attack the vampire?"

"I did as commanded, Guild Master." Sterne's smile was vicious.

She could barely think with the trauma of events, yet the words sent her mind into a whirl. "Nobody was ever to make it out, were they?" she asked. "The vampire would be dead and Leo and Blade with it.

Three of the prince consort's enemies gone in one fell swoop with him left to cry false tears over the fallen 'heroes.'" The thought sickened her, but she knew only too well how the Echelon worked.

Leo sucked in a breath, fury sliding harsh shadows over his face.

"Don't." Honoria held out a hand to stop him. "It's futile."

Blade caught at her fingers. "What are you about?" His voice was low and desperate, his gaze searching hers.

A fresh wave of tears scalded her cheeks. She stroked his face, fingers pausing on his lips. "Please look after Lena and Charlie." Leaning close, she kissed his lips, but he caught her hands, dragging her face up, shaking his head.

"No. No!"

"He only wants me," she replied.

Blade glanced at the towering metal legion. "We're dead anyways."

"Then use the water," she whispered and pressed her pistol into his hands.

Black bled through his eyes. He was going to fight. Honoria took the choice away and stepped toward the handler.

"I'll come for you," Blade snapped as she stepped within reach of Sterne.

"*Water,*" she mouthed, meeting both his and Leo's eyes.

"You won't be going anywhere," Sterne said as he grabbed her and dragged her behind the metaljackets.

There was a little click and then a roar as the Spitfire's jets fired. Light blinded her, burning her eyeballs with the fury of its heat. The tears on her cheeks dried instantly, and her hair whipped behind her like a blazing corona. "No!"

When she could see again, the tunnel was scorched with thick black streaks of soot. There was no sign of the three men. Honoria's heart pounded and she started forward, but Sterne grabbed her wrist.

"Don't give me any trouble," he hissed, grinding a knife into her spine. "And start walking."

Honoria shot one last glance over her shoulder as the hulking metaljackets fell into step behind them. It might have been her imagination, but she thought she saw a ripple move on the surface of the water. *Please.*

A sob caught in her throat, but she swallowed it ruthlessly. The weight of emotion sitting on her shoulders was enough to drown her if she let it. She had to think. Had to keep her head.

For she knew that she was finally heading toward the confrontation she'd been fleeing from for months. She was now in the hands of Vickers.

Chapter 27

Water dripped somewhere in the darkness. Fire burned in Honoria's hands. They'd been bound behind her so tightly that she'd long ago lost feeling in them. Occasionally she tried to wriggle her fingers, but it only shot a flash-fire of pain through them.

A black velvet hood covered her head, the golden tasseled ropes tied just tight enough around her throat for her to be aware of them. Though she had not seen him, she knew it to be Vickers's personal touch. He overlooked nothing.

Honoria was afraid, not of darkness, but of the wait. The anticipation. Vickers had trained her body so well during the years that he'd stalked her. Goosebumps erupted along her flesh, and sweat trembled on her forehead. Each panicked breath she took was hot and refracted back into her face from the hood. She felt as if she were slowly suffocating inside it.

Fight it. She closed her eyes as a hiccuping gasp leapt up her throat. *Don't let him win.*

But how was she ever to escape *this*? He would

never let his guard down again, and the Ivory Tower's dungeons were inescapable—for a mere human.

Tears leaked from her eyes, burning a trail down her cheeks. The only consolation was that Charlie and Lena were safe. Blade would protect them. She couldn't have left them in better hands. That is, if he had survived.

Don't, she told herself. She had lost her father. She could not bear to think of losing Blade too. He had to have survived. There had been that ripple in the water. And he was strong and clever and…injured. A groan choked in her throat. *Don't.*

The thought of him alive was the only thing keeping her sane in this hellhole. Unless Blade ruined it all. Unless he came for her.

Honoria ground her teeth together. He wouldn't. Though he might have escaped the tower once, he could never find his way back in and get her out safely. She'd seen the guards that Vickers had placed. Not only the silent metaljackets but a handful of Nighthawks too. Blade wouldn't do something so foolish, would he?

She knew the answer to that and it scared her. "Don't come," she whispered, as if he would be able to hear the words. "Leave me here to rot, I beg of you."

"Ah, but you're not going to rot, my dear. Not yet…not until I've had my way with you."

The words tore a gasp from her throat and she sat up straight, hunting for any further sound. He was here with her. Vickers was *here* and she'd never even heard the door open. How long had he been watching her, enjoying the sight of her struggles?

Boot heels crunched on the gravel and grit that covered the floors. Deliberately, she was certain. The thought oddly stirred her anger. Damn him. If he thought she was going to cower before him like she had years ago, he was mistaken. She'd been younger then and unused to a life of hardship. Her six months in the rookery had been a trial of fire. She had faced Slasher gangs and a vampire, starvation and poverty. In comparison, Vickers's mind games suddenly seemed incredibly petty.

"Have you nothing to say to that, pretty?" Humor laced his voice. She heard the distinct sound of his snuff tin opening and then a snort.

Honoria said nothing. This time she would not play his games. He could do whatever he liked to her body, but he could never touch Charlie, Lena, or Blade. She was strong enough to survive anything he did to her, even if the thought made her skin crawl. He could not break her. He *would* not.

A hand came out of nowhere, tugging at the cords around her throat. She flinched, but as he jerked the hood off, the cool air of the dungeon touched her face, taking away the suffocating cloy of her own breath. The room stank of moldy straw and urine, but she had smelled worse in the 'Chapel.

Vickers stepped back, wearing pristine white and gold from head to toe. Golden tassels clung to his boots and his breastplate gleamed. Powder from his hair flavored the air with its sickly sweet scent, and there was a rapier sheathed at his belt. A powerful figure. Even a handsome figure if one did not know the man. Unlike many of the dukes, he had kept himself trim and fit over the years with daily bouts with the sword.

He smiled at her once he saw he had her attention. "I told you I would find you. You can run and hide, my pretty. But I will always find you."

Silence became her greatest strength. She forced her expression to a placid contentedness, as though she were merely waiting for him to leave. And then she stared through him.

A flicker of anger swam through the depths of his icy gray eyes. She had won the first bout. The next one would be bloody, for she knew him too well, but she would not yield.

"Your arrogance always was your downfall. It was the first thing that caught my eye all those years ago."

A knife appeared in his hand. Honoria stiffened then forced her body to relax. He would not bloody her, not today. This was to scare her. Vickers preferred the slow build of terror.

"I thought it was my relative youth and naïveté," she said. "You never did like to confront someone who could fight back."

"And now you think you *can* fight back?" Vickers said with a laugh. "Ah, my dear, you always were my favorite. I think I shall remember you the most when you are nothing but dust and ashes."

Her heart thundered in her ears. "Will you visit my grave too? Will I haunt you too?"

His eyes narrowed as though he wasn't quite certain what she referred to. "Perhaps I will forget you instead. Like all the others."

"*All?*" she asked. "Surely you are mistaken? You

have not forgotten all of your victims. There is one you'll never forget."

A slight tension was visible in his shoulders where before there had been none. "Ah, the mongrel has told you of his poor, pathetic past. What story did he fill your ears with? How I wept tears of blood when poor, sweet Emily was torn apart by that brute?" He laughed again. "No, my sweet. I am afraid that little Emily does not haunt me. She was nothing more than a diversion to while away the years."

"Blade has told me little," she replied. "I refer instead to your silent vigil beside her grave." At the sudden gleam of his eyes she allowed herself a small smile. "I was hiding within, you see. Oh, Vickers, the look on your face. It almost made the womanly part of me weep and long to take you in my arms to comfort. But, then, one does not take an asp to the breast. We all know how that turns out, do we not? You were so close to finding me. You see, I had returned for my father's diaries, which I had hidden within. All these months and they were right under your nose. It seems, even in death, that Emily denied you what you wanted most."

Vickers was as frozen as a statue, the knife dangling, forgotten, from his fingers. "You have the diaries," he murmured, half to himself. A mad light came into his eyes. "Where are they?"

"Where you shall never find them."

There was a blur of movement and her cheek erupted with a hot sting. He'd cut her. She gasped but then forced her body to still. Vickers had never been driven to violence before.

A drop of blood dripped from her jaw onto her shoulder. He watched it fall and a muscle in his cheek twitched. "It seems you may still have a use then, my sweet." He put the tip of the knife to her other cheek and pressed hard enough to cut. "You will tell me, sooner or later. Later is, of course, so much more enjoyable. Do hold out for me. Please."

"I gave them to Blade," she said defiantly. "I gave him the cure and then I asked him to burn the diaries. It works, even now. He has taken what you want, and you shall never get your hands on it. You are condemned to your bloody damnation, Vickers, while he shall survive. You will be nothing more than a wretched monster, put down by the sword before it can wreak more havoc on the city." She deliberately took a breath through her nose. "How long do you think your perfumes can hide the scent? It's starting, isn't it? The Fade. How long before you are nothing more than a vile, filthy, stinking monster?"

The force of his fist snapped her head to the side. Her ears were ringing, but she barely had time to notice, for he struck her again. And again. White-hot pain speared through her cheekbone. The world narrowed to the feel of Vickers's closed fist and the taste of blood.

It seemed an age before he let up. Honoria blinked through swollen eyes, her head ringing with the sound of his blows. She spat blood, her entire jaw feeling as though it had been branded with red-hot metal. Through it all, she could hear the sound of him panting.

He caught her chin in a cruel grip and she cried out.

"A mistake," he hissed. "For that cure could have been the only thing I'd have traded you for." With that he let go of her and stepped back, wiping his bloodied fists on his pants, smearing red across the flawless white.

Through the pain and the coppery taste of blood, somehow she found the strength to laugh—a short, choking hack. "I would rather see you in hell," she whispered.

His nostrils flared and for a moment darkness rose in his eyes. Then he took a step back, breathing in slow, controlled breaths. "No. No, not yet. You will have to wait until I can deliver your broken, battered body to your lover. We shall see how much you laugh then, you little slut." And then he turned and stalked from the dungeon, leaving her to her pyrrhic victory.

Chapter 28

Blade thundered down the stairs, his hand on the hilt of his short sword. Five hours. Five hours since that treacherous bastard had taken Honoria. It had taken that long to return to the warren and see the wound in his side stitched. It was still deep, an angry throb that clenched with each movement, but the stitches would hold it together.

How much could Vickers do in five hours? Blade's thoughts were full of time, and he could almost hear the tick of some silent clock echoing in his head. It had to have taken at least two hours for the handler to return to the city with her. Another hour perhaps to summon Vickers. Which left two hours, maybe less, for the duke to have done whatever he willed with her.

Fear turned Blade's gut to lead. How long would it take him to get to the Ivory Tower? If the streets were crowded, he'd go insane. He couldn't bear the thought of her in Vickers's pale hands.

The lightweight black leather armor he wore made no sound as he moved. Overlapping plates shielded his sword arm, and the gleaming steel breastplate protected his chest cavity and the wound at his side.

Storming the Ivory Tower would be suicidal. It had taken Barrons's cool logic to see that. In the first few moments after Blade had emerged from the water into the humid, ash-stained air of the tunnel, he'd barely been able to see for the sudden, flaring storm of fury. Both Lynch and Barrons had held him down until Barrons's words finally penetrated.

If he went after Vickers alone, he would die. And Honoria would be lost. The only way to get her back was to challenge Vickers on his own ground.

As he hit the ground level, the smell was the first thing that gave him warning. Blade looked up with narrowed eyes as he stalked down the hallway. Familiar faces looked back—Will, Tin Man, and even Rip, standing there and leaning heavily on his sword, using it like a crutch.

"No," Blade said flatly.

Will was the one who lifted his chin in defiance. "How you goin' to stop us? You go and we'll follow."

"This ain't a scragger's fight," Blade said. "You can't 'elp me with this. I go to duel."

"Then we'll watch your back," Rip replied.

He met their gazes and saw no yield in them. His jaw clenched. "If I don't succeed, who'll protect me people? What 'bout Esme? And Lark?"

Rip straightened. "Esme were the one as told us."

"You can barely stand straight," Blade hissed. "And I ain't bringin' a newly infected craver 'neath the noses of the Ech'lon. They'll collar you for sure."

"You don't 'ave to," Rip said. "I'll follow 'long behind."

"You stubborn, bloody fool—"

Will grabbed Blade by the arm. "Time's wastin'."

Damn him. Damn them all. Will was right.

Blade shook out of the verwulfen's grip. "I can't protect you," he said. "If they see you, they'll lock you up. You won't escape again."

"Ain't your choice," Will said. "We knows the consequences. And we're prepared to pay 'em."

Blade tried one last time. He looked at Tin Man. "And you? What 'bout Lark?"

In response Tin Man slowly hefted the massive spiked axe he held in his hands.

"We've given Esme money. She knows 'ow to make 'em and the Todds vanish," Will said. "If need be."

"You're fools, the bloody lot o' you," Blade snarled, pushing past. "Aye, then. Come and dance with the Ech'lon. You can be me bloody retinue. King o' Fools and 'is merry band o' jesters. If they don't laugh us out o' the tower, it'll be a bleedin' miracle."

Barrons was waiting for him at the gates to Caine House. He leaned out of the gilded carriage, his face whitening with pain. A rapier dangled from his belt, and he wore the same heavy armor-plated manica that Blade did. His was painted red, with the golden hawk emblem of the House of Caine embossed upon it.

"You're late," Barrons said. His gaze flickered over the hulking trio behind Blade. "Bold. But it might work."

"Not much choice in the matter," Blade muttered. His heart tightened in his chest. He'd been trying not to think about it, but the sight of Barrons..."'Ave you 'eard of 'er? Is she alive?"

"She's alive. He's got her in the dungeons." Barrons's lips thinned. "She's not pretty, Blade. By my man's reports, he's bloodied her up."

A vision flashed through Blade's mind: the thought of slashing the smirk from Vickers's pale face. He breathed in slowly and then let it out. *Kill*, whispered his demon. *Not yet*, he told it and clenched down on the urge to destroy the world.

"Will 'e fight me?" Blade said aloud.

Barrons gestured him into the gaudy carriage. "I'm going to try to force his hand on the matter. If he won't fight you, then I'll challenge him."

Blade glanced down at the way the man favored his right leg. "You ain't fit to stand to piss, let alone fight."

Barrons returned the look. "Are you?"

Blade fingered the dagger at his belt. "This 'as been a long time comin'. I've got reason to kill the bastard."

"So have I," Barrons replied. "He slit my father's throat."

Blade glanced up at the mighty facade of Caine House. "I thought the duke were enjoyin' good 'ealth."

"He's currently indisposed," Barrons replied. His voice dropped. "A little dash of laudanum and hemlock in his blud-wein. If he knew what I was about, he'd hang me up by the heels and flog me. He and Vickers have an alliance." Barrons looked grim. "And I'm about to destroy it."

"'Ow long till the poppy wine wears off?"

"Not long enough. We'd best hurry. Your men can follow mine."

Blade gave the order then sprang into the carriage. Barrons followed with considerably less agility. Whatever the depth of his injuries, it was vibrantly clear that he couldn't carry the duel himself.

Blade fingered the hilt of his dagger. That suited him perfectly.

❧

The Ivory Tower speared halfway to the heavens. Marble columns and gothic arches supported each level, leaving a balustrade around the edge for the Echelon to take air upon. Half the business of the realm was conducted there, it was said, during those long, slow strolls between allies and enemies alike.

Barrons alighted from the carriage with an attempt at his usual grace and started toward the double doors, hobbling slightly. Blade fell in behind him, examining the outlay of the place. Two metaljackets at the main doors, another twenty in the perimeter. All of them Spitfires.

There would be none within the tower, Barrons had explained on the way. Metaljackets were dangerous but unable to use initiative—and under strict control of their handler. The Coldrush Guards were comprised of blue blood rogues from the lower families of the Great Houses. Boys who'd been ineligible for the blood rites, but infected by circumstance or accident.

Though Barrons stalked toward the doors as if he simply couldn't fathom being turned away, Blade couldn't help holding his breath. A pair of ladies strolling in the forum beyond glanced their way, their eyes widening as they recognized his face. They should. There'd been enough cartoons drawn and printed about his continued defiance of the Echelon. Complete with horns. One of the women's eyes darted toward his head as though searching for them before her companion tugged her away with scandalized glee lighting her eyes.

"It starts," Barrons murmured. "They'll spread the word."

The enormous gothic arch of the doors shadowed them for a moment and then they were inside. A strange hush fell. Blade looked up through the central spire of the tower. A pair of staircases circled upward, sinuously winding around each other. Rooms and chambers speared off them at each level, but the core was hollow. The top of the tower—the atrium—was almost lost to view.

Hushed whispers came from above as the members of the Echelon in all their brilliant-colored clothes came to the rails to see what was causing so much fuss. Fans fluttered and feathered headpieces bobbed as their owners whispered behind their hands to each other.

Blade's nerves tightened and a thrill of darkness surged through him. Honoria was beneath this roof, somewhere. He wanted to run, his sword cutting through these peacocks like a hot knife through butter. To rain blood down upon the tower like they'd never seen before. *Teach them the meaning of the word* bloodlust. *Teach them what it meant to steal his woman from him...*

There was a moment where the world blurred into two; one vision was shadows, the other was brilliant with color.

"Blade?" He barely felt the hand on his arm. Barrons peered at him warily. "Did you speak?"

A thrill of fear shot through him. He blinked and his vision cleared. But they were nearly halfway up the stairs and he couldn't remember any of it. "No," he ground out. "Not me."

"We ought've taken the elevation chamber," Will muttered, eyeing Barrons's leg.

The man was no longer limping, but not without effort. And there were reputedly a thousand steps to the atrium.

Barrons shook his head, the silk of his scarlet cloak draped over his arm to maximum effect. "Too fast. I want them to have time to gather. The council is in session this morning. I need them in the atrium. You need them."

"Aye, but are you sure you can make the top?" Blade asked.

"You cannot fight pain. It must be accepted," Barrons replied, with the odd sound of rote, "in order to be defeated."

"Who said that?"

"The duke," Barrons replied, his gaze intent on the stairs and the curious flock of blue bloods that was swarming from every bloody room in the tower, or so it seemed. "He had the words beaten into me as a child, so that I should remember them."

"And what'll 'e do when 'e finds you've defied 'im like this?"

Barrons glanced down. "I don't know." Gone was any sign of the arrogant young blue blood. World-weary cynicism now shone in Barrons's dark eyes.

"You need an ally, I got your back." A sudden announcement, but Blade always paid his debts. Barrons was going out on a limb for him—and for Honoria. "She's not going to like this, you know?"

"Who? Honoria?"

"She's got you pegged in a neat little 'ole. This is goin' to disrupt 'er ordered view o' the world."

"The wicked half-brother?" Barrons asked.

"You. Carin' more 'n you should."

Silence greeted this statement. "Don't tell her that," Barrons finally murmured, looking up. "Here we go. That's the duke of Goethe about to challenge our right to be here. Let me do the talking."

The duke was an imposing figure, standing directly in the path before them. They both stopped three steps down, and Barrons tilted his head in a slight bow. "Manderlay."

"Barrons," the duke replied. Icy blue eyes flickered past him to Blade. The last time they'd met, the duke had been a young Coldrush Guard of barely sixteen—not even through his blood rites yet—wielding a sword and standing between him and the only exit of the tower. In his madness, Blade had nearly torn the man's head off. The heavy scarring across the duke's left jaw was a grim reminder.

Dressed in an immaculate black velvet coat with a spill of lace at the chin and leather leggings, the duke looked to have aged well. Though that could have been the unexpected rise to leader of his House, something no other rogue had ever achieved. The black attire was evidence of the recent death of his consort.

"We meet again," the duke said as he turned to

Blade and cut him a sharp little smile. "And the scene remains the same. Only…slightly less bloodier than I recall."

"Give us a moment," Blade replied in the same cuttingly polite tone. "And I'll remedy that."

Kill him.

Not yet.

The duke looked at him, considering. "You carry a dueling weapon."

"He's here for Vickers," Barrons replied.

"The prince consort—and the queen—are both in attendance," the duke said. It was clear that the queen was almost an afterthought.

"And his quarrel is not with them." Barrons held out a soothing hand. "I give you my word: no harm shall befall any but the Duke of Lannister."

"Have you proper grievance?"

"Vickers kidnapped Blade's thrall. He holds her here in the dungeons."

Manderlay was clearly tempted. "The law is on your side should your claims prove true." He stepped out of the way. "You shall pass. This is a matter for the council to consider." Then his smile widened. "But not your men." He glanced at Will. "Nor the abomination."

Will bristled on the steps behind, looking like he wanted to pick up Manderlay and throw him over the railing. A tempting thought. Blade met Will's amber gaze and shook his head.

"I want your word they won't be 'armed," he demanded. "Or imprisoned."

"No harm shall befall your men," the duke replied, "should they not provoke it."

"Nor the wolf." He wasn't going to be caught out with word games, and no blue blood thought a verwulfen anything but an animal.

A minute hesitation. "Nor the wolf," Manderlay repeated.

One obstacle out of the way. Blade shouldered past the duke but didn't take his gaze off him.

"He won't stab you in the back," Barrons muttered under his breath. "Not here. And not until he sees how this plays out with Vickers."

"Let's 'ope their curiosity is stronger 'n their 'atred o' me."

"I'm counting on it."

They climbed through the silken-clad flock of people thronging the stairwell. Women whispered behind their fans, more than one of them casting an appreciative eye over Blade's figure. He ignored them all, women and men both. The one man he was looking for wasn't among them. Vickers was the only one who mattered.

Unconsciously, his hand opened and closed on the hilt of his sword. The grip was smooth and polished by years of handling, but there was no sweat in the leather. He felt curiously distanced, his mind disassociated. His mouth spoke, but in his head all he could hear was the *tick, tick, tick* of the clock.

A half dozen guards waited at the entrance to the atrium, their pikes held low and at the ready. Dozens of young ladies and lords waited to see the ensuing confrontation with malicious glee on their faces.

Barrons strode toward the atrium. Blade followed. His nerves were leaping. What if he lost? What if they would not allow him to take her back?

Darkness flickered through the edges of his vision. If they denied him, he would wash the walls with their blood.

"Easy," Barrons murmured, his hand coming out of nowhere to squeeze Blade's wrist. "You cannot afford to lose control. Not here. Not now."

Just as swiftly, his vision cleared, but Blade could sense the dark, hungry part of himself pacing. He couldn't afford to let it loose. He needed to focus on Vickers. The man had fought more than a hundred duels in his lifetime. This was no pup he faced, but a fully fledged master of the sword.

The atrium was perfectly rounded, columns circling the room. On the dais beneath the stained-glass window stood a small group of people conferring in low tones. As he and Barrons entered, Blade looked up and counted six. The prince consort, with his red-rimmed eyes, stood almost six and a half feet tall in the center of the dais. He wore a gold cloak, held together with a pearl clasp, and his wavy brown hair was not powdered. At his side was a human woman, gowned in midnight blue silk, with the golden diadem of the realm on her brow. The queen's features were pretty but human in their ordinariness. He had heard rumors that she was clearly under the prince consort's control, but her gaze, when he met it, was clear and firm. As she glanced away, pasting a smile on her face, he had the feeling the blue bloods surrounding her didn't realize what was in their midst. The queen had the same cool mask as a cardsharp. He recognized the type.

"Morioch," Barrons murmured, "Malloryn, Bleight…

and Casavian." His gaze fell on the Lady Aramina and narrowed. "That's four of the Great Houses."

"Vickers ain't 'ere," Blade observed.

"He'll be waiting to make an entrance," Barrons replied. "He knows why you're here."

"Perhaps you would care to enlighten the rest of us, then." The voice came from an elderly man upon the dais. He stepped forward, instantly capturing the attention of everyone present. The swelling murmurs silenced. A carnival showman if ever Blade'd seen one.

"The duke of Morioch," Barrons murmured, "who simply won't die, much to his heir's disgust."

The swish of skirts was loud in the room as dozens of newcomers lined up along the walls, jostling for a better position to view the proceedings.

Barrons opened his mouth to speak, but Morioch cut him off. "You dare bring a rogue among us?"

"Considering who infected him, perhaps he is not a rogue after all but a sanctioned blue blood," Barrons replied, his own voice loud enough to cut the air like a knife. "After all, was Vickers not absolved? If there was no crime committed, how can Blade's turning be considered unlawful?"

The crowd stirred. Whispers upon whispers. Unease rolled through Blade. He just wanted to fight. He just wanted to get Honoria back. Where the bloody hell was Vickers?

A pair of light brown eyes met his in curiosity. Blade stilled then slowly tilted his head to the queen. Two outsiders in a world that could kill them with one word. He had to respect that.

"If he is not rogue, then he is also a nothing,"

Morioch countered. "And a man not born of the blood has no right to challenge a duke."

"I wasn't aware that you were speaking with Vickers's voice, Your Grace," Barrons said. A laugh or two came from the crowd. "Tell me," he continued, looking around with widespread arms. "Where is our good duke? Can he not speak for himself? Or does he prefer to hide behind his friends?"

Blade swung his body in a circle, hunting through the crowd.

"Unless he is…afraid," Barrons suggested.

A chain clinked. And then Vickers's cold voice cut through the crowd. "I am afraid of nothing, you little cur. I was merely preparing a gift for our guest."

Honoria staggered forward as if she'd been shoved and landed on the cold marble with a gasp. Her wrists and ankles were locked in the finest of gold chains, and a black silk cravat served as a blindfold. A thick gold band circled her throat, with the delicate chain winding sinuously across the floor and leading back to Vickers's hand.

He'd put a fucking collar on her.

Blade started forward, jerking back as Barrons grabbed for him.

"Not yet," Barrons cautioned. "This is not how we get her back."

"Get your 'ands off me. Get 'em off!" he snarled, his vision washing of color.

Sound amplified and the stink of perfume hit his nose like a punch. Through it all he caught a faint hint of burning flesh. As if drawn, his gaze settled on Honoria's arm, and the crest that Vickers had branded her with. The three roaring lions of the House of Lannister.

Blade saw red.

There were hands clutching at him, a voice shouting no, and through it all, the smirk on Vickers's face as he stepped through the ring of avid spectators. Somewhere nearby someone was bellowing in anger.

Kill, Blade's hunger whispered. *Yes.*

Chapter 29

A SCREAM OF RAGE TORE THROUGH THE AIR. DESPITE her pain, Honoria pushed herself into a sitting position and tore at the blindfold.

The sudden light streaming through the airy chamber nearly blinded her. The crowd she heard appeared as merely a splash of vibrant color in the background. All she could see was Blade, his eyes gone completely black as he strained for Vickers.

Leo held him back, both arms locked beneath his shoulders as he pleaded in his ear. Finally she saw what the crowd saw: the Devil of Whitechapel in all his infinite fury, a beast pushed to its limits, its entire focus narrowed on the man it wished to kill.

And she found no fear. For there was a man there too. A man she loved. Full of kindness and gentle touches. Sweet little smiles as he gave her pieces of his heart without asking for anything back. A man afraid to touch her for fear of unleashing the monster within.

"Blade," she called, her hands grasping in the air for him. "Blade, *look* at me."

He threw Barrons off him with the ease of a man

flicking lint from his shoulder. As if time slowed down, she could see his hand dipping for his sword, hear the steely rasp of the metaljacket guards as they reached for their weapons, and she knew he would never get to Vickers before they slew him. As Vickers had, no doubt, planned.

"*Blade!*" she screamed in desperation. He barely slowed. "This is what he wants!"

The metaljackets streamed past her, locking their automatic recurring pistols on him. Blade stopped dead in his tracks as they fanned into a circle around him. His nostrils flared as he waged an internal battle she could only guess at. Then his gaze—still black as the ace of spades—locked on hers.

"Honoria." The word was crisp and cultured. But the frown drawing between his brows was not. There was a hint of puzzlement to it, as though his darker side could not quite fathom what she meant to him.

"Don't let him win," she whispered. Her throat was suddenly thick. "I love you."

A tremble ran through his frame. His fist clenched around the hilt of his sword. And yet finally he seemed to see the towering metal legion that surrounded him. He looked around, his dark gaze taking in the room with a calculating gleam.

Honoria barely heard the crack of boot heels on the marble. Her entire focus was on Blade, on holding him to his sanity. She felt as though his tenuous control would break if she so much as blinked.

A rough fist caught in her hair, and she couldn't help grabbing for the hand to ease the searing pain. Her chains rattled and she froze as the movement leeched out of Blade. He stood like a statue of Vengeance, his gaze narrowing on Vickers's hand. A muscle in his jaw ticked.

"Who allowed this monster, *this animal*, to present before the prince consort?" Vickers spat.

Blade stared at Vickers as if shaking off a spell. The black faded from his eyes replaced by grim determination. "I *ain't* an animal," he said, each word clearly delineated.

Relief flooded through her.

"No?" Malicious humor flavored Vickers's words. He appealed to the crowd, his hand wrenching her around. "Who could tear his own sister apart and still call himself a man?" Shocked gasps abounded, but Vickers continued. "Or live in the filth of the rookeries with vermin and verwulfen and not be tainted?" Vickers sniffed the air. "You stink of vileness, you beast. How dare you enter this tower?"

"At least I ain't stinkin' o' rot," Blade countered. He stepped forward and the metaljackets moved as one, taking a threatening step toward him.

Frustration danced across his face, and he looked at the group on the dais in silent appeal. The prince consort had seated himself in an enormous throne-like chair, his left ankle hooked up on his knee. The queen stood at his side, her hand resting on his shoulder as he idly stroked it. She stared at the tableau in front of her with a distant, unfocused look on her face.

"Come and fight me," Blade snarled. "Or aren't *you* man enough?"

Vickers let her go and wiped his hand on his thigh as though it had been soiled. "A duke doesn't duel with dogs. You have no cause—"

"Honoria is *mine*," Blade interrupted.

"I was her father's patron," Vickers explained, as if to a child. "My claim takes precedence over yours. And I shall do whatever I like with her." He yanked on the chain at her throat.

"So the question is," someone said in a quiet, yet firm voice, "whether a man of no quality may duel a duke?"

A hundred heads swiveled toward the dais. The queen stepped forward.

The prince consort glanced at the queen with hooded eyes, but his thoughts were concealed. She might have been acting his desires, or this might truly be her own whim. Honoria could not tell.

"Your Highness," Vickers said, his voice turned to treacle. "This is no matter for the court. Allow me to see the creature removed."

The queen speared him with a look. "I have not finished, Your Grace."

A hush fell across the room. This time the prince consort did not look entirely pleased. "Alexandra," he murmured.

The queen half glanced behind her. In that moment she looked incredibly young. Perhaps little older than Honoria. And so fragile and human.

She wavered for a moment, and then a spark of defiance lit her gaze and she swept down from the dais. The metaljackets parted before her and the prince consort half rose to his feet, his face flushed with a flicker of anger.

Blade stared down at her. "Your 'Ighness."

"I have heard word of you," the queen said crisply.

"They say you are a monster. A killer." She held out a hand toward the nearest guard. "A sword, please."

Honoria made as if to move, but Vickers hauled her up short.

The queen struggled to lift the heavy sword. "On your knees."

Blade looked for her and Honoria slowly shook her head. "No," she whispered. "No." She could not lose him. Not like this. But how could he defy the queen? They would tear him to pieces.

Blade had always owned an odd sense of honor. As the crowd of blue bloods watched in fascination, he went to his knees before a mere mortal.

"The Devil of Whitechapel," the queen pronounced. "And yet you are also a savior of the realm, responsible for the single-handed execution of a vampire, or so I am told. My people—I—cannot thank you enough."

Shocked gasps met this statement. The prince consort was on his feet, his nostrils flaring with rage. "Where did you hear of this nonsense?"

"It isn't nonsense," Leo replied. He bowed his head as the prince consort's gaze fell upon him. "I was there. He killed the creature himself." Leo didn't dare look at her.

"What is your true name?" the queen asked, resting the sword tip on his shoulder.

Blade looked up in shock. "My queen?"

"Your name?" she repeated gently.

He had to think. Honoria could barely breathe for the sudden gleam of hope. Beside her she could see Vickers quivering with rage, his knuckles whitening on the chain links.

Blade cleared his throat. "I were born 'Enry Rathinger."

"For your services to the realm, I name thee Sir Henry Rathinger." She touched the tip of the sword to each of his shoulders. "Arise, my knight. And greet your peers."

The room erupted into mayhem. Vickers went pale with fury, and the prince consort stared at his wife with a deadly look on his face.

Through all of the shouting and shocked gasps, Honoria found and met Blade's gaze. He looked stunned. He knelt on the floor still as the room raged around them. Honoria found herself grinning stupidly, and then he was grinning too. The room faded away. All she could see was her love, and there was a chance now. A chance!

His laughter faded away. He pressed his fingers to his chest, then his lips, and then held his hand out toward Honoria, palm upward.

The moment gave him strength. Determination washed over his expression and he surged to his feet, silencing the roar of the crowd. The queen stepped back, trailing the borrowed sword along the marble tiles. Her gaze met her husband's with a little flare of defiance.

"You," Blade said, focusing on Vickers. "I challenge you to a duel."

Vickers glared at him, then gave an ugly little smile. "I accept."

Chapter 30

"He favors his left side, but don't overextend, for he's used it to his advantage in the past." Barrons helped Blade slide his hand into the grip of the dueling sword. Blade gave a slight twist, and the overlapping plates of the hand guard extended up, enclosing his hand. The sword truly became an extension of his body. The only way to remove it would be to remove the arm.

Blade took an experimental swing. It was heavier than he was used to, but perfectly balanced.

"What other weapon do you want?" Barrons asked. "The shield? The mace?"

Vickers was hefting a shield. Their eyes locked on each other. "No," Blade said. "Just this." He flicked open the razor in his palm, feeling it settle there like an old friend.

"Unorthodox," Barrons murmured, glancing around, "but it should give the crowd a thrill."

"I don't give a damn."

Barrons grinned. "Aye, but, Sir Henry, you're one of us now."

Blade grunted. He was nothing like them and he never would be.

The floor had been cleared to reveal a brass ring cut into the marble. This was where the duel would commence. Any man who stepped outside that circle instantly declared forfeit.

He had to focus. Vickers would be no easy kill, Blade knew, and the darkness within him was bubbling up, threatening to overtake him again. He couldn't let that happen. There had been a moment when he'd woken from that monochrome nightmare and realized that he'd been about to tear his way through the Echelon with no thought to Honoria or his own safety. All that had mattered was Vickers and killing him.

Blade looked down and clenched his fist within the protective casing of the sword hilt. If he lost control like that again, Vickers would have him. And Honoria would be better off dead.

She stood by the dais, her chains placed in the hands of the Lady Aramina. The plain white robes of a blood slave revealed more flesh than was courteous, but she held herself still, ignoring the speculative glances of the men around her. There was a certain untouchable feeling that she projected, as though she had forgotten the world around her and focused only on Blade.

When she saw him looking, she gave a weak little smile that didn't fool him for a moment. She was scared. For him.

"Are you ready, or should you like a few more moments to stare at your whore's face? To memorize it for your years in hell?" Vickers taunted.

Anger flashed through Honoria's eyes, and Blade smiled. There. That was how he wanted to remember her.

Turning, he favored Vickers with a cool look. "Are *you* ready?"

"I've been waiting for this moment for years. You were a dog that should have been put down after you murdered your sister. An oversight I am about to correct."

Blade stepped into the brass ring. Silence fell across the room as the crowd craned their necks to see. He knew what Vickers was trying to do: rile the monster within so that he lost control. Nothing would ever ease the pain of Emily's death—or the press of guilt he felt whenever he thought of her—but Vickers had his share of blame in that too. Yes, it had been Blade's hand that ultimately caused the killing stroke, but he'd only been Vickers's pawn.

Thank you, Honoria.

"Ain't nothin' less interestin' than a man who keeps repeatin' 'imself. Any time you're ready, Your Grace." He gestured to the ring. "I wouldn't wanna keep you waitin' after all 'em years."

"You will learn that I am nothing if not patient," Vickers said as he swept the luxurious fur-lined cloak off his shoulders and tossed it at one of his cronies. He stood for a moment in his gold-leafed armor as though testing the edge of his sword, but his position placed him within a ray of light that shone through the glass panes in the ceiling. Some of the ladies in the crowd gasped.

Knowing the figure he presented—strong, tall,

his armor gleaming like an invulnerable god from legend—Vickers stepped into the circle.

And Blade attacked.

Vickers parried the blow with ridiculous ease, despite the fact that the edge of his heel was dangerously close to the brass ring. But Blade didn't want to force him out of the circle and win by default. He wanted the man dead. He backed off.

Vickers smiled darkly as though realizing his opponent's intentions. He took a mocking step forward. "Come. Do your worst. Show us your little alley tricks."

A glimpse of Honoria drifted through the corner of Blade's vision, white-faced and stiff with tension. *Mine*, whispered the darkness within.

She's bloody mine, he snarled back silently, feeling the press of the demon upon him. It wanted Vickers's blood. For once they were in agreement.

Forcing himself to block the hunger—even Honoria—from his mind, he lunged forward and met Vickers's sword. The duke parried each thrust with economical skill, a little smile playing about his lips.

"You have strength," Vickers commented, whipping his shield up to block another blow. "But little skill or grace. Perhaps you should have chosen the broadsword. It seems more suited to your rudimentary style of hacking."

"You talk too much," Blade said, slashing across Vickers's guard. The wound at his side gave a warning throb and he pulled the blow unconsciously. It scattered harmlessly off the shield.

As Vickers danced back, his guard lowering for a moment, Blade kicked him in the face.

Vickers went down, his head cracking against the cold white tiles. The crowd gave a collective gasp, surging toward the circle with bloodthirsty glee. Blade leapt forward, bringing the sword down in a sweeping stroke. The duke saw it coming and rolled. Sparks showered off the marble as Blade's sword bit deep.

"Do try not to mark the atrium, Sir Henry," Morioch called. "The marble is Italian. Very costly."

Blade circled Vickers, balancing low on his feet.

Vickers got up and scrubbed blood from his nose. His eyes were darkening with fury. "You fight like an alley cur."

It was intended as an insult, Blade assumed. "Aye."

"Whatever was the queen thinking?" Vickers said, countering the next two strokes with exquisite ease.

"Mayhap she wanted to see me slit you a new smile." Blade waved the razor at him. "I don't think she likes you."

Vickers's gaze narrowed on the deadly weapon for a moment. "I grow weary of this toying. I thought to give you a somewhat honorable death, but why bother? You have no honor, and there is none to be gained from defeating you as a gentleman. Let me show you what a sword is for."

The rapier streaked toward Blade with vicious speed, but he blocked it. Barely. Then Vickers flicked his wrist and the tip sliced across the overlapping leather plates of Blade's manica. He danced back on light feet as Vickers showed him just how easily he could pierce his defense. The swords tangled, Vickers lunging forward with elegant appeal and disengaging just enough to score a strike. Something stung hot and furious across Blade's cheek. The scent of coppery blood filled his nose as the duke actually turned his back on him and bowed to the crowd. Blade wiped at his cheek with the back of his hand.

Barrons caught his eye, gesturing swiftly with his hands as though trying to show him what to do. Someone clapped for Vickers. The duke of Morioch, of course, a smile on his thin lips. On the dais, the queen was watching, her hand secured beneath her husband's.

And Honoria was staring at him, her lip clenched between her teeth. She gave him a reassuring smile when their gazes locked, but he saw the truth written in her eyes. He could not defeat Vickers like this. The man was incredibly fast. Monstrously fast. And his skill with the rapier was superior in every way.

"That is called the botta-in-tempo. A simple form, but highly effective," Vickers lectured. He held the point of his sword low, as though daring Blade to attack.

All right, then. Blade hefted his own sword. If he couldn't win fighting Vickers's way, then he would do it with his own. He made another preemptive strike.

Vickers met the expected attack with a disdainful expression. "Pathetic, really—"

Blade spun low under the point of the swords, his heel sweeping Vickers's left foot out from under him. The little razor sliced in beneath the edge of Vickers's breastplate. Blade felt it bite in, and then Vickers was falling with a surprised snarl, trying to bring his shield up in time. Blade leaped forward, the heel of his boot crunching into the breastplate. It crumpled beneath the force, the breath leaving Vickers in a rush.

The duke's head hit the marble, and his eyes widened in horror as his hair started shifting.

What the hell? Blade missed the chance for another crushing kick as Vickers rolled. His hair tumbled half over his face as though he'd been scalped. A bloody wig.

Blade flipped the tip of his sword and the wig sailed through the air, landing outside the circle. The room gasped as one, and Blade froze as Vickers looked up with a murderous gleam in his eyes. His scalp was pasty and bare, the skin flaking around a few straggling tufts of wiry hair. The sudden stench of sweet rot escaped him.

"You son of a bitch," he swore quietly. No wonder Vickers was faster than Blade. This was no blue blood he faced but a man well into the Fade.

Shocked cries rang through the room as they saw the duke's changed appearance. A man wearing enough heavy powder and rouge to hide the effects of the albinism. No doubt beneath the heavy breastplate and the padded shoulders, they would find the duke's body starting to wither into the lean, stringy muscle tones of a vampire.

"A vampire," Blade spat. Elation soared through him. It didn't matter now. Vickers would die. By his hand or by the executioners. And Vickers knew it.

A look of fury and despair flashed over the duke's face as he scanned the horrified crowd. They drew back from him, surging for the exit. His peers and so-called friends, and they turned their noses up at the first sign of the Fade.

Slowly, Vickers's gaze locked on Blade.

"You're done," Blade laughed in sheer amazement. "You die today."

"Damn you," the duke spat and launched himself at his opponent.

He was no longer playing. This time he meant to kill. It took everything Blade had to turn aside a furious strike that almost decapitated him. He staggered back, step after step, barely keeping the rapier between them.

Launching a rebutting kick against Vickers's shield, Blade somehow turned the man off balance. The razor slashed across the duke's face, almost an echo of Vickers's previous blow. Blood splashed off the end of it, and a lady screamed as it spattered across her face. "It burns! It burns!"

Blade ducked, sweeping under the next strike. He saw a chance and barreled forward beneath the edge of steel, his shoulder striking Vickers in the chest. They both went down, but a twist of Vickers's hips sent Blade rolling over the top of his shield arm, momentarily leaving the duke open.

Wrong bloody side. His razor was in the other hand, but he tried to slash at the duke's face with his rapier. It was too unwieldy, and Vickers jerked his head aside as the sword harmlessly raked over the tiles.

Both of them rolled, coming to their feet in low crouches. Vickers ripped at his shield and flung it aside, crumpling a quartet of youths with the heavy steel.

As Blade watched, he wiped at the blood staining his cheek. Smooth, pasty skin met Blade's incredulous eyes. Vickers's wound had healed itself.

"There are advantages, it seems," Vickers said with

a deadly smile. "I shall die, but by God I shall take you with me."

The line of metaljackets had formed up between the pair of them and the crowd on the dais. The prince consort had not shifted, his face a blank mask of cool interest. He meant to see this duel finished. Only then would he move to destroy Vickers. And perhaps see two enemies vanquished in one day.

This time Vickers was prepared for his opponent. As Blade swept under his sword, Vickers countered with a dagger that had somehow appeared in his hand. It sank with a meaty thud between Blade's ribs, opening up the vampire's claw marks from the tunnel. Blade staggered, blood patterning the floor with dark, almost violet drops.

Vickers gave him no time to catch his breath. The rapier slashed down Blade's face from eyebrow to jaw. Blood dripped into his left eye and he turned instinctively, barely avoiding the responding attack. A reflective strike with the razor glanced off Vickers's crumpled breastplate with a steely shriek.

Blade barely had time to blink before the sole of a boot appeared in his vision. For a moment the world disappeared, and then he found himself on the floor, his head ringing from the crack of the tiles. As his head lolled to the side, he caught a glimpse of Will's furious form trying to force his way through a pack of restraining blue bloods.

And then Honoria, her face white with terror as she shoved her way through the metaljackets, the chain around her throat hauling her to a halt. She ripped at it, and though the duchess of Casavian had twice her strength, the end somehow sailed free. Honoria swung the chain and it sailed through the air, wrapping around the duke's raised weapon.

He jerked almost contemptuously, and Honoria gave a cry as she fell onto the floor in front of Vickers.

Vickers straightened, curling his fist around the chain. An ecstatic laugh burst from his lips. His eyes were flooded with a demonic matte black. "And now I have you both." He raised his sword, looking straight at Blade. "This time, you watch *your* love die."

"*No!*" Blade screamed.

No, the darkness echoed.

A moment of the constant fight, the edge of control slipping through his fingers. And then he made a conscious decision. He could not win, not against Vickers's superior strength and speed. And so he let the darkness flood over him, through him, sinking itself into every cell of his body.

The room fell away. Color leeched from the world. And Blade leaped for Vickers.

His body cut through the air, almost as if time slowed around him. Vickers lashed out with the rapier, sending the stroke meant for Honoria toward him. Blade twisted minutely and it swept past him, the cool air of its passing rippling against his throat. The edge of his rapier sank through Vickers's crumpled breastplate like cutting through soggy bread, the force of the blow driving the duke back.

Twisting his wrist inside the hilt, Blade felt the wrist guard unlatch, and then he was free of its cumbersome weight. He rode Vickers to the ground, ignoring the sudden flood of heat as the dagger pierced his side again.

Somewhere in the distance someone was screaming "mine!" over and over again. Blade drew his fist back and smashed it into Vickers's face. Blood burned his skin like acid, but the thought was distant, the rational notation of pain for a form long since gone.

The darkness wanted only to kill, to protect what was his. Blood sprayed across the floor, darker than his own but not quite the viscous black fluid of a vampire. Then bone gleamed in the pulpy mess of Vickers's face.

"Blade!" A hand caught his arm and he spun, drawing back his fist with a snarl. Honoria froze, her shackled hands held in front of her in a placating manner.

"You must come back," she whispered. "I need you to let him go."

"I am always me," Blade replied in a cool voice. The body on the floor in front of him was nothing but a mess of flesh and mangled bone, the face crushed to so much pulp. He looked down in puzzlement. There was blood all over him, a mixture of black and gray. His hands hurt.

Honoria reached out, taking his hand in hers. They trembled and he gripped them strongly. "Please," she said. "They will not allow you to live."

He looked around at the shocked crowd. Though danger stalked the arena, none of them had fled. Bloodlust now overruled their fear, and the metal-jackets that surrounded the circle gave them a feeling of invulnerability.

His lip curled. He could mow the metaljackets down before they even saw him coming. It was simply a matter of...

Honoria squeezed his hand. "No."

He stroked her face, leaving a smear of blood across her cheek. "You are mine. They tried to 'urt you." The clink of the chain caught his attention and a growl curled through his throat.

"No," she said, catching his hand and pressing it against his cheek. "Vickers tried to hurt me. He is dead. And you must let go before they decide to kill you too."

"I can kill 'em all," he said. Could she not see how easy it would be? They were peacocks, fluffing their feathered fans.

Honoria hesitated. "Please. For me."

He shifted uncomfortably. He wanted to kill. He had only just begun. "Wet the walls with blood..."

Honoria caught his face in her hands, drawing his attention back to hers. "For me."

He didn't want to. But she was insisting on it.

"You're bleeding," she said. "I need to see to your wounds before—"

"It doesn't hurt."

"It hurts me to see you hurt."

"For you, then," Blade said. As he closed his eyes he sought the burning flame deep within. Honoria's presence helped calm his racing heart and the dark hunger inside him. "Because I love you."

"I love you too," she whispered.

The darkness evaporated from his mind at her words, and he opened his eyes, wincing at the sudden rush of color. Pain flared like someone had stuck a dozen or more holes in him. He looked down at the bluish blood spattering his clothes and the floor.

"Bloody 'ell," he muttered, his knees giving way beneath him.

Honoria caught him under the arms. Her breath was a half sob. "Thank God. Oh, thank you."

Chapter 31

Blood covered Honoria's hands, warm and slippery. Blade staggered against her, his eyes blinking with the onslaught of weakness. And the danger wasn't over yet.

The crowd drew closer, as though lured by the thought of weakness. Leo stepped within the circle and wordlessly slipped beneath Blade's other shoulder. Honoria had not quite forgiven him yet—perhaps she never would—and yet she thanked him with a quick glance.

A hush fell over the spectators as the prince consort stood. "There is a reason we do not allow rogues to live freely," he said with the kind of quiet assurance that made people strain forward to hear. His icy blue eyes locked on Honoria's and the muscles at the corner of his mouth shifted slightly. "Their dangerous lack of control and breeding can lead to catastrophic misfortune."

"As catastrophic as having a vampire in your midst, beneath your very noses?" Honoria said and then shut her mouth as Leo grabbed her arm and gave it a warning squeeze.

Morioch examined his nails. "The duke of Vickers is dead. The point is moot. The question now—after that vicious showing—is whether we allow a rogue, so blatantly on the verge of bloodlust, to live."

Leo swore under his breath.

Honoria glanced around the room helplessly. Anticipation lit not a few faces in the crowd. "What does he mean? Leo?"

"He's going to put it to a vote for the council," he replied under his breath. "I can sway one or two, Honoria, but the rest are either in the prince consort's pocket or playing their own games."

A little stirring of panic started to tighten her chest. "No," she whispered.

"For Blade's sake, keep your mouth shut." Leo relinquished the weight of his burden to Will, who had forced his way through the crowd. Then he stepped forward. "Bloodlust presumes that one cannot return from such a state. The lucidity in the man's eyes begs to differ."

"By what right do you dare speak?" Morioch's lip curled in disgust. "This is a matter for the council."

"True. However, my father, the duke, is indisposed. In his absence I have been granted right of vote according to law."

A little flicker appeared at the prince consort's lips. Almost a smile. Honoria's heart fluttered in her chest. Behind him the queen stood quiescent, her head slightly bowed. She had dared much today. There would be no further assistance from that quarter.

Morioch held Leo's gaze for a long moment. "So be it." He turned to address the rest of the council.

"Does he live, or does he die?" He held his hand out, fist clenched. Then he slowly turned his thumb down. A whisper started in the gallery.

Leo held his chin high and responded with his thumb firmly pointing toward the ceiling.

Honoria held her breath. Blade stirred, his gaze barely focused as he studied the scene. She shot Will a frightened look over Blade's head then pressed her hand against one of the worst of his wounds, to stem the sluggish blood flow.

"Who speaks for the House of Lannister?" Morioch called.

Alaric Colchester stepped forward, his gaze burning with hatred as he stared at Blade. "As the late duke's heir, I so claim the right. Let the mongrel die."

The young duke of Malloryn, Auvry Cavill, gave a shrug and a rueful grin. His coppery hair gleamed in the sunlight, and he stood, the height of fashion, as he faced the crowd. "I make it two all. For sporting odds." He shot Honoria a grin, full of amusement and mischief.

Gazes turned toward the middle-aged duke of Bleight standing on the far side of the dueling ring. He stared hard at the prince consort then slowly turned his thumb down.

Oh, God. Three to two, with two of the remaining council left to vote. Honoria's head swiveled toward the dais. The duke of Goethe and the duchess of Casavian could have been carved from marble, their faces carefully neutral as they surveyed the scene. If only one of them voted for death, it would be a simple majority.

Barrons swore under his breath.

"They ain't no friends o' mine," Blade managed to whisper. "Neither of 'em." His weight was starting to grow heavier. Honoria didn't know how he held himself up.

"I'll get you out," Will promised in a low, firm voice.

"No. Get 'er out instead. You stand between us, and they'll go after you as well." Blade and Will exchanged glances and Will slowly lowered his eyes—but not before she saw resentment burning in them.

Blade turned to Honoria.

"No," she replied to the unspoken demand in his eyes.

"What about Charlie? And Lena?" he reminded her.

Honoria shuddered under his weight.

Before she had time to deny him, the duke of Goethe stepped forward. "A curious spectacle," he murmured. There was a look of uncertainty on his face, unusual in the stoic duke. But, then, some said that he still grieved for his beloved consort. He climbed down the steps and circled the three of them, his hands clasped behind his back. "Before today I have never seen a man come back from the depths of his bloodlust." His voice softened and he looked Honoria in the eye. "You remind me of Sophia." A flicker of grief went through his pale eyes, and then he looked at Blade for a long moment. "We still have blood between us. But not today. For your young woman's sake."

Turning on his heel, he strode back to the dais. "Let the man live. It shall prove interesting if nothing else."

Honoria exchanged shocked glances with Blade. "Three to three," she whispered, shooting the duchess of Casavian a terrified look. The woman became the center of all eyes as she graciously soothed her violet skirts. A fine shawl of black lace dangled from one slim shoulder.

Honoria's breath caught. *Please...Oh, God, have mercy...*

The duchess examined them with her stunning, brandy-colored eyes. At long last her gaze settled on Leo, as though some challenge shot between them. And Honoria remembered how much the duchess hated the House of Caine. Her hope stuttered. Would the duchess vote against them simply because Leo had voted for them?

The duchess held out one small, perfectly formed fist. The crowd leaned forward, hungry for the result. The sound of Honoria's heart pounding in her chest filled her ears, a slowing, marching beat that seemed to halt the stem of time around them. *Please.*

Slowly, the duchess's thumb tilted upward. "Let him live," she called in a commanding voice. The prince consort shot her a dark look, tempered with surprise. The duchess's cool expression never changed. Her catlike gaze flickered over the three of them as if weighing and measuring them and then finally settled on Leo.

Honoria's knees nearly buckled beneath her.

"Let it be known," the queen announced. "The Devil of Whitechapel has been granted leniency." A slight pause. "But not without reservations."

Chapter 32

The first thing Blade felt was sunlight, warm and golden on his skin. His eyelashes flickered against his cheeks, the sudden flood of light making his pupils retract painfully. The air was redolent with rose-scented soap, a hint of crisp linen, and the fresh, clean scent of sunshine. Blade opened his eyes and winced.

A throaty, low-voiced hum came from the corner of the room. He blinked up at the red velvet curtains surrounding the bed and rolled his head to the side. His cushions. His bed. His room. And Honoria, muttering under her breath as she folded something by his armoire.

Sweet lord. A spear of pain shafted through his head, the remnants of a headache. The last he could recall, he'd been standing in the atrium, the floor rushing up to meet him as the queen pronounced her sentence.

Blade shifted. Honoria was oblivious. The lacings of her gown pulled tight. It was new. Printed lavender cotton, the swells of the skirt sweeping in loose waves toward the floor. Little silver fleurs-de-lis graced the fabric, and there was a pretty, silvery pin in her neat chignon. She had begun to fill out, her frame no longer bearing the gaunt, starved look she'd first worn. Beautiful.

He stared at her for a long, painful moment. A muscle clenched in his chest. So beautiful. And he was going to have to let her go.

No, the darkness within whispered. *She is ours.*

Not ours. Mine. His fingers curled into his palm at the thought. He shut his eyes against the sudden hot dryness. There were no tears. He could not cry, just another piece of humanity that his illness had stolen from him. Not for Emily, and not for Honoria. But he could still feel the crushing burden of grief deep within.

Honoria's head slowly lifted, her hands stilling on the shirt she held. As if she sensed his gaze, she glanced over her shoulders, her eyebrows drawn together in that serious expression he so adored. The shirt dropped from her suddenly nerveless fingers. "Blade," she whispered, a smile lighting up her face with a radiance that almost made him change his mind.

Three steps and he was engulfed in a tangle of warm skirts. Honoria caught his face in hers and kissed him. He couldn't help himself. He caught her to him, arms gripping far too tightly, and kissed her back. Their tongues clashed and he tasted the sweet dash of cinnamon on her lips.

"Oh, Blade. You're awake," she whispered.

He drew her face against his shoulder so he would not have to look at it and held her close. She was safely away from Vickers and the monster. Now he had to keep her safe from himself.

"Aye." His throat was hoarse, but he cleared it. Honoria sprang from the bed for the pitcher of blud-wein and poured a glass for him. Somehow he found the strength to sit up. The scent of the blood stirred hunger through him, dark shadows chasing his vision. His hand snatched at the glass and he paused, forcing himself to move with controlled slowness as he brought it to his lips. A tremble started in his fingers and a cold sweat broke out on his brow. Avoiding her glance, he drank deeply.

The bed dipped slightly beneath Honoria's weight as she settled on the edge of it. Too close. His nostrils flared, filling themselves with the heady scent of her warm skin. Strength was returning in leaps and bounds as the blud-wein filled his cramping stomach. He drained the cup and stared at it, his thirst barely quenched.

"More?"

Honoria dutifully filled two more glasses until even he was sated.

"That's a full pint and a half," she noted, a flash of seriousness filling her dark eyes.

Blade couldn't stop himself. His fingers found her cheek, stroking the smooth skin. "Aye, luv."

She slid her hand into his, drawing it between her clasped palms. The heat was intoxicating. He bathed in it, wanting to draw her down, rub his naked flesh against hers, and steal more of it.

"Do you remember what happened?" she asked.

Blade dragged himself upright. The sheets pooled around his waist and he realized he was naked, the silken drag of the sheet an exquisite torture against his engorged cock. He bent his knee up to hide the evidence. "The council voted on whether to allow a monster to live."

A flash of confusion lit her eyes. "You're not a monster."

"Honor." He dragged her hands to his mouth and kissed the knuckles. "You know what I am." A pained whisper. "I lost control when I saw Vickers with you. And I lost it again—willingly—when I thought 'e was goin' to kill you."

"But you came back."

The touch of her hair was soft as he stroked it. Imprinting the feel of it into his memory. "I can't control meself 'round you." A first sign of the Fade's nearness. Despair was a heavy weight in his chest. "I came back. This time."

He could see his words start to penetrate. Honoria dragged herself into his lap, a fierce little twist of denial on her face. "Don't you dare. Don't you dare do this to me! I fought for you, damn it! Now you fight for me."

"I am." *Fighting for her life.* Another kiss, full of thwarted passion and tinged with pain. Honoria wrapped her arms around him and straddled his hips, her mouth firm and demanding on his.

The heavy skirts rode up. Blade's hand ran over her stockinged thigh, clenching in the smooth curve of her bottom. He groaned, pressing her hips against him. Burning need tightened in his groin. What he wouldn't give for just once more…

Honoria's greedy little mouth possessed him. Her hands plucked at the sheets, at her skirts. He shook his head, coming up for breath. "No." Grabbing her wrist, he froze as he felt the smooth, wet skin of her quim brush against his heated cock. "Honoria."

Another kiss. He couldn't resist her. Groaning, he gave a little half thrust, feeling the skim of her curls and then the teasing breach of her body.

"Damn it." He rolled them both, pressing her into the bed. Her skirts splayed over the red silk sheets, her thighs wrapping around his hips and trapping him. Pinning her wrists to the bed, he tried to ignore the intoxicating feel of her.

Just once.

No. He buried his face against her throat. "We can't do this. I'm a danger to you. To me people."

"You would never hurt anyone you'd sworn to protect."

He met her passionate gaze. She was so fierce, so protective of those she considered her own. And she would fight where there was no longer any cause.

"Me CV levels 'ave been at seventy-eight percent for the last three months," he growled. "Tell me, what does that mean? How long 'ave I got—you, with all your numbers and facts?" He saw her lips firming and shook her lightly. "Damn you, Honor. You know what that means. Don't turn a blind eye to it."

"They're not at seventy-eight percent," she replied stubbornly. "They're—"

"I took a friggin' measure a week ago," he yelled, pushing away from her. Ignoring the sudden dash of tears in her eyes, he turned away, wrapping the sheet around his waist as he staggered from the bed. The room seemed to tilt. He barely saw it, stumbling over furniture and even his slippers as he tore a small diary from the drawer of his escritoire.

He flung it at her. "I can't read or write much. But I always knew numbers. I jot 'em down each week." The anger faded from his voice and he sank into a chair, dropping his face into his hands. "They've been risin' steadily for years. I've told Esme. If they 'it eighty, then I'll give meself up to Will."

Silence. Then the sound of her fingers rifling through the pages. "This doesn't make sense."

"O' course it does," he snarled. "It's the course o' the disease. The body can only 'old it off so long, then the decline starts." He ran a hand through his hair. "I can see me 'air and skin gettin' lighter. I can feel me body gettin' colder. I ain't a fool. I knew what was 'appenin'."

She looked up. Instead of hurt or despair, a sudden gleam of burning intensity lit her face. Her skirts tumbled around her thighs as she straightened off the bed, Blade's diary clutched in her hand. "I tested your CV levels yesterday. They were at seventy-six."

Blade froze. "That ain't possible."

Both of their gazes shot toward the small brass spectrometer.

"I know they were seventy-six," she said, sweeping toward it. "I was surprised at how…high they were. You've never spoken of it."

A polite rebuke.

"I 'ad a few things on me mind," he replied, striding after her.

Honoria held out her hand, the other reaching for the small needle. Blade hesitated.

"I won't hurt you," she said, misunderstanding.

"I'm very accomplished at this. I've done it for years at the Institute."

He sucked in a deep breath. "It ain't that. Me levels ain't ever come down before. It's unheard of." He slowly put his hand into hers. "What if it were just an error?"

Honoria stroked his fingers. "Then we'll find out. Together." She eased his finger onto the brass plate. The sharp little needle spiked down, driving into his flesh with a stinging ache. Blood welled. Honoria tilted his hand and held it over the small glass vial, squeezing the skin to encourage the blood to flow.

One drop. Two. Another for good measure. He watched it sluggishly spread across the bottom of the vial. Honoria stoppered three accompanying drops of hydrate of soda into the vial, then slid it into the spectrometer. Pressing a button, she toyed with the pair of dials until she'd found the right frequency. Depending upon the level of acidic reaction, the little brass cogs would whirl into place, giving them a readout of his virus levels.

It was a breathless moment. He couldn't look.

"It will be all right," Honoria murmured. "I still have my father's notes if I need them. I *know* he was on the verge of something. He spoke of little else in the days before he died. And we have time, a little of it anyway."

There was a sharp click. Honoria leaned forward, the sound of her weight shifting on the timber floorboards.

"Well?" The words stuck in his throat.

"Look," she whispered.

The little dial hovered at seventy-six.

"I know I wrote 'em down right," he said, the strength in his knees starting to give out. Honoria caught him under the arms as he looked down in surprise. "They was seventy-eight. I know they was." The last was a whisper.

Honoria staggered back, guiding him to a chair. "It's not the sort of mistake you would be making for months." An enormous smile lit her face. "You've got columns of figures and dates. March the thirty-first was the last time you were at seventy-six."

"The machine might be skewed—"

Honoria settled on his lap, her hands cupping his face. "We'll buy a new one, but it looks perfectly fine to me. I don't know how…" She shook her head in bewilderment. "Nothing has changed? Your dietary intake? Sleep patterns? Living habits?"

He gave a raw chuckle. "A lot's changed, luv." His hands were trembling. For the first time he allowed himself to hope. He'd long thought himself immured to the thought of what was going to happen. But then Honoria had come into his life. For the first time in years he *wanted* to live. "But nothin' unusual. There's always problems to deal with in the rookery. Me sleep falls by the wayside, and I drink more chilled blood, but it's been done before. Ain't never caused me levels to fall."

She kissed him. "You stupid fool. You were going to send me away, weren't you?"

It hit him then, like a circus performer's mallet. If his levels were falling, he might be able to avoid the grim fate waiting for him. The hunger's hold on him would lessen—though it might never ease completely.

Blade scooped her up and swept her toward the bed. "Absolutely not," he replied with a straight face. "You come into me life and turned it topsy-turvy. I ain't 'bout to let you go."

He tossed her on the sheets and followed her down. Honoria laughed beneath him, fighting at his hands.

"Wait! Wait, let me think."

Baffled by the sudden push—as opposed to her very recent pulling—he drew back, kneeling over her. "What for?"

That same burning intensity fired her dark eyes. "That's it. *I'm* the only true difference in your life."

"I don't see as 'ow that'd make any changes to me virus count," he said dubiously.

"I'm the only recent change to your diet." She sat up. "Don't you see? There must be something in my blood that created the change. The only thing I can think of is that I was vaccinated. That's got to be it. Once father developed a vaccination that worked, he offered it to the staff and volunteer feeders at the Institute. Some accepted, some didn't. Three of the test subjects started showing a decrease in their levels, but others didn't. Perhaps those three subjects were feeding from volunteers who had been vaccinated." Excitement shone in her eyes. She had never been more beautiful to him than in this moment. "Father must have guessed. He kept speaking of a common element in that last week. He could barely sleep, barely eat..."

Honoria could contain herself no longer. She bounded off the bed, hands gesturing wildly. "The vaccination doesn't affect blue bloods. We tried that.

Yet when a blue blood drinks the blood of a vaccinated person..." She looked around, raking a hand through her hair. "A notebook. Do you have a notebook?"

Blade let his head sink back onto the bed, a faint smile tugging at his lips. "I've just returned from the dead and you want a bleedin' notebook?"

Her wide brown eyes blinked at him as she slowly returned from whatever mental plane she'd momentarily existed on. "You don't understand. I have to get this down."

"I've got time." He rested his arms beneath his head and lazily surveyed her. "Charlie's got time. It's enough to know that me blood levels are goin' down. But you and me, we needs to 'ave a little chat. I'm feelin' awful lonely and neglected over 'ere."

Honoria's gaze dropped to his waist—and the tented suggestion beneath the sheet. Blazing intellect faded from her gaze, replaced by a sultry look that made him freeze. She climbed onto the bed, dragging her skirts up over him as she straddled his hips. "You poor, starved blue blood. Or should I refer to you as Sir Henry now?"

"Only," he murmured, drawing her hand against his mouth, "if I may refer to you as Lady Rathinger."

Her breath caught. A little hint of vulnerability shot through her eyes. "Are you asking me to marry you?"

Blade kissed her palm, stroking his tongue across the tactile skin. Honoria shuddered a little, her lips parting and her gaze blurring with desire.

"Aye. Whoever thought I'd get 'ammered for life? But it's the only way I can be certain of reinin' in your 'eadstrong impulses," he replied. "No more facin' down vampires, ravenous dukes, or a hall full o' blue bloods. I've died a thousand deaths over the last few weeks. Me poor old ticker can't 'andle so much trauma."

"Then you must not face such dangers either," she told him, leaning down and brushing her nose against his with a smile. "For I only do battle for those I love."

Blade caught her face in his hands and kissed her. Hard. He was almost afraid to let her go, for fear that the words had been nothing more than a hallucination—like his memories of them from the Ivory Tower.

Mine, whispered the dark little voice inside his head. His darker half. Himself, he finally realized. The part that was ruled by his passions and hungers. A part he had once feared and fought.

I am the darkness, he thought wonderingly and tugged at Honoria's laces. She laughed, the dress pulling free and revealing the crisp white cotton of her stays.

But the only ones who would ever have to fear him now would be his enemies. Not her. Never her.

Ours, he corrected, finally surrendering to the inevitable. *Always ours.*

Read on for an excerpt from

HEART OF IRON

by Bec McMaster

London, 1879

Fog clung to the Thames like a light-skirt to a rich patron. Here and there, gaslight gleamed, flashing will-o'-the-wisp in the shrouding pea soup mist. It was the perfect night not to be seen.

Will Carver loped across rooftops and gables, leaping across an alley and coming to a halt behind a chimney near Brickbank.

A man landed lightly on the tiles beside him, breathing hard from the exertion. He wore black leather from head to toe, and the only weapons he carried were a pair of razors, tucked in his belt. "Bloody 'ell. You tryin' to run me to death?" Blade muttered.

The words were quiet, but the sound carried in the still night. Will's lip curled, and he glared at his master.

"They won't be listenin' for *us*, bucko." Blade straightened, staring at the ruddy glow ahead of them. "Not with that burnin'. And none of 'em 'as your hearin'."

A column of red glowed against the night sky

ahead, barely muted by the fog. Every time Will breathed, he could taste the ash in the air. Ahead, a massive brick gate and wall blocked the way into the City. A company of metaljackets paced in front of the gate, gaslight gleaming off the shining steel plates of their armored chests. With the flame-thrower appendages in place of their left arms, they looked formidable enough to keep the general rabble at bay. They were, however, automatons and not human.

He'd long since learned they didn't look up.

"Over?" he asked.

"I got me pardon now," Blade said. "Could waltz right on through them gates, and they'd not say a word." The devilish light in his eyes said he wanted to try. There was nothing Blade liked better than thumbing his nose at the blue bloods who ruled the city.

"Yeah, well, we ain't all that lucky," Will reminded him. "I've still got a price on me head."

Blade sighed, eyeing the massive edifice. "Over it is then."

"You're gettin' lazy."

"I should be at 'ome, tucked up with me cheroot and a nice glass of mulled blud-wein." What he didn't add was that he most likely wouldn't have been doing either of those things. If the fire hadn't called them out, Blade would be in bed with his wife, Honoria.

Will took a few steps back. No point him being at home. The flat he rented these days was cold and uninviting. There was nothing for him to go back to.

A wide leap took him sailing across the street and onto a rooftop beside the gate. Taking a running start, he bounded up and over the wall before the guard on top had finished shaking out the flame on his match. Human eyes were sometimes just as bad as the automatons.

Boot steps echoed him on the rooftops as he flitted lightly through the night. Fog parted around him, drifting in his wake, but he was moving too fast for anyone watching to see.

Here in the City, the streets were a touch wider, the buildings not as jammed together as they were in the Whitechapel rookery he called home. Blood rushed through his veins as he leapt from rooftop to rooftop. He'd been cooped up for too long; he needed this.

Screams caught his ear, and the organized shouts of people trying to marshal water pumps. Little snowflakes of ash floated through the air, almost thick enough to choke a man. Will paused in the crook of a chimney.

Ahead, the world looked like it was on fire. Billowing gouts of orange flame licked at the skies, and a thick dark pall of smoke hung over the river. Lines of people manned water pumps desperately, trying to stop the flames from spreading.

"Jaysus," Blade cursed as he knelt at Will's side.

"The draining factories," Will said. "Someone's fired the draining factories."

It was unthinkable. The line of factories down by the river were owned by the ruling Echelon to filter and store the blood gathered in the blood taxes. This would be a huge blow to them.

Blade's eyes narrowed. "You and I ought to get out of 'ere quick-smart." His nostrils flared. "The place'll be swarmin' in metaljackets before we know it."

Will backed up a step. He knew what Blade wasn't saying. Two more perfect scapegoats couldn't be found. Most of the aristocratic Echelon had been furious with the Queen's pardon and knighthood of Blade three years ago. And Will was just a slave-without-a-collar to their eyes.

A clink of metal caught his ears. Iron booted feet on distant cobbles. A legion of metaljackets by the sound of it. "Go," he snapped, shoving Blade in the back.

Blade needed no urging. He scrambled up the tiles on the roof, a break in the clouds bathing him in moonlight. Once, a few years ago, his hair would have lit up like a beacon. Now it had dulled to a light brown, and his skin was no longer as pale as marble.

Will followed at his heels in an easy lope, his ears alert to the slightest sound behind them. They'd seen what they came to see. No doubt word of it'd be all over the streets by morning.

Movement ahead caught his eye. A swirl of a black cloak stirring the fog. Will leaped forward and shoved Blade flat, covering him with his body.

"Ooof," Blade wheezed. He lifted his head. "Thanks, but I've already got a wife—"

"Shut up." Will pressed his hand between the other man's shoulder blades, coming to a crouch. His gaze raked the fog. There. A metallic chink. Voices in the shadows.

From Blade's stillness, he'd heard them too.

"Stay here," Will breathed close to his ear. "Keep your bloody head down, and I'll check it out."

"Do I look like a need a friggin' nursemaid?"

Will shot him a look. Three years ago, no. Blade

had been the most dangerous thing to stalk the night. But his hair and skin color weren't the only changes in him, since he'd started drinking Honoria's blood.

"You go left," Will finally murmured. Short of tying Blade to the chimney with his belt, there wasn't much chance of him staying here.

Both of them faded into the fog. The voices ahead were getting farther away. Will moved like a wraith through the night, his dark wool coat rippling around his hips. Beneath it he wore a heavy leather waistcoat that had been modified with steel inserts, as well as steel caps over his knees. You couldn't be too careful in a world where a man's main weapon might be a shiv or a heavy wrench. His loupe virus could heal almost anything, but being knifed still hurt.

Metal clanged and a pair of curses littered the air. Then silence, as though both people froze to see if they'd been heard. Will slowed, creeping across the tiles with one foot placed carefully in front of the other. He knelt low, easing on hands and feet around the edge of a chimney. There was no sign of Blade, but then Blade was even better at this sort of thing than he was.

"You drop that again, and Mercury'll have your head," someone snapped.

Two figures. Both dressed in black and moving with a footpad's efficiency. The shorter one picked up something heavy. A hollow metal tube, like the flame-throwers the spitfires used.

"Mercury ain't here, is he?" asked the shorter man, hefting the flame-thrower over his shoulder. "And when he hears how well we done, then he'll be burying us in ale and whores."

"That's if the Echelon don't rip your guts out first," Blade said pleasantly, materializing out of nowhere.

Shit.

Will leaped forward, even as the two men turned on his master. Despite their bickering, they moved with military efficiency. The shorter one snapped the flame-thrower up, just as the other drew his blade. The tube coughed, then bright orange flame spewed through the fog, highlighting the roof and everyone on it.

Blade spun low, sweeping the knife-wielder's feet out from under him. Will grabbed the barrel of the flame-thrower and elbowed the man in the face. There was a satisfying crunch, then his mind registered just how hot the tube was. He dropped it, and it rolled toward the edge of the roof, catching in the gutter.

"Just the two of you boys?" Blade taunted, not even bothering to draw a knife. He bent backward, avoiding the swipe of the knife with a gravity-defying movement before snapping upright.

The man he was facing stiffened. "Frigging bleeders!" He reached into his pocket to press something, and agony screamed through Will's head.

The sound was like an icepick to the brain, wiping out all sense of time and place and even connection to his body. He hit the tiles, scrabbling blindly for purchase as he started to slide.

Something hit him hard under the chin, snapping his head back with resounding force. Words sounded, distorting the high-pitched scream, but he couldn't make any of them out. Then movement blurred at the edge of his vision. Another smashing blow against his cheekbone. Blood splashed over his face, wet and hot.

Will clapped his hands over his ears, collapsing back on the tiles. That sound! Like razors in his head.

In...his pocket. Something in the man's pocket. A device of sorts, making the noise.

Grinding his teeth together, he saw the shorter man lifting the flame-thrower high. No time to think. He kicked out, aiming for the man's knee.

A heavy weight landed on him, and they both grunted. The throbbing squeal of noise pounded in time to his heartbeat. Will clawed to his feet and staggered forward, searching for Blade.

There. On the roof. The other man knelt over him, and Will realized he had a knife buried deep in Blade's chest. Trying to cut out his heart.

"No!" He roared, seeing red.

Anger rushed over him, swallowing him whole and burning him in its wake. He grabbed the man by the collar and flung him away. Blade gasped, clapping a hand to the knife hilt, but his reactions were still slow, disorientated.

The noise.

Will slammed the man down and yanked at his pocket. A small, vibrating device came free. He crushed it in his fist, and the world fell silent.

Will staggered, throwing aside the crushed pieces. His ears were still ringing, but at least he could think. Breathe. Move.

The scent of hot, coppery blood washed over him.

"Blade," he growled, leaping over the gasping man on the roof and sliding to his knees beside his master.

Blade lifted his head, then collapsed back down. "Bloody... Get it out... 's silver." He lifted his fingers and flinched as they brushed against the knife hilt.

"Hold still," Will snapped. A cold ring of sweat beaded on his forehead. The knife was buried to the hilt. He had no idea of the damage it had done or what would happen if he removed it.

Behind him, the two men helped each other to their feet. Will spared them a glance, but they were trying to get away, now that the advantage had shifted once more to him and Blade.

"Gutted by a human." Blade laughed incredulously. "Always thought...it'd be one of the Echelon. In the end."

"Stop your whinin'." Will wrenched his shirt off, a frisson of icy cold trailing down his spine. Blue bloods were notoriously difficult to kill. That was one reason the French revolution had guillotined their aristocrats. The only other way to stop them was to cut out their heart or cause severe damage to it. He swallowed hard and shoved his shirt around the wound to stop the bleeding. "Nothin' more'n a scratch. We'll have you hale in no time."

Blade met his gaze. His fingers were surprisingly strong when they closed around Will's. "Swear you'll look after 'er," he snarled. "If... If I don't..."

Will dropped his gaze. "Aye. You know I'll do it." He owed Blade his life, no matter what he personally thought of Honoria. "Hold still. You need blood."

Darkness slithered through Blade's pale eyes. His head rolled to the side. "Feels... numb..." he murmured.

Panic speared through his gut. "Don't you dare!"

Ripping at the heavy hunting knife he carried, he cradled his friend's head in his hands. "Here. Have me blood. It'll help."

Short work to slash the vein in his wrist open. He cupped the back of his head and held Blade's mouth to his wrist.

A moment of hesitation that never used to be there. He knew what Blade was thinking. He'd stopped taking directly from any of his thrall's veins when Honoria came into his life. Now he drank his blood either from her or cold, out of the icebox.

"Don't be a fool. She won't mind," Will snarled.

That hint of darkness swept through Blade's irises again. Will's chest caught. Not in fear. Gods, not that. Anticipation swept through his veins, lighting them on fire. It'd been a long time since he'd been one of Blade's thralls. He'd not realized how much he missed it.

As Blade's mouth closed over his wrist, his tongue sliding over the ragged wound, Will collapsed forward onto his other hand. A gasp tore from his lips. Feeling flooded through him that he hadn't felt in years. It had confused him when Blade first took him as a thrall, but it was nothing more than his body's reaction to the chemicals in his master's saliva.

But the moment of closeness...

This was all he'd ever have of that.

He ground his teeth and tried to deny the pull. Twice as harsh after three years of abstinence. And just as confusing.

He didn't feel this way with females.

Or he never had. Until Lena walked into his life.

And I'm not *thinkin' of her*. Will bit his lip, trying to ignore the flush of pleasure that thought brought. Dark hair, dark eyes, that flirtatious little smile that drove him insane... His groin tightened and he growled, head bowed as the sensation against his wrist increased.

It was over all too quickly. Will collapsed onto his backside, clutching his wrist against his chest. The skin throbbed, still feeling the imprint of Blade's mouth. Heat flushed through the ragged edges of the knife cut, his loupe virus rapidly healing the wound. It would be gone by the end of the hour, barely a pink pucker against his swarthy skin.

Blade gasped, drawing his feet up. His eyes blazed with black fire, and he grabbed the handle of the hilt and ground his teeth together. Crying out, he drew it out of his chest and collapsed back on the roof, panting for breath.

The wound was still bleeding, but sluggishly now. With his blood rushing through Blade's system, there was a strong chance he'd pull through. Verwulfen blood was thrice as potent as a human's.

"Honoria'll... kill me," Blade gasped.

That's if he survived. Will took one look at the ashen color of his face and looked away swiftly. Damage to the heart was always dangerous. He had to get him back to the Warren, where Honoria, with her medical background, might be able to help.

Rigging up a makeshift bandage, he held his coat in place to suppress the bleeding, then tied off the ends of his shirt. "There. That'll hold until we get you home." Sliding his arm under Blade's shoulder, he helped him to sit.

Blade gasped, clutching at his chest. The sight tore another shaft of ice through Will's gut. Followed by a hot stab of anger. Three years ago, Blade would've laughed this off. He was no longer standing on the edge of the Fade— when the craving virus finally overtook a blue blood and he turned into something else, something worse—but for a moment, Will didn't know if that was any better.

"Can you stand?"

Blade struggled to his feet, his eyes glassy with pain.

"You have to hold on," Will warned, bending and easing the other man over his shoulder. "I'm goin' to get you home. To Honoria. She'll know what to do. Just you hold on."

❧

Honoria eased the blankets higher, then turned the knob on the gas-lamp lower. Muted light cast a variety of shadows across the room as Blade slept. Will paced in front of the fire, his wrist tingling as the skin healed.

Honoria washed her hands, moving away from the bed. Her face was composed, but deep shadows lingered in the hollows beneath her reddened eyes. As she turned, the light caught her profile, and for a moment Will stopped breathing, seeing another's face in the shadows. Then she looked up, arching a brow at him and the image was gone. She shared the same dark eyes and rich mahogany hair as her sister, but Lena's face was prettier and she was a good inch or two shorter than Honoria.

Just the ghost of her image lingered, haunting him.

A quick jerk of the head meant Honoria wanted to talk to him. Outside.

Shooting Blade one last look, he strode to the door. An old shirt of Blade's hung loosely over his chest. He couldn't quite button it, and the sleeves stretched taut over his arms. Foolishness. But he wasn't knocking on Rip's door—Blade's other lieutenant—and asking for a shirt that might have a better chance in fitting him.

Honoria eased the door closed. "I think he'll be fine. The bleeding's stopped, and I'll get some more blood into him. Thank you for bringing him home to me."

Will nodded. He never had much to say to her. They'd tried, after she first married Blade, to find some common ground between them. But he knew what she thought of him—had overheard it in quite explicit detail the night before he moved out of the Warren.

Dangerous.

Unpredictable.

A threat to her sister.

Sometimes he wasn't sure if she hadn't been half right.

Her gaze dropped to his wrist. "Do you need tending—?"

"It'll heal."

"Something to eat then? There's stew... In the kitchen. I'll just—"

"Ain't hungry." He nodded his leave of her, then turned on his heel. The back of his neck was itching.

"Will. Please."

He stopped moving and glanced back over his shoulder.

"You know you can come home now. It breaks his heart that you're living on your own. And you know... She's not here anymore either."

Honoria would never understand. He shook his head. "She weren't the reason I left," he growled. *Not the only one anyway*.

Then he turned and stalked out into the darkness, feeling her eyes on his back the entire way.

No point going home.

Will stared at the fire in the distance, still raging out of control. Something bothered him about the attack. The mysterious device. The flame-thrower. Two men who had been prepared to face blue bloods and incapacitate them.

He breathed deeply through his nose. It was hard to pick up a scent trail with the overwhelming cling of ash in the air, but not impossible. Moving east, he loped across the rooftops, his unease growing as the men circled back toward the north. Toward Whitechapel.

Just before the wall that circled the rookery, they dropped off the rooftops and disappeared into an alley. Will knew the area well. It was a dead end.

He followed them in and stared at the brick wall. The ripe scents of the rookery spilled over into the surrounding streets. He wrinkled his nose and looked around. There was a grate in the cobbles, but surely they wouldn't have gone down. That led to the sewers and from there into the notorious sprawl of Undertown. Weren't nothing living there now, only ghosts and whispers. People had tried to move back in once the vampire that had slaughtered its residents was killed, but something drove them back out.

If they came back at all.

All that space, the caverns and homes carved into the old underground tunnel scheme. Empty. Or was it?

Will hauled the grate out of the cobbles and dropped down into the dark, landing lightly on the pads of his feet. His nose told him there was nothing nearby. Nothing but refuse and the odd rat skittering away.

Without the ash or a breeze, it was easier to follow the trail. The men weren't moving fast, probably thinking they were safe from the Echelon and their metal army down here. Will shook his head. Dead men walking. The Echelon didn't just rely on the metaljackets. Give them an hour and the tunnels would be full of Nighthawks, the infamous guild of trackers that did most of the thief-taking in the city. Rogue blue bloods who could smell almost as well as he could and track a shadow over stone, or so it was said.

Not a lot of time if he wanted to get his hands on them first.

He waded into the sluggish stream, his nose almost shutting down. He'd smelled worse things—the vampire sprang to mind—but right now they were only a distant memory. It was the curse of heightened senses. He could smell everything, from a woman's natural musk to the slight hint of poison in a cup; he could see for miles, and if he listened, he could hear things people didn't want him to hear.

Like stealthy footsteps, a few hundred yards in front of him.

Will made no sound as he stalked them. Whispers echoed and then a light appeared. A shuttered smuggler's lantern by the look of it.

"Got him," the short, fat one crowed. "Right in the chest. Won't be so high-and-mighty now, will he?"

Will's eyes narrowed.

"Shut up," the taller shadow snarled. The acrid scent of fear-sweat washed off him. "Didn't you see his bloody face?"

A shrug. The short man sloshed through the water carelessly. "All looks the same to me. Pasty-faced vultures."

"It was him," the other man replied with a shudder. "The Devil himself!"

"The Devil of Whitechapel?" The shorter man's face stretched in a delighted grin. "Cor, Freddie! All them years, and the Echelon themselves ain't been able to get near him! And you done him in! You're famous now!"

"I'm bloody dead is what I am," Freddie snapped back. "If that were the Devil, then you know who the other one was!"

Will took another step forward, drawing the blade at his side. He smiled. *That's right, you son of a bitch. You're in trouble now.*

"Who?"

"The Beast," Will hissed, his voice echoing out of the darkness.

Acknowledgments

A huge thank-you to my editor, Leah Hultenschmidt, for taking me on and giving me this wonderful chance, and to my agent, Jessica Faust, for helping me navigate these new waters. To my wonderful critique partner and one-woman cheer squad, Michelle de Rooy, who helped whip it into shape. Your turn's next, mate. And to Kylie Griffin for all of her insight and advice. Couldn't have done it without you two! Last but not least, to all of my friends and family, for putting up with my writerly ways.